Five Years After

By

LeRoy Clary

Five Years After
1st Edition
Copyright © 2021 LeRoy Clary
All rights reserved.

Cover Design Contributors: Karen Clary
Cover image: Used by license from www.bigstock.com
Editors: Beta Readers

Acknowledgments

Good books are a team effort, written by several exceptional people, all of whom have my thanks. This group sets my limits and helps establish the foundations for my books, keeping me on track as they progress.

My beta readers, Lucy Jones-Nelson, Laurie Barcome, Paul Eslinger, Dave Nelson, Sherri Oliver, Joel Mobley, and Pat Wyrembelski, all found lots of things for me to correct, and to improve. Thank you all. I want to publish the best books I can, and they are certainly better with your help.

My wife puts up with me and deserves extra credit for her help with the covers and her ideas—and she gives me the time to write.

And my dog, Molly. She sits at my feet and watches me write every day.

Contact LeRoy Clary at leroy.clary@gmail.com or message him on Facebook at: LeRoy Clary's Facebook Page if you have questions and/or suggestions

You can "follow" LeRoy Clary on Amazon by going to: LeRoy Clary's Author Page. Amazon will then notify you about new releases.

If you'd like to receive earlier notification of LeRoy Clary's latest novel releases, books in progress, or other cool stuff, please sign-up for his mailing list by going to: leroyclary.com. Your e-mail address will never be shared, and you may unsubscribe at any time.

4

Contents

Books by LeRoy Clary

The 6th Ransom
Blade of Lies: The Mica Silverthorne Story
Here, There Be Dragons
The Last Dragon: Book One
The Last Dragon: Book Two
Humanities Blight
Nine Years After

The Mage's Daughter Series

The Mage's Daughter: Discovery
The Mage's Daughter: Enlightenment
The Mage's Daughter: Retribution

Dragon! Series

Dragon! Book One: Stealing the Egg
Dragon! Book Two: Gareth's Revenge

Dragon Clan Series

Dragon Clan: In the Beginning (short introduction)
Dragon Clan #1: Camilla's Story
Dragon Clan #2: Raymer's Story
Dragon Clan #3: Fleet's Story
Dragon Clan #4: Gray's Story
Dragon Clan #5: Tanner's Story
Dragon Clan #6: Anna's Story
Dragon Clan #7: Shill's Story
Dragon Clan #8: Creed's Story

6

Chapter 1

*A quick note: All the books in this series were intentionally written to be enjoyed in any order. Please feel free to start and finish with any.

"Pen, we have to get you out of here," Jake whispered as he snuck up on the door to my jail cell just after the evening lights dimmed in the Monroe underground sanctuary.

"Are you crazy?" I snorted in surprise. "You were there in the courtroom. The judge sentenced me to death. She has always hated me."

He fumbled his keys at the lock and finally pulled the door of the only jail cell open. Jake was my two-timing ex-boyfriend. He was going to get himself into serious trouble for being here.

I backed away to the far corner, not in fear of him, but for him. There was no reason he had to attempt the impossible. I'd brought the sentence down on myself. After five years below ground after the war began, the future held nothing for me. I tried to convince myself that death was welcome.

I pleaded, "Come on, Jake. You know the outer doors of the sanctuary were sealed when the war started. There's nowhere to hide down here."

He reached inside the cell and took my wrist in an iron grip. "There's a way."

"No, you're going to get yourself killed along with me."

He pulled me out and started walking down the deserted

hall as he hissed, "Shut up and walk faster."

"Jake, let go."

"I can get you out," he muttered.

I shut up and started walking. We passed others in the hallways, the few who were still awake and about. They looked at us in shock. Everyone knew about my trial. It wouldn't take long before everyone in the sanctuary knew I'd escaped, and that Jake had helped me. Rumors fly faster than a pair of fugitives can run. We ran faster.

Our footfalls echoed down the corridors as he turned away from the community area and the residential section and rushed down a few levels on concrete stairs. We entered a maintenance tunnel. The dim night-lights were barely enough to see by. We jogged past several closed doors and made another turn. I didn't recognize our location, but I'd never had reason to visit there.

Jake urged me to move faster.

The seldom-used overhead speakers crackled to life and a tiny bell chimed for attention. The voice of the young woman judge, the one who had ordered my death a few hours earlier, spoke, "Attention, attention. The woman prisoner, Penelope has escaped with the help of the soldier known as Jake. They were last seen in the lower sections."

Penelope paused to listen.

The excited voice on the speakers continued, the voice louder than before, and rushed, "Please report any sightings to me. All military are to report to the armory."

"They're getting guns," I blurted.

Jake huffed, "It'll be alright, Pen."

I snarled, "They're going to kill me, you friggin idiot. It is not ever going to be alright."

"Shh."

Jake had shushed me, something that was somehow more offensive than the judge's words. My instinct was to slug his shoulder with my free hand. He'd never done that to me before. My anger flashed—and as quickly, subsided.

He wouldn't shush me without a good reason. A glance around found that a door a few steps away stood open an inch. An eye was watching us, and no doubt an ear listening to our every word. He tugged my arm to make me move faster.

Rumors spread quickly among the three hundred of us locked away down there, like rabid foxes after a flock of chickens. A good, juicy, rumor like the death sentence of a troublemaker, even one who received a punishment undeserved, moved even faster. Nothing similar had ever happened before.

The overhead speakers came back to life with a burst of static. "All residents are ordered into the safety of their personal residences. Do not come out until the emergency is under control." The speakers shut down with a final burst of static.

Back when the war began, I'd been accidentally swept up along with local government officials, senior military personnel, and a few financial leaders designated by those in charge as *survivors*. Important people. Including Witch Hazel, the judge who had sentenced me.

More than one of those notables had made it a habit to drink at the tavern where I worked. They rushed us from there to the federal land in crowded busses, SUVs, and in the beds of pickups, to an entrance in the forest as simple as crossing a cattle guard and a swinging metal gate. I hadn't noticed the camouflaged guard shack or the machine guns until we passed by.

Not that I was a great waitress or good at serving schooners of cold beer. Sure, I was cute and perky and chatted with the boys. However, mugs of beer from my tray regularly spilled on customers, sometimes intentional, some not. But I was always the kind of person who enters a room, and something nearby breaks or spills. My body moved through a doorway and a glass vase that had been sitting on a shelf across the room for three years chose that moment to fall and shatter.

The thirteen of us who were not on that survivor list were never accepted by the privileged who were *worthy*. We never socialized with them before the war and didn't after the massive outer doors of the sanctuary sealed behind us. They relegated us to third-class citizens. The military, including Jake, along with those with skills like welding or electronics, became second-class citizens, only a small step above in the social structure. But we were still at the bottom, no matter how you looked at it.

They assigned menial chores to those of us who had been scooped up in the confusion of the impending war. We became the cooks, cleaners, and laundry workers—if we wanted to eat, as they reminded us frequently. Our duties rotated until they assigned more permanent positions. The cooks became the top rung of our lower ladder of hierarchy.

I didn't cook.

About year number two, I'd started a succession of my many small revolts, and became a regular pest. I wanted better treatment and I wanted some of them to help with the laundry, cooking, and the rest. Depending on one's outlook, I was fighting for equality, or I was a danger to the tranquility of life in the sanctuary.

Serving beer in my old life had kept me busy. One night a new girl entered and hit on my boyfriend. She claimed to be the judge in traffic court, and the daughter of one of the richest men in Monroe. In front of half the crowd that night, I gave my boyfriend the option of which of us he would leave with.

He chose me. Our female war began. Hazel and I were at odds for a year or more. Then the other war began, and we ended up in the sanctuary together.

The first time I had formally faced judge Hazel in the sanctuary, the young woman we called Witch Hazel, I did my best to explain the feelings of all of us they treated as slaves. I hoped to improve our lot, not cause trouble. Witch Hazel, had ignored my words and simply asked in the judicial tone that she had learned in traffic court, "Do you enjoy eating, Pen?"

I'd told her, "Yes."

"Then you will do as we tell you or that privilege will cease."

Those things flashed through my mind, as Jake strode down the tunnel with me in tow, his jaw set, his eyes challenging any who dared look at us.

We angled left again, and our speedy footfalls slapped on the concrete floors announcing our approach in the empty passage. A door ahead opened only enough for us to slip past. I tripped over the sill and Jake pulled on my wrist to keep me on my feet.

"Hold up," Jake said.

The hunt was on. Even in the warren of tunnels, it wouldn't take them long to find us. Those in the passageway would eagerly point out our direction. Jake shrugged off my questions, which seemed flippant considering the circumstances. We had entered one of the many mechanical rooms that allowed the sanctuary to thrive.

From the hum of the huge fans and air in the ductwork, I knew it handled air distribution. Inside the room stood three anxious people, all known to me, one of whom I liked, and two I didn't. All looked scared. They were members of the same lower class as me.

A little man with an annoying voice named Gerry said, "We have to hurry."

I kept my attention on all of them, trying to understand and control my confusion. Together, there had been endless hours washing dishes, clothes, and scrubbing floors. They had seldom spoken up for me. Yet all were looking at me as if we were old friends.

"Hurry?" I asked, totally confused with their friendly demeanors, and excited expressions.

"We're all here to help you, Penelope," Jake said as if the five of us were going to complete a task before attending a party.

"They'll just find us, kill me, and you'll all be in trouble," I said, trying to bring the subject back to normal.

Any temporary hope I may have held of escape or freedom fled like a startled deer in a forest glade. My concerns turned to those who were offering their help, even the two I disliked.

Jake said softly, in a rushed and tense voice that petrified me, "Penelope, there's a way out of here."

"It's too late. They know we're here. Soldiers are coming with guns."

"No, I mean, *out of here*. This place. The sanctuary."

"Come on. I've seen the entrance," I told him. "The bank-vault doors sealed us in. There is no way to open them without the combination and special keys, and I know for a fact we don't have either."

I awkwardly turned away from Jake and looked at the other three for answers.

Gerry wore a homemade backpack and almost danced in place with nervous excitement. Danny held a blanket rolled tightly into a tube under his arm. A piece of twine looped over his shoulder to hold it in place. Grace carried a small canvas sack in one hand and wore a determined, worried expression.

Gerry and Danny were the two I didn't like. They were mice among men, never complaining about the assigned work, and always doing what the others ordered without any backtalk. Grace was loud and abrasive, always ready with a sharp comment to anyone. I liked her.

"What is this?" I asked them, my eyes quickly shifting from one to the next.

"A jailbreak," Grace said evenly, without mincing words. She looked the calmest of the lot, a woman well over thirty, but looking over forty after a hard day's work. Life had been hard on her. Before the war, she had worked nights at the Circle M convenience store in town, was on her third husband. The war forced her to leave five kids up there the day the bombs fell.

We all had our stories, but my emotions were peaking and screaming that we had little time to reminisce. My mind refused to cooperate as it flashed across what I knew of each.

Gerry not only looked the part, but he had been a young computer geek that barely made ends meet by repairing residential PCs for people that often didn't or couldn't pay. He had shared a shabby one-bedroom apartment with a guy that co-managed the Burger Shack out on the highway.

Danny, the youngest, had just finished his first semester at community college on that fateful day. He was about three years younger than me, but without any experience in the world since he had still lived at home with his parents and two sisters. Entitled might best describe his personality. The world owed him—until he arrived in the shelter with us.

My eyes went back to Jake, the guard who had brought me here. He was the lousy two-timer. When he should have been with me, he dated one of the elites. Yes, he'd dated the young judge I called Witch Hazel on the sly. I wouldn't forget or forgive.

He met my gaze. "I have no choice but to go with you because everyone knows you were in my custody. Henry had been assigned to escort you, but I told him we were still close, and I wanted the chore of guarding your cell."

I must have looked as confused as I felt.

He continued quickly, "In a few minutes, all hell will break loose down here when the military arrives. By now, they know where we are."

Instantly, I understood that part. He was right. No excuse could cover the reason he'd let me out of my cell and accompanied me here. In rescuing me, he'd committed himself to whatever we were up to, which would probably end in the deaths of both of us.

I partially forgave him for two-timing me with Hazel. N totally, of course, but a little.

I turned and backed away a step to see them all at once, Jake, Gerry, Danny, and Grace. Five of us had ended up in the sanctuary by accident. A hell of a crew to escape with.

My mind took another leap. There must be another way out of the tunnels. If there was, we were going to escape into a devastated world where mutants killed, radiation burned, and people starved. Me, an ex-beer server in a cowboy tavern, along with a two-timing soldier, a clerk from a gas station, a half-assed computer geek, and a college kid who'd finished less than a year at a community college.

It could have been worse.

Maybe.

I forced a weak grin. "You must have figured something out or we wouldn't be meeting like this. Tell me."

Grace said, "It'll take a while for the cavalry to get down here, and I doubt if they are going to rush in with guns blazing. They'll have to talk about it and decide on a plan, so we have a little time."

Jake pointed to the rear of the machinery-room. The whir of fans that pushed clean air to the rest of the sanctuary and other fans that pulled it back, created a steady hum. The ducts were massive, taller than his six feet, with smaller arms branching off to carry clean air to different levels and sections.

It was easily one of the largest rooms in the complex, but I doubted that any of the ducts reached up to the surface. It would be stupid to do that and pull down biologically contaminated or radioactive air to spread in the sanctuary. Expelling our air up there was almost as bad because replacing it with contaminated air was worse. Besides, leaving a dangerous penetration from the sanctuary to the surface was dangerous.

Where Jake pointed, the wall was *oddly* blank, I realized as I tried to see what he pointed to. A whole section of the wall four feet wide stood flat and empty of electrical outlets, attached pipes, conduit, or anything else. A glance around revealed the other three walls had the normal stuff attached everywhere, things that I had no idea what most of them did, but that one section of the wall was as empty of attachments as a movie screen in a theater.

Jake said quickly with a jab of his finger at one of the others, "Gerry figured it out."

"What?" I asked.

"Gerry found a notebook hidden behind some equipment when he was cleaning. It was handwritten by one of the workers who originally built this place. It said that during construction, they had accidentally opened an old mining shaft from a hundred years ago. The workers decided not to tell their supervisor in case they ever wanted to get into the sanctuary, should something happen—like hundreds of bombs and missiles falling from the sky. In effect, they left a backdoor for themselves behind that wall."

I looked at Jake in disbelief. "You're risking your lives over an old notebook some construction worker made a dozen years ago?"

Jake said so fast the words almost ran together, "Think about it. Imagine the frustration of workers building this place and then not being allowed inside when and if the time came? Gerry came down here where the notebook said and cut a hole in the sheetrock. He shined a light inside and found the old tunnel just as described."

"What hole?" I asked.

"Over there," he jabbed a thumb. "After that, he patched it so nobody would notice. That was about a year ago. Gerry's been waiting for the right time to do this. Months ago, he shared the information with Grace, Danny, and me, and we needed the right people and the right time." Jake stood taller and continued, "Besides, you were sentenced to death, so we all decided the time is right."

I demanded, temporarily forgetting the people hunting me and that these were my friends, "And why wasn't I told?"

Jake stammered and finally turned to Grace with a shrug of his shoulders.

Grace snapped, "For God's sake Penelope! You were included from the first. We just didn't tell you because of your temper and your big mouth. Leave it at that. Right now, we have to get our butts moving or get caught."

Eying the group, I still didn't like Gerry or Danny. Both were weak and had refused to take my side during the numerous times I'd protested or refused to do the menial work assigned to me. While they complained in private, neither had had the balls to join me. If we had all refused, things may have changed.

If we reached the surface, and the world outside was a desert wasteland of dead, twisted plants from radiation, would they want to turn around? Would we descend to the sanctuary again and beg forgiveness? Maybe. It could happen.

Of course, if we got up there and the radiation caused our teeth and hair to fall out and boiled our skin, or the mutants ate us for evening snacks, or if whatever remained of humans captured us and had their way with us, would that be so much worse than facing a needle filled with a clear liquid that was to kill me in the morning?

Maybe not. Hell, I might survive two or three more days up there.

We heard shouting echoing down the hallway beyond the door. They were coming.

Gerry slid a wedge of wood he'd probably made for the very purpose under the bottom of the door and kicked it securely in place. It might hold the door closed a few minutes. Not long.

"Food, weapons, and clothing. What if it's winter up there? Or a caveman is waiting at the entrance?" My wild ideas were escalating and coming faster. My breath was rapid, and I felt faint.

Gerry said, "Firearms down here are all locked up. But we have food, lots of it. MREs, the dehydrated foil packet kind. We've stolen them from the military supplies, along with blankets. We also managed to pilfer from the medical unit. Shit is going to hit the fan in a few minutes and we're standing here talking instead of running."

He'd never spoken before with that kind of conviction. I said as a last attempt to let any of them change their minds, "Are you sure you all want to do this? There is no going back and we'll all probably be dead by morning. Right now, you can still deny helping Jake and me. Say we took you, prisoner."

Nobody responded. I guess they all were going, or better said, they were coming with me because if there was a mining shaft behind that wall, I intended to use it. We stood in absolute silence until Grace huffed her answer. "I'd rather die."

Fists pounding at the door jarred us from inaction. Gerry leaped to the wall behind one of the massive units containing a giant fan and reached out to the base of the wall. He took the end of a dangling string between his thumb and forefinger. With a steady pull, the string cut a piece of drywall tape covered with a thin layer of painted joint compound that blended with the rest of the wall. In my mind, he should have done that while we stood around for a couple of minutes talking like idiots. Yes, that description included me.

From where I stood, it looked almost like a zipper. A square of sheetrock about two feet on a side came free. He held it in place for a moment, then carefully removed it and set it against the wall as he waved us forward.

Jake dropped to his knees and quickly crawled inside. Soon after, a light came on inside the tunnel and it didn't look as intimidating as it had. His hand motioned for another of us to follow. Danny, the young man from a local community college who had said little, so far, silently dropped to his knees, flashed a smile in my direction, and quickly crawled inside. Grace followed.

That left Gerry and me. He said, "Go. I need to put the sheetrock back up to delay any pursuit. It may take them a while to find it. We can use that time to move."

That sounded optimistic to me, but I crawled in, smelling the chilly, dampness, and feeling the sour, cool air rushing past. Water ran in rivulets down the rock walls in the dim light, which made me wonder if the walls were solid rock, where did the water come from? The floor was mushy, inches deep in yuck, and incredibly distasteful smells entered the air wherever we knelt, or placed a foot.

I moved a few steps ahead so Gerry could enter. The tunnel roof was higher than my head, the width about four feet. Round timbers, which were old tree trunks with the bark removed, braced the sides and roof. They had placed them every five feet. Again, if it was solid rock, why the need for supporting timbers? And how rotten were the old timbers?

My illogical, logical thinking was worrying me. Who in their right mind would worry about seeping water when armed soldiers were searching for them?

Jake handed another flashlight to Grace, who shined it around, examining the floor, walls, and roof, as well as the darkness where we would soon travel. The beam of light settled on a pile of things near the entrance we'd crawled through.

Green slime and blue mold grew on many of them, telling me Gerry had been stashing items in the tunnel a long time. He was right. Our attempt at escaping was not a spur-of-the-moment idea. He'd planned well.

Another stray thought flooded my mind. How many times had he removed the panel and replaced the string and joint compound? Several, from the number of items I saw.

He'd made carry-bags out of scrap material. Each was about eighteen inches square, with a pair of handles handsewn, looking like the reusable green grocery bags we'd used before the war. Each was bulging with contents, although I had no idea what. Foul water soaked and stained the outsides, which meant the contents were in an identical condition.

It didn't matter.

Suddenly, the shouting was closer. They were inside the mechanical room. We said nothing. Our actions became frenetic as we silently snatched whatever was closest at hand. My mind ignored the soldiers searching for us as it shifted to other, more immediate concerns.

If we managed to get outside and died later this day, I'd be happier than dying underground. The five years of constant dull work, verbal lashings for work not done to our leader's demands, and poor treatment had forced me into complaining, offering solutions where others, members of the upper class, helped with our work, and I offered methods to make it easier on us.

The same woman who had sentenced me to death had recently assigned us fourteen-hour workdays, instead of twelve, with only eight hours off—providing us with time to do whatever we wished, as she put it. Dropping exhausted into our beds was what happened. That was the way she liked it. If we were either working or sleeping, we couldn't make trouble, meaning me.

Except I had made trouble. Lots of it. Much directed at her. Somehow, she had used her limited experience as a judge in traffic court to have herself appointed as the judge for any disputes. She decided that meant she could give orders to those of us who had become the servants.

Four of us in the tunnel were those workers with the expanded hours. That made five out of twelve. Almost half of the menial workforce was about to disappear. The workload stretched thin. All sorts of bad stuff were going to hit the shelter walls after this when there were not enough to do all the dirty work. Others would find themselves demoted to replace us.

That made me smile as Jake selected two more carry-bags and handed them to me. He almost squealed with joy when he noticed a pair of compound bows and four quivers of arrows standing against the far wall.

It seemed Gerry was a packrat of the highest order. How he had managed to steal so many things amazed me. Even Danny was impressed enough to whisper, "Dude, you're a hell of a thief. Nobody ever suspected?"

Gerry already had the sheetrock for the hole back in place and stood. The voices outside the mine shaft were suddenly almost silent as they searched, dulled by the steady drone of the loud machinery. He allowed a slight smile as he said softly,

"Everything I stole was set up so that if discovered, someone else got the blame. There were some very enjoyable arguments I observed over this stuff going missing."

I said, "They never suspected you?"

"Me? I'm just a half-assed computer geek without a computer in sight, thus a master dishwasher, and toilet cleaner. To them, I'm invisible. I might cheat at cards, but stealing and hoarding for an escape attempt? Come on. Look at me. I'm a hundred-twenty-five pounds of flab standing five-five."

"Underestimating people is a vice of the powerful," I said. It sounded so intelligent and insightful it impressed me, and I think I said it first. Sometimes I impressed myself. Other times caused me to curse those same impulsive ideas. I looped two bags over my right shoulder.

"We gotta move," Jake hissed, turning his back on us.

I felt the movement of air on my bare skin that Gerry had talked about. There had to be a vent or shaft behind us to let it in and the flow was to our right where it had to get out. I drew in a deep smelly breath and tried to calm my breathing. This was it. An unexpected chance at a new life, or death. Either way, there were mysteries to solve and a possible future, if only for a short time.

Everyone carried a shopping bag or two. Jake also carried a bow and quiver. Grace carried the other bow, after saying she had hunted deer with one. Nobody objected.

We slogged, and that is probably the best word to describe our progress. The muck on the bottom of the mine floor was inches-thick goo, wet, cold, and stinky. We wore the same thin scrubs everyone else in the sanctuary wore, looking much like nurses in any hospital before the war. No underwear. No shoes. However, we did wear cotton booties with elastic around the top.

I managed almost twenty steps before slipping and falling the first time. Stuff spilled from my bags and I groped in the dark and mud to find them.

My first slipper came off about three steps later in the sucking mud. The other lasted a few more. Retrieving them was hardly worth it, so I didn't. My shoulder ran into one of the timbers and I almost fell again. With my clumsiness, it's a wonder I didn't bring down the roof of the shaft on us.

I ended up last in line by the time I gathered what I'd spilled again, so Grace handed the flashlight back to me. I shined it ahead, on the ground, so those in front could see. When I dropped it into a pool of filthy water, the light in the tunnel failed until I found it. The other flashlight was off, to save the battery for later. My finger wiped across the lens got enough mud off to allow it to show our way again.

There were little railroad ties when the narrow tracks started. Walking on them was awful. I had to take small, tiny steps or long ones to skip every other tie, but my legs wouldn't reach that far. The ground was flat for a while. Then we reached a place where the tunnel ended in a wall of solid rock.

A crooked ladder made of old two-by-fours went up into the darkness, rickety and missing a few rungs.

Jake said to me, "Pen, how about you go up first. I'll follow and if you fall, I'll try to catch you."

"Try? You'll *try* to catch me?" I hissed.

"Hey, you're the lightest. I'm the heaviest and strongest. If the ladder holds up under your weight and then mine, everyone else should be fine."

"Except me," I said, "I'm the one that's most likely to fall. And you *might* catch me."

Jake drew in a long, exasperated breath. "Okay, Pen, can you think of a better plan?"

"Any plan is better than one where I'm the person supposed to fall."

We stood there glaring at each other. Grace stepped forward and said, "I'll go first."

She was nearly five-eight with wide shoulders and before the war had been heavy-set, probably close to two-hundred pounds. If she went first and fell and hurt herself, I'd never forgive myself. I gave in. "No, he's right. It should be me."

Jake said, "Keep three points of contact on the ladder. Two hands and a foot when you move the other foot, etcetera. One hand, two feet. That way, if you slip or if rungs break away, you won't fall."

I slipped the straps of the bags up to my shoulder again

and grabbed the first rung before I lost my nerve.

It instantly came free, the wood wet, soft, and mushy.

Not even one step up before the ladder came apart. It was not a good start.

Looking at where the rung had attached, a steady drip of water from the wall fell on the rusted nail, or what little remained of it. I reached higher and tugged on the next rung. While damp, it held firm.

Jake put a hand under my butt and lifted it when I reached for the missing rung. I ignored the intimate placement of his hand, thinking that he had been a little too familiar, but his strength was impressive and comforting. I went one rung at a time as he said. Two feet or two hands two were always in place, while the fourth appendage moved, and then again. Often, I had four points of contact instead of the recommended three.

"Take your time," he told me unnecessarily while meaning for me to hurry.

I climbed what seemed like thirty rungs, changing ladders once, the filthy flashlight held in my mouth so I couldn't scream. Jake stayed right behind. If I slipped, he was there, and my weight would probably rip him free of the ladder and we'd both die. If he allowed me to fall, he had better go down with me or I'd give him hell.

Instead, we made it up to the next level of the tunnels.

"In here!" The shout came from far down the shaft, but it was clear that one of the soldiers had found our point of exit. Others would follow. They had guns. My hands and feet flew.

There were only five soldiers in the sanctuary, not counting Jake. No doubt all five were searching for us, along with a few eager volunteers, all armed and ready to kill. I reached down and helped Jake up the last few rungs. He helped the others while I did a three-sixty, looking for the best way to go.

They wouldn't have flashlights, I realized. Not yet. The guards hadn't followed us yet, for that reason. That gave us more time while they went to fetch them. Hell, I didn't even know there were flashlights in the sanctuary because nobody I'd ever known had needed one. I mentally thanked Gerry again.

The mine shaft had other levels, other ladders we moved past, but the tunnel we stood in was the tallest and widest. I followed the narrow tracks built for the oar carts with my eyes, deciding they were probably the best route to follow.

Before now, I hadn't even known they dug gold mines on different levels, but it made sense. Where the veins of gold went, so did the miners, and the tunnels wouldn't always be horizontal. The new tunnel was not as wet as the one below, but the rocks on the floor were sharper and they moved and shifted when my feet landed on the side or edge of one. The chunks of rock varied from fist-sized to watermelon. Even the thin booties I'd left behind wouldn't have helped.

"Good. We have lights. Let's move," the familiar voice of another soldier I'd once dated echoed from far below.

"We have guns," I screamed. "You don't want to come up here."

Grace whispered, "Not smart, Pen. Now they will bring guns for sure if they haven't already." Without another word, we all turned to follow the rails, moving quicker as isolated calls sounded from below.

"Halt where you are and I promise a fair trial," a familiar female voice shouted.

"Does that include me?" I called.

Jake snarled, "Will you shut up? You're telling them where we are and how far ahead we are. Just move."

A few moments later, the same voice called, in a loud but calm voice, "Turn Penelope over to us and we'll forget about your escape attempt. We can say she took all of you as a prisoner."

Witch Hazel couldn't believe any of the five of us were stupid enough to believe what she was saying. The better news was that her voice sounded no closer. We continued moving at a slow pace. I only fell once more.

Nobody answered her repeated calls and promises, not even me.

I stubbed my toes a hundred times, sharp rocks cut my soles, I slipped, and fell again and again, at least, ten times. Still, I kept moving, the others stumbling and cursing behind me. When my feet were about to give out, I caught a whiff of something strange and familiar. It brought my head up and I pulled to a stop.

In the damp stinking muck on the floor, each step of ours forced foul smells to rise, and now others didn't belong. I sniffed again and recognized a difference, one long forgotten. I drew in a deeper breath and savored the sweet scent of evergreen trees.

More calls came from below for us to give ourselves up, different voices and threats. I moved a little more ahead and asked softly over my shoulder to the others, "Smell that?"

Nobody answered. Maybe I had been wrong. I went ahead another dozen steps and felt a subtle change in the air. It was a dampness in the air. I heard increased dripping from the ceiling and walls. The scent of evergreens became stronger— and the smells of other trees. Just as I was about to say that I told them so, I decided to be quiet.

A minute later Jake said, "I smell it, now. We're almost outside."

18

Chapter 2

It was not only the smells and moist air anymore that I sensed. Ahead, there were familiar sounds and others I had nearly forgotten. An owl hooted somewhere in the distance. I paused long enough to hear the answer from its mate and smiled to myself as we moved ahead again, a sudden smile plastered on my face. The answering owl hooted. Now I could die happy.

Not that I'd ever paid much attention to owls. The familiarity of the sound combined with the smells of the evergreen forest was like coming home. Five years locked in a sanitary hole in the ground working as a slave and receiving threats if I didn't work harder had taken their toll. One more deep breath and I took another step forward while ignoring the appreciative sounds of my friends. I didn't have time for them.

There was no need for any of us to explain that the soldiers were going to catch up with us if we didn't move faster, if not in the mine shaft, then outside. Failing to escape now would kill me literally and physically. They would not take back my body if it was alive.

"Let's get out of here," I said in more of a grunt than words.

Gerry laughed without humor at the tension in my voice, a poor-sounding substitute, but he understood. The others, almost forgotten for the moment, remained as respectfully quiet as they might if entering a new church for the first time. They understood the importance of the moment as well as I did.

I kept shuffling ahead, ignoring my painful feet, and I noticed a spot of faint light that was different from the surrounding area or the glow cast by my flashlight. The smells were stronger, the sounds louder, and after fifty more steps, the spot of light had grown to the size of a basketball. It was the tunnel entrance.

"Damn," Grace said in a voice full of wonderment. She'd said it for all of us, and as if she didn't believe we'd ever do it.

Although we still had fifty steps to reach the world outside, the expected history of the war challenged in my mind. A desert has a certain dry smell and few sounds. Those familiar memories from our daily lives at the foot of the Cascades rushed back. Here it was damp with a faint evergreen smell. There were owls. Outside was not the desolate and waterless wasteland we'd expected and feared.

There were more voices from far down the shaft. While we'd hurried, a closer noise, the splash of a foot in the water inside the mine. It spun all of us around. Someone was close behind us, too close. Not within a few steps, but not far away. I heard a huff of expelled breath, probably from the exertion to catch up with us. I readied myself to sprint outside, no matter who was behind, or how close. I considered taking the bow from Grace on my way. Whoever emerged from the mine would get an arrow of mine.

If only I knew how to use a bow.

I tried to tame my imagination. Nobody moved after the initial sound. Probably trying to sneak up on us. I think we all believed much of the awe and potential possibilities outside, despite the dangers behind and those we would face.

Not only were we about to escape the confines of the sanctuary, but our destination was also nothing we'd anticipated or dared think about. The fly in the ointment was the steady advance of splashes from behind us, hopefully still on the level below with the rickety ladder between us. We should have destroyed the ladder. It was the other sounds from nearby that worried me. At least one of them had managed to almost catch up, and that one would have a gun. I tried to convince myself it had been a trick of sound in the tunnel and failed.

Tried is the operative word. I'd also heard a few drops of nearby water falling. That was no trick of sound. I kept a close watch behind, ready to burst into a sprint.

As I turned to look back again, the flashlight in my hand illuminated the others. They were my crew. The five of us were going to walk out of the mineshaft and face whatever was outside. We'd do it together. That was my goal. We had to get into the free air and whatever happened then was fine with me. It was as if we all felt it, the knowledge that the next few steps would take us into our futures. I let the light briefly linger on each of them while I let my mind rove over them as if it was another kind of light.

Despite my physical awkwardness, and the universe breaking or destroying things around me, I believed I could see inside people, understand what made them tick. That was my secret power. I read them as if their thoughts and feelings were printed in large text on their foreheads. I saw their intentions, loyalties, and instinctively knew who to trust. To demonstrate the quality of my unique abilities, one only had to look at my relationship with the lying, two-timing Jake who had fooled me for months.

Grace seemed the calmest of our lot. Her clenched jaw aside, she was ready to go outside and face the world. If it resisted, she'd smack it down. I'd follow her and Jake anywhere. The other two were less likable and had few redeeming qualities I could put my finger on.

Jake broke the silence as he held up a bow and asked us, "Anyone else ever use one of these?"

Gerry and I shook our heads. Grace had indicated familiarity but quickly gave it up when Danny said, "I've used one. Never hunted or anything, but lots of target practice at summer camp. I was accurate. Won a trophy, once."

"Good enough for now," Jake told him as Grace handed him the bow and quiver. She looked relieved.

Danny slipped the quiver over his shoulder and wore it crosswise on his back so his right hand could reach an arrow near his right ear. He pulled one and fit the arrow to the string, tested the pull and feel of the bow. He gave a curt nod, more to himself than us.

I noticed Jake give him a small smile of approval. That small amount of respect had Danny walking taller. Jake had that way about him when he was not cheating on his girlfriend.

Jake held the other bow above his head as if it were a source of power and spoke in a soft tone, "Danny and I will go outside first. We have no idea what's out there, but I guess that it's not what we've been told, and it won't be the first lie we've heard. So, expect the worst and hope for something better."

To my surprise, nobody objected. No comments, questions, or suggestions. Nobody even made obscene statements about those people below who had mistreated us for so long.

As if to punctuate his speech, a splash sounded right behind us, only yards away, if my guess was right. Everyone looked back this time, probably thinking the same thing. Our flashlight didn't reveal him but why wait? A few more sounds of nearby movement convinced us our pursuit had caught up with us and we started almost jogging.

Movement from farther away erupted, and a few curses sounded. A voice used to command shouted, "We will forgive all, but the woman who was convicted of treason, Penelope. Give yourselves up. You'll die out there."

Grace said as if speaking for all of us, "Well isn't that nice of them. We can return to our duties of drudgery and fourteen-hour days . . . if we're nice, all we have to do is give Pen up to die, and all is forgiven."

Jake glanced at me. "Turn that flashlight off."

"Why?" I asked.

"Save the batteries and besides, it'll draw the attention of anyone back there and tell them where we are, or if anyone is outside."

Outside? People? That indicated how little we knew.

Jake didn't mince words when it came to military stuff. It hadn't occurred to me that those behind would see our lights, and to show what a dunce I can be, it hadn't entered my thinking that there might be anyone alive outside the tunnel.

The reality of emerging into the outside world hadn't set in. His order to turn off my light hit me like a punch in my belly.

Danny moved to the front, to Jake's right, and they started moving towards the mine entrance, step-by-slow-step, which was our jogging speed. I didn't imagine anyone behind would go any faster. Jake and Grace had arrows ready to fly. Neither commented on being ready to kill someone, which surprised me. They were already adapting to our new world. None of us talked anymore, but those behind did. I heard more swearing and the mention of a broken ladder along with curses, so we all knew where they were. We were not in immediate danger from them. However, there was still one that had been a lot closer.

My mind split into two equal parts. One part observed the world around us, the smells, tastes in the air, sounds, and the coolness of the night. The chill was a welcome difference and proof we were about to leave.

Dread occupied the other part, dread, and the life-threatening danger behind—and possibly in front. If only a small portion of what they'd told us had happened on the surface of our world was true, the five of us were about to die. Perhaps before the sun rose on our first day, but a week seemed too much to ask.

Fifty small steps would take us to our new lives, I calculated as we took the first. Not that there was any way to measure, but it felt right to know how far until I saw my death. Forty-nine left. I forced myself to quit counting and concentrate on the freshness of the air, the sounds that might indicate danger, and any possible dangers from other sources.

Images of wild Indians attacking us with flaming arrows, or outlaws shooting six-guns into the sky, or a pack of rabid wolves slavering and waiting for their next meal as we went out the exit filled my mind. The ideas of mutated pink lions, which were tan colored but now stained from the blood of people escaping from underground sanctuaries crowded out giant snakes writhing and twisting to be the first to reach us at the mine entrance. My imagination was not a beautiful thing to have active in my head.

We stumbled along over the railroad ties for the light rail. In the darkness, we couldn't see them, nor the dips in the ground or larger rocks and boulders. Anything waiting for us out there knew exactly our position because of our grunts, groans, and curses.

The light at the mouth of the tunnel grew stronger with each step. Thirty-six to go. Then, suddenly, we were standing at the edge of the entrance. The mine entrance. My count of the footsteps had been wrong, and we arrived before I was ready.

There had once been a wooden wall, probably constructed to keep people out of the mine for their safety, but it had either fallen in or was torn down. Only parts of it remained and the broken boards looked like fingers pointing into the night sky. The wood appeared rotted, even in the darkness. In the dim light that filtered through heavy clouds, we saw dark shapes that might be mountains in the distance through the trees. More noticeable was the light rain falling.

We hadn't felt rain on our skin for five years. Below, we had bathed with reusable wipes when needed. I'd forgotten the damp smell of Washington forests as water soaked into the soil and moistened the decaying leaves on the forest floor.

What we didn't see outside of the shaft were artificial lights or campfires in the night. The world was ominously and forebodingly dark. That struck me immediately. It was as if we were the only people alive—and that might have been accurate.

However, the road we'd traveled to get to the sanctuary entrance was a two-lane blacktop that went nowhere but to here. It dead-ended a little past the turnoff we had taken. There were a few more farms and houses up that way—or there had been. People had no reason to travel up the road.

From the tales we'd swallowed, I was also certain there were *things* out there in the dark of night, mutated by radiation. Huge slathering beasts, many with two heads. I didn't have to know what else they were, only that they existed, and that they were probably waiting to eat me. My hands shook. My eyes darted side to side, up and down, and ahead. I was ready to spin around and run back into the mining tunnel and huddle with my arms wrapped around my knees while waiting for the soldiers to get me and return me to safety, for my remaining day.

Jake said easily, in a reassuring voice, "Rain. I like it. Always have."

That stupid expression at a critical time revealed how unintelligent he was—or how stupid he thought we were. He had to tell us what we already knew. He likes gentle rain. Woohoo. Just like a soldier. I ignored his one-word description of our new home and instead watched for the first mutated *thing* to mercilessly attack. For all the years we'd been below, we hadn't seen a wolf, lion, spider, dog, cat, snake, bird, or any creature other than the people we lived with.

Before any of us arrived, Monroe Sanctuary faced monthly cleanings. Disinfected, fumigated, antiseptic applications kept it sterile. No pets, livestock, or insects allowed inside. Periodically, they closed off sections of the warren of tunnels and sanitized them. Later, my crew and I went inside to further clean every surface by hand.

The leaders were paranoid about outbreaks of disease, insects, mice, or other vermin. In their opinion, I was only a single evolutionary step above any of those.

They even sanitized the air. It smelled of chemicals and unwashed people, but every cubic centimeter of air recycled through purifiers again and again. There were people whose primary job was to keep the air clean and to change filters as a critical function.

I shivered at the idea of what biologicals had already attacked us since climbing through that square hole in the wall of the machine room into the muck of the mine. Names of human enemies like molds, fleas, mosquitoes, flies, midges, and ringworms flooded back. There was so much we'd forgotten. Well, not forgotten, but had gone unused for so long it may as well have been.

Jake spoke again, and I hoped these words would be more intelligent than his last. "We should stay in here at the entrance until dawn."

"No," I heard my voice say. It was one of those times when I speak before thinking. Blurting out my innermost thoughts had been a huge part of why they sentenced me to death, but I knew I was right. "We don't know how long until morning but there is a good chance those soldiers behind us have climbed the ladder by now. They may reach us before daylight. Do you want to have a shootout with your little arrows at soldiers who have rifles?"

"We don't know they have rifles," Jake said.

"We do know they are kept in the armory, along with pistols. That's because you were one of them. They might be less than five minutes behind, in fact, nobody has mentioned the sounds of someone right behind us. It will only take one to capture or shoot us."

It was all true. The splashes and other noises had been a lot closer than the ladder, although we hadn't seen a light. I didn't know how they moved that fast to catch up with us. The army used to have things they wore that let them see in the dark. I'd looked through one once. Everything was greenish. Maybe the first ones to come after us in the mine wore them.

Jake said in resignation and acceptance, "Pen's right. We can see well enough to find a nearby place to hide and wait for morning."

I said, "Well, for me, I'd prefer to stand naked outside in the cold rain and let it rinse all the accumulated *whatever* off me. I would if I had a change of clothing."

"You do," Gerry said from the darkness behind me.

"Do what?"

"I brought extra clothing for us. It might not fit perfectly without a little adjustment, but we have it in the bags."

I could have hugged him—and probably should have.

Jake interrupted my thoughts. "We should move—and while doing that, make plans. Think about what comes next. What happens after the sun comes up?"

"It gets light outside," I muttered under my breath. Maybe Jake was not as stupid as I thought. For me, all I could think about was a rain shower to rinse the gunk off my body. The globs of stuff from the bottom of the mine shaft clung like contact glue.

Jake was planning our future, thinking about coming dangers and options. I thought about getting clean. I focused only on that. Different goals for different people. I forgave his stupid earlier comments about staying in the mine shaft until dawn. A *rain* shower would wash away many sins. It always rained around Washington. Right?

We climbed gingerly over the soggy wood at the entrance

and emerged into a clearing, of sorts. Small trees and shrubs grew here and there as our eyes adjusted to the light, but overall, it was open. Perhaps a small forest fire had burned the larger trees years ago. Maybe it had been cleared during the construction of the sanctuary. Bulldozers and digging equipment might have sat in the clearing.

Jake took my flashlight. He also took the lead and used it to find his way between the trees, over boulders, and around stands of briars. We meekly followed in a single-file line, our eyes wide with excitement and filled with amazing things we hadn't seen in years.

There were trees on the sides of a nearby hill. Alive. The lower branches where the flashlight swept were the new pale green color of spring, April, or May. I held my arms out to my sides and allowed the misty rain to wet my entire body. At least, that was the idea. The reality was that the rain was little more than a mist and it washed little off me. I used my hands to skim off the worst and looked for a puddle.

Enjoying myself in a way hard to describe, my mood shifted. I was free. I could do anything I wanted and when the sun came up, I wouldn't face a needle filled with stuff to kill me. I said in my snarky voice while suppressing a giggle, "Got any more good ideas, Jake?"

The others were keeping pace as we moved through the thick underbrush, always up the side of a hill. There were several exclamations of pain as we stepped on sharp rocks or thorns with our bare feet. A vine tripped me and another with barbs scratched my arm. I wondered what our pale blue scrubs would look like in the light of the coming day. We wouldn't be pretty. Not after the trip through the muck in the mine and what we were traveling through now. Chilly air cooled my thigh where I assumed the thin material had ripped.

Jake whispered urgently, "First, everyone needs to keep quiet and keep your ears open. If you even think you hear something, warn us in case they are following right behind. Talk softly, if at all. They will send people after us with guns. We want to slip away without being heard or seen and find a hole to hide in until they return below. Until dawn, I want to watch the mouth of the tunnel. Everyone keep your bags close and be ready to run."

That all made sense to me. If they captured us, I still faced a deadly needle. The purpose of the sanctuary cells was the short-term holding of a prisoner. There were no long-term cells. Besides, it was a waste of the dwindling resources to keep me alive. I vowed to escape, no matter what the cost. Those escaping with me had to either keep up or get caught.

"Spread out?" Gerry asked.

That would allow more of us to escape if trouble came, but we shared supplies and I didn't like the idea at all. If anything happened, I intended to hang onto Jake's shirt for the first ten miles, no matter what others did or which direction he went. He was a soldier and trained for this stuff. I hoped Grace would be at our side.

Grace said sternly, "No, we stay together. Later, after we divvy up the supplies, if anyone wants to split from the group, so be it. Tonight, we are five. Tomorrow, who knows? But first the supplies."

Danny said to her, "Are you going after your kids right away?"

"Not kids anymore, but yes. We lived in town, just across the river from here. I'll start looking there."

I tensed as I felt words about to spill from my mouth. "I think we should all stay together for a few days, even if that means we go looking for Grace's kids as a group. I know others have a family but until we know what the hell we're getting into, we should help each other."

Danny sounded like a petulant child complaining over which toy he should have gotten on his birthday, "I want to find my family as much as she does."

I found my anger rising and attempted to force it under control. Jake kept walking and the conversation continued in harsh whispers. We were not yet out of sight of the entrance to the mine and already our group was splintering. I snapped louder than intended, "It's been years, Danny. A few more days before looking for your family won't matter."

He didn't like my answer. He didn't object or say anything out loud, but in the dim light, his body went rigid. Maybe I'd overstepped. I momentarily closed my eyes, and as my nose drew in the myriad of luscious scents, I ignored him. I listened to the few insects that made noises during the fall of the rain, and to the steady large drips falling from the leaves above to the ground from the drizzle accumulating above. A frog croaked. I smiled. I loved frogs. Always had. My room, while growing up, had statues and pictures of them, and there was a little gold pin with a frog I used to wear.

My thin clothing was getting wetter—and colder. The anticipation of leaving the mine and entering the edge of the forest offset my imaginary sounds of the uniform footsteps of marching soldiers coming after us. Twice, my eyes flashed open, and my ears perked to focus on what I imagined followed. Once I heard a low huff of sound that could be a guard following us.

I asked the others about it, but they hadn't heard the noise.

When I reconsidered, and thought back, trying to be logical, no guard from below could be that quiet in the muck on the floor of the mine shaft. Not if they were right behind us. None could have traveled as fast as us without flashlights, and it would have taken time to locate them since we did not need them in the sanctuary. Only Gerry's planning had made them available to us. My mind was swirling with stray thoughts and creating scenarios where we never made it outside after being so close.

Besides wet and cold, I felt afraid, anxious, sleepy, tired, and eagerly anticipated the coming sunrise; our first in five years. There were not any emotions that were not present in my confused head, all fighting for attention and superiority.

In the darkness, I sensed Grace was sharing much the same ideas and on a more personal level as the mother of five children. I said, "Grace, no matter what, I will go with you and help find your kids."

"What if," she began, then sobbed loudly without finishing the statement.

She was right. There were a hundred "what ifs," and she would find part of the answers within a day or two. Like me, her home was not far from the entrance to the underground compound. Once we adjusted ourselves, either of us could walk directly to our old home if we could walk across a river.

My mind drifted to the others. Each of them had a story of their own. All but Jake were natives of the small town, and a few of us had met at social functions before the war, working teenage jobs at the state fairgrounds that were on the outskirts of town, or back in high school. Although separated by a few years, Gerry, Danny, and I had all graduated from the same one.

Jake came from somewhere in the middle of the country. Kansas, maybe. Or Wyoming. And Grace had probably sold all of us gas or snacks from the mini-mart at the gas station on the state highway that cut through the city.

But Grace also had older children who had still lived in the area. Had lived in the area. Whatever. That was probably no more than five miles from where we walked. While I had a few relatives, and none living close to Monroe, I shared her concerns. There were friends I'd left. Lots of them. People who came into the tavern for a beer after work, or to dance on Saturday nights. It had been that sort of place. We were all friends.

My mind took one of those leaps again. Were there still any people alive in the world but us? That basic question hadn't yet been answered. I know there had been no communications contact because of the EMP, the Electromagnetic Pulse, which had destroyed all computer chips within range of the nuclear explosions, so cars didn't drive, phones didn't work, and neither did anything else with computer chips in them. An EMP event was often the center of speculative discussion at the tavern, so from fragments of overheard conversations, I had a basic understanding.

There were some old cars and old trucks built before computers were in them that some said would work—for a short time. When they needed a new tire or part that was not on a nearby abandoned car that would fit, it would sit. If gasoline were not available, and some said it gets old and useless amazingly fast, cars wouldn't be going.

Maybe diesel ones? Not battery-powered cars because there was no way to charge them. Electricity for that came from coal or oil plants, maybe a few windmills or solar, too. Without cars and trucks, there is no way to distribute food and repair parts. That's what they told us down in the sanctuary . . . they had either lied or spoken from fear and ignorance. Maybe both.

Danny finally whined, "What about my family?"

Grace snapped back, "For God's sake, go see about them. I'm going to look for my kids."

So much for sticking and working together. It was a repeat of the earlier conversation—but with more bitterness interjected. Probably time for me to shut up about it. Whatever I said was going to make no difference unless it made things worse. I just wanted to be clear of those chasing after us. We could decide what to do after sunup.

We were moving slow. Each step hurt our sore feet, the muddy terrain didn't help, and we were in near darkness, with only filtered light from the stars behind low clouds.

Jake hadn't spoken much since we left the mineshaft but after a while, he said, "I agree with Pen. We stick together and go look for Grace's kids first. What we learn doing that will tell us how to proceed with locating your families. For now, unless someone has an objection, we can plan to go look for Danny's right after we find Grace's."

I liked it. I also liked him finally speaking up about something. But nobody spoke up to argue or support his idea and it sort of died a quiet death as the dark sky to the east grew lighter, just a faint glow behind the mountains at first, and then it gained in intensity and the mouth of the mine shaft behind us became clearer. We had only traveled a couple of hundred yards, so far.

We'd traveled a circular and upward course so that we were above the mine entrance, where we huddled on the side of a rocky hill looking out over a small meadow. Our position was maybe half a football field length away, and fifty feet above. Below us, the rotted boards of the entrance were dark and broken. They were the only signs of civilization.

Traveling in the underbrush at night in unknown territory with enemies on your tail means you travel slow and carefully. I considered our location. Not just near the mine, but also in relation to the small town or city we called home. It was on the state highway that traveled over Steven's Pass, the local main route to get from the coastal part of Washington to the high desert to the east.

Our small city, Monroe, lay only a few miles away from us. The town of Gold Bar was not much farther east. Some said the name came from all the gold pulled out of the ground from there, that in the old days they pulled enough gold from the mines to make it into bars.

A little north of us was the ghost town of Monte Cristo, where they had mined so much gold a hundred years ago, that they had built a railroad to it to carry supplies for the miners— and the gold back to Everett and Seattle. They claimed the Count of Monte Cristo had once visited but that sounded like a hometown rumor to me. Hundreds of abandoned mines were up there. A boyfriend and I had explored several. Mines like the one we had just left.

With those stray thoughts semi-contained in my jumbled mind, I forced my thinking back to the present. In the growing light, Danny wore a scowl, so I guess Jake's suggestion hadn't been accepted by everyone. Grace's face appeared red and puffy from silently crying, whether from joy or fear, there was no way to tell. Gerry and Jake were anticipatory, almost jittery to do something. Anything. It was the overflow of energy from youth. Sitting and waiting patiently were alien ideas.

It took a little work to figure all that out from the faces and clothing covered in dark brown muck. Not mud, stinking muck. It was still wet on my skin in most places, caked on my scrubs, streaked on my exposed skin. A coating of a crust of mud a quarter-inch thick went from hair to foot. I'd already learned not to touch my eyes with a muddy finger and the drizzle of rain was not washing it off fast enough, if at all.

In other circumstances, we would have laughed at our appearances.

Instead, we squatted and silently glowered at each other as the light increased. The light was a soft gray, filtered with morning mist and fog, all of which was normal for western Washington.

The sun rose above the tops of the mountains on our right. We believed the sanctuary was a few miles to the southeast of Monroe, certainly across the Skykomish river that flowed along the eastern side of the city. The trucks that carried us there had crossed the old bridge on Lewis Street, and not long after we had turned north off highway 203 to the east.

If all that were true, we knew exactly where Monroe should be. Probably no more than five miles and one river to cross, and we'd be home. Grace had lived just off Lewis Street, in a small white house in an older section of town where former presidents were the street names.

Looking out in the direction of where my hometown was, reminded me of the signature feature of Monroe. The Monroe State Reformatory, the largest construction in the city, and a nice name for a four-hundred-acre prison built a hundred years ago. It included everything from minimum to super-max security for inmates.

Six or seven hundred of them. We could see the penal complex from the high school, a good daily reminder to grow up and become good law-abiding citizens. At least, that's what our teachers and administrators continually told us.

As if reading my mind, Gerry said, "What if the prisoners are out there? Or worse, they escaped and live around here."

A rifle shot sounded. It came from inside the mineshaft and sounded more like a cannon as it echoed off the stone walls and burst into the stillness of predawn. Shouting followed, but we couldn't make out words. A long and lingering scream that raised the little hairs on my neck and chilled me, followed that. I shivered, but not from the cold.

I assumed one of the soldiers had fired at a shadow inside the shaft that he believed to be me, or one of us. The bullet might have bounced off the granite walls and struck one of them. The scream became a whimper, then nothing. My reaction was to leap to my feet and run away so fast and far the shooter could never keep up.

"They're coming for us," Grace muttered in a shaky voice.

Chapter 3

I gave Grace a wink intended to reassure her. Until we spotted a flashlight or saw the soldiers in the clearing, we still had choices. For myself, I didn't believe they would pursue us any distance outside. An unprecedented situation called for unique responses, but one item remained at the forefront of my thinking.

For years, they told us about the anticipated horrible conditions of the world outside. Even if they never caught us, the soldiers would return below with tales of a far different world. People below were going to ask questions and demand answers. At a minimum, they would send scouts.

Gerry and Danny were the two of our group we had to worry about. A young geek and a beginning college student, both scared and undisciplined. No telling what their reactions would be, however they might not be good for us. Mindless sprinting away from danger was a possibility. More likely, they would want to talk to our pursuers or debate with us before acting, which was their normal method of making decisions.

Making matters no better, Jake had been a soldier before entering the sanctuary, trained to confront enemies, to charge straight ahead, no matter the odds. He might want to go to war and fight them instead of attempting to talk our way out of a situation. That was also a problem as great or greater than the younger boys.

I whispered in Grace's ear, "We need to know who it is down there and how many. Maybe we can negotiate."

She nodded.

Danny turned to me. "What?"

"I said that we need to move into a position that we can either defend or flee while unseen. Quickly."

Gerry had also turned to us, his face pale and fear taking control as he understood that at any moment five armed soldiers could appear.

Grace came to my rescue as she said softly, "It only makes sense. There was a movie with a scene like this. We have to take the initiative and do what's best for us."

Without a word, Jake, who had listened but said nothing, motioned for us to follow him. He silently took us a few hundred feet to our left, then started climbing higher up the steep granite slope. It was not sheer, but very close in parts, and it took both hands and both feet to almost crawl vertically up some areas. The bags we carried did nothing to help. They threw me off balance and threatened to carry me back to the bottom.

There were steeper places where we helped each other climb, either by pushing from behind or pulling arms. Jake's hands touched where normally ex-boyfriends are not allowed. Jake's hands adjusted to *balance* me again. It was not the time to discuss it with him, but we'd have that conversation. Soon. Two-time me with that witch of a judge and there is no more touching.

He grabbed my arm as my foot slipped and I lost balance. One of the bags tumbled down the slope. I kept climbing, but not before noticing that Gerry and Danny saw the bag fall and that I didn't return to get it. In that instant, they understood something was happening and they climbed faster.

We initiated a few small rockslides but were soon a couple of hundred feet above the entrance when we located a shelf of flat rock that would hold twenty people or more.

Jake said, "Everybody get down. Stay out of sight and peek over the edge. I'll do any talking."

Suddenly sensing the seriousness of his tone, Gerry and Danny dropped down to their bellies. Grace and I were already there, watching the empty meadow below.

Jake said softly for all to hear, "I saw movement. There is

someone in the mine. Close to the entrance. Be ready to fight but stay hidden until we know what to do."

The boys exchanged fearful looks.

Jake went on, "I think we can slip away unseen if we want. Danny string your bow and place the quiver where you can reach it. We'll try to stay hidden and sneak away. I may try to talk our way out of this if they will listen. If they decide to take us back, that'll be their problem."

"Why?" Gerry asked innocently. He was asking why it would be their problem.

Instead of chewing him out for talking, Jake nodded at the slope we'd just climbed and said, "Think how long it took for us to climb up here. They'll be in the range of our arrows the entire time if they try climbing that. Guns or no guns."

That was a silly comment. We had heard the gunshot a while ago, and they would have more than one bullet. Gerry looked over the edge as if to remind himself of what he'd climbed and seemed to relax despite the obvious danger of troops coming after us. He asked me, "Are you sure they will come out here after us?"

"I don't know but think they will if they know we're here," I said.

Jake said to Danny as he made up his mind about something. "Will you have trouble shooting whoever it is?"

A long silence ensued. Finally, Danny said in a calm tone that sounded far older than his years, "I'm not going back down there into that hole to do their dirty work for the rest of my life. If I must kill a few people who are trying to make me do it, I guess it will happen, not that I want to kill anyone."

"Good answer," Jake said. He turned to look at Grace and me. "Can the two of you quietly gather some rocks, big ones? Larger than your fists?"

Gerry was pale. He said in a voice with a tremble, "We're going to throw rocks at soldiers?"

Jake said, "How would you like to try climbing up that granite face to reach us with rocks falling on you? Or being thrown at your head?"

From my standpoint, Gerry wouldn't fight in any circumstances. Nobody asked him to help the rest of us defend ourselves. He was one of those who considered himself entitled to share everything but didn't expect to work for it. I also had my doubts about Danny, but if he didn't use his bow, either Grace or I would take it and let the arrows fly. They might not hit anyone, but we'd try. I felt better as I got to my knees and spotted several rocks that had rolled down the slope from above and gathered at the edge of the shelf we were on.

I located three bigger than my fist and carried them to the edge. I caught sight of Grace struggling under one larger than my head. Damn, if she rolled that one down and it struck a person, he or she was going to die.

I went for more, settling on most somewhere between the size she was gathering and my first ones. Jake abruptly held up his clenched fist and we froze. He motioned for us to drop to our bellies again and we did, then both of us crawled to the edge and looked down. We heard sounds from below.

Heavy breathing, more splashes, and the sucking sounds from feet in the mud on the bottom of the cave floor. My stomach tensed. My fist clenched a rock, then moved to find a larger one.

Directly below, a snatch of movement drew our attention. I held my breath.

The movement emerged and waddled into the small clearing in front of the mine where it stood on hind legs and snarled at the world. It then moved a dozen steps further into the clearing, sat, and scratched its neck with a hindfoot. It was a bear. A skinny black bear. Tan muck from the floor of the mineshaft coated it, the same color muck as our scrubs were now.

Two smaller versions of the mother bear tumbled out and joined her. She roared again, darting a few steps toward the mine entrance again, huffing and snorting as if angry. She smelled us, or the scent of us in the mine. Her home for the winter.

It slowly came to me that during the night we'd walked right past a momma bear and her cubs somewhere in the maze of shafts. They must have been in a side tunnel. She had probably been hibernating, probably spent the winter there, and was ready to wake.

But if we'd awoken her fully, she would have protected her cubs and we'd be dead.

My breathing was coming as fast as that of Gerry at my side. He must have thought the same things. If that bear started climbing the slope in our direction, it was going to find my rocks hitting it in the face. The bear and cubs moved to the edge of the clearing and suddenly pulled up. The momma spun and looked back at the entrance.

A man emerged, blinking in the morning light. I recognized him. We all did. He was one of the soldiers, but he held a flashlight instead of a gun. He looked around cautiously, searching for us.

The bear charged.

He saw it and screamed. He didn't turn or run. Terror filled him, paralyzing his legs. He stood and waited with his arms thrown up as if they would protect him.

As if attracted to attack by the man's scream, the bear was on him, slashing, biting, and grunting. A few seconds later, the bear tossed the limp body of the soldier aside as another soldier ran into the light, took it all in with a single look, then darted back into the mine shaft. For a moment, it looked like the bear was going to follow him, but instead, it stalked around the clearing for a few turns, paused to sniff the carcass of what had been a man, then turned to the entrance and charged. It went inside.

Another man emitted a sorrowful scream that didn't seem to end until it suddenly cut off as if it had never been. Moments later, a series of grunts replaced it, then a roar of a successful kill from the bear. At least that's the way I heard it. There had been no more gunshots.

Five soldiers had made up the entire amount in Monroe Sanctuary, all who happened to be on guard duty that fateful day five years earlier. They were not supposed to be included in the population of the sanctuary any more than those of us who became the worker-bees for the colony. The leaders used them from the beginning to enforce their stringent rules. Not that there was a lot of crime, but a small force dedicated to keeping the peace seemed to benefit all. Two of them remained.

I chanced a glance at Jake. His face was understandably white, his lower lip trembling. He'd just witnessed half of his coworkers die since in my mind, there was no doubt the one inside had died. Any lingering doubt disappeared when the bear rumbled into the early morning light again. Its fur around its neck and mouth had turned red with fresh blood, and it chewed on a piece of what could only be flesh.

We remained still and quiet, stunned speechless, and scared. Meanwhile, the bear cubs tussled and explored the meadow. Both nudged and prodded the limp body of the first soldier before moving on to explore a hole at the base of a tree, probably where a rabbit lived. When one of them squealed, the mother bear raced to find the problem. A few minutes later, she waddled away from us, with both cubs trailing after.

Jake said in a tight voice he obviously tried to control, "That was close. We had all night to wake that bear and have it attack us, and somehow didn't."

Gerry said, "Maybe we did wake it and that's why she came out now. I'm scared as hell. My hands are trembling."

Jake turned on him. "And I'm proud as hell of our response. All of us. If the bear had charged up the hillside, it probably wouldn't have made it because of us shooting arrows and throwing rocks. Don't forget, those people down there were after us with the sole purpose of killing at least one of us."

I couldn't help noticing that his fellow-soldiers had also been regulated to being included in *those people,* who sounded like his way of compensating and pushing the reality of relations he'd enjoyed with them from the front of his mind.

"I don't care. I'm still scared," Gerry said. "I wish I'd have never come outside. I shouldn't have told anyone about the book or mine."

Jake stood to his full height, which was almost a foot taller than Gerry, his face drawn tight as his clenched jaw. He said in a dead-serious tone, "Hey, this was your discovery and your idea, but I'm beginning to wish the same thing. We may not all belong together. So, I'll tell you what. I'll escort you back down to the sanctuary if you wish. Chances are, they haven't missed you yet, and you can always say we took you captive and that you escaped and went back home. Point out the way we went to them. It won't matter, we'll be long gone and there are only two soldiers left down there to chase us and I doubt the leaders will send them up here again."

The blood seemed to slowly drain out of Gerry's face, more with each sentence.

Jake continued, "And just to make myself clear; from this time on, any of us can leave this group at any time, for any reason. You are free to go. We banded together to escape. We did that, so there are no more obligations."

He paused to look at each of us individually. It dawned on me that our lives now depended on each other and our actions despite his words. A glance at Gerry confirmed I was not comfortable placing my life in his hands. Danny was questionable but fell a little more on the plus side than a day earlier. Jake and Grace, I trusted with my life.

Jake continued in the same flat tone, "That includes being kicked out for complaining too much or not doing your share of the work or what needs to be accomplished. Gerry, if you took the time to notice, the four of us were willing to fight for our freedom, even if it meant throwing rocks to protect each other. You were not."

"I don't know anything about fighting," he whined, sounding like a spoiled child. "Besides, I'm too small."

That comment nearly set me off. We were about the same height and weight. It was not about size, but attitude. He could have gathered rocks and readied himself to throw them if attacked but hadn't.

He looked at me as if pleading. Maybe it was something else, but I was angry. Not at him. At an undefinable something else. In high school my junior year, a new kid enrolled. He was about the size of Gerry and me, which made him about five-five and a hundred and twenty pounds. Of all things, the kid had tried out for the football team.

It had been the talk of the school for a day or two, then the talk turned directions when the players quit laughing at the new kid. He could fly. Better than that, he caught anything thrown in his area—even passes intended for others. To top all that off, when the ball was not going in his direction, he blocked for the running backs and other receivers.

It took less than a week for him to earn his way from joke to hero. The next year they voted him co-captain. It is not about size, but attitude. Maybe I needed to get Gerry off on his own and tell him the story.

Jake turned to the rest of us. "Vote? Should we allow him to stay with us or banish him?"

"No, please don't vote," Gerry said quickly, realizing a vote would probably go poorly for him. "Okay, okay, I'll do what you say."

"Not good enough," I heard my voice ring out before my mind had the good sense to make my mouth shut up. "Jake is right. Despite finding the way out for us, you're like a weight around our necks. You're bringing no value to the group, but when we eventually find food, you'll want your share. You won't fight for us to keep us all safe, but you will let us do it for you while you stand back and watch. You won't even help with the hard work. That has always been your way."

"I cut the hole in the wall and stashed everything in there. I already did my part." He almost seemed defiant until the tears fell. "Without me, you would be dead this morning, Pen."

He was right about both things. Grace waited and let him sweat for a moment before finally saying, "The vote can wait a few hours or days, I suppose. But I'm ready to cast mine now."

If possible, even more blood drained from Gerry's face when he faced Grace. His eyes were flashing and moving from side to side looking at the rest of us for moral support and found none. However, Grace had raised a handful of kids and probably knew better than the rest of us how to handle him.

I said, "Grace and I talked last night. She lived closest to here and knows the area best. It makes sense to try and find her family, first. Any objections? From anyone?"

Jake said, "My family is a thousand miles away, so I may never search for them. If we can find hers, we should do that. I'd feel better if one of us managed to locate loved ones."

Danny nodded sagely after looking at me and surprisingly said in a manner that was a complete change from the person he had been inside the mine when he insisted on going to his home first, "Agreed. Then what?"

"You and I lived closer to the new shopping area on the

west side of town. Let's just leave it open until we see what we're facing and make it up as we go along," I told him. "It's just a few miles, so it makes no difference if we look for yours or mine, next, but what we find between here and there might make all the difference."

He seemed happy enough with that. At least for now. My anxieties were growing with the realization I might see my family again—or those who remained alive. It had been so long that I'd pushed any ideas like those aside, so they didn't make me crazy.

Jake said, "Right now, we need to get off this hill and away from the tunnel entrance and the door for the sanctuary. It must be near. We can carefully work our way towards town." He paused and looked down at the ragged lump in the clearing that had been a man we all knew before continuing, "We already learned things we didn't this morning. The leaves on the trees are new growth, the bear cubs were young, so it's early spring. I'm cold and wet. We need to change our clothing but before doing that, we need to wash some of this off."

"What else?" I asked with a grin, expecting to draw a laugh or two and lighten the mood. "You are doing so well at making serious plans. We're filthy, so you've decided all alone that we need to clean ourselves up?"

He smiled as he said, "Aside from running from armed soldiers and avoiding bears, from here to town there is only one bridge across the river. The water will be high this early in the year, so we probably want to use the bridge to cross, if possible."

Danny asked, "Why wouldn't we cross it?"

Jake shrugged. "It might not be there. A hungry bear might be sleeping on it. Any number of reasons."

Danny continued as if Jake knew more about what we'd find than him, "People?"

Jake sighed and spoke slowly as if considering each word before uttering it, "If people are living in Monroe, they will be watching the bridge, for sure—which is a complete contradiction to what I just said about crossing the bridge. It is exposed and anyone nearby who is watching would see us."

That last statement prevented any laughter. In effect, he'd

first told us to boldly cross the bridge, then told us to avoid it and the guards posted there. As the only way into the city from where we stood, we didn't take to the advice.

Danny said in a more upbeat tone, "You know, I had a friend who lived on this side of the river. I've thought about him a lot since being here because we passed his place the night we were captured, and I knew he was close. I watched the route when we were in the trucks. His house is on the side-road we took, not far from this spot. Maybe he can give us information on what it's like up here on the surface now."

That sounded good. If Danny's friend still lived close, that was a step in the right direction. We were woefully lacking in information. But clean clothes came first. Whenever I looked at the others—I refused to look down at myself—the shock of their filth and caked-on mud offended me, let alone their smells. I certainly didn't want to be one of them. Mud coated their hair as if they had stood under a mud waterfall, as well as the same stinking brown slime covered everything else. Besides all that, I was cold from the damp gently falling from the sky. Not shivering, but the kind of wet cold that never lets you get warm which is far worse than simply being chilly.

Jake peered around looking for landmarks. "We have to find the road to go home, first. Any ideas?"

"It has to be on our left," I said pointing, almost as quickly as Grace said much the same. We had grown up in Monroe. Despite never having been to the location of the sanctuary entrance, we'd spent our lifetimes within a few miles of it. When the war began five years ago and they rounded up important people for transportation, the vehicles turned north off the main road, highway 203, that crossed over the Skykomish River on one of the few truss bridges remaining in the area, painted green as were most in Washington.

It seemed funny that it had all happened so fast back then, all the cars going fifty or sixty down the road, but I remembered every detail in my excitement. Ten minutes of fear while bouncing in the rear of the truck, not knowing where it was going or what was happening with the sirens screaming in the distance, we had gone only six or eight miles. Less than ten minutes. One terrifying word was on the lips of everyone.

War.

To travel on foot the same distance the truck had taken me, it might take us a couple of days, especially if we went across country instead of finding and following a road. So close, and so far, away. I hadn't understood that phrase until today.

But Danny was right. The most critical lack we had was information. We had no idea what had happened to the world after the massive door to the Sanctuary closed. The communications, computers, radios, and all else that used computer chips had died at the same time. Even digital watches, computer tablets, and cell phones ceased to function from what people called EMP.

However, since everything looked and smelled as we'd left it, maybe they had called off the war and we spent all that time below for nothing. Nobody mentioned it but I'll bet the thought crossed all our minds.

Everything else could wait. The gathering of information came first, in my opinion. No, it was about to come in second if we found water, meaning a pond, lake, or stream. Washing came first.

As we struggled to move ahead in the forest, my mind swirled and raged with new thoughts. While not paying attention to walking in thick undergrowth, I'd let go of two or three branches that swung back and hit Danny. Disgusted, he increased his pace and got ahead of me, grumbling all the while.

After the look he cast my way, I fought to keep my mouth and smile in check. He could have lagged a few more steps behind instead of making such a big deal about getting slapped by some tiny branches that couldn't have hurt. Or he could have moved in front without making such a drama of the action.

I tripped and stumbled forward, my hands reaching out reflexively. I accidentally shoved his back to regain my balance. Danny paused to glare at me. His expression asked if I had done that on purpose?

"Sorry," I mumbled. He seemed to accept that—for now.

I shifted to think of other things. For five years we'd heard no news, not a single radio broadcast, email, or even a newspaper. We had a five-year blank in our lives as far as the world outside the sanctuary went, and until we figured out what had happened in that time, we were vulnerable in a thousand ways.

They told us repeatedly, while below, the surface was a vast desert wasteland probably occupied by mutants and worse. Green trees didn't exist. Radiation killed most people and warped all other life and would continue to do so for thousands of years. Twisted beasts roamed while searching for scarce food, mostly surviving humans. Water was more than scarce. Of the few humans alive, most would be living in bands of thieves and killers.

Most of that was untrue. Therefore, information was more important than clothing and we didn't know what to believe. We could maybe find blankets or clothing of some sort, build a shelter perhaps, but without accurate information, we were certainly going to die, if not from one thing, then another. I felt that belief deep inside but was too frightened to express it out loud.

On the flip side, just before the bears had emerged from the mine was when it had first hit me as solidly as if someone swung a baseball bat at my head. *We were outside.*

No matter that we were covered in mud, almost comical in appearance. We were breathing uncirculated air and looking at trees that were leafing out in spring, and above was the normally gray sky of Washington and rain. Smelling those evergreens and feeling the touch of the breeze on our cheeks after years of living below filled me with passions remembered. Even as a bear tore apart a man we knew, the feeling of lost freedoms tore at me. The duality of that moment is one of those I'll always remember. Joy and revulsion intertwined.

This was the morning they were going to inject that needle. By this time, I'd have been dead if not for Gerry and my friends. I hadn't stopped to realize what had happened this morning in its entirety, the good and bad.

To fully understand, I forced myself to think back a month. Thirty days of working endlessly and thanklessly, for fourteen hours and sleeping for eight in almost exhaustion. The two-hour gap in the twenty-four that allowed our shifts to overlap, so there were always six or more of us working at the same dull jobs—always under the threat of having food held back if we didn't obey.

We were the lowest of the low, but there were times when I believed we had it better than the other three hundred people down there. For those I sometimes called the "Dirty Dozen," work filled our time, or better said, consumed, with the performance of our duties. Our hands were always busy. Those people who were the top-tier, the old politicians, wealthy, and powerful had it worse in some ways. They had to devise methods to fill their waking hours.

I'd watched them play endless and mindless card games that nobody cared who won or lost. I'd seen two men whose faces had been on the front pages of newspapers and every TV channel, staring at a chessboard for an hour with neither moving a piece. We called them *trances*, and it seemed most of them entered them at times.

Suicides were frequent. As a lot, the people living in the sanctuary were bored, scared, resentful of the status they'd lost in their previous lives, and they often took those things out on we twelve. It was as if there existed two separate races of people. Us and them. Them and us. Dogs and masters.

But my mind was not on them. It was on me. Because of Gerry, and the others, I had now lived beyond the death sentence given me. The overlords had warned me to behave myself often enough. It had only been a matter of time, I suppose. But I was still alive.

I had not cared about the future, and that was a major difference between then and now. In some ways, the trial had taken the responsibility of ending my life from me. I don't believe I would have lasted another six months. Another suicide.

Now, it hit me as hard as running into a closed door. I was free. I'd managed to get out of the Monroe Sanctuary alive. If I died within the first day, it would still be better than what I'd faced.

I drew in a breath so deep my chest swelled, and my nose identified dozens of individual scents, damp, moist, and half-forgotten. My eyes closed as my body relaxed. The evergreen forests of Washington smell like nowhere else, or that's what I believe. Clean, wet, fresh, all shadowed by fir, pine, cedar, and a dozen others.

Jake said, "Are you okay, Pen?"

Through eyelids opened only enough to reveal his outline, I said, "Better than okay. This is the morning I was supposed to die. Instead, I live. I need to thank each of you for what you've done."

Unexpected tears trailed down my cheeks. I'm not one to cry. Grace's arms circled and pulled me close.

Danny said, "We couldn't let you die because you were the one that always spoke out and defended us."

Even Gerry mumbled a few nice words.

I said, "They found out how we escaped in no time. Are they going to come up here trying to recapture me, and all of you? If they do, will they find what it's like? If so, will they also come up here to live?"

Jake said, "I don't think so. If they do come up, or if any of a couple of guards left that were after us returned, I wonder what they'll tell everyone? It's a secret too big to smother and ignore. People who see that things haven't changed will insist on returning to the surface. So, if they learn what we already know, I can't believe they would remain below."

He had a good point. When those below learned that the surface was much like we'd left it, they would want to come up. Of course, they would expect to still be wealthy and powerful, but that was not going to happen as far as I knew. Maybe I was wrong.

Gerry said, "I can't see them wanting to leave the easy lives they have."

Danny rolled his eyes. "With us gone, who is going to be their slaves?"

"Should we take a good look around and then go back down and tell them what is up here?" I asked.

Grace spoke first, when none of the others did, "Why should we do anything nice for those people? We've been working as their slaves for years. We never asked to go down there, and they would have been glad to keep us doing their dirty work for another five years while they sipped their wine and played board games. No, you can do whatever you want, each of you is on your own for the future. But me? I don't owe them friggin anything but a punch in their guts and maybe a kick in their teeth."

Gerry said, "That's pretty harsh."

"They took my children from me," she said, each word dripping with venom. "I don't forgive them for that. With me down there, I couldn't protect my family, and they wouldn't let me come up here, so don't tell me about being harsh."

Danny said quickly, "I know it's still morning, but we don't know how far it is to my friend's house or what we'll find when we reach there. I think we need to change clothing before we spend another night outside, not just more medical scrubs. They are too thin. Besides, while wearing these, anyone who sees us will wonder who the hell we are and know something is strange about us. Maybe we need to eat, too. Save our dehydrated stuff for emergencies."

"And gather news," I added as I steeled myself for their negative reactions, which didn't happen. It seemed we all needed to know what had ensued while we were below. But we must get this muddy crap off us. Our immune systems are probably weak and who knows what biological things that were living in the bottom of that mine are attacking us right now?

Jake flashed a wink in my direction. I didn't know why he did it, but it made me feel better. He took the lead again, marching strongly and yet, slowing to help Gerry over rough places a few times. Gerry walked right behind him, but his footing was as poor and as clumsy as mine. I saw why he may have gone into computers instead of something more physical. I'd bet he had never participated in organized sports—and that was too bad. It would have helped him.

It was my father's belief, and thus mine, that no matter how uncoordinated a person, sports could improve them, mentally and physically. Teamwork to accomplish a goal unreachable by a single person was a good example.

When young, I'd been the sort of seven or eight-year-old who ducked fearfully when a ball came my way. My legs were too long for my body, and I was all knees, elbows, and feet too big for my skinny body.

One spring, he'd made me go into the backyard and kick a soccer ball with him every day after he got home from work. Spring, then summer. I hated it. Every day, kick, kick, kick. Control the incoming ball with one foot, place it on the ground in front of me, and swipe it back with a kick from the inside edge of my other foot. Control. Place. Kick.

Later it became control and kick. No need to place it anymore. Months passed and one day I realized that my father's kick returns came at me with zip, and I controlled them and returned them equally fast, two touches, without conscious thought, and often without looking at my feet. Rarely did one get past me. I no longer ducked. He had me dribble the ball with my toe for an extra ten minutes a day, which meant that I chased a lot of balls—until I got the hang of it—then it seldom touched the ground.

He put me on a team that year, one at the lowest level of soccer competitiveness. He did that intentionally. After a week of practice with other girls who ducked when a ball came in their direction, I went to my father and demanded to be moved to a better team with players who had foot-skills. Ones like mine. I never won a soccer game. My team did. That is a lesson Gerry needed to learn.

While never becoming a top-level soccer player, I'd found I could also swing a bat at a softball, put a basketball through a hoop much of the time, and even hit a tennis ball with some power. It was all because of the initial learning-curve my father put me on.

However, it was not about sports, I came to realize. It was about facing an opponent, any opponent, and squaring off. Win or lose, I would give it my all. He taught me that. His philosophy carried me through life.

Gerry never had that privilege.

With my father as his father, things would have been different. While thinking those thoughts and forgiving Gerry for his ineptitude and weaknesses, we moved along various paths and game trails through the forest, careful to watch out for other bears that finished hibernating.

Danny was not much of a woodsman either. To our delight, he discovered you can never tell how deep a puddle is until you step in it. The rest of us had walked around it. He should have—and if there were any soldiers from the sanctuary, nearby hungry bears, or outlaws in the area, they would have known exactly where to find the four laughing hyenas we became. Our tension seemed released by over-laughing.

I didn't expect anyone from the sanctuary to chase after us. Of the two who had, both were dead. They might send more, but probably not, mostly because there were only two left. There had been five soldiers. Jake was with us, and the bear had attacked two. Most of the other people in the sanctuary were too scared to attempt the wet slog through the dark mineshaft. Maybe in a year, or another five, someone would remember the seven who had left and never returned, which were us, and the two guards. Maybe others would eventually follow us outside. More likely, they would build wild stories of what nasty creatures we faced and how we'd died in the wasteland filled with mutated creatures, so the prudent thing would be to remain in the sanctuary.

Yes, I tried hard to convince myself we were safe from those below. It was mostly true. Not all, but mostly. Still, I also convinced myself that once I'd searched for my family, Monroe would be a distant memory. Where I'd land up was in question, but not that it would be far enough away that retribution from the sanctuary. They wouldn't forget.

The ground beneath our bare feet was damp or wet, or both. Moss covered old logs and rocks. We were cold. Water soaked the legs of my pants to my thighs, and the heavy overcast suggested we could expect more rain. Five years ago, I'd have complained. Not today. Today, I couldn't seem to keep the silly grin off my face.

I hadn't seen any rain in more than five years other than the slight drizzle this morning. Bring it on. A briar snagged my left foot, and I hopped a few steps. No, I didn't *have* to hop, but I did, and we shared a few chuckles because my feet were so muddy it was hard to tell which foot was muddier and which was not, and if either still wore a bootie.

The morning was quiet as they often are in the forests of Washington. It's as if the noises of the wildlife are muted and the green coating on most surfaces absorbs sounds, the ferns growing to our knees softened noise, and the air is so heavy with moisture sound cannot pass. It almost encourages people to be quiet.

I noticed Danny now held back as we walked in single file, protecting our rear. He carried his bow in one hand and a single arrow gripped in his fingers along with it. Both he and Jake had strung the bows right after we left the mine and we believed we were pursued. I assumed that at some point they would relax, especially as we put distance between the mine and us.

Maybe we still were in danger. It's better to be prepared than not.

Other than our raucous outburst over Danny stepping into the deep puddle, we moved quietly. Jake took us along animal paths and gave every indication he knew where we were and our destination, but I knew differently. His military personality dictated that if he had doubts, he was to charge ahead and pretend he knew what was ahead. That was what he was doing.

To a substantial extent, I was doing the same.

Chapter 4

We moved in a generally southern direction, as determined by the location of the brighter part of the dark clouds that revealed where the sun hid. The highway had to be ahead, somewhere, and not too far. At an infrequent rest stop, Jake explained an old hunter's trick for traveling in unknown thick forests where people tend to get lost. He said we needed to always go downhill until we found a stream, then follow it. Sooner or later, it would either join a larger stream or river, flow under a bridge, or reach the ocean. Those were the only three options.

The shallow stream we followed was a few inches deep and narrow enough to step over without stretching our stride. It eventually reached a small concrete bridge.

As the old hunter's trick predicted, a bridge passed over the stream right where it joined with a larger one and where culverts under the bridge allowed the water to flow past. We stood on the pavement in something akin to awe. At first glance, it was just a country blacktop road like most others in the northwest.

Then my eyes picked out details. The pavement had cracked in several places. There were no repair crews to maintain it. Dirt managed to find its way into the cracks and from those cracks grass and small shrubs and grass grew. Some might eventually grow into large trees as the roots split the openings in the blacktop wider. Moss covered much of the road where the sun didn't reach due to overhanging branches that hadn't been trimmed. The result was the road was no longer smooth, black, or flat. It spread before us, broken, chunks uplifted, lumpy, and more a deep shade of green from the layers of moss, than black.

The forest was taking the road back as if eating at the sides, a little at first, then more each year. At least, that was my take. The forest encroached until a time would come when a stranger wouldn't even know a road had existed here. That wouldn't be too many years into the future.

The next thing I noticed was that with the vegetation creeping into and onto the buckled blacktop, no wheeled vehicles had passed this way, or it would have crushed the plants and left clear evidence. No feet had traveled the road either. No passing feet had crushed or broken them; the grass stood upright.

The water flowing underneath the bridge was only a foot deep, rushing quickly, but pooled just before the culverts. We removed our clothing and spread replacements drawn from the sacks we carried. Gerry has been smart enough to seal them in plastic bags from the kitchen before hiding them in the mine.

The water was so cold it stung my feet and ankles, but we entered together and rinsed mud off with the help of using our removed clothing as washcloths and helping each other by wringing water from that same clothing over our heads to get most of the muck off. If Gerry had only enclosed a little soap.

It took a while. A long time standing in the cold water that was barely above freezing. Laughter and squealing filled the air as we returned to human forms. Smiles filled our faces and our eyes sparkled.

Finally, cold, clean, water wet our skins and turned them pink. When finished washing, we were cleaner and wearing fresh clothing. Blue scrubs were the clothing of the day, the same thin material we had worn below for years. We looked like a troop of itinerant nurses from a poor nation, the scrubs ill-fitting. While standing and admiring each other the rain began again.

The soft drizzle wet the new clothing and soon it was

almost transparent. I pulled another shirt from my bag and pulled it over the first, not for modesty, but warmth. The others did the same.

We discarded part of the empty bags we'd carried because they were now empty of clean clothing, or the contents combined with others. We tossed away the old, muddy scrubs. A quick inventory confirmed there were items in some bags that we didn't need. We left them, too. It was mostly thin bedding and maps printed on now soggy paper. We kept only the MREs, military Meals-Ready-to-Eat packets, and a few other items. We were down to four sacks and the scrubs we wore, along with the bows and arrows. Our total of earthly belongings for five people. It was not much.

We followed the blacktop road, still maintaining our single-file method of moving despite plenty of room to walk alongside each other. No reason to do so, except that it felt like the right thing to do. I said, "Danny, how far to your friend's house do you think?"

He did a mental calculation and said, "We turned off highway 203 and only went a few miles to the sanctuary entrance, which was probably no more than five. His house was about half-way. All that is guesswork from a long time ago."

I did my calculations to confirm or deny his estimate. Not that I believed he lied, but it was just my way. "So, no more than three miles from here, at the most, and probably closer."

He nodded absentmindedly, his eyes darting from one side to the other. He flinched when a bird flew over.

"What is it?" I asked.

After a tense moment, he said unconvincingly, "Nothing, I guess."

I turned to the others and fell back into line, however, remained more alert. Danny's reaction to the bird reminded me of naked fear, far more than any bird should have induced. My hands wanted to hold a weapon, even another rock. My ears searched for sounds that didn't belong. I watched him closely. Danny was holding back.

He was not doing it to place us in danger, I felt, but that was what I believed was happening. Maybe he didn't want us looking at him in the same cowardly manner that we looked at Gerry, thus he was not about to show his fear or tell us when he sensed something wrong—or that might be wrong and have us laugh at him again like at the puddle.

As if to prove my thinking correct, a man, old and withered, stepped out from behind a tree at the side of the road ten yards ahead. He casually allowed the rusty barrel of a shotgun held in cradled arms to swing in our direction. Jake stopped, while the others of us moved to his side as if the shotgun didn't terrify us.

Jake smiled in a friendly fashion as he casually and slightly turned his hip to allow the bow to shift into a position easier to raise. Behind his hip where the old man couldn't see, his fingers set the arrow he carried in his free hand on the bowstring as he said cheerfully, "Good morning, sir. Can we help you?"

"That you can, my boy," the old man rasped with a dry chuckle. "Put your things in a nice, neat pile at your feet and keep walking on down my road and maybe I won't kill you today." The voice crackled, the rheumy blue eyes challenged, and for a man who stood about as tall as my five and a half feet, his confidence was supreme. I noticed the shotgun was a double-barrel type, twin barrels beside each other. That meant only two shots without reloading, and there were five of us.

However, he was too sure of himself and that attitude seemed shared by my friends. Danny caught my attention. With a flick of his eyes, he told me where to look. I shifted my gaze to where he indicated. That glance revealed there were more people behind us. I turned to look. There were two of them, one holding a menacing-looking hunting knife and the other a large kitchen knife.

I seethed. If Danny had said something when he first suspected lurkers in the undergrowth, we might have been in a better position. He and I would have a talk—if both of us survived whatever was coming.

All three men appeared as filthy as we had been before bathing, their beards long and tangled. Matted and uncombed hair contained twigs along with dried leaf fragments. All dressed in baggy jeans and filthy shirts with poncho made of a waterproof material, probably plastic tablecloths with holes cut for the necks.

The two standing behind us were young, both maybe twenty-years-old and they held a resemblance to the old man beyond dressing alike. The man with the shotgun was closer to fifty. Maybe even sixty. Lean and evil would be the way I'd think about him in the future.

Jake, from the side of his mouth, said, "Penelope, can you talk to this nice gentleman for us, and explain that there is only our food and nothing of value inside our bags? Be nice for a change."

He always called me Pen, not Penelope, which increased my tension when he used the longer version. "What else?" I said as I moved a step ahead of Jake.

"Tell him we're not giving him anything. If he chooses to walk away with his friends, we might all live another day."

"He can hear you, you know," I said. "Just talk louder."

"Talk to him."

Jake wanted me to draw his attention. The problem with that was that if the old man got angry, I'd be the first one shot. I took another step forward, mostly because Jake sort of bent back and placed his shoulder behind mine and gently pushed my back with his fingertips.

I found myself between them and suddenly realized and understood that had been Jake's intention the whole time. I tossed my arms wide to attract the old man and moved a small step to my left where more of my body hid Jake's, despite his larger size. I tried to use those actions so he would look at me while concealing whatever Jake was up to.

Jake had said to be nice. I assumed that was for the old man's benefit because it was not my way. In that tavern, I'd learned to use my tone and attitude to talk to drunks and those belligerent. I said in a loud and demanding voice as I leaned forward, like a mother scolding a child, "Who the hell gave you the right to take our things?"

He screwed up his face and peered closer at me. He drew back and at first, I believed I'd succeeded. He raised his forearm and held it over his mouth. "Why are all of you people so white? Are you sick?"

If I had been quicker, I'd have coughed and agreed. That might have made him back off and leave us alone. We had all lost our tans years ago in the sanctuary. We no longer noticed our whiteness so hadn't noticed until he mentioned it. I ignored his question and raised my voice louder as I stamped a foot and raised a fist for show. "We are not giving you anything. Besides, we have nothing of value, so leave us alone."

He swung the barrel of his gun forward until it centered on me. I expected to do some fast backtracking and change my attitude quickly, but instead, an arrow suddenly appeared in him, a few inches from the center of his chest. More specifically, only the fletching appeared on his chest, because the rest of the arrow had penetrated his ribcage and now protruded from behind his back.

His eyes went wide, the barrel slowly lowered as he slumped and looked down at the little bit of the arrow still in sight until his body tilted sideways and hit the ground as the shotgun clattered to the pavement.

Jake had used my body to shield his actions. He'd fired from behind me. Now there were other sounds from behind. I spun and dived to one side.

Danny, bringing up the rear, had also let an arrow fly, and it had struck one of the young men's throat. In the panic and haste to remove it, the filthy young man tore at his internal flesh loose until he held the entire shaft of the arrow dripping with blood and gore. As if in denial, he closed his eyes and fell forward, his face making a wet sound as it struck the blacktop.

The third man froze in place a few critical seconds, but now charged us, the kitchen knife poised high to stab the first person he reached. Jake had also turned to look behind. He'd readied another arrow and hit him high on his shoulder with the quick shot, spinning him around until his feet tangled in each other and he fell over the body of his dying friend or brother. He screamed in pain, fear, and rage, using inventive cursing I'd never heard, and I thought I'd heard some rather good stuff while working at the cowboy bar.

Jake had done what he trained for. I ignored him while I looked at Danny in complete surprise that he had just killed a man. When needed, he had come through. He had another arrow ready to finish off the other attacker if needed.

Jake said, "Don't shoot him."

Danny slowly relaxed the pull on the bow. He said, "The other one. I was aiming at his chest and hit his neck. Bad shot."

Jake said, "Grace, get that shotgun and search the old man for more shells or anything else we want."

He didn't have to tell her twice. Jake moved ahead of Danny and went to the man lying near his friend, an arrow still protruding from his left shoulder. He kicked the knife in Gerry's direction. When Gerry didn't move, Jake snarled at him, "Pick it up."

I watched Gerry, expecting him to refuse, which almost happened, but he saw my judging eyes on him. He reached for the knife while I went to the first man, the one with the hunting knife clutched in his fingers, and found he wore a belt with a scabbard. I took the belt, scabbard, and the knife.

The belt was too big, so I'd cut it off when I had a chance and make a new hole for the buckle, in the meantime, I tied it in a knot and put the knife back in the scabbard.

Jake was kneeling beside the last one alive. He said, "Where's your camp?"

"Screw you." He winced in pain with the venom he'd put in the words.

The man, not much older than me, if that old, looked horrible. Thin to the point of malnutrition, dirty ragged clothing, a tangled beard, and he smelled like he hadn't had a bath since last summer. Jake drew in a long, slow, breath and allowed it to escape through lips pursed so it almost became a whistle. Without warning, his empty hand darted out and slapped the end of the arrow protruding from the man's shoulder.

A howl of pain erupted.

Jake waited a few moments, then calmly repeated the question, "Your camp?"

"No, don't do that again. Please," he pleaded. "Damn, that hurt me, man."

"Answer me."

A quavering finger lifted and pointed, then fell to grasp the arrow where it entered the shoulder.

Jake said, "I thought so. Thank you."

"W-what now?" he asked as snot ran from his nose and blood seeped from the shoulder in a red expanding stain.

Jake stood and placed his hands on his hips like a modern-day Paul Bunion. "Now, my friends and I are going to visit your camp and take whatever we want. You can go anywhere but there. Understand?"

"That's our stuff," the man protested angrily, seemingly more upset at what we might take than at the arrow in his shoulder or the deaths of the other two. "That's simply wrong, man. You can't do it. It's stealing, that's what it is."

I stood in absolute wonder at his words and attitude. Not more than two minutes ago, he and his friends had tried to rob us and were probably going to kill us, yet he now accused Jake of stealing. I didn't know if stupidity ran in his family but suspected it did.

Jake hesitated. He finally said, "I'm sorry, son. You're right and I wouldn't want to steal from you. Tell you what. I'll fight you for it. Winner takes all."

That brought an abrupt giggle from Grace who now held the shotgun in one hand as she searched the pockets of the old man. I didn't laugh. Neither did anyone else. All I could think of was that we'd killed two men and put an arrow into the third, therefore the police would arrive soon and take us all to jail. That's how things worked up here the last I remembered.

The young man on the ground clenched his teeth and didn't say anything.

Jake motioned to us with his thumb, and we followed him across the road. Behind a stand of briars, a trail angled up the side of the hill. Jake moved as if he knew exactly where we were going.

Gerry said with a weak voice and a face that looked ready to puke, "From the looks of them, they have nothing we want. We should move on, Jake."

Jake never slowed.

To be fair, I sort of agreed with Gerry and would have been happier to continue looking for the house belonging to Danny's friend. Instead, we climbed the side of the hill until we came to a campsite with three battered tarps providing shelter for people and things. A fire smoked under one.

Jake said, "Search the place. Tear it apart if you must. There must be things we can use."

Again, Gerry was about to refuse. After receiving a glare from me, he began to slowly pretend he was helping. The other three of us separated, and as we did, Grace carried the shotgun to Jake and held it out for him. "Four more shells in his pocket. I got a good knife off him, too."

"You keep the shotgun. The bow is quiet. I'll keep that."

Danny rushed out from under a filthy tarp. Trees supported it on two sides, and metal poles on the others. His face flushed red, his voice became a shriek, "Hey, you guys got to see this."

We ran the few steps to him at the excited tone of the scream he'd used. More tarps hung from the top to the ground around the outside to make sidewalls for a crude tent about ten feet square. Inside, in the far corner, sat a young woman. Her eyes were big, scared, and dark brown, her knees pulled up to her chest.

At first, it was difficult to tell it was a woman or her age. She sat in her filth and mud. The stench was enough to gag me and forced me to take a step back, where the air was cleaner. I took a deep breath and held it before entering again.

Soon, we were all stopped at the flap that served as a door. Grace raised the edge and pinned it open. Then she rolled up another sheet of canvas and tossed it on top, so one side was open, and part of the stench escaped while allowing light inside.

At our slightest move, the woman flinched but was going nowhere. A heavy, rusted chain looped around her neck; the other end secured to a tree stump a foot in diameter.

Grace handed me the shotgun without taking her eyes off the woman. She advanced, speaking softly, "We're not going to harm you, honey. We're here to free you."

The girl drew back and extended her splayed fingers as if about to rake her nails across Grace's face. She screeched. Tears filled my eyes.

Grace pulled to a stop, just out of her reach. She said over her shoulder, "I don't see a lock. What's holding that chain in place?"

"Zip-ties, I think," Gerry said.

I noticed the woman was rail-thin under the coating of excrement and mud. She wore a filthy plaid skirt and a wool shirt better sized for a large man. Barefoot. Her hair was greasy, tangled, and despite the filth caking her, the skin showed bruises, cuts, scratches, and welts from insects or worse. She sat on what had been a sleeping bag at one time. Layers of feces coated the material.

The smell of urine and feces mostly came from one side of her, at the limit of where the chain would reach. There, she had scooped out a small depression, probably with her bare hands, for a toilet. Grace suddenly reached out and took the woman by her wrists and used her superior strength and weight to control the emaciated girl without causing any pain.

Jake stepped forward and as he passed me, he slipped the knife from the scabbard I wore.

The woman drew back in fear. Jake ignored her as he got a grip on the chain and cut at the zip-ties but her near-maniacal convulsions and twists prevented him from doing it without causing harm. He turned and softly tossed the knife back to me, handle first.

Of course, I fumbled it and the damn point on the thing almost stuck me in my instep, but I hopped too fast, and finally retrieved it from the mud. He could have just handed it to me instead of throwing it and risking injury to any one of us by my hesitant reaction.

Jake said to Grace, "Let her wrists go and leave her alone. She understands English, so let her hear us talk and maybe she'll know we are here to help and are not going to hurt her."

Grace did as he said and leaped back to avoid a wild kick that missed her by a hair. The girl was snarling and spitting, more like a trapped animal than a human. We settled ourselves in a sort of ring and waited for someone else to have a good idea.

Danny moved nearer to her, drawing a fierce look. She seemed prepared to attack. He ignored it. In a normal voice, he talked, "Hi, I'm Danny. I went to school here and lived in Monroe my whole life."

She watched him as if he were a bug and her fist curled in readiness to squash it at the first opportunity.

He ignored that and continued, "We've been held captive in some underground tunnels for five years, better than this, but still captives and slaves. We escaped last night, so you can imagine what we thought when we found you. A prisoner like us. We want to free you, which you may not understand now, but you will. In the tunnels, they made us work all that time, but we hated it and risked our lives to get away."

She was watching him closely, every slight move, tensed and ready to fight if he advanced any more. But more importantly, she was listening.

He kept talking in soothing tones without attempting to move closer. "Seeing you like this makes me want to kill someone for putting you in this situation. The old man and one of the two younger ones who kept you chained up here are dead. The other has an arrow in his shoulder and is probably far away by now. If I had known what they did to you, he'd also be dead."

The anger and fear in her slowly subsided with his calm words.

Danny was probably only a year or two older than the girl. We realized that now as our eyes adjusted to the dim light under the tarp. The overwhelming stench had numbed our senses of smell. I could breathe without gagging.

He said, "So, here is what is going to happen. My friend Penelope, the one who can't catch anything tossed her way, is going to come over here when you are ready, and she will cut the rest of those zip-ties from the chain on your neck. None of us men will come near you. After she is done with that, you are free. We'll back away. You can run, and we won't chase you. Or you can stay with us and we'll care for you. Your choice. Just tell Pen when you want her to cut you free."

With that, he backed off two full steps and waited.

Jake said, "Everybody but Pen needs to leave here and continue to search of the camp. Meet back here, *outside* this tent in ten minutes. Pen, you stay with her and do what Danny said."

They left us. I heard them rustling through things, talking

softly, while I sat and waited. I didn't expect her to speak to me, but she said in a voice that made her sound like she was younger than I thought, "Will you really cut me free and let me go?"

"I have no use for making a girl a prisoner."

"How will I eat?"

"We have food. We'll share if you remain with us. Or you can go to join your family. We'll help you find them," I told her softly. "Whatever you want."

"They took me from my family."

I sat there and closed my eyes, letting my mind drift. When I opened them, she was staring at me in anticipation. I said, "Listen, we only escaped our imprisonment yesterday. We don't know shit about what we've walked into since we were taken below ground years ago, so I can't make you any promises. I don't know what will happen to us by the end of the day, let alone tomorrow."

"I don't understand. Underground?"

"We were kept below ground in a government sanctuary. We did the washing and cleaning for others. We know nothing about what has happened up here for the past five years. Who is the president? Hell, we don't know if this is even part of America and if there is a president."

"I can tell you some things, I guess."

Now she had my attention. I scooted one step closer without her asking and pulled the knife free. Before raising it, I said with a smile, "You already saw how poorly I handle a knife, so hold still or I may cut off an ear by mistake."

She snorted a giggle. Not much of one. But enough. I got the tip of the knife under a zip-tie and managed to cut it free. There were two more, but instead of prying them off because they were closer to her neck, I sawed with the edge of the dull knife. It finally cut through the tough plastic.

The chain rattled free as it symbolically clattered to the ground.

She stood up slowly and awkwardly, almost losing her balance.

For the first time, I noticed she was very pregnant. Her knees drawn up to her chest, hid the swell of her belly. The baby-bump was well defined. I hadn't seen a pregnant woman in a couple of years. Maybe more.

I remained sitting, not wishing to frighten her by standing. "Your name?"

There was a hesitation. She whispered, "Does it matter?"

"Nope," I said in my normal smart-alecky, snarky voice. "We can call you, Hey-you. Or Girl-with-the-dirty-hair. If you like Mary, that name's fine, too. Grace and Penelope are already taken by us but choose any other and it's yours."

She didn't smile or laugh. Her eyes drifted off and her voice sounded wistful, "I like Sara. I once knew a girl with that name. She was nice to me."

"Sara, it is, until you tell us otherwise. Listen, we're trying to find a friend who lived near here and maybe he can help us. We have some food, and we washed ourselves down by a stream close to here. We also have a few clean scrubs like mine if you would like to change." I touched the thin material I wore.

She slowly nodded, then asked in a little girl's voice, "Where are they?"

I knew she meant the dead men who had held her captive. "Down by the stream. Two of them, anyway."

"I want to see them."

"They are not looking well. Take my word for it. You don't want to see them."

"Yes, I do."

"Why?" I asked.

"I have to know they will never come after me again. I have to."

I nodded in sudden understanding. She couldn't take our word for their deaths. My eyes went to her belly. "One of them is the father?"

It was her turn to nod.

That confirmed they had held her prisoner for at least six months if the size of her belly was the measure. A half-year chained to a stump under a stinking tarp, using a hand-dug hole for a bathroom. I said, "The third one has an arrow in his shoulder. He may have left a blood-trail. The last we saw, he was alive."

"Will you let me kill him?"

"Sara, only a damned fool would get between you and him," I told her. "We'll also help you try to find him and then you can use my knife if that will help."

I stood and opened another flap. They were all standing right out there, listening. I said, "We have to go look at the dead men and search for the other."

"We heard," Danny said somberly. "Jake, can you lead us?"

I took a second look at Danny; one of the two men I hadn't liked yesterday. Maybe I needed to reconsider what I thought about him. Even Gerry seemed deferential to Sara. We hadn't been outside the sanctuary for a full day and we'd already watched a bear rip a man apart and kill another inside the mine, we'd killed two others with arrows, seriously injured another, and rescued a pregnant maiden. Now we were going hunting for a third man to allow a young girl to kill him.

It was a lot to consider for our first day of freedom. However, there seemed no choice but to continue.

Grace took up the position last in line, the shotgun carried in one hand as if it had been there a month. We followed the same path down to the road and I started to worry. Had I promised a fifteen or sixteen-year-old Sara that she could kill the lone survivor? I knew I'd promised to help track him and as I walked, I tried to figure a way out of the other.

Could I stand by and let her kill him? She was a young girl, little more than a child. That action would remain with her for the rest of her life. Then my mind went off on one of those sideways tracks again and it asked me, how long would she remember the treatment she had received for the last six months? Another lifetime?

Chained to a stump and used for sex by three men for half a year would affect her forever. Killing one of those three might make it all set a little better with her. Provide a little closure. The problem was that I didn't know what the right thing to do would be. Maybe Jake could take charge and get me off the hook, no matter what the choice we came to. I resolved myself to not criticize whatever decisions he made.

We reached the road and found the two dead bodies quickly. A pool of blood revealed where the third had lain. He was gone from sight. I'd expected the one with the shoulder wound to be alive and waiting for our return, but this felt unexpected, and that delayed my thoughts about allowing the girl to kill him.

The arrow must have cut a vein or artery because the drying pool he left on the blacktop was two feet across. A series of drips told the direction where he'd fled.

Sara went to each of the other two bodies, slowly, almost as if stalking them, and she paused at each to assure herself they were not strangers but the ones who had abused her. She rolled one with her foot enough to see his flaccid face. Then, and only then, she turned to me. "You said you have clean clothes I can have?"

I reached into the bag I carried over my shoulder and pulled out a pair of pants. "Anyone got a shirt?"

Gerry still had two in his bag.

Sara walked calmly to the edge of the stream and out into it as if it cleansed more than her body. She let the dirty plaid skirt fall to the ground and used the wool shirt to dip into the water and wash, after repeatedly rinsing and wringing until the water no longer ran dark brown. She took far longer than us— and again I thought she had more to clean than we had.

Without her clothing, more cuts and bruises were obvious on her legs, back, and upper arms. As she sluiced off grime, even more bruises came into view on her pale skin. Scrapes, black and blue bruises, and scabbed insect bites. Hundreds of them. Fleas and worse infested where she slept. At night, the mosquitoes had feasted. There was barely a smooth, unharmed square inch of skin.

She ignored us as she washed, her back usually to us, seemingly lost within herself. The water was barely above freezing. She ignored the cold. My instinct was to rush to help her, but a secondary instinct warned me to let her have this time alone. If she wanted company, she would let us know.

Once dressed in the scrubs, she looked like one of us and smiled with her lips but not her eyes. Still, she was young and beautiful. Her hair was light brown, and her features full. With the clothing covering most of the wounds and bruises, as well as the baby bump, both Gerry and Danny were looking at her differently.

It was her first-time bathing in months, I'd wager.

We walked along the road, six of us now, armed with knives, bows, and a shotgun. It had been a productive day, and it wasn't yet noon. The drips of dried blood left by the third man on the road led the way.

Chapter 5

When we reached the home of Danny's friend, all that remained was a blackened pile of ashes with small trees and weeds growing out of it. A concrete set of five stairs showed where the front porch had stood a year or two ago. The ashen remains were not five years old, which was telling. At a guess, maybe a year. There was still the faint scent of charred wood, so maybe less.

We paused on the road. Danny stood dejected and pointed, "There was a garage over there." His hand waved vaguely to one side as he almost whispered, "That was the house."

"He may still be alive," I said, feeling inside that it was a lie to say that, but required to make Danny feel better.

Sara said shyly, "Up ahead is another place where he might be. It was another spot for thieves to gather half a year ago. No people were there, last time I saw it, but it's a barn and if it hasn't fallen in, we should go there. It's going to rain again tonight."

That was the longest she'd ever talked. It showed she was gaining a measure of trust and thinking ahead, which was a major step for her.

The dried drips of blood-trail were still on the road, fewer than before. Either the wound was sealing itself or he was running out of blood. I expected him to come into sight at any moment, but the blood-trail continued. So, did we.

The roof of the barn came into view as we crested the next

hill. Only the roof because of the surrounding forest that encroached on the building hid the sides. Unlike barns I remembered, the small trees and underbrush grew right up next to the walls, making it hard to see if not for the roof standing high above. While watching for signs of the farmhouse that should be nearby, my foot found a rabbit hole, throwing me off balance, and I stumbled ahead a few steps before falling and skinning my left knee.

The others came rushing to me as I cried, "Frigging hole. What're the damn road crews doing the last five years?"

It was not meant to be funny, but the jokes started as Danny pushed my pant leg above my knee and pulled a bandage from the first-aid kit. I was trying to hide my embarrassment over being so clumsy with anger and shouting, but everyone already knew about that, everyone but Sara—and she did now, after hearing the multitude of jokes aimed at me.

Danny paused, one hand holding the back of my knee to steady me, a bandage in the other, and his eyes shifted to Sara. A guilty expression flashed across his face as his eyes fell to her many injuries while he made an issue of mine.

He said to her, "We have supplies, and you're welcome to them. It's just that . . . well, none of us wanted to frighten you by getting too close so we could put them on you." He paused; his eyes still locked on hers. "We weren't trying to hide our supplies or anything. You need a few patches here and there if you're up to it."

Sara smiled at Danny with a slight tip of her head. When she spoke, it was soft and understanding, "Yes, it would have scared me. That's about the nicest thing anyone has said to me in a year. Taking my feelings into consideration, I mean."

There was already something developing between them. An attraction. It had happened so fast I wondered if I was reading things into their words and actions. I'd also caught a hint of dislike as her eyes passed over me. Then I looked at his hand holding my knee and said, "Are you going to put a bandage on me or what?"

He fumbled the wrapper off and used white medical tape to secure it in place, his eyes diverted from her. I had the feeling he would rather be holding one of her knees. That should have mattered to me because until today I hadn't liked him—but that was way back yesterday. Today, a pang of jealousy flared, then quickly faded.

I got to my feet feeling somewhat silly. A skinned knee compared to what Sara had suffered was like the attack of a single midge compared to that of a mountain lion. No matter how much it hurt to bend my knee as I walked, I wouldn't complain.

The lessening number of drips of blood angled off to the side of the road.

Jake pulled to a stop and motioned for Sara to come ahead and join him. He handed her his knife without a word and she accepted it. Head down, she followed the thin line of drops to the side of the road where the stream flowed, and stood at the top of the bank, feet spread apart, looking down. She held the knife loosely in one hand.

From where we stood, it seemed like she was talking but with the rush of water, we didn't hear a word. She turned and came back to us, returning the knife to Jake as she walked past.

"Is he dead?" Gerry asked.

Sara said, "Not yet. Soon."

"Did he talk to you?" Gerry continued.

"He ordered me to help him. I left him to suffer. A quick death is too easy."

Grace snorted in contempt and said, "You did right, girl. We'll leave him there to die alone, hopefully in the dark, and hope it's a long and lingering time after what he did to you."

Sara just nodded and her eyes focused on the barn a quarter of a mile away. She started walking in that direction and we silently followed her.

The barn was large, weathered gray, the side walls twenty feet high. It was generally in good shape, all things considered. A few boards and some missing. Cedar shakes covered the roof and appeared like new. From our vantage on the road, a stone rectangle filled with charred debris and new growth plants told us where the house had stood and why the barn was there by itself.

Someone had left the barn door open and a hundred silly jokes ran through my head. However, before getting too funny,

I observed the tall grass in front of the door and found it without evidence of recent feet crushing it down to get inside. The morning incident with the bear leaped to mind, and the barn looked like a perfect place for another.

We left the road. Jake had us circle behind and walk near the walls to prevent a trail of our passing through the grass in front of the door for anyone walking above to notice. We paused at the door long enough to look inside. The dim light revealed a vast, open chamber that was dry and somehow alarming. The smells were earthy and musty. Birds nested in the rafters and we disturbed them. They fluttered, scolded, and a few flew in circles. About half flew out the door. Others went out a hole on the wall near the roof.

Jake said as he pointed, "There's a ladder to the loft."

"So?" I asked.

"Easier to defend ourselves up there and anyone poking around down here would make a lot of noise to warn us." His tone was sharp, and his lips pinched as if he was tired of me questioning his choices.

I said, "Hey, that was not a criticism. Just a question." He seemed to relax and reached for a rung. I continued as if I couldn't keep myself from irritating him when the opportunity arose, "Want me to go up the ladder first again? So, you can put your hand on my butt and *help* me?"

It didn't come out as humorous as intended. Nobody laughed. It was like finding a dog turd in the center aisle of a church on Sunday morning.

Sara looked away quickly.

Jake turned his back to me and wordlessly started climbing. A small animal sprinted along the edge of the back wall and exited through a hole before I could identify it. The smell of hay, decay, and damp assaulted my nostrils, all vaguely remembered until now. I watched him climb and avoided the accusing eyes of my friends.

"It was a joke," I explained. However, even to me, it sounded lame.

Once on top of the second level—the loft as I remember the name, Jake said softly down to us as if afraid of using a louder voice, "It's dry and a good place to spend a night. Come on up."

It was early afternoon on a wonderful day to be above ground. It didn't make sense to stop traveling. Not to me. We could reach Monroe by nightfall if we hurried and encountered no obstacles.

Before I could insult Jake again by asking a silly question about continuing to town, Gerry made those same points—however, in a voice that whined and offended so much that it convinced me to remain where we were, so I didn't have to listen to it anymore, before Jake spoke.

However, Jake took his questions as legitimate inquiries and addressed us like he would a group of soldiers, "None of us got much sleep last night and some are a little cranky."

I felt eyes resting on me but refused to meet them. Later, he might pay for that insult if the opportunity arose. In fact, he would.

He quickly continued, "Besides, we can keep a watch on the road through windows up here. I also want to talk to Sara and pick her brain about what we're likely to find around here. We still need to know a lot, and she can help with that. It might save us from making a mistake that will cost lives. We'd be silly not to make use of her knowledge."

If I'd asked the same questions as Gerry, Jake would have given me a short, terse answer. It was not fair. I like it when things are fair—if they favor me.

At the top of the ladder, we found a flat, open area behind a short wooden wall probably placed there for safety to keep anyone from falling off. The end of the barn faced the road, and a series of open windows let light in while keeping most of the rain and wind out. The wood floor of the loft was hard but reasonably clean. A few brushes with my hand cleared an area and I sat.

There were feathers and white, dried bird poop on the floor under the beams. A lot. Birds of several kinds must roost inside if the variety of feathers littering the floor told the story. There was the ammonia scent of urine and old scat, not from birds. Animals had lived inside the barn and probably still did.

The sleepless night before, while escaping in the mine shaft and then waiting for those below to catch up with us and kill me left me tired and sleepy. Maybe I was a little cranky, after all. But that was a matter of opinion and perfectly understandable. Walking the distance today made my legs feel heavy. It was probably more walking than I'd done in the last five years in the sanctuary.

Added to all that, the emotions of killing Sara's keepers and freeing her from the chain around her neck, the physical ups and downs of our travel, and the emotions I tried to keep in check ripped at my body and mind, trying to tear it in pieces. Everything rushed at me like a tree falling on my head.

I closed my eyes to sort things out. When I opened my eyes again, darkness filled the barn. The others were asleep. I saw their outlines in the dim light and identified their distinctive breathing and small snorts and snores. If needed, I could tell each of them from what I heard, although no reason came to mind of why I might need to know them in the dark.

The original plan had been to talk among ourselves during the afternoon, gather information from Sara, and make plans—then sleep. It seemed as if I had slept all during the afternoon and into the night. There was no way of telling when the others had drifted off, but no matter, we'd talk in the morning. Sara could tell us a lot about the world we were entering. We all wanted to hear all about the news and the war we'd missed.

Jake sprawled right beside me, snoring softly, one arm akimbo in my direction. I wanted to believe he was trying to protect me in his sleep. More than likely, he had a cramp in his arm. The chill in the air evaporated sweat and my skin felt hot. I wanted to reach out and draw him closer or roll over and snuggle. We were adults. Everyone else was fast asleep. His quiet touch had probably been what had awakened me.

While those thoughts bubbled around in my head, and before I could move closer to him, the creak of weight shifting on the wooden ladder that went down to the ground floor brought me instantly to my senses. A quick mental count of the heavy breathing near me and the five shapes of lumps in the dark beside accounted for all of us and said something was very wrong.

A similar groan on the ladder may have been what had awakened me. Perhaps I'd heard a sound that didn't belong.

Not a lot of noise, just the creak of a board, as if a foot put pressure on it. I'd already accounted for everyone in our group, so my brain decided that the soldiers from the sanctuary had tracked us and were sneaking up the ladder to take us, prisoner.

My initial reaction was to wake the others or scream to warn them, but instead, I waited. Whoever was on the ladder climbed slowly and probably listened for any movement from us between steps that would tell him or her we were aware of his surreptitious advance. The slightest change in sound in us would cause the intruder to either charge or flee. Maybe he would shoot if startled and he had a gun. A single shotgun blast could hit us all with one burst, I decided. My brain shifted into higher gears with possibilities and dangers real and imagined.

We were sleeping behind the short wood wall standing waist-high, at the top of the ladder, so whoever it was on the ladder could only guess at how many of us there were, our sexes, ages, and the weapons we possessed.

Unless he had watched us enter and knew. I dismissed the soldiers in sudden inspiration. I didn't believe they could exit the sanctuary and track us and there was only a couple of soldiers left of the original five. Those in charge of the sanctuary wouldn't allow the last two to chase after us.

A stranger climbed the ladder. I was certain.

I didn't like that idea entering my mind nor the possible consequences.

If we scared him off, yes, I'd decided it was a man and not an animal, he had all night to plan another attack or ambush us when we went outside in the morning. Where all those ideas came from was unknown. I was no frontier woman, had never hunted, and nobody had ever hunted me. However, a primal instinct took hold as fear became secondary.

Unconsciously, my fingers wrapped around the handle of the hunting knife on my hip and gently pulled it free without making any noise to alert the intruder. The most likely person on the ladder was probably Sara's injured captor, to one with the arrow wound in his shoulder. Maybe he had feigned more injury than we believed. If so, we'd restrain him, and let her throw him over the side to the floor below if she wanted. With his loss of blood, he couldn't have much strength left.

She deserved that privilege.

I heard the barest whisper, vague words from one mouth to the ears of another, followed by the sound of someone beginning to climb faster. There were two of them. At least two, I realized. It couldn't be Sara's captor unless he brought a friend or two.

My level of fear doubled.

Grace's finger reached out in the darkness and touched my lips to keep me quiet. I knew it was her on my other side because the old steel of the barrel of the shotgun touched my bare forearm as she raised it, the barrel pointed to the top of the ladder at the end of the half-wall, and we silently waited.

She wouldn't shoot until they identified themselves as enemies, I decided. Even then, she would warn them before pulling the trigger. That was the civilized thing to do. Grace might be a little crude in her language and manners, but she was honest and treated others well.

I thought of the young pregnant girl and the punishment she'd faced. I instinctively knew there were more like the three men who had kept her prisoner. Whoever climbed the ladder might be more of them. Everyone on the surface might be like them. We didn't know what hell we'd entered.

My mind raced faster than words could form in my brain. Concept replaced fear, survival replaced flight, killing replaced peaceful talk.

The strong survived in today's world on the surface. I lay still in the dark trembling and suddenly realized another truth. Good people would have called out to us and requested permission to enter the barn, making their presence and intentions known. Let us know they were friendly. Even if they hadn't known we were there, they would never climb a ladder so silently and stealthily unless they were up to no good and knew of us.

That idea kept repeating in various forms. Seconds passed. There was no reason to wait until people tried to harm us before killing them. If they intended to do us harm, we should strike first. All those thoughts rambled around in my head in mere instants. I'd only been awake perhaps thirty seconds.

A darker shade of black moved quietly where the heavy bolts held the ladder to the wall, as a person reached the top and moved noiselessly across the floor of the loft in our direction. A stray shaft of either moonlight or starlight revealed his darker form against the wall. A floorboard under him creaked.

Grace fired the shotgun.

The blast lit up the inside of the barn for an instant and revealed a man who had been crouching, ready to rush forward. The explosion of the shotgun lifted him off his feet, a mass of red at his waist in the wink of the light from the shell. The blinding darkness returned and what I'd glimpsed had only been impressions and my imagination. My ears felt as though someone had punched them with fists.

No groaning or cries of pain came—or if they did, my stunned ears failed to hear. A single thump a second or two later may have been him falling from the top of the ladder to the ground floor. I felt it more than heard it.

Grace leaped to her feet and raced to the edge of the loft, me right behind, my knife in hand. Jake was shouting questions, Danny called out for Sara. Grace started to look over the edge to see if anyone else was on the ladder when I realized that was a bad idea. I grabbed her shirt and pulled her back as I shouted, "No."

Three shots quickly followed from below. One after the other, in a space of maybe two seconds. Wood chips flew from the loft edge where her head had been, and holes appeared in the roof as bits of wood floated down. Whoever was next on the ladder had been waiting for a head to appear and eyes to look over the edge and investigate.

Our friends were leaping to their feet now, calling questions to us that we didn't have time to answer.

"Down," I ordered in a shout. Just the one word.

Grace had initially resisted my pull on her shirt because she had intended to look over the edge and see down there. Now she understood the second person on the ladder had to only point a weapon up and wait for her to look over again. Their other option was to shoot through the thin boards we stood on. She shoved me to one side and darted to the other and dived near the base of the wall where she could ease out and see the ladder from an angle.

Before she could, four more shots erupted through the floorboards where we had been standing.

Grace eased the shotgun barrel near the edge without looking over it. She braced the butt against her shoulder and angled the barrel to point down the ladder without exposing herself. Her brief move placed the gun over the edge. She fired the second barrel and leaped back.

There was the huge blast of her gun, followed by a grunt, then the thud of a second body falling onto a wooden floor below. She called softly, "Pen, see any more of them?"

"Just those two, I think."

Our friends were on their knees but didn't move or talk.

It was quiet for a moment, then Grace said in a calm voice that traveled the quiet expanse of the barn, "Okay everyone, grab your shotguns and flashlights. Let's search this freaking place top to bottom. Shoot at anything that moves, just don't hit me."

A single set of heavy footsteps raced across the wooden floor heading for the open front barndoor. There had been a third person, after all, probably waiting for us to show ourselves before he or she shot.

Jake whispered and my still ringing ears heard, "You two are bad-asses."

"You better believe it," I said, not believing a word that came from my mouth. My hands shook, my mouth was dry, and tears trickled down my cheeks.

"What was all that?" Danny asked in a voice that was more of a croak than his normal one.

"Three people tried creeping up on us," Grace snarled as she hit the thumb lever on the shotgun and the two empty shells ejected high into the air and they clattered to the floor, at least I imagined them doing that, but in the darkness. I couldn't see them. She loaded two more shells and snapped the barrels back, ready to shoot twice more. The sounds of her movements were easy to follow, as easy as if we were outside in daylight. Besides, I'd seen how it works in countless westerns.

Gerry's voice wavered weakly, almost a whisper, "Did you kill someone up here? I woke up and there were gunshots."

"Two dead, with any luck," Grace said in a tone that sounded angry to me. "I shot one up here, and one down there."

Gerry gagged, rolled to his side, and vomited. The stench filled the still air in the loft, but I ignored it. Would the third person attempt to return? Would he bring more armed men with him? After coming so close to dying—again—and the shotgun blasts and smell of gunpowder strong inside the barn, my adrenalin was raging. Oddly, I felt safer. We had protected ourselves.

Sara said, "You killed two more people?"

She sounded disapproving but obviously didn't understand. We all talked for a while since we were awake. Our decision came down to manage the unknown again. Climbing the ladder in the dark and going outside where the third person who had tried to sneak up on us was stupid. Up in the loft, we could defend our position, provided they didn't attempt shooting through the walls. Danny offered to stand the first watch. My eyes closed and I fell asleep as Gerry continued to spew his guts accompanied by disgusting sounds only ten feet away.

I semi-woke later, hearing Jake's soft snores on one side and Grace's on the other. I may as well have been in a bomb shelter because of feeling so safe with them on either side to protect me. I went back to sleep. Danny was still on guard when I whispered his name. Not that I distrusted him, but I wanted to verify he was awake and offered to stand the next watch.

"Jake already offered," he said. Of course, he had. That was the way Jake worked. He did his share and more.

When the first of the morning light flooded the barn, we woke almost as one. Small shafts of sunlight came through the new holes in the roof. Dust motes floated in each. I looked over the edge of the loft and located the bloody body of a man cut almost into two pieces at the bottom of the ladder near the wall. Swarms of flies had already found him. The second man lay in a heap on the floor a few steps away, half of his head missing.

Grace came up behind me and looked over the edge of the loft at my side and said, "I owe you one for saving my ass, Pen."

"You already paid me," I said, looking at the one who had been within a few steps of hurting one or more of us. I noticed the handgun he'd carried lying a few feet away on the floor of the loft. It had been worse than I'd believed. He had carried a gun, no doubt pointed at us and the first of us to move would have been shot, then the rest.

The ugly black thing on the floor was built to kill. It was a modern pistol, the kind with lots of bullets stored in the handle. He had carried it ready to shoot us. He had been only ten feet away. One or more of us was only seconds away from dying. I felt like adding my vomit to the pool beside Gerry. Only Grace firing the shotgun without giving a warning had saved us.

I gingerly picked up the pistol between my thumb and forefinger. It was heavy, black, and menacing.

Jake asked me, "Know how to use that?"

"I know not to touch the trigger unless I want it to go bang," I said, despite my earlier experience. I didn't want to pretend I knew more than I did. "That's about all."

He laughed without amusement and said, "Smart girl. Hand it over here." After a brief examination, he said, "Nine-millimeter, Glock, semi-automatic. A thousand-dollar weapon back in our day."

"You can have it," I said. "Now, you owe me a grand."

He tucked it into his waistband. Conversation stalled. I saw and smelled the drying vomit from beside Gerry again. He hadn't even bothered to move away from it, and it coated his shirt on one side.

It was not that he was a coward. He couldn't help it if his parents raised him differently and he knew nothing about weapons or fighting for survival. I could almost forgive him for the scowl aimed at me, but his accusing, red-rimmed eyes bore into me.

He must not have slept after the attack and perhaps blamed me for what happened. Some people are like that. They accept their safety as something due to them and hold a grudge against those who protect them and risk their lives to do it. They also believe in multicolored unicorns and that everyone in the world should live in peace and harmony as if that is ever going to happen.

Maybe we all should, but don't. Not for the last ten thousand years, or so.

Sara was also awake. She aimed a stage-whisper in my direction, in a tone of pure condemnation, saying what Gerry was thinking as her eyes locked on mine, "How many people do you people kill a day?"

"Lately? Two-and-a-half, on average," I said flippantly without a smile. It was the plain, simple truth since our break-out. Three dead yesterday and two today, for the average I gave her. Well, the sun was barely up this morning, and we still had all day to add to the total carnage and raise our average higher, so we might have to adjust that number.

The way she had spoken to me curdled my stomach. I wondered why she had singled me out as an enemy. She had no reason to talk to me that way. I was trying hard to be her friend but that might end quickly.

I wouldn't apologize or explain. I refused. Grace was a hero. I owed her my life again. Of all people, Sara should understand that there are people in the world who don't deserve to live. Gerry's passive attitude, I could understand. Sara's escaped me, especially after what we'd found at the camp where her kidnappers held her.

Only yesterday, we'd liberated her from months of torture and forced sex at the whims of three terrible men, and last night we'd saved her from the intentions of three more. She had no right to judge. Those who had tried to kill us in the dark of night would still be alive if they hadn't meant to harm us. If we hadn't protected ourselves, none of us might be alive this morning.

My mouth was about to remind her of those things. But my mind was off chasing tangents again. I hadn't liked the tone of her question and my response had been automatic, which was most of the reason for the death sentence Hazel gave to me. My mouth spoke before my mind thought. More than anything I'd done, which was little enough, it was the way I'd done them—and the *how* of things said. Perhaps I needed to work on that. Perhaps it would get warmer in the summer. Perhaps tomato seeds would grow tomatoes instead of grapes.

Danny made a stern face and aimed it in my direction. He'd heard my flippant answer and went to Sara to console her over my sharp-tongued cruelty, and to ingratiate himself with her. I felt a small pang of guilt over speaking to her that way. My eyes went to the wounds on her exposed skin, her arms, neck, and face. There was barely a square inch that didn't have an injury or insect bite, yet with all that, she was a beautiful young woman.

Danny could do worse than befriend her.

I could do better.

Jake said quietly, "We should leave and eat while we walk. Remember the third one that came in the night is still out there, and probably not fond of us. Keep your eyes open. We'll go out slow and careful and try to find his tracks."

"So that you can kill him too?" Sara snapped.

"Hopefully," I muttered before I could stop the word from slipping out. Then, I quickly went on, "Before he kills us, I hope we kill him."

We filed past the two bodies on the ground floor that we had to step over one to leave the ladder, and our nearness increased the buzzing of a thousand flies. Jake pushed the second body aside with his foot and exposed another gun, one just like the one I'd found. He stooped, grabbed the gun, patted the man's jacket pockets, and found a fistful of loose bullets. He removed the magazine and refilled it. The remaining bullets went into the bag with the food he carried. We had no pockets on our scrubs.

Nobody suggested removing their clothing. The material on both was not only old, but patched crudely, and dirty. Then there were the flies. Thousands of them. No, we didn't need their shoes or clothing.

I had reconsidered giving Jake the gun last night and intended to talk with him about returning it and giving me a few instructions on how to use it. Grace had a shotgun. It would make me feel safer. In the darkness of early morning, I'd planned my words to him. After all, I'd given it to him in the first place, hadn't I? I never said he could keep it. But now he had two. He should share.

I had none. He had two. Fair is fair.

He caught my eye and my look of disapproval in his direction, and he handed me the gun he'd just picked up as if he read my mind. "Please don't shoot anybody until we talk about how to use it."

Sara didn't think the comment was funny if her expression revealed anything.

I did. The smile on my face almost became a laugh. With that ugly black thing in my hand, I felt safer, even if I didn't know how to fire it. There had been a session with a boyfriend on a shooting range years ago, but most of it was forgotten in the intervening years. I intended to learn quickly.

Grace gave me a friendly slap on my shoulder as she shifted the shotgun to her other hand. She and I were getting to be good friends. Well, I guess we always had been friendly but now there seemed to be a difference.

Not surprisingly, Danny walked alongside Sara as we went out the door. Jake took the lead again, and Grace and I brought up the rear. Gerry got stuck in the middle, head down, eyes red, as he glowered at the world in general.

Jake paused and examined the ground. The third person, man, or woman could be anywhere. Whoever it was would either try to kill us or had fled hours ago. Jake tried to determine which. He pointed to one lone set of boot-prints leading away from the barn, up the incline to the road.

I watched his back the entire time. At the very least, I could point the pistol as if I knew how to shoot if the third person appeared. My finger could pull the trigger. If the gun fired, so much the better.

The attitude of both Danny and Sara upset me more than I wanted to admit. In response, I started to review what I knew of each person in the group again. Gerry had been the one who figured out there was a way to escape. He'd smuggled the things into the tunnel including the clothing I wore. If I had to guess, if he had a choice, he would return to the sanctuary and never mention the mine tunnel.

Which was odd in another way. If things outside had been

as we'd initially expected, meaning a vast, waterless, wasteland, ravaged by radiation, he would be well on his way to death by now. Finding a lush, vibrant, place where people tried to kill him made him unhappy. Either way, he would die soon if he didn't change his thinking.

On impulse, I said, "Sara, why not come back and walk with me? I want to talk."

She looked at Danny, hoping he would refuse the invitation for her. Then she reluctantly slowed and walked beside me while Grace fell back a few more steps to cover our rear. Sara eyed me suspiciously.

I said, "Tell me about what's happened to the world in the last five years."

"You don't remember?"

The five of us had agreed to keep our lives in the sanctuary a secret, at least, for a while, even though we'd already shared part of it with her. We didn't know how people would react, and there was a good chance they would not like us for that reason. We'd heard that our leaders had closed the outer doors as the first bombs exploded, and we shut outside and left them there to die. She knew a little about it, of course. But not all.

I said, "We were out of touch, and I want to hear what you experienced. Here, in Washington."

My words were not lies. They simply didn't reveal the entire truth—or much of it. She wanted to tell me as little as possible.

"Bombs fell. And missiles, they say. Things blew up. All in one damned day. Houses caught fire. There were sirens and shooting."

"What else?" I asked.

"Isn't that enough? I suppose you want me to give you all the gory details. That's the part you like best, isn't it?"

I held my tongue. When I trusted myself to remain calm, I went on, "No, it isn't enough. I have a lot of questions."

She snapped at me, "A whole war isn't enough for you? How much bloodshed do you want?"

"No, I mean what you're telling me isn't enough. Who were we fighting? How long did the war last? Start there."

"I don't know."

I slowed and looked at her face, at the extended belly of her pregnancy, and the condition of her skin. All of her. I found that I wanted to strike her. Push her down. Anything to make her talk in full sentences and drop the attitude. We'd saved her ass twice and now she looked down on us for killing the people who had enslaved her and tried to kill her in the night.

From behind, Grace said softly, "Take a deep breath, Penelope."

She was listening and probably was as upset as me. Grace simply handled it better. I took more than one deep breath and said to Sara, "Who were we fighting?"

"Nobody seems to know. It was like a sneak attack. There were soldiers. Not ours."

That was better. "How long did the war last?"

"Tuesday, I think."

"What?"

"It could have been a Wednesday, I guess, but why does it matter?"

I took a few more deep breaths and then said, "The war lasted a single day?"

"I don't know. They didn't tell us anything. I just know the bombs and explosions were all the same day. The fires and shooting lasted two or three more. Then people started killing each other. Soldiers came. Different ones in uniforms. They spoke another language. They killed people, each other. Like you do."

Grace warned me, "Penelope, your neck is getting red again."

"Me?" I snapped at Sara and ignored Grace. We had killed both men in the night, but Sara must have thought it was me instead of Grace for some reason. At least, she was blaming me. The day before it had been Jake and Danny who had killed, but I'd have gladly killed any of the three who held Sara hostage. Still, the girl seemed to only want to blame me. I turned to her.

She looked away as she rolled her eyes the way teenage girls used to do with their parents.

Grace said, "So, back then. There were a lot of people killing each other?"

"For food. Or guns. Or anything else. It was terrible for

months. Going anywhere was sure to get you shot. Then more soldiers arrived and there was a lot more fighting between them and the ones with guns who were not soldiers."

Grace continued, "What did you do?"

"My father, a man of peace, took us, our whole family, and our neighbors, in his old RV and drove fast to get us out of town and into these mountains. We went up on this road, and where a dirt lane broke off, we went along it to a small clearing with a stream. My dad knew about the place and parked the RV up the road a bit and we all got out and dug up small trees and bushes, and we kids gathered pine needles on blankets and spread them over the dirt road at the beginning to hide it and the RV's tracks. From the pavement, you couldn't see anything. Then we drove up to that clearing by the lake."

"Very nice," Grace said as if discussing a family picnic. "Then what happened?"

"Nothing."

"Explain," Grace said.

"Well, Dad hunted for rabbits and deer, we all fished for trout and sunfish, and we grew some food. We had a small stream and we used water from it for the plants."

I asked, "Where did the seeds come from?"

"Oh, my dad went to town by himself and got them after things calmed down some."

Grace continued asking my questions without evidence of anger or pointing fingers, which drew reasonable answers in sentences longer than three words. "In town? Did he get anything else there?"

"Oh, sure. He always got the clothes and stuff we needed. He even got a motorcycle one time and rode it back and forth until he didn't come home one day."

I glanced over my shoulder at Grace and understood her finger across her throat meaning to cut off the line of questions. The girl had no idea that her father had been raiding others to get the seeds, clothing, and motorcycle. He'd probably killed several people to do it. Sara had no idea.

It was not my place to insert myself into her history. I said, "So, you lived in the forest for about four years before those three men captured you. How'd that happen?"

"They put a blanket over my head and took me away. I was sleeping."

"Your family?" I asked.

Sara faced me and I saw through the bruises, cuts, and insect bites. She was younger than I'd thought. Her voice was almost that of a little girl when she said, "They are probably worried about me."

More like dead, from what her story told me. Three of those men had gone into their camp at a remote stream and took her away. I didn't believe they had left any others alive, but you can never tell. I said, "Can you find your way back to the place?"

Caution closed her face.

Grace said, "Listen, Sara. From what you've told us, your home is nearby. We'd like to take you there."

"Why?"

I answered first, "Because we are going into Monroe and have no idea of what it's like there. Bad people may run the city. We don't know what we're going to find and would feel better if you were safe with your family where you can have your baby."

"I agree," Grace said with a sideways nod of approval to me.

Sara walked on, her eyes averted as she seemed lost in thought, probably deciding the right course of action. I wanted to interject my ideas. However, it was better that she assessed the facts and came to her conclusions, than for me trying to tell her what to do. My eyes fell to her growing stomach. Six months pregnant, maybe more. It would only get harder for her from now on.

She needed a family to provide support, medical care, food, and shelter. I asked myself if we'd done her a favor by removing her from a place where those evil men fed and cared for her after a fashion. She was helpless on her own. I compared her future with those around me. Chances were, in my mind, one or two of our group would almost certainly die in the next month or so. Maybe more.

If yesterday and last night were examples of how we would be accepted by those living up here, that death might occur within another day. So far, we'd been lucky the sanctuary guards hadn't caught up, the bear hadn't eaten any of us, the three men on the road lost their ambush because of Jake, and the three sneaking up the ladder in the barn shouldn't have made the noise to wake Grace and me. All luck.

It couldn't last.

Nothing said the outcomes of the next four encounters would be the same as the last four.

Taking a very pregnant girl along with us was folly. No, stupidity better described it. She would eat our food, contribute nothing to our success, and slow us down. With her attitude about us, she might find my finger poking her eye out. We needed to find a nest for our little mama bird.

After about five minutes of walking down the side of the blacktop road, she said, "I'll show you where we lived."

Grace said, "Which way?"

Sara pointed in the direction we were walking to a hill about a quarter of a mile away. "There. I was going to slip away when we reached it, but I guess that would be wrong."

I called out to Jake, who was about fifty steps out ahead, and motioned for him to come back. In a few words, I explained the situation.

He understood and agreed. If she had a family living so close, we would leave her there.

Poor Danny was heartbroken at the idea. She went to rejoin walking beside him. After a few steps, she took his hand in hers.

Of all things, Gerry fell back and walked beside me. It took him a while before he spoke, but finally said, "I'm not like you, you know."

"Maybe that's a good thing."

He shook his head sadly. "No, it isn't. Maybe five or six years ago it was, but that was a different world. In today's world, I'm not going to make it am I?"

"Come on," I said encouragingly while inwardly completely agreeing with him. "You can learn."

"That's why I came back to talk with you. I want to learn. I just need a teacher."

"I'm not a teacher," I said with a snort of genuine humor.

"I can barely take care of myself."

We walked on a few more steps and he said, "Okay, I need a sergeant to guide me. I'm a private."

"Grace would be a good choice. Hell, Jake *is* a sergeant. Ask him," I said.

"Nope. You. Jake's good at what he does, but he's a foot taller, a hundred pounds heavier, and all muscle. He smashes through doorways. Others back away from him because they know they will lose to him in a fight. They take one look at me and start swinging, knowing they will win."

"All that is true," I agreed.

"We're about the same size, you and me. But you don't back down from anything or anybody. I can never be like Jake, but maybe I can learn to be like you."

I think he was trying to compliment me. I said, "Nobody has ever said something that nice. I'm not sure being like me is a good thing, but we can work on it."

"It looks like *good* people die early. I was raised differently but I'm smart and can learn. If we have to bet on which one of us dies first, who will you put your money on?"

"I see."

"Me too. And I don't like that answer. I need to change or die."

Sara pointed to the side of the road, where there was a stand of pine trees, a few small fir trees, and underbrush. She said apprehensively, "That way."

Chapter 6

We moved ahead as a group until we stood at the edge of the road. My eyes found the pavement had broken at the edges long ago, probably from the tires of vehicles turning off the main road onto the dirt road that had existed. If I hadn't known the family RV and others had used the unseen road, the broken blacktop wouldn't have drawn my attention. Of course, the RV had been driven down it, years ago.

Sara said happily, without indicating anyone as she started moving into the brush at the side of the road, "Are you guys coming?"

"Damn right," Grace said, speaking for all of us. We were not going to allow Sara to go off by herself now that we'd rescued her.

For me, a sense of foreboding had descended. The three men who had taken her in the dark of the night would have been afraid of pursuit from her family. They had taken her to their camp which was less than a mile away. That meant the family could locate them at any time. Also, Sara hadn't mentioned hearing the protesting voices of her family as they whisked her away.

All that added up to one of three things. One was that my paranoia and negative outlook had taken over rational thinking. The second was I was right in my expectations of what we'd find, which was not much of anything, possibly we were even at the wrong place. And lastly, I might be completely wrong about everything. At the end of the dirt road might be her loving family. Sara and her expected child would live long and fruitful lives in the valley with the small lake full of fish.

A gambling woman would give long odds on the last scenario happening.

Sara spoke up in a direct manner we hadn't heard, "Listen, what we need to do is go off the pavement fifty yards from here and slip into the trees without leaving any tracks for others to find. Then, after we're hidden by the trees, we will move to the old road and follow it to the campsite, maybe a half-mile from here."

She took the lead and delegated Jake to be the last and make certain there were no stray footprints to indicate where we'd left the road. She had taken charge and missed the looks exchanged between the rest of us. Being more aware than I'd given her credit for, she ordered Jake to remain hidden for at least ten minutes beside the road to make sure nobody followed.

My estimation of her increased. It had done so almost hourly since rescuing her. From the simpering prisoner that we'd found huddling in the corner of the tent, to the confident young woman before us was a change I couldn't see myself making. Putting myself in her circumstances made me come up far short.

It reminded me of Gerry coming to my side earlier with his questions about how to be stronger. I quickened my pace until I was alongside him again, determined to help in any way possible. I'd been wrong to rebuff him.

"Gerry, we didn't finish our talk. I'm sorry if I was rude. You know me. I'm awkward, clumsy, break things, and I trip and fall. I mean, handing me a knife usually means someone is going to bleed, probably me, and the blade will probably shatter or snap."

He turned to me as we walked; with no trace of the humor that I'd tried to inject into the conversation. He said, "I know all that. And still, you have to admit that you won't back down. That's why they sentenced you to death. If you had cooperated, that Witch Hazel of a judge would have dismissed the ridiculous charges. Who ever heard of someone sentenced to death for being rude?"

"I couldn't do that." I shrugged. Back down, I mean."

"Exactly. You are a little taller than most women, thinner, too. That makes us about the same size. But men and women respect you. That's not true for me."

"Maybe they just don't want to take a tongue-lashing from me."

"No, that isn't it. Not entirely, but maybe a little." He walked a few more steps and said, "If one of those important people down there gave you shit about something like they said you were too slow to serve their food, or you laid out their clothing incorrectly, what would happen?"

"I'd tell them to pound sand. Maybe scratch their eyes out. Sometimes, I'd manage to keep my big mouth shut."

"Then what?"

"I don't know," I admitted.

He said, "Me neither. Not exactly, but *something* else would happen. You'd water their liquor, trip and break their last bottle of fifty-year-old-scotch, or a seam on their favorite clothing would pull free and embarrass them. Maybe something else, but you would do a little *something* to get even."

"Maybe," I smiled.

He didn't. He said, "I'd fall all over myself apologizing and asking for forgiveness. I might think about revenge but wouldn't ever do it."

His admissions and admiration of me were making me embarrassed. He had never once told me anything like that in the last five years. He had barely spoken to me. While never rude, he seemed to pull away. Maybe he feared what I might do to him, or the fallout from things I did. Well, it seemed what he watched was me getting arrested and sentenced to die, also. That was not a feat to be proud of. It revealed my stupidity more than anything and why would he wish to copy those actions?

The words to tell him how to live his life wouldn't pass my lips. I could see that he had a hero-worship crush on me and that he doubted himself. However, it wouldn't hurt to give him a little push in the right direction.

The two-track road through the forest we followed was

overgrown and looked like nobody had traveled on it for . . . six months or more. About the same amount of time Sara spent away from her family. I noticed others were exchanging wary looks as they realized the same things. If Sara's friends and family still were alive, there should be signs or fresh evidence of habitation this close to the camp, not that any of us were woodsmen or trackers.

A veil of impending dread descended as if a fog moved in. It was as if I stood in front of the judge again, knowing what her ruling would be, yet hoping for a different outcome. Our pace slowed.

Nobody dared speak. A glance at Sara revealed her excitement and impatience. She wanted to break away and run to her family. Only she expected something different than us.

"Just over the next hill," she merrily called over her shoulder as she outpaced the five of us.

While avoiding the others because of trying to hide my feelings, I walked on, even when Sara pulled to a stumbling halt. I joined her and stood at her side. The beautiful little stream and clearing in the forest she had described spread in front of us, small but from our elevation, the cold, clear water of the lake sparkled. The bottom of the clear stream feeding the lake was as clear as the sides. A tangle of dead trees was at a bend in the stream, the result of a past flood.

On the shore stood a leaning cabin built of local wood thrown together for shelter, and beside it sat an RV, coated with a veil of green moss, vines, and bits of grass growing in the cracks. Four flat tires and tall grass made it look squat. The blackened stones of a fire pit sat beside a variety of chairs and homemade benches, all covered with vines and moss, unused for months. A silver aluminum rowboat sat upturned on the beach of the small lake.

The grass in the camp was green and already knee-high. There were no trails within it, no spirals of smoke, and no movement.

As beautiful and alive as the camp appeared at first glance, it supported all but living people. Sara's knees buckled and I helped her sit. A motion brought Grace racing to her side, and then came Danny.

I said to her, "Jake and I will go down there. No need for you to see."

To my surprise, Gerry pursed his lips and said, "I'll go too."

His eyes were on mine, pleading for permission to accompany us. Suspecting what we'd find, I almost refused. However, Gerry wanted to learn to be tough and gain respect. It was a start. I nodded once.

His expression said he wished I'd refused.

Jake put an arrow to his bowstring, a symbolic gesture from my standpoint. What was he going to shoot? New plant sprouts or trout?

Of course, he took the lead, which was fine with me. I nudged Gerry ahead of me so I could reach out and pull him back if what we found was as expected.

The road to the camp ran a hundred yards down a gentle slope. I realized why Sara's father had selected the location. Only one small access road that was easily concealed led to the place. No other roads, no cabins on the shoreline, and it sat in a small, almost circular depression.

The surrounding forest would absorb sounds. Anyone on the blacktop a half-mile back wouldn't hear a shout, probably. Campfires were built low, below the mound we traveled down to arrive at the bottom. The camp was hidden from accidental discovery if the smoke from their fires was accounted for. Fires were probably only used at night so the smoke wouldn't be seen.

The prevailing wind came from the west, which moved the smell of smoke east, into the larger portion of the National Forest where there were few people before the war, and probably fewer now.

The stream and lake probably teemed with fish. A large flat area had been planted with crops, but now the forest was reclaiming it. A few brown cornstalks remained upright.

It was a perfect location to live but for one item. The three who had taken Sara lived to the east, perhaps a mile away. The scent of smoke may have carried to them. Or the three may have been hunting deer and stumbled on the camp by accident.

Whatever the circumstances, I had no doubt the three were responsible for what we were walking into.

I said softly, "Gerry, are you sure you want to go down there?"

"No."

"Why don't I send you back to take them a message or something?" I saw Jake stiffen with puzzlement. Gerry was willing to help, and I was pushing him away.

Gerry said, "I'm going. I have to do this."

Jake said for only our ears, "He's right. He goes with us. It's a new world we have to live in."

My foot caught on an exposed root and sent me stumbling ahead. I almost ran into Gerry and realized that if someone like me was going to make it, Gerry was not alone in learning how to survive.

At the edge of the clearing, we found a motorcycle laying on its side, rusted, coated with algae, and the grass growing between the spokes of the wheels told of how long it had been there. At least, for the winter.

"Go slow," Jake ordered, his bow ready to shoot at anything he didn't like.

As we reached the RV, one of those large bus-like things, we found the side facing the stream missing. Much of it lay fallen to the ground in a sheet, as if someone, or three somebodies, on the inside had kicked the thin wall until it fell.

We moved on. At the cabin, a makeshift structure of small branches covered with tan tarps, we found the bones of a person. Then another nearby.

I saw a pot beside the firepit. That was something we could use. I considered gathering it then left it alone. No reason I could determine for that choice, except that it felt wrong to disturb anything, let alone take it.

Gerry fell back beside me. His eyes were wild, taking it all in. His expression was what I felt.

"If not for Sara, I'd run from this place and never return," I said.

Gerry said, "For her sake, let's keep looking."

Altogether, we found seven bodies.

"We can bury them," Gerry said. "That might make her feel better. It's the right thing to do."

Jake spoke for the first time in a long while. "First, we talk to Sara. People are funny about their dead. They sometimes want things handled differently."

A half-hour had passed while we explored, during which none of us looked back up the hill to our friends. To my utter surprise, Gerry morphed into a clinical describer of all we saw. His emotionless voice pointed out the sleeping cots, the broken crockery that had to have been in the hands of people, the lack of weapons, knives, and a dozen other things that indicated the useful items had been spirited away, the rest destroyed in what must have been a rage of insanity.

"They're waiting for us," Gerry said, his hand flicked in the direction of the road.

As one, we turned and began the long walk back.

When we were within speaking distance, Sara said, "Are they down there?"

"All dead," Jake replied, then waited. "Seven. We can bury them if you like."

Without a tear shed, Sara said, "No. It's just bones, right? Let them return to the dust they came from. Digging holes and filling them with old bones isn't going to help my family and it will tire us out."

Her eyes were hollow, her voice sounded weak and pleading. I couldn't help myself. "You don't have to go down there. We can do it for you."

She sniffed and drew in a deep, relieved breath before saying, "They would have done that for me, I guess."

Danny leaped to his feet. Jake turned and headed back down to the camp, his back stiff and his jaw set in determination. Gerry went with him. I stayed with Grace and Sara for a while, then went down to the campsite to lend a hand. Sara didn't seem to want to talk to me or look my way. The few times our eyes met, she scowled.

That puzzled me. She seemed to be fine with the others, but for some reason, she didn't like me. I could live with that but would like to know why she felt that way.

They had located two shovels, one with an unbroken handle. The dirt beside the stream was soft and easy to dig, so I went down and helped with that.

As seven holes were completed, I noticed something was

wrong. Nobody was moving. "What?" I ventured.

Gerry said, "How do we get them here? The bones are scattered, we don't know which belongs to each person, and—how are we going to carry them?"

Jake said, "I was thinking the same. Maybe if we take a tarp from that shed, we can pull them down here. One skull to a grave and distribute the other bones as well as we can. Anyone got a better idea?"

"I'm not touching them," Gerry said, his face pale.

I moved to his side, understanding he'd gone far beyond his capacity for such things. Even though he was refusing to do more, a surge of pride at what he'd accomplished swept through me. I said, "Can you help cover them?"

He closed his eyes and then made a sound that may have been a grunt of agreement. He might have been on the verge of spewing his last meal, instead. I chose to believe the former.

The other three of us removed a tarp from a sidewall and gathered bones. Touching the first few gave me chills. After that, I picked them up quickly and placed them gently on the tarp without issue. It took us two trips.

Before the second trip, when the tarp was partly full, Jake had his back turned to us, and as I moved to gather a few more bones, I noticed him intently studying one. His finger ran along the length of what looked like a leg bone to me. He put it down and went near the shed to gather more.

I couldn't help myself.

I deposited those I carried near the one Jake examined. Then I picked up the leg bone he'd been staring at while wearing a suspicious scowl. On it were parallel marks, or maybe striations is a better word. There were other flatter scratches on the surface. My first reaction was to wonder what sort of animal made them.

My stomach suddenly wrenched. No, they were not made by the teeth of any animal. The lines were too regular to be a natural occurrence, and I realized where I'd seen similar marks. They were caused by a knife.

The cuts were made by a knife hacking through a slab of meat. The other marks came from where a knife had cut alongside the bone to remove the flesh. I'd seen the same sort of marks on venison roasts from deer my father had killed.

The bone fell from my lax fingers and clattered onto the others. People had made those cuts as they removed the meat from the bones.

Jake's hand touched my shoulder and startled me. I screamed and jumped.

"What is it?" Gerry asked.

My eyes went to Jake. He gave me the smallest shake of his head.

I turned to Gerry, "Nothing. This burial is getting to me. I'm jumpy."

I went back to work while thinking that if there is a god, he should allow those three bastards to return to life a dozen times—so I could kill each of them twelve more times, each time a slower and lingering punishment.

Gerry helped fill the graves without mention of the marks we found on the bone. Hopefully, if he saw them, he didn't know what they meant. We walked slowly back to where Sara waited and asked what sort of service she would like for her family and friends.

She stood, back straight, chin up. "I've been thinking. That bunch of bones is not them down there. Not my family. The bones are just stuff they left behind. You've done what was needed. Thank all of you."

She turned and walked back along the dirt road in the direction of the blacktop, leaving us all to look at each other wordlessly. Then we followed behind.

At the edge of the blacktop, we turned left and walked along the edge in the early afternoon. The day was warm and clear, with only a slight chill from the breeze. Before long, we would come to the intersection of Highway 203 and turn right to reach Monroe, our homes.

There was little talking.

Again, I brought up the rear and noticed that all but Sara now carried weapons. Thirty hours ago, we'd had a pair of bows. We were adapting. A deer leaped from cover and darted across the road startling us. Six weapons trained on it.

We moved slowly, watching cautiously ahead and to both sides. Now and then I quickly spun to look behind because if anyone crept up from there, I was the last in line, thus the first victim of an attacker.

The trees were more than leafing out. The foliage was the pale green of early spring despite the warmth in the air and a few were opening blossoms. Had the climate changed very much? It was a silly question. If it had, there would be different varieties of trees, the previous varieties dead or struggling to remain alive. Maybe palm and mango would someday dominate the area. Who knows? What I saw was the same as always.

At the junction of the highway, we turned west and spread out, leaving ten or twenty steps between each of us, not because anyone told us to. That was the odd thing. We realized we were on a more traveled road, heading in the direction of a small city, so the chances of encountering unfriendly or antagonistic people increased with each step. Being too close together made it easier for attackers to take us all out at once.

All six of us were city-dwellers, yet we instinctively understood that concept. My mind took over again. Admit it or not, all people feared the dark. Some more than others. The same with spiders and snakes. We were born with the tools to help us survive, and that often means avoiding certain things. Sure, some overcome the fears or pretend to. I'm not sure they do.

Every year we used to hear about people that kept poisonous snakes who were killed by their pets. A boa constrictor strangled a woman not far from Monroe. Wait, that was just a story I'd overheard in the tavern where I served beer, so it stood a good chance of being a tall tale instead of truth. No matter, those things had happened.

Despite many arguments to the contrary, I believed that like most animals, perhaps all of them were born with certain amounts of knowledge. Baby ducks imprint on the first animal they see after hatching. That animal becomes its "mother." No other ducks teach it to do that. Raise a kitten with a puppy and the cat will chase mice. Elephants shy away from the same mice, yet they may have never seen one.

Why? It's that inborn knowledge, by whatever name we choose to call it. The six of us sensed we were approaching danger and caused us to separate, to put distance between ourselves and the others for safety. If something happened, the entire group wouldn't die. Some of us might escape.

While my brain analyzed those thoughts, my ears twitched in response to the slightest sound, my nose searched for smells out of place, and my eyes flicked from side to side, searching for movement, shapes, colors, or anything that didn't belong.

The rusting car on the side of the road didn't belong in nature. It was the first we'd passed, and both Gerry and Sara reacted by pulling away as they walked past. As I drew alongside, I looked inside and found white bones in the driver's seat, the skull on its side, empty eyes still looking at me. I shuddered.

A pickup truck with a camper was ahead. Between the car and pickup, grass and moss grew undisturbed in the cracks of the blacktop. The road was narrower than I remembered. A glance to the side showed that plants encroached on each edge, narrowing what remained of the blacktop. In a few more years the two sides would converge, and the road consumed by the forest.

Jake pulled to a halt. His fist raised into the air to stop us. He bent at the waist, examining the ground. Then he stood upright and pointed near his feet.

As each of us passed that point, we paused to look. There were two sets of footprints in the soft dirt left by a dried puddle. Human. Wearing boots or shoes. They were walking in the same direction as us.

They were also fresh.

Chapter 7

The footprints didn't need an explanation. They were there. They were fresh and going our way. If we moved faster, we might catch up to the makers, or perhaps catch a glimpse of them. If they had friends up there ahead or had set an ambush, we might be in trouble.

Or they might be our saviors.

That was the problem. We didn't know who they were. We didn't know much as facts, but we speculated on everything and considered it all dangerous. Jake paused and knelt as he examined the ground again. When I reached that spot, it was clear two more had joined the original pair. There were now four people ahead of us.

An unknown four against us six. I couldn't help but calculate the odds. Remove the pregnant Sara from the equation and it was four against five. Remove Gerry—I didn't have to continue the math.

I looked at my footprint and compared them with a shoe or boot my size. All four sets were larger than mine, all different, so it was not the same two people walking in the same direction twice. Chances were all four of them were men because of the sizes. For some reason, they had split into two groups or pairs, before entering the forest. We had found where they came out and joined together.

Why they had gone into the forest was beyond us. What we knew for sure was there were four men ahead. Our pace needed to slow from my perspective. We needed a plan. A good one. Going the other way would be a plan I might like.

Fortunately, Jake seemed in agreement because when we reached the next rise, he veered off the road and stepped carefully on the exposed rock until he concealed himself in the underbrush, leaving no telltale footprints behind. At the wave of his arm, the rest of us carefully followed.

When we gathered in a tight group, he said softly, "Well, we know we're not alone in the world. That is good and bad. There were four of them. They were heading toward Monroe, to cross the river on the Lewis Street bridge, I'd guess."

"What does all that mean?" Gerry asked.

Jake didn't ridicule or tease. He shrugged. "Who knows? I think we should slip through the woods until we can see the bridge from a concealed location and watch it from a distance for a while."

"Why?" Danny asked.

"Because," Jake said slowly as if explaining to a child, "if I wanted to control Monroe or know who was going or coming into town from this direction, I'd choose to watch the bridge from the other end. There I control who passes or does not. I'm assuming, they are doing the same."

Grace said, "Makes sense to me. There are two places reasonable to swim across the river near here if the water isn't too high. Upriver of the bridge is an island. The water is shallow enough we can wade out to it. On the far side of the island is the main channel, but it's only about fifty feet wide. A person can swim a dozen fast strokes and reach the other side. Did it a hundred times when we were kids."

"The other one?" Jake asked.

"Below the bridge. Not far from where we are. A sandbar and again, the main channel with fast water. We'd all get wet, but there's a park there beside the river to hide in and my house is only a few blocks away." Grace spoke as if she was going that way, with or without us.

Gerry said, "I'm not a strong swimmer."

Grace turned and said, "Don't have to be. Let a couple of us go first. You can use a piece of wood to help float you, but I'd suggest you just dive in and paddle like hell. We'll be waiting on the other side to grab you."

Danny said, "What about Sara? She's pregnant."

Grace made one of those faces women sometimes use for men. "I had four kids. I was pregnant, not crippled. Sara, how's your swimming?"

"Not bad. I've swum across that river a few times like most kids from Monroe."

Grace said, "Again, if a couple of us get to the other side, maybe downstream where the current will carry you to the others, we'll grab and pull you out."

Jake said, "Okay, downstream it is. But first, I want to find a perch and watch the bridge for a while. They might be watching who is coming and going from the other end, but I'd like to see too. It might tell us a lot."

"You're worried," I said, for no reason other than I detected it somehow in his words or manner.

He didn't deny it. "Probably four men passed by here. Or four people with feet nearly my size and long strides, which means over six feet tall, came out of the woods and walked along the road, going into town. If they had left the road and entered the woods, I might think they were sneaking up like we are. As it is, I'd guess they came from town, entered the woods in pairs, and met up again later, before going back. Or they came from somewhere else and joined up to go into town. Why did they do that? It sounds military."

"That's what bothers you?" I asked. "Maybe they just went hunting. Kill a deer and take it back. Might take four to carry it."

He said, "Nice try. But if they were hunting, they would have brought a wagon to carry it, but it is possible, I guess."

Danny said to Jake, "Then what do you think?"

Jake shrugged.

Gerry said, "If I was guarding my city with a choke-point like the bridge, I'd send scouts out to search the road and forest on either side for intruders every day. Look for people like us— or signs of invaders sneaking up and spying on them. Other soldiers."

Jake bit his lower lip and said, "That makes sense, too. Where'd you learn strategy like that?"

"Video games. I used to be fairly good at first-person shooters."

Games, I thought derisively. An instant later, I changed my mind. He had a point. The bridge was not only a chokepoint for travel to the north, but it was not the only chokepoint. There were others to the east and west, the north was mostly mountains, and they were a barrier easily defended.

If Gerry were right, and I assumed he was, we'd been fortunate to miss encountering the scouts. They might venture our way once a day, or even twice a day on patrol. In any case, by tomorrow, they would find where six people had traveled this way unless they were blind or inept.

I said, "We need to cross today, if possible. From the bridge, they can see too far, so it must be right after dark when we go. I think we should find that perch Jake spoke of and nap while taking turns watching. It may be a long night."

Jake took my statement as an agreement for all. He said, "Okay, I'm going to be out in front about fifty yards as a scout. Keep me in view and be ready to stop or hide at my signal."

We exchanged looks. Gerry pulled his shoulders back and tried to stand taller, which made him only a little shorter than me. But his chin was up, his jaw set, and he appeared ready to go. I was beginning to understand what he'd told me about admiring me. He was trying to be stronger. Maybe stronger is often a mental issue and not physical.

I made it a point to give him a little wink of encouragement as we moved off, and promised myself that when we stopped, I'd teach him a bit about the Glock he carried in his left hand. Jake had entrusted him with it. Not that I knew so much about guns, but I had twice fired a nine-millimeter semi-automatic at a target range while working at the Happy Rodeo Bar and Grill. A boyfriend at the time had taken me to a local outdoor range.

His clumsy instruction amounted to being familiar enough to not shoot me or my friends. Hitting targets was for those who used guns frequently, not him. His aim, pardon the pun, was for me to learn to hit an area the size of a man twenty feet away. That and to make himself look good as he put bullet after bullet into the center of the round target.

Within a couple of minutes, he taught me to raise the gun, sight-aim down the barrel, and pull the trigger while hitting the target almost every time. He said I wouldn't be shooting anyone fifty yards away, only ones nearby. It was those less than twenty yards away I needed to worry about. My goal was to protect myself at close range. In retrospect, it was a better lesson than I understood at the time. I'd try to teach that much to Gerry and see how it went.

Danny was helping Sara along as if she couldn't walk without his support, and she seemed to be eating up his attention with her big doe eyes. It may have been my imagination, but it seemed there were fewer bug-bites on her flesh today, some of her bruises had faded slightly, and after washing and tying her hair back, she was far prettier.

I would have suspected she would have been more depressed over what we'd found at the RV camp and her family, but on second thought, maybe she had suspected what we'd find all the time and had been mentally prepared while hoping for the best. It hadn't been a shock to her, but a confirmation.

Grace walked methodically ahead of me. Determined, was a better description. Shortly after dark, we'd cross the river, enter the wooded park, and come within six blocks from her home. If even one of her family still lived there, or maybe a neighbor, she could find the information about the others.

I couldn't see Jake out ahead of us but assumed the others could. I did see glimpses of the river to my left, and the reformatory beyond.

People from other places used to talk about living in Monroe and having the prison right there as the largest employer in the city. The first question was always, aren't you scared? Our stock answer was that if any inmates escaped, Monroe was the safest place to be because the escapees were doing their best to get away from our town.

Those ahead of me pulled to a halt almost as one. Gerry knelt. He was at the front of our group. When he did, we did too.

Gerry motioned for us to move up.

Ahead stood a small knoll or rise. Jake was below the crest, on a knee, only his head above the top. Jake motioned for us to move away from the road, closer to the river, where we peeked over the underbrush to see the green bridge, looking like a resurrection from seventy-five years ago.

Technically, it was a truss bridge, built of heavy iron beams in the fifties. Most just called it the Lewis Street bridge. No cars or trucks were driving across it, however, there was a pile of them at the far end, perhaps ten, or more. Stacked two high, acting as a barricade with a narrow, gated opening in the center, wide enough for one person at a time to pass.

There were, at least, two guards at the gate. More importantly, a makeshift platform stood at the top of the bridge, higher than the barricade. Another man was up there, wearing a pair of binoculars around his neck. Now and then he paused in his pacing to scan the area on this side of the river with them.

We didn't need Jake to tell us to stay down, out of sight.

Three guards on the bridge and presumably more on call at the first sign of trouble. That brought up the question of why? Who were they on guard against? Were they expecting an attack?

I wondered if the entire city was guarded in the same manner. From our position, I could see the river below the bridge, and across it. Were there more guards there?

Behind us, a little lower in elevation and farther from the road was a stand of evergreens, firs, or cedar, I'd guess. Jake pointed to it and motioned for us to retreat to the trees.

Once safely under the low-hanging branches, we settled in a ring facing Jake. He said to all of us, "Okay, what do you think?"

Gerry said instantly, "If they have that many guards all day and night, it's a lot of resources to assign. Three per shift, probably four shifts a day, are twelve people dedicated to watching one entrance. Besides, you don't do that for one place. You do it for all."

Danny said, "So, you think they have similar blockades at both ends of highway two, and highway five-twenty-two?"

"Those are the four main roads into town," Grace agreed. "It's where I'd put them."

Gerry used his geek skills and probably his gaming skills to put forth a problem worrying me. "Assume six-hour shifts, the bridge has three people on duty, which is twelve men a day, seven days a week. If the other three roads have the same, you have fifty men or more dedicated to standing guard-duty. That is a lot of resources."

Danny screwed up his face and demanded, "So?"

Gerry went on, ignoring the rudeness, "Fifty guards, plus replacements for illness, and give them each a day or two off now and then, and you're nearer a hundred. Those are a hundred *unproductive* men, or guards, who are not helping provide food for the town, or building shelters, or doing anything of value but standing guard detail."

"Again, so what?" Danny said in a challenging manner.

"That is a lot of idle people," Gerry said. "In the studies of armies that I've read, guards seldom make up more than ten percent."

Jake nodded. "About right. Probably less."

Gerry said, "That means there are possibly a thousand soldiers in Monroe, certainly several hundred at minimum. My question is, why so many?"

Danny spun on him. "You've been playing too many video games."

I said, "Maybe he has. Who cares? Two thousand soldiers is a crazy number, but so what if there are *only* five hundred there? How does that affect us?"

"Meaning?" Danny asked, after a critical look at Sara as if he'd taken a stance in front of her and didn't want to back down for matters of his pride.

Sara snuggled up next to his arm and they held hands. That didn't bother me. What did, was that I'd been watching the bridge when a mosquito landed on my forearm. Without thinking, I slapped and quickly turned in her direction. She directed an expression of pure hate at me. Then, she saw that I'd seen her, and it melded into a phony but sweet smile.

Jake said, "Meaning, that if they have guards posted, they are fearful of outsiders. They do not want outside people getting inside the city, which is us, and others. What they do to intruders is unknown, as well as why they don't welcome them."

Grace said wistfully, "I can almost see my house from here."

Jake said, "I have a plan. Grace is right. Her house is close to the river. The two of us can swim across and gather information. If there are five hundred or two thousand troops over there, they must eat and sleep somewhere. We can locate that place and listen to what's being said."

I found my mouth speaking again before thinking about what I wanted to say. "What about us?"

He looked at everyone and spread his palms as if asking forgiveness before talking, a skill I needed to learn. He said, "No disrespect, but taking Gerry with his lack of skills could get us killed. Penelope would trip over her feet or shoot someone and get us killed. Sara is in no condition to swim the river and get into a firefight with soldiers. Danny would do well, but I think he should stay here and take care of the other three."

"Just you and me?" Grace asked.

"The more of us that go into Monroe, the more likely we'll be discovered. You know the part of the city we're going into better than anyone."

I couldn't disagree with his reasoning. Looking around, I realized others were coming to the same understanding. "What do we do while you're gone?" I asked.

Jake turned to me. "We need more information. Getting it in town is one way. Another is to scout along the highway, south of here, beyond where the sideroad to the sanctuary breaks off. Say, two people move and spy on anyone they find. Are there others living out here? If so, perhaps they will talk to you, especially if you say you're from somewhere else, far away. Just strangers passing through."

I looked at Gerry, certain he would refuse to go with me. He didn't. I glanced at his attire and smirked. Sure, we were going to tell them we worked in a hospital far away and had no other clothing, not even shoes or a jacket. No one was going to believe that lie.

Danny said quickly, "I should stay here with Sara and guard Grace and Jake with my bow if they run into trouble."

"You can't stay here," I said. "You'd be spotted too easily, and You can't make a fire for warmth tonight. How about we all meet back at the barn? It's only a walk of a couple of hours."

"Where the dead bodies are?" Sara asked her lip curling at the idea.

For someone who had survived half a year as she had, you'd think she would be used to death and what came with it. "You and Danny can pull the bodies outside and into the woods while we scout around for information," I snapped. I'd about had enough of her bad attitude aimed at me. Our intention was her safety in meeting back there at the barn, not because I wanted the additional walk. So, her objections landed on deaf ears. "We can all make our way back to the barn by tomorrow night and share what we find."

There were more subjects for discussion and details to decide, but the basic plans didn't change. We became three pairs, each with a different objective.

We left Jake and Grace under the cover of a few imposing evergreens. They would wait until dark before making their move, while the other four of us worked our way back the way we'd come. At the turnoff, we said our good-byes and let Danny and Sara return to the barn and their grizzly task.

Gerry and I moved on down the road in the direction we had not explored, generally to the south. I'd made sure we had the two nine-millimeter pistols with us, but we carried them in our hands because we were still dressed in scrubs and had no other place to put them. Besides, I felt better with the weight of the pistol there, ready for use.

We paused at the edge of the road long enough for me to explain how the basics of the Glock worked. A thirty-word introduction to the use of weapons designed to kill. Point it this way and shoot. Just like video games. Do not shoot if the person is farther away than you can throw a large rock. Aim for their middle, not the head, leg, or shoulder like heroes do on TV. Until you are ready to shoot, keep your damn finger off the trigger or you'll lose a toe. Worse than that, I might.

I ejected the magazine, found it fully loaded and showed him, and slammed it back home with the butt of my hand. He hadn't said a word—but he listened and repeated my actions without hesitation.

We moved on. There were houses located up ahead along the highway, a small community. I remembered that. Not exactly a town, but several houses clustered along both sides of the road.

There were footprints here and there on the pavement where a thin layer of mud had formed. Once there were the imprints of horseshoes, old prints, but I had no way of knowing how old. But that was encouraging. Signs of other people meant there were options to explore.

Later, while standing at the top of a small hill, a farm spread out before us, the fields neatly laid out, and newly plowed dirt in regular rows. People lived at the farm.

I moved off the road and settled down where a fallen log provided convenient seating. Gerry looked confused. I said, "We're here to talk, not fight. But, if capturing a person and questioning them is what happens, so be it. We need information."

His impersonal eyes told me nothing.

I said, "Listen, you came to me and wanted to—well, to be more like me. Right?"

He grudgingly nodded.

I lifted my gun, hit the magazine release, and snapped the slide almost in one motion. I snatched the ejected shell out of the air with my hand. "Do the same."

He fumbled the magazine as it shot from the handle with more force than he had expected. The difference was, I'd been taught to place my palm under it, not catch it with my fingers. His ejected shell flew off to one side and fell to the ground. He stood and looked at me in fear of my next words. He expected me to bawl him out.

Instead, I said firmly, "Wipe the dirt off, insert the bullet into the magazine and do it again."

My lesson went on until he had done it all but shoot and clean the gun. He no longer had to look at the gun as he did each part of the exercise. There isn't that much to learn, but what there is, he caught onto quickly. I showed him how to line up the sights, but Gerry claimed to know the process learned in playing his games.

I said, "This is important. If you must shoot, do it. No

hesitation. You only shoot if the other person is going to kill you or me. Got it? Especially me."

He did.

I gave him a hard stare.

He said, "I'll be scared, you know."

"Me too. So, we have that in common."

"What if I can't do it?"

I gave him a weak smile. "Remember, the scenario is that they are going to shoot you or me. If you let them kill me, I'll never forgive you. I promise to shoot anyone I think is going to kill you, in return."

In a sort of echo of Sara's words earlier, he said, "We've killed a lot of people in two days."

"Nobody since breakfast," I snapped back, more irritated than I should have been, but the remark hit home in the same way that Sara's comment had.

He mumbled to his feet.

"What?" I asked.

He looked up and met my eyes. "The day isn't over yet."

"You're the one I have to trust with my life, and you give me a ration of shit like that?"

He pulled away. "I didn't mean anything. I'm scared."

"Well, get on your damn feet, and let's go find somebody to shoot." I stamped my foot for emphasis and stormed in the direction of the road to hopefully allow my temper to cool. In my frame of mind, he was lucky I didn't shoot him.

He meekly followed with his head hung low.

I knew he hadn't meant it the way it sounded, but he'd touched a sensitive nerve. Twice in one day, I'd felt insulted about killing too many people and I hadn't killed anyone. The other way to look at my killing spree was to calculate how many lives of friends I'd saved. Did anyone even mention that? No, of course, not.

We watched the farm from another hillside, hidden behind brambles climbing the base of trees and just leafing out. Within a few minutes, I spotted four workers and three barking dogs. I stretched and said as I stood, "Let's go."

Gerry meekly followed. I wanted to shout at him to man-up or something similar to force him to take a stronger position. Following me along like a puppy was not cutting it.

The farm, like most we saw, had too many workers and dogs for us to venture nearby. What I wanted, was a person to sit down and talk with over a friendly cup of coffee. A little conversation between new acquaintances. I'd settle for taking one a prisoner and tying him or her to a large tree trunk while waving my gun or knife around to get the conversation flowing.

Hurting or scaring people was not the ideal plan. We needed the information they had. Good information came voluntarily. Lack of that vital information could cost the lives of my friends, not to mention mine.

We walked along the side of the road, ready to dive into the underbrush if anyone should approach. I considered and rejected a hundred ideas. I hoped for a person alone, maybe a talkative housewife who was out gathering mushrooms to use in the evening meal for her family. I'd help her pick them as we talked. Now, I simply needed to locate a friendly mushroom picker.

That's another example of my mind taking what I expected, smoothing off the rough edges, and making a task palatable. Reality said we'd perhaps find a victim to kidnap and slap around. Nothing too serious. But the mushroom picker scenario probably wouldn't evolve.

Motion ahead drew my attention. Not much, but movement where there should be none. We slipped off the road a dozen steps and hunkered down where we hid. As we waited for what might be a combat situation, I found, like many warriors have described in books, that the brain has its methods of preparation. I needed to stay still despite my hands shaking. I had to focus and remain calm.

So, I thought about the last time I'd used the words, *hunkered down.* If ever. While concentrating on that puzzle, two men strode into view.

Young men. Both were in their early twenties from what I could see of their faces past their full beards. Shaving seemed to be a thing of the past, from what little we'd seen so far. No razor blades equaled beards, some trimmed short, others hung to their waists as did the three we'd killed. Both men wore jeans, so there must still be sources of them. There had been millions of pairs before the war, probably five or ten pairs for each person in the country. They were probably getting scarce after five years, and in a few more, would be as dated as shaving.

They wore shirts and light jackets, not the same patterns or colors, but the guns strapped to their waists by similar belts. Similar suggested military. Web belts went around their waists including nylon holsters. Velcro secured flaps held the weapons in place. Knives rode on the opposite side of their hips, the sheaths leather.

Hats, like floppy cowboy hats, again both the same shade of a brown color adjusted to their head sizes. The brims drooped all around, protecting from the sun, but mostly from the gentle rain as it sluiced any water off their heads.

The pair walked along the road, almost like moving through a city park five years ago as if they didn't have a care in the world. The word, confident, summed it up. One was talking, jokingly and telling a story the other laughed at. The talker's hands waved as he explained.

After consideration, I decided they'd do for gathering information. Not exactly what I was looking for, but close enough.

I wagged a finger behind my hip to catch Gerry's attention since he crouched there, several steps away. When I glanced back, he raised his eyebrows in a puzzled response and gave me a small shake of his head. He wanted to let them pass and find others. His response didn't surprise me.

I pointed to the gun in my hand and then to them, and where they would be as they passed by us. Gerry was on my right, twenty feet away. I'd prefer that he was on the other side because the two men were going to walk past me before I could act. It would be better if Gerry stepped out on the road in front and drew their attention while I came out of the trees behind them to enforce his words.

Gerry, not intentionally, forced me to act as if alone. I couldn't depend on him at all despite his recent improvements. I hoped that he didn't get in the way or screw it up.

All those thoughts and more flashed through my mind as the men took a few more steps. They would quickly be out of range for my idea to work. They drew even with my position. I forced myself to remain still. Their peripheral vision would catch any movement.

When they were a few steps past, I darted quietly to the edge of the road and paused for a brief look in the direction they came from to make certain there was no more behind. The road was clear. I slipped quickly ahead on tiptoes until they were within ten feet.

"Hold it right there!" I ordered while deepening my voice to be intimidating and looking past them in the other direction. The road was also clear down there. Having others like them within sight while we held up their friends would ruin a good day.

Both spun to face me instead of doing what I'd said.

My gun pointed at a space between them, my finger on the outside of the finger guard so it wouldn't accidentally pull and shoot if I flinched. Their eyes went to that finger. It may have convinced them I knew what to do.

The one on the left said with limited bravado, "There's two of us."

Gerry stepped into view, right beside them. "Two of us, also. And we already have our guns pointed at you."

My biggest fear was that one of them was an idiot and would go for his weapon. The one on the left bent his knees slightly. His fingers splayed as he tensed. His eyes drilled into me.

I shifted my aim to point the barrel between his eyes, although if I had to shoot, it would be at his chest. However, it was a threat that worked. He looked into the barrel of my gun from ten feet away and relaxed. Well, relaxed is not the proper word to describe his actions, but he no longer looked ready to try and pull his weapon. He realized he'd lose that gunfight. From that distance, he couldn't get to me before I'd shoot, and there was no way I'd miss from so close.

The other one asked in a shaky voice, "What do you want?"

I pointed to where we'd been standing in the trees. "Right now, I want you to move off the road so we can all get out of sight. As you pass by, hand me your guns. Use two fingers to do it and move slowly so I don't flinch and pull my trigger. One hiccup and you are dead. If you have a spare gun, better hand that over too."

No sense in threatening them more. They would either do what I said or not. They hesitated again, exchanged looks, and the sound of Velcro ripping from two holster flaps came as they each pulled a nine-millimeter much like the ones we held, but a different manufacturer or model. Both men used their fingers on the grips with exaggerated motions to extract the guns, so there would be no misunderstanding that they were doing as asked.

They exchanged fearful glances before taking a tentative first step to the side of the road. To help them along, and because we didn't want to hurt them, I said, "Do as we say, and you can go free when we're finished talking. That's all we want. A little information."

"We're going," the first one said in an irritated voice that made me want to shoot him where he stood.

He was the one with the chip on his shoulder and the one I needed to watch. "Just speed it up and keep going until we can talk without being overheard."

Fifty yards in, I called a halt. Gerry had moved out to my right side for the walk, twenty feet away, where they couldn't catch both of us off guard without the other shooting. Maybe he had learned that on his video games, too. Whatever. It worked.

They turned to face me. Gerry positioned himself a little further away, his gun held steady in front of him.

The pair of prisoners waited, but like most people, couldn't remain silent very long. The belligerent one said, "You nurses?"

They recognized scrubs. I understood men, especially young ones. Their modesty overrode their swagger. I'd heard tales while working at the Happy Rodeo. All the time. It was a testament to those stories I'd heard, often in the women's dressing room. Men become weak without clothing.

I said, "We need to talk. What we don't need is for you to attack or try to deceive us." They could have rolled their eyes, for all that statement got me.

"Talk? About what?" the calmer of the pair asked

stubbornly.

Instead of answering him directly, I said to Gerry, "Please promise me you will not kill either of these men for no reason like you did those others. You've done enough killing in the last two days."

"Huh?" Gerry responded, which was fine with me. That utterance served its purpose as they believed he was questioning why I wouldn't allow him to kill them.

I continued, "I really mean it, this time. No more killing. If you must, shoot either of them in his leg or foot, and then maybe they'll be more willing to tell us the truth."

Gerry caught on. A maniacal grin appeared on his face that would have forced me into gales of laughter at another time. He lowered his aim to their legs. If the men could have climbed trees to get away from him, they would have. I bit the inside of my cheek to keep from laughing.

The calmer one's face flushed, he looked scared, and said to me in a voice that had almost become squeak, "We'll talk. Make him stop. Don't let him do anything to us."

Gerry hadn't done anything but point his gun. Still, I said again, "Don't shoot."

Turning back to them, I continued, "I do not want him to shoot your legs, kill you, or have to chase you down. To prevent any of that, I want you to strip. And be careful with those gun belts. Toss them this way very slowly. Sudden movement makes my friend anxious."

"Strip?" the other asked.

"Strip," I confirmed. "As in, take off your clothing. Do it now and quit wasting our time."

My voice had increased near the end as if I were becoming impatient. After a glance shared between them, they removed the gun belts, and the clothing came next. Even the hats. Remembering the conversations in the women's dressing room about how nudity caused men to react, I motioned for them to remove their underwear.

"Off," I ordered. "Boots, too."

They reluctantly removed the items, both men trying to hide their private area with their cupped hands, which served me well. If they attempted to attack, they would have to raise their hands—and neither seemed likely to do that.

"Sit," I told them.

Each of them sat on his clothing because the ground was damp. I moved forward and retrieved their gun belts then took a few steps back, to maintain distance. I said, "This isn't going to be intensive. The questions are few and easy. Where are you from?"

"Oregon," one said.

"Seattle," the other told me at almost the same time.

"No, no. I mean now. You both look like you eat regularly. Where do you eat and sleep?"

"Monroe," one said. "Now."

"You're in an army?" I asked.

He shrugged. "I wouldn't exactly call it an army."

"What would you call it?"

"Militia," he said instantly, telling me that he'd heard that term, and probably recently.

"How many militia soldiers in Monroe?"

"Counting women?" the other asked.

"Of course."

They exchanged another of those looks. Before they could answer I raised my gun and threatened them by shifting it back and forth between them. I heard only silence and told them when satisfied, "Turn around so your backs are against each other."

They did. Both looked scared.

I said, "Now, just to make sure nobody is lying, hold up fingers like in grade school. One finger for every hundred troops."

One held up four fingers. The other vacillated between two and three.

I said, "Your numbers don't match."

The one who wavered said, "Are you counting slobs and cripples like cooks and cleaners, or just fighters?"

That statement pissed me off. Until a day ago, I'd been included in that lowly grouping of cooks and cleaners. I drew in a steady breath and said, "Yes, everyone."

He now held up three fingers. Then a fourth that didn't seem to want to remain up as if he couldn't make up his mind.

They generally agreed about four hundred militia occupied Monroe. I asked, "Do you have all the major ways into the city guarded?"

"And some of the others, too. Just not as many on duty as the bridge. Snipers, mostly. Their job is to sound the alarm, not defend the city."

All the answers were coming from the man on my left. The other still looked ready to rip my head off. He needed to be watched closely, and Gerry had shifted positions so he could better cover him, a good instinct by him.

"Defend against others? Like where are they posted?"

He shrugged. "Like the river crossings."

River crossings! Where Jake and Grace planned to go. I needed to warn them but one look at the sky told me we'd wasted a whole day and the sun would set long before I could return. Hopefully, they would be careful and avoid the extra guards.

I looked Gerry's way. I turned back to the prisoners and said, "My friend has moved over there so he can shoot you easier and not hit your buddy. Have you noticed that?"

He slowly nodded and seemed to put more respect into the nod.

"Give us no trouble and you go free. You have my word. Otherwise, you will get a bullet in your leg, at the least. If it seems either of us is in danger from you, there will also be one bullet in your head. Just a few more questions."

That seemed to register. I asked, "Why are you guarding the city?"

"Raiders, of course," the other said in a manner that suggested we already knew the answer. "We're protecting it."

"Raiders from where?" I asked.

He waved an arm that generally encompassed west. Then he said, "We also have to watch out for slavers sneaking in from over the pass. They're always looking for people to grab."

Slavers. There was a word I hadn't heard for years unless I was talking about those in the sanctuary.

Despite asking dozens of additional questions, we got little else of value from them. I grew weary of the process. It was not as if they were holding back, but more that they were lowly privates in a militia who followed orders. Returning to Monroe in time for a warm bed and food their goal. They watched the main road for intruders and if found any, took them, prisoner. If "Raiders" approached, their orders were to race back to the city with a warning. Shooting into the air would do. They stood guard duty every other day. Not much else. They seemed to think it was a good deal.

"Up," I told them. "On your feet."

They stood, both covering themselves again with their hands. They eyed their clothing, expecting to either put it back on or to be shot. In other circumstances, their thought processes might be humorous.

I gave them a stern wag of my pistol and said gruffly, "Go."

"Go? What about our things? Our clothes and guns?" the angry one snarled, his feet as still as if planted in the soil and taking root.

"Everything here is now mine. Go. I'll keep my word."

They sprinted away. Men and their silly pride. They did not want to go out onto the road naked. I thought briefly about giving them my scrubs and decided not to. Instead, I spoke to Gerry in a soft voice, "You wanted to shoot them earlier. If they insist on staying here, you have my permission."

Gerry, who hadn't said a single word, smiled, a slow grin again that spread into a wide, wicked, smile. Before it had fully formed, both were sprinting away, hopping and skipping as their bare feet encountered stones, sticks, and nettles.

I turned to Gerry after they were out of sight. "You are learning. I'm proud of you."

He scrunched up his face. "Maybe that's not something to be proud of."

I gave him a slight shrug. "Do you have an objection to what we did?"

"At least you didn't kill either of them."

"*I* have not killed anyone. Not me! Not the guards behind us in the mine, the three of Sara's captors, and not the men in the night at the barn. I don't know where you get the idea that I did. You and Sara."

"We did it," he hissed at me. "You and I just performed a holdup like in the old west. We took guns and clothes. At gunpoint. Us."

"Yes, we did."

"Are you proud of that?"

I thought about it for a moment and gave him a curt nod. "Yes, I guess I am sort of proud of it."

Chapter 8

Gerry suddenly seemed delighted. Not because of what the militia had left behind, but because of how we'd handled the encounter and his participation. He'd received respect—and I suspected it was one of the few times that had happened in a situation involving animosity, brawn, or weapons.

My eyes had followed the pair as they scurried to the road, and I had watched them gingerly hopping from foot to foot as they went down the road without shoes. Stones and barbs seemed to attack their feet. They might run into more of their militia at any time, and send them chasing after us, so my next goal was to get us out of there and to anywhere else.

But first, we went to the clothing they'd worn, two distinct piles on the ground. I pulled my top off and was sliding the pants down when I felt Gerry's eyes on me. "Unless you want to wear those scrubs to your grave, you had better get changed instead of watching me."

He turned away and was busy trying on boots when I looked his way again. Both militias were larger than us, but we were not going to a fashion show and anything was better than the paper-thin scrubs we wore. They had been serviceable in the sanctuary, but on the surface, they were almost worthless. The material was too thin to add protection from the elements, it ripped easily, and the color of blue stood out in the forest, drawing attention.

My bare feet had been sore since we crawled out of tunnels and into the mine shaft.

My *new* boots were too big, and Gerry had the same problem. I wadded some of the material torn from my scrubs and stuffed it into the toe, then pulled the laces tighter than normal, but they fit snug enough. They looked funny when I glanced down, and my feet extended an extra inch or more than usual.

I rolled the pants cuffs, and the shirt was flannel and so large I tied a knot in the front, which solved part of the voluminous problem. I rolled the sleeves about four times each and tried to imagine what I looked like.

With no mirror, I did the next best thing. I looked at Gerry, fitting himself into a similar set of clothes. I saw a boy of twelve dressing in his father's things.

His eyes met mine coldly. "Laugh at me and I'll tell you how you look."

He was deadly serious. That set me off. First came a smile, followed by a chuckle, and then we were on the ground grabbing our bellies as we laughed with pure joy. Later, it dawned on me that any enemies within a mile should have come running and killed us because we were so loud.

It was worth it.

Gerry and I somehow bonded at that moment. We became friends. Well, maybe that description pushed the relationship more than intended. I hadn't liked his smarter-than-everyone geeky computer attitude when we were below, and I'm sure he didn't like my mouth sounding off and getting us both into trouble.

I said as I pirouetted, "We both might not have dressed like this five years ago. Now? Different story and we're lucky to have these."

"Lucky? How do you figure?" His gaze fell to his oversized clothing, the waist held up by a belt cinched in bunches around his thin middle.

He seemed genuinely puzzled by the comment. He didn't see things in the same way I did. I said, "Listen to me. It's all about attitude. We were lucky the two soldiers were not smaller than us, so we couldn't wear them, for one thing. Lucky that we have better, heavier clothing now that will keep us warm at night and won't tear every time that we pass a bush with thorns, no matter how silly we look, as if we didn't look stupid like a pair of nurses in a forest. We're also lucky we were able to take them away from those two without a problem. Nobody got hurt. We could be dead if one of them had shot us."

"I think I liked you better when all you did was complain." His smile took the sting from his words as he reexamined himself.

I had a stray thought that needed to be said before forgetting it. "Listen, when we head back to the barn tonight, we need to call out and let them know it's us in these clothes and not an intruder."

His concerned look told me he hadn't thought of that. Gerry was fumbling with the web holster and belt. I picked up the other and from the scabbard pulled a hunting knife with a ten-inch blade, good for cutting, slicing, stabbing, or chopping. The long, curved blade looked like new. Not a nick on the edge or spot of rust.

That discovery brought me up short. In five years of use, the knife should show extensive wear, and probably from several owners. Nobody today could make a knife like it. The manufacturing processes didn't exist. Not that it was perfect, but it was an exact copy of the one Gerry had, therefore it was made in a factory. Near the hilt, each blade listed a model number. It was a knife from before the war, yet unused.

Aside from the knives, I had three nine-millimeter guns laying at my feet, one of mine, and two of theirs. Gerry had his gun beside him. All were in like-new condition. After strapping on the utility belt and pulling the thing tight around my waist, the buckle and series of brass holes fit me perfectly, with an excess tail that I planned to cut off.

"Now to see which gun is best for me," I said playfully to distract Gerry from my examination.

However, there was not much play as I lifted one of the new weapons and turned it this way and that while looking closely. Its handle was somewhat shorter than the one I carried, molded for a smaller hand, and it fit mine perfectly. Although it was older and had a few small scratches, it was a better weapon for me.

Just for the hell of it, I lifted the other new one and found it much too heavy. After ejecting the magazine, I counted nineteen bullets inside. The one I'd carried so far had only five. A few more would fit in my magazine, maybe another five, but the difference is five and nineteen made the newest gun feel far too heavy for me and the magazine protruded probably two additional inches.

Gerry was watching, not buying my casual inspection at all.

I handed him the larger gun while keeping the smaller one for myself. I remembered to carry one in the chamber and racked the slide on mine. I had eleven shots and number one wouldn't have to wait.

Gerry didn't like the larger gun I'd handed him, either. He placed his Glock in the holster and pulled the Velcro flap down over it. He stuffed the other under the utility belt in front.

I did the same.

He said, "We need to get away from here and from the road."

"I saw a trail a while ago. Follow me." I headed out, going deeper into the forest, and climbing at the same time.

Our legs were weak, and we rested several times, but eventually reached a rock face that overlooked the road where it made a wide bend around the base of the mountain we stood on.

He said, "Nice. We can see anyone on the road from either direction up here."

Pointing, I added, "Unless I'm mistaken, our barn is right over there. If you look closely, you can see where the tops of the trees are open where the other road is."

"It makes a sort of line. I see it. If the highway is there," he pointed, "and below is the other road to the sanctuary, the barn must be about there where you said. And it's all downhill when we're ready."

I wanted to compliment him on being so positive for a change but didn't know how. My skill set lacked that ability in favor of pointing out things I didn't like. Instead, I sat and gave the highway a good, long look, expecting to see a platoon of soldiers returning to search for us after the two we released reached their friends and ratted us out.

I wondered what tale they would tell. Would they attempt to make themselves look better by swearing there were ten of us? Maybe they would tell the truth, but I doubted it.

Gerry sat at my side and I tried to ignore how silly he looked in the baggy clothing. His voice came firm and authoritative, "Four-hundred militia, they said. The only reason you need that many is that you have an enemy of more than three-hundred."

Turning to him, I asked, "How do you figure?"

"Easy," he said. "If there's an enemy army of only fifty out there, you don't need four-hundred. You need maybe seventy-five to deter them from attacking. Four-hundred is a total waste of resources and costs too much to maintain against fifty soldiers."

I saw his point but couldn't let him get away with something I should have seen for myself. I said, "You might use four-hundred militia to keep out a force of six-hundred, since you have a good defensive position and supplies at hand."

"Maybe, but that goes to prove my point of why they have so many."

"Maybe? That's all you can say?"

He wore that silly smirk again. "Oh, you might keep out five-hundred-fifty with your four-hundred militia. Not six hundred. I think six is a bit of a stretch."

Even I had to admit he'd bested me. I shut up and watched the road. A horse and rider trotted past. The rider dressed more like a farmhand than a soldier from our distance. Later, a deer edged into the thin grass in the open field where we sat. It was about fifty yards away and watched us as it snacked on the new green shoots.

A fire had recently burned off all the trees where we were, probably no more than a year ago. The rain had washed away the charcoal and added nutrients to the soil. Those, coupled with water and sunshine, had the area rejuvenating.

"Look," Gerry said softly, "but don't move."

Two men dressed as we emerged from the cover of the canopy and walked slowly along the two sides of the road.

Their heads tilted forward as they looked at the ground.

"Searching for us," he said. "You know what that means?"

I didn't, so shook my head.

"We may not be sleeping in our barn tonight."

"How so?"

"You and I have to go down this damned hill again and set an ambush. If they track us, and I'm sure they can because their bosses sent them instead of others, we'll have to kill them, or they will follow our tracks right to the barn and put all of us in danger. They are much better at this stuff than us."

Damn, Gerry was surprisingly good at warfare tactics he had learned from his stupid video games. I'd have to stop thinking that since he was not a fighter, he was stupid.

With them trying to locate us, going to the barn was our last option. We had to devise another plan. I glanced at Gerry.

He may have been thinking the same thing. With a sigh, he said, "We can go back and ambush them, or we can lead them away from the barn and then attempt to lose them. Set a false trail that will take them somewhere else."

My initial reaction favored the false trail. We could do that. With a little luck, we could take off through the forest, maybe even take them to the entrance of the mine shaft where the bear might be roaming around. At a safe distance, we could elude the bears.

If we knew how to *elude*. However, my tricky brain kept going. If the bear didn't get them, and we managed to sneak away in some manner, what would they do? Go home and forget about us? I doubted it. They would follow our backtrail and perhaps bring in more people to search. They would return to where they had found the kidnapping took place and begin again. I had no doubt they would find that place quickly.

Oh, yes. They would find us. Maybe not today. Certainly tomorrow.

"We have to kill them." The words simply flowed past my lips as if I was a ventriloquist's dummy.

Gerry sat still. His eyes focused on the ground near his feet. Eventually, he said, "I know."

He'd come to the same conclusion and couldn't think of a better answer. I said, "Even killing them won't solve the problem, you know. Those we sent back reported to their superiors and they dispatched these two to find us. When they don't return, they will send others. More of them."

"We, all of us, will have to be gone from the barn before that happens."

I didn't leap up to charge back down the hill and kill two men. I waited for Gerry to come up with a plan.

He said, "Think back on the way we came up the hill after leaving the road. Where's a place where we can set an ambush and be likely to succeed?"

I gave it some thought and remembered a rock formation that had forced us to move between it and a ravine. Most of the rest was a tree-covered forest, evergreens, and not a lot of underbrush. "Those big rocks were near that ravine? Is that a good place?"

"Nope," he said instantly. "When playing my games, that was a place I either went around or proceeded carefully. Ambushes placed there always failed because the enemy also knew it was a choke-point."

"So, what worked?"

"Two-against-two warfare? A setup in what seems an open and safe area."

"I don't understand," I said.

"Okay, I see that. Ideally, we'd go back on our trail and scoop out depressions on either side of where we traveled and cover ourselves with leaves or branches. Then wait. No warning. Just sit up and shoot when they get even with us as they follow our trail."

Blood rushed from my head and a wave of dizziness had me faint at the idea of killing without warning. My knees buckled, but I pulled myself together and forced my body to obey. "I can't do that. There must be another option."

Gerry said quietly, "There maybe is another way if they are tracking us slowly and carefully. We can outrun them. Pick a direction and run for two, maybe three days. Eventually, we might lose them."

"What about the others of our group?"

"Those two following us will return and begin another search. Or their friends will while they are chasing after us.

They might also send for more help. Or they may find the barn or Jake and Grace as they're sneaking into Monroe. So, even if we run off, they still may find and kill our friends."

I turned to him. "We're wasting time doing all this planning."

"We don't have a choice." His voice was as dull as my thinking.

"What do we do?"

He turned and looked back the way we'd come up the hillside. Where the fire had burned the trees a year or two ago, small bushes and trees had taken root. Most were knee-high at most. We'd chosen here to watch because we could see over the tops of the trees downslope and had an unimpeded view.

I anticipated his thinking. After creeping through the forest while following our trail and watching every movement on either side in the depths of the shade under the trees, the openness of the bare spot we stood on would give them a sense of security. Up here, they could see for a hundred yards in any direction.

Gerry said, "They will relax as they leave the trees and enter the openness of the burn."

My eyes went to where we'd emerged while following a game trail. It was a hundred yards back. On one side, perhaps thirty yards from the trail was a blackened log. I pointed. "I could lie there, with just a few leaves covering me."

Gerry said, "That will work. I'll circle around and find a place on the opposite side of where we walked. We wait until they pass us by ten steps, so they can't dart back into the safety of the trees. Ten steps. Count them, then open fire. Sit up if you must, but do not hesitate. These guys are a lot better at this than us."

He could have gone on to warn me not to move or show my head, or a hundred other things, but didn't. He turned his back and swiftly walked across the path to the far side and made a sweeping turn to avoid leaving any footprints for them to follow. Before they reached where he crossed, we would attack. I went to the log, keeping an eye on him.

Last fall's leaves piled by the wind behind the log. It didn't take much to scoop them aside and lay down where I could see the trail they would come from—and watch their progress until it was time to shoot. I felt ill. I was about to shoot two men.

My fingers went to the tree trunk and the tips of them were black. I smeared charcoal on my face, then added more and more. While I couldn't see myself, the coloring would match and help hide me. I was using my limited knowledge.

Gerry settled directly across from me. He had been in sight, then he was not. He must have found a depression or something because there seemed to be nothing like my tree trunk nearby. If I couldn't spot him, the trackers wouldn't either.

I felt better, if a little scared and revolted by what we were going to do. Too much thinking brought doubts.

We waited.

My mind raced. Could I shoot a man following us? For a while, I played the "what if" game. What if they didn't come? What if we didn't hit them with our bullets? What if my gun jammed? And a hundred others.

In preparation, I placed both guns in front of me so one failing was not a problem. I forced my thinking to understand that we were not only protecting ourselves but the lives of our friends. We hadn't started any of this. They didn't have to come after us. We hadn't hurt their friends, only taken clothing and guns.

I estimated when the pair should arrive. They didn't. I forced myself to relax as the anxieties grew. I couldn't. Each passing second increased my unease.

Had they turned around and gone back to wherever they came from? I didn't know.

A few black ants crawled up my hand to my wrist. I told myself black ants don't bite, but I also told myself that the trackers might be in the shadows at the very edge of the trees, watching for movement—like idiots shaking ants off their hands.

The leaves covering me felt like they had ants on them too. My imagination had ants crawling all over my body. None bit and I remained still. Let the ants use me for their path. I didn't care.

Then, they were there.

Two men entered the bright sunlight at the edge of the clearing and pulled to a halt. If I sat up and fired, I might hit one. They were that close. Perhaps forty or fifty yards.

To my way of thinking, they should have looked ahead and when they saw no sign of us, they should have speeded up, not pulled to a stop, and had a conversation. They should have rushed ahead and made up some time as they closed the distance to us.

Then, they did the unthinkable. They split up.

One went Gerry's way as if he knew where my friend would be. The other left the trail and went to his left, along the tree line, then after a hundred yards, which put him far out of range of my gun and my shooting abilities, he turned up the hillside in my general direction.

He was much too far away for me to hit.

I chanced a glance at the other. He was moving slowly, directly for where I'd last seen Gerry.

Oh, shit. Gerry would have to react, and that would tip off the one on my side.

I refused to move. I was safe for now. Whatever happened next was up to Gerry.

It was impossible to see both without turning my head. I decided the most likely thing was between Gerry and the other. My target was a hundred yards away and moving farther with every step.

Two shots. Bam-bam, so fast they ran together.

I couldn't see who fired.

The tracker near Gerry covered his belly with both hands and slumped to his knees.

Gerry leaped to his feet and ran. He was running away from me! I should never have had faith in him. He was a coward. His back was all I saw as he raced down the hill to the path at the edge of the forest, right below me. He would run into the trees and disappear. I nearly called out to him but heard noises behind me.

It was the other man.

Still not turning my head because he might see the movement, from the corner of my eye, the second one was racing to intercept Gerry, gun in hand. In that instant, I realized his direction would take him within a dozen yards of me, while his attention fully focused on Gerry.

Gerry was not running away. He was drawing the other into my field of fire.

Instantly, I understood that if I panicked or missed my shot, Gerry would pay for it with his life. I held my breath and waited, still as a boulder, my finger near the trigger, but not touching it because a twitch would cause it to fire and give my position away. The crashing of the tracker's boots in the dry ash and burned trees grew closer.

Only a thin layer of dried leaves protected me from sight because according to our plan, our enemies were supposed to be on the other side of the log that would hide me. When I moved, there was no going back or second chances. I remained still.

He was only twenty yards from me when I rolled over. Fifteen, when he saw me and attempted to leap to one side. My first bullet hit higher up on his chest than I'd intended. The second was dead center, and that phrase took on a new understanding. Dead. Center.

His momentum carried him a few more steps and he hit the ground twenty feet from me. I leaped up and held my gun in front of me as I cautiously went to him.

He was dead.

Gerry walked up the hill to join me.

When he arrived, I was still looking at the man I'd killed as my mind tried to process what had happened. Gerry said, "Go check on the other and get his weapons while I strip this one."

"Strip?"

"Our friends need warm clothes, too."

I found the other dead man with no problem. I started removing his clothing. Now I had four nine-millimeter semi-automatics and a bundle of clothes. I'd stuffed all the clothing inside the man's jeans to carry them. Gerry joined me and we rolled the extra guns inside the other pair of jeans and used the sleeves of a shirt to tie the bundle securely.

Neither of us spoke.

We now had six guns, extra ammo, four knives, clothing,

boots, and two hats. When we were ready to leave, I started to walk in the direction of the barn.

Gerry said, "No. This won't be the last of them. We need to make a false trail to send the next group the wrong way."

Confused, I waited for more.

He pointed away from the barn. "We go that way since our goal is Monroe. We point them away."

"How do we get back to the barn?"

"On the road, of course. After dark, we use the road where we won't leave footprints."

"What if soldiers are hiding beside the road?" I asked.

"We shoot them. God knows, we have enough guns to start a small war."

At another time, I might have laughed.

We made no effort to hide our trail, but we didn't leave intentional signs of passing either. A good tracker would realize what we were doing if we attempted that. At least, that was our decision. We moved fast, as if running scared, which was easy for me to do.

We hit the road just before dark and waited at the edge of the blacktop where we could see in both directions until full-dark. Gerry offered to go first. I was to stay twenty yards behind and protect him.

I think what it meant was that if there was trouble, he would be killed or captured while I had a slim chance to escape—or perhaps to rescue him. For a computer geek I had little use for a few days ago, he was making himself well-liked.

Chapter 9

Gerry and I crept through the dark. The usual spring cloud cover obscured the stars, but a near-full moon spread filtered light below. I kept a distance behind, with the flap of my holster turned back so I didn't have to pull it open to draw the weapon. That way I could quick-draw, but my real reason was the ripping sound Velcro makes on a quiet night.

Things flittered in my head like a bee that had found a new flower garden. One nasty thought was that I'd soon have to talk to Sara again and revise the daily body count. It was increasing.

Another was wondering what my friends had encountered in town. Grace and Jake had the most dangerous job of entering a small city with four-hundred militia guarding it against intruders. I was anxious to hear their tale.

Twice we heard voices and left the road to circle the speakers. We didn't catch sight of them, so we didn't know if they were militia, farmers, or travelers, but the more important thing was that they didn't catch sight of us.

We were becoming regular creepers.

While we would need sleep, we moved through the dark, damp night air like shadows beneath the trees, shadows within shadows. I only tripped three or four times and dropped my bundle of guns once. The clatter was enough to bring an entire army our way.

We eventually reached the turnoff to the sanctuary and the barn. Instead of turning, we continued ahead for a quarter of a mile to make sure nobody was there watching for us. Gerry led us back down the highway and up the side-road. The barn was perhaps a mile away, maybe a little more.

We found it as a darker black in the dark of the forest. Not a light was showing. We moved to the front door and slipped inside without opening it more than necessary. I called softly, "It's Gerry and me. Don't shoot."

"Come on up," Danny called.

We made our way across the floor and climbed the ladder. Only Danny and Sara were there. I tossed my bundle to the floor with a solid thunk and said, "How are you guys doing?"

"Scared," Danny answered.

Sara was awake but hadn't spoken. I could barely make out her reclined form.

Gerry said in a tone firmer than his norm, "Pen and I had some trouble."

Some trouble. I tried to see his face in the dark and failed.

"What happened?" Danny asked solemnly.

"We found two militia on the road and crept up behind and took them prisoner. We went into the forest and questioned them."

"I suppose Penelope killed them afterward," Sara said flatly, not a question.

"No," Gerry said. "She threatened them. Threatened to shoot them in their legs, but in the end, we made them take off all their clothes and give them to us. We took what they wore and their guns."

I waited. There was more and Gerry said nothing about the others we had killed. In the morning, there would be too many guns and clothing for his story of only two people. Questions would be asked.

Gerry reached to my shoulder in the darkness and gave it a squeeze.

"Better get some sleep," Danny said. "Hopefully, Grace and Jake get here soon."

I put my head on the bundle of clothing and used it for a pillow. After pushing either the barrel or butt of a gun aside, it felt good. My back and legs hurt. I was worn out. However, sleep wouldn't come. My mind centered on two people, Sara and Gerry.

Sara, I still couldn't figure it out. She blamed me for all the killing, no matter that I hadn't even had a weapon for some of it. No matter what happened, she thought the worst of me, and I had no idea why. Finally, I gave it a mental shrug and decided that in a day or two, or five, I would see the last of her, so it didn't matter what she thought.

Gerry was another story. Scared to stand up for himself in the sanctuary, probably had never been in a fight, and he seemed to have the opposite opinion of me. I'd never liked spineless people. He had been one of them. But he had changed, or tried to. In only a day or two, he'd evolved, as if he'd been waiting for the push.

He relished what was happening, but I worried. It's easy to talk tough until the opponent hits you for the first time. Knocks you on your butt. Then, and only then, do you make a choice. Get up or not.

There are no other options. Getting up means you might get knocked down again. Probably will. However, staying down means you never forget to remain there instead of fighting. That is far worse than losing.

Somewhere you learn that there is no shame in fighting and losing. There is shame in not fighting. When the time came for Gerry to decide, I hoped I would be there at his side. I would help him stand up that second time. That's what friends do.

My eyes finally closed.

When I opened them again, Sara was watching me, a slight curl to her upper lip. It was morning and the two men were still asleep, but she was half-sitting, her eyes fixed on mine. I said quietly, "What's up with you?"

"You," she answered quietly.

"What did I do to you?"

Her eyes flicked to Danny, then back to me. "You're after my boyfriend. Don't bother to deny it. I've seen it from the beginning."

So, that was her problem. Jealousy, a reaction I should have expected. A shake of my head didn't convince her. "Jake is my kind of man. We used to be a couple."

Her face twisted and she spat, "You're saying you're too good for Danny?"

Oh, great. First, she was angry because I wanted her new

boyfriend. Now, she was angry because I didn't. I stood and said softly as I strapped on the web-belt and nine-millimeter, "I'm going to look around."

"I knew you couldn't get up in the morning without carrying a gun or looking for someone to shoot." Her eyes glared as I went to the ladder, turned, and climbed down while resisting the urge to stick my tongue out at her.

My feet went down the ladder before I examined the ground floor, a stupid mistake that managed not to kill me—this time. The bodies of the two dead men drug off. Drag marks in the dirt coating the wooden floor showed where Danny had pulled them by their feet to the door, and presumably far enough away we wouldn't smell the decaying bodies, and animals attracted wouldn't enter the barn. I was sure Sara hadn't helped him.

Having made my first mistake of the day by entering a space without checking to see who was waiting to attack me, I avoided the second when I pulled my gun free, worked the slide, and checked the magazine. I tucked the Velcro flap behind the butt of the gun, so I could pull it free quickly and quietly.

Outside was chilly, a mist was falling, and the sky was flat gray. I stood for a moment, taking in the fresh trail through the grass we'd trampled. Anyone passing by would know people had been there. That was another dangerous mistake.

Under the eaves of the barn was an area a foot or two wide without any tall vegetation. It would be a little longer to walk into the woods and enter the clear area from the back side. After a morning pee, I went to the road and examined the ground carefully. If anyone had passed by, they were too good at covering their tracks to fool me.

I stood there in the center of the blacktop and made a full turn. There were people out there, maybe not close, but they were there. Enemies.

My instincts were kicking in. Climbing down the ladder without checking bothered me and haunted me. Since then, I'd examined our surroundings, readied my weapon, and searched for danger. It was not about strength or intelligence. It was survival. A new way of life after the peace and serenity of the sanctuary.

Some would survive in this new world. Others wouldn't. Jake and Grace would do fine. Danny's preoccupation with his new love slowed his learning. He probably wouldn't make it. Gerry was an enigma. Two days ago, he didn't stand a chance. Today? Maybe.

I decided to watch him. Not help this morning but watch him. If he was going to be an anchor, I'd leave him. If he could contribute to my future, he'd be welcome. After yesterday, I suspected he would come along.

Back inside the barn, I climbed the ladder and found everyone awake. Danny went down the ladder to go pee, his hands empty of weapons. Stupid. I didn't correct him. I heard his footsteps across the wooden floor and out the door. Gerry stood, stretched, and glanced beside where he had slept. His gun and belt were there, within easy reach.

Instead of putting it around his waist, he slipped the belt over a shoulder, paused at the top of the ladder, and took a good look down before descending. He also pulled the pistol and gave it a quick once-over.

Not bad. He could have done better with the gun, but he'd done better than me before climbing down, so we were even. Danny had failed miserably.

Sara said nothing but her eyes seldom left me.

Neither did I talk to her. As far as I could see, she and I had no future together.

When the men returned together and settled down, she gave me a sly smile and turned to Danny as she said sweetly, "Do you think it's a little odd that they captured only two militia but returned with four sets of clothing?"

Her tone was what I called snarky. Her timing with waiting for Danny meant to target me. I made my tone as sweet as summer honey, "Gerry and I knew you both were tired last night, and God knows we were, so you got the short version of our adventures so we could all sleep."

"You did that just for us?" she asked, her tone emulating mine.

"We did," I said enthusiastically. "We brought you warmer clothing and weapons to protect yourselves. You can thank us later but there is no need. We're all working together, right?" Yes, I'd heard the disapproval and ignored it. And I expected the questions to begin and to hear more of her veiled comments.

Gerry wore a blank expression. What was behind it, was hard to guess. My suspicions told me he was wary and a bit angry at Sara. He was also taking direction from me.

Danny said, "She's right. Where did the extra things come from?"

His tone was not accusatory however, her wry smile revealed her inner thoughts. "As I said, we were too tired to tell you all that happened. Other men, trackers, were sent after the two who returned naked. We realized that if we came back, they would follow us and kill us all while we slept."

Sara couldn't hold herself back as she blurted, "So you killed them, of course."

"Yes. We did."

My voice held no give. Her games tired me, and so did her dancing around and cute but cutting remarks. Being blunt has its advantages. Danny gave it a little thought and made a small nod in my direction. He shifted to look at Gerry with unasked questions.

When Gerry didn't speak, I continued, "Gerry was a tremendous help."

Sara hadn't missed Danny's approval of our actions. A scowl formed and her lips trembled. She looked ready to cry. I wondered if it was phony.

Danny said, "I'm going to look around outside, just to be safe."

"Stay next to the barn and leave through the woods, so you don't leave a trail to our front door if you don't mind." While I spoke to him, my eyes locked on the girl. Her lousy attitude had worn thin, and my vote said she could leave at any time. If she didn't, I might. Jake and Grace returning were all that held me back.

Gerry remained oddly silent.

It was easy to see he was sorting things out and hadn't reached any firm decisions. Or maybe he had and didn't wish to share them.

Five Years After

The silence in the barn was of three parts. First, was the protective roof over our heads, the sounds of the breeze whistling softly between the boards, and the hundreds of small creaking sounds a large structure makes. The second part was Gerry and his evaluation of our situation and his involvement in it. The third was the absence of Grace and Jake.

To avoid conflict, I shifted positions slightly and placed my back against an upright beam of solid wood that must have been sixteen inches square. My eyes closed, shutting out much of what I worried about—and Sara.

I dozed. Danny returned and said, "Everything looks okay out there. I stood the tall grass in front of the door upright to try and hide the trail we made. It helped, but anyone looking will still see it until the grass regrows or rights itself. There is no sign of Jake and Grace. I think we should go look for them. Maybe we'll meet on the road."

"Bad idea," Gerry said.

I liked his attitude. There was no give in the two words. No reason was given. None needed.

Danny faced him, looking ready to argue and thinking better of it. He simply asked, "Why?"

"If they see us, the militia will recognize the clothes we took from them, and their weapons. They will attack as soon as they recognize we're wearing them."

"We can wear scrubs," Danny shot back.

"Like the scrubs that Jake and Grace wore when they snuck into town? What if they were caught or killed because their scrubs stood out? The militia would want to ask a lot of questions about that. With a little torture to make us talk, any of us would lead them back here. Of course, I may be wrong." Gerry was on a roll.

I wished he'd left that last sentence unsaid. Or all of it. He was right on all counts. Little Gerry who had been pushed around by all of us for years, who never argued or fought back, had turned into a fierce confrontational animal. Thinking I had a small part in his transition, I felt proud.

And I couldn't leave him hanging out there alone. I said, "Gerry is right. What we need is for a couple of us to get into town and collect clothing like the civilians who are not militia.

Maybe clothes like the farmers. We need to observe, and then capture someone to interrogate so we can make a plan."

Gerry pulled off a boot and exposed a huge, swollen blister.

"Why didn't you say something?" I asked.

"Would you have complained?"

I gave it a tenth of a second consideration and snarled, "Damn right."

Danny took his foot and then helped Gerry remove the other boot. That revealed an even larger blister. Blood seeped from the edges. Danny said, "You can't wear boots that slip around on your feet when you walk. Too tight is probably better than too loose."

"You can't go anywhere with feet like that. They need time to heal, at least a couple of days," I told him.

Danny said, "The boots will fit me better. My feet are larger. I'll go with you."

I didn't miss the pained and hateful expression Sara flashed, somewhere between disbelief, surprise, and fear. Unaware of her feelings, Danny examined the boots and said, "Hey, they are my exact size. I need socks, too. Listen, Gerry, I'll try to find you a pair that will fit you better, okay?"

Gerry didn't look happy. I believed it was because he was not going into town, but it may have been over the loss of the boots. I didn't think he'd get them back.

Sara was not the only one surprised at Danny. The idea Danny would leave her side hadn't occurred to me. They had latched onto each other from the first. Now his eyes slid over her when he looked in that direction. While we'd been gone, their situation had perhaps changed.

Danny held up his bow. "I'd like to take this."

"As long as you also take a gun." My statement was a challenge, and I expected an argument from him. Instead, he reached his hand out and I gave him one. He put on a belt and holster while I selected and examined another weapon, an exact duplicate of his. All four of them were the same. That was more than odd. It said that there had once been many identical guns stored in one place. Not even a sporting goods store had that many.

That got my mind working again. There must have been a

hundred manufacturers of nine-millimeter semi-automatics before the war, and each made several variations. The only way all of those we had captured were the same was if they came from one place. Like an army arsenal. Or a police station, or a store that was having a gigantic sale of one model. At any rate, they had originated in one place. Then distributed to the Monroe militia.

All the while, I kept Sara in the corner of my eye. She said nothing. Her face had turned impassive, her eyes cold. I could have liked her but for her derogatory remarks aimed in my direction. Hormones from being pregnant could be part of it, but as the person on the receiving end, my immediate goal was to get away from her.

Danny tied the boots, adjusted the belt, and looked at me.

"I'm ready," I told him. My boots were on and a gun was on my waist, along with a knife. I pulled a hat lower over my brow.

He said, more to Gerry than Sara in my opinion, "We'll try to be back by dark, but we might need to spend the night in town. Tomorrow, late we'll return. Or we're in trouble."

"Then what?" Gerry asked.

I shrugged and smiled, "Let's face facts, okay? If Grace and Jake didn't make it, and Danny and I don't return, the last thing the two of you need to do is follow us and run into the same trouble. Go the other way and run all the way down to Seattle, if you have to, because something in Monroe is killing or capturing people."

"You're not funny, you know," Sara said with a snarl that irritated me more than it should have.

I said playfully, "Sometimes I am. This isn't one of them." With that, I went to the ladder and scuttled down like a rat avoiding a cat about to pounce. Surprisingly, I got in the last word. Sara was getting stranger by the day. Her smaller bug bites were healing fast and without new ones, her skin was already smoother. Scrubbing in the stream had helped, too.

When I looked at her in dim light which also helped hide the bruises and injuries, she was beautiful. In a few more days, she would turn heads wherever she went.

Danny was right behind me when we reached the ground

floor. At the door, instead of walking through the tall grass and leaving a more defined trail for others to follow, I put my back to the wall and sidestepped into turning the corner away from the road. Then, I moved into the forest and paused to allow my eyes to adjust to the dimmer light.

Danny stayed right on my heels.

I said over my shoulder, "What's with you two?"

"Sara?"

"Who else?"

He slowed and I turned to face him as he pulled to a stop. We were a hundred yards away from the barn, well out of hearing range, but he still looked around before speaking as if afraid Sara might have snuck up behind us and was listening. "She is getting strange."

"I thought you liked her."

"That first day, I did. Felt sorry, at first, but then . . . well, underneath all the dirt and stuff, she is a very pretty girl, you must admit. It's been a long time since I met and talked with a girl I didn't know in the sanctuary, not that there were more than a few. It was exciting. Then, things changed. She made snide remarks about everyone, but mostly about you. I think she's jealous of you. Whatever it is, she makes me uncomfortable."

That was quite a speech from Danny, and I wondered what she had said that put him off like that. There must have been something very distasteful, or a lot of smaller things. While working in the tavern, I'd seen relationships develop in a single evening and fall apart just as quickly. That seemed to be the case today.

He had his lips pursed. He wanted to add to what he'd said and was searching for the right words. I waited.

"She is not right in the head, you know. She twists things to suit her purposes. Have you ever heard the saying, don't confuse me with facts?"

I had. "Maybe she can't trust people yet. Give her time."

He paused again. "Ever hear of the Stockholm Syndrome?"

"No."

"After a person has been kidnapped and mistreated, they often become attached or affectionate to their captors who provided their food and water. It's a well-recognized mental condition."

"But they beat and raped her, then left her chained inside that tent. How can she not hate them?"

"I can't remember the reasons the syndrome exists, just the result. I think she is like that. And a little crazy."

"Give her time."

"No, it's not like that. She hates you like nothing I've ever seen. But she thinks Gerry is sneaky and that Jake wants to get her alone for sex. Grace reminds her of her mother, a woman that bullied her, or so she says. I'm the only one that she thinks will protect her."

"Do you feel that way?"

He walked on a few steps and then said, "I will admit she influenced me that first day. Who wouldn't be? But then, reality struck me like a semi on a highway. One wrong word and she would turn on me too. She is sick in the head."

The whole Stockholm Syndrome sounded like a load of horse manure. The problem was that after he started explaining, I remembered hearing something similar about a girl willingly helping her captors rob banks. Maybe it was all true.

No matter, I kind of agreed that she could turn on him at any moment, and possibly do him harm. It surprised me that she felt that way about the others, but thinking back, I should have seen it for myself.

It seemed time to change the subject. I said, "Listen to me. If Jake and Grace were captured, I will do whatever it takes to rescue them."

"What about revenge?"

"That's why I'm telling you this. As much as I like both, attempting revenge is an easy way to die. Oh, I might go away and learn how to build a bomb and sneak it back there, but I will not charge in with my nine-millimeter futilely lighting up the night sky with deadly shots."

"So, you're on a rescue mission?"

"That depends, Danny. If I see a way to get them free, fine. I'll risk it. To a point. This trip into town is just a fact-finding mission. Not a battle. If you have other ideas, why not wait until tomorrow and then you can go in alone and play the hero."

He didn't like my tone, words, or that I challenged him. His face turned red, his jaw clenched, and his eyes squinted. He snarled, "Why bring me instead of Gerry? It seems the two of you are getting along well. Not romantically, but as a team. His blisters?"

"I've asked myself that a few times."

"Gerry is a wimp, and you know it." His voice had turned cruel and judgmental. That concerned me and I wondered if Sara's opinions hadn't taken hold on some level.

"No, he's not anymore, Danny. While we were out there, he did what was needed. Someday I'll have to tell you how he used himself to draw one of the trackers right up to me, which would have cost him his life if I failed to act or missed the shot. He's learning fast and maybe I should have brought him instead of you. If you want to trade places, go back, and tell him to come to meet me here. I'll wait."

He took a couple of deep breaths, as he thought it over. "I'll go with you."

With that, I turned and started walking. Not that I was convinced it was the right choice. Danny had a hero complex to go along with Sara's Stockholm Syndrome. Gerry was an introvert who was emerging like an insect entering the next stage of its life. And last, I was a stubborn radical that didn't like being told what to do. We all had our problems, and I should be more forgiving of the failings of others.

The ground was damp, as always. In places, ferns grew head high. The vines and creepers held last year's dried berries and they tried tripping any people walking, especially me. The firm-looking ground often let our feet sink into the swampy muck below. A brown bunny darted in front of us and hopped down our path for a few seconds before disappearing.

That bunny made my day. The smile held for a long time and my eyes searched for another. Just a rabbit hopping along a bunny trail. Our escape to above ground was already worth it, if only for seeing that one creature that was the prey of all local predators. I felt I was more like the bunny than wolf, cat, bear, or whatever. I found myself grinning so much that my cheeks hurt.

We waded across two small streams, and climbed three small mountains, or tall hills, before coming out of the forest far below the bridge. From our vantage point, the barricade of old cars, refrigerators, sofas, and pallets left only a small access on the bridge for people walking.

If enemies, like us, were approaching from our side of the bridge, the guards stationed at the top of the pile had a clear view for a quarter of a mile. Even a poor shot would hit his target as we moved closer, and it was impossible to get closer unseen.

I liked the idea of crossing the river below the bridge, even with the extra guard posted there. The water was swifter and deeper, but the channel narrower than above the bridge. More than that, I liked where we'd be when we came out. Almost right behind Grace's old house, only a few blocks away. And yes, I remembered there were guards posted there. However, after dark, with cloud cover, guards would depend more on their sense of hearing because they couldn't see anything. The rustle of the fast water hid most sounds.

Grace had headed for her old house and neighborhood, so that is where we'd locate her and Jake. In that part of town, there were houses built fifty or seventy-five years ago. Maybe older. The streets were narrow, the trees and shrubbery tall, and a careful person could move undercover the whole way.

It sounded so easy from our vantage on this side of the river as we talked and planned. Our fingers traced out possible routes in the sand indicated places to avoid and likely positions where the guards were stationed. Finally, we spotted the pair of them at the river below the bridge, right where we expected.

Evading or avoiding their position would be no problem, so there was no reason for an encounter. They were bored, talking while sitting on a log beside the water in plain sight, and their attention, when they looked, was always upstream where the water was shallower, and moved slower. We decided to swim across below them where large trees grew right up to the edge of the bank, so the shade underneath would be darker and conceal us better. We would be far enough away that any stray sounds of our swimming wouldn't carry, but to be honest, our plan also depended on the guards remaining sleepy or inattentive.

If they came alert and made rounds to inspect the river's edge for footprints, we were in trouble. However, each time we looked, they were in the same location. They may have guarded that location a hundred times before. With that, they became careless.

Chapter 10

Danny said, "What are you thinking?"

"Really? Do you want to know what I'm thinking at a time like this?"

He turned to me; his face serious. "Yes."

I allowed a long breath to escape. "I'm thinking the hard part is what comes next. And after that. I'm thinking the odds of both of us seeing the sunrise is smaller than I like."

"What else?" he sighed.

"Honestly, I'm thinking that if there is trouble, I can outrun you, so the militia will chase you instead of me and I'll probably get away if either of us does. How is that?"

A smile almost formed, but a tremble prevented it from fully forming as he realized I was not joking.

I said, "You can always go back to the barn, you know. I can do this alone."

"Not a chance," he said. "Do you want to go in the water first, or me?"

That was a loaded question. I wanted to lead, of course. That was my way. However, Danny was growing daily. Not physically. Mentally. He deserved some credit if not all that Gerry did. Neither were the meek boys I'd known in the sanctuary. "Listen, why don't you go first, and I'll follow right behind. If there is trouble, use your bow if you can. Keep it silent. One gunshot will bring every militiaman in the city searching for us."

He gave me a curt nod. "Where do we go after crossing?"

"We travel in the woods to an old part of town south of Lewis Street. Find their kitchen. The barracks will be close to that. Grace and Jake are probably near those, watching and listening."

Danny kept to the edge of the shrubbery at our side of the river. Out of sight. Quiet. He took us a few hundred yards further downriver where we couldn't be seen from the bridge or guards posted below the bridge and we waited.

We watched, listened, sniffed, and remained still. After that, he moved in a crouch down the rocky bank to the sandbar, quickly and quietly. At the edge of the water, he didn't slow, despite the cold temperature.

I followed a few steps behind. When my ankle hit the water, I sucked in a breath. Cold didn't begin to describe it. The water had probably been ice or snow a day ago. My other foot landed deeper. Then the next step carried me deeper and my feet went numb. The water only went part of the way up my calf. I sucked another mouthful of air, anticipating what came soon.

By the time the water was thigh-deep, the current was swift and threatened to carry me downstream. My jaws clenched from the cold tight enough to crack teeth, and a shiver went through me as I watched Danny dive ahead and take powerful strokes into the darkness.

If he could do it, so could I. A deep breath and I followed. The water that had numbed my feet did the same to my hands instantly. I gasped, despite trying to be quiet.

Only one way to get out and get warm, I mentally repeated to myself over and over. Swim faster and get out faster. My arms pumped. My fingers lost feeling and no longer cupped but I kept on.

The stroke of my left hand finally jarred my shoulder as it touched the rocky bottom. My shirt went tight at my neck as Danny gripped me by the collar of my oversized shirt and pulled. We were out. We stumbled into the shrubbery and fell to the ground, gasping for air and hugging each other from a combination of fear and cold.

If there had been a guard within fifty yards, they would have raced to us. There was no hiding the breathing and panting sounds we made. I rolled over and lay on my back, wondering if my gun would shoot bullets or squirt a stream of water. It wasn't funny. I didn't know if a wet gun, one that submerged while swimming, would fire.

I said, "Your bow. Is it ruined?"

He hissed softly, "Nylon string. If anything, the fletching on the arrows might come loose, but they probably used waterproof glue."

We left the edge of the river and followed animal trails and paths. There were lights in windows ahead. Not electric, but yellow and pale. Candles. We reached the first houses and found a place to wait where we had a view of the length of a side street.

People were moving about. They all seemed to either head for what had once been a hardware store I think, or they were emerging from it. I smelled meat cooking. My stomach growled in answer to Danny's. We shared a smile, the first in an hour.

Everyone carried a gun of one kind or another. Rifles in fists, pistols in holsters, and a few carried both. I saw shotguns, revolvers, automatics, and rifles that had probably provided venison for families years ago. The people, the men, at least, were coarse, rough, and bearded. It was not the beards that drew my attention.

Beards and flannel were normal in Monroe before the war. No, it was the men themselves. These were the survivors of the war and the chaos after. Weaker men, and women too, had probably died in the first few days after the attack. Those willing to fight and kill had probably thinned the herd during the next phase, but the truth came like the unexpected flash of a camera in a dark room.

I was looking at not only the toughest and hardest of survivors, but many were men who had been in the Monroe Reformatory and were now free. Hardened criminals, bank robbers, and murderers—and worse. They filled the city. As a result, anything goes. Fights and killings probably happened almost daily. Hell, some of the men I watched were seeking them out.

It reminded me of old western movies about Tombstone,

Dodge City, and Abilene. Monroe probably also attracted bad men who were not in prison but had heard about the wild, wide-open city. *Bad men*, what a poor excuse to describe the present inhabitants. Swagger, anger, intimidation, and drunken brawls were better choices, but I couldn't think of a single word that described the debauchery we watched unfold on the streets.

"Night scopes?" Danny hissed at me. "Think they have them?"

"Those need batteries. Probably not many of them around so, no."

We watched for an hour, people coming and going, their conversation relaxed, and laughter sounded now and then. Occasional shouting occurred, along with crude humor and cruel laughter. Most on the streets were men, but not all. They were universally dressed in jeans and flannel shirts to the point that I tried to remember if there was a warehouse in town for similar clothing. If so, that probably supplied the army with warm clothing. Maybe there was a cargo semi-trailer that had stopped on the highway nearby or rail cars on the tracks that held the clothing where it came to a final stop.

There had been a new distribution store for an online company built just before the war. They received orders and packages were sent all over the world. It had been a clothing outlet.

When I mentioned my ideas, Danny replied, "That makes sense. The distribution centers. There was an accident when I was a kid. A cargo container that a truck was hauling was filled with expensive sneakers. The news said it held over twenty-thousand pairs or something like that. Imagine how many pairs of jeans a whole building could hold. It makes sense."

It was a good answer for several reasons. The first was that he agreed with me and that indicated his high intelligence. I held in a smile at the conceited thought.

However, thousands of trucks a day had driven over the mountain pass through the Cascade mountains to either reach the rest of America, or to bring goods from there to the Pacific Northwest coast, meaning Seattle, Tacoma, and Everett.

We found an abandoned house on a side street. The back

door stood open. Leaves and clutter covered the porch. Danny whispered to follow him. I wanted to remain outside where we had options for defending and escaping if discovered, but he moved ahead, and I followed.

Our footsteps were careful not to disturb the debris on the porch, most of which were leaves from a tree in the back yard. Inside smelled of rot, mildew, and old things. The carpet was soggy and fell apart where our feet touched. I wanted to get back to the fresh evergreen smells and take my chances out there.

Danny went to the little hallway leading to the bedrooms and reached up. He pulled on a small rope and a rectangle, hinged on one end, lowered with the snap and protest of large springs. He unfolded an attached ladder and motioned for me to go up first.

I reached a smelly attic and carefully stepped on the top edges of two-by-sixes. Behind me, Danny refolded the ladder and pulled the access ramp up into place again. It was dark. Only a dribble of light came from air vents at either end.

Danny took us to the vent on the front of the house. He inserted the barrel of his pistol into the wire mesh and shoved it, then twisted. With very little sound, the vent pulled free, leaving us with a rectangle a foot wide to see though, a surreptitious place where we saw most of the street in both directions.

The street lay right below, twenty feet away. Yet our hiding place kept us concealed. It was perfect to watch from, even if it meant discovery and wouldn't provide an escape.

At the left corner, maybe six houses away seemed to be a makeshift tavern in a converted carpet dealer's building. As a former employee of a tavern, I recognized the comings and goings. A fair stream of people, mostly men, entered with eager enthusiasm and anticipation. Others stumbled out, not having found what they hoped in the bottoms of their glasses. We watched two fistfights in the street an hour apart. Nobody attempted to break them up.

The fights barely attracted attention. One man still lay bleeding profusely from a head wound and a deep cut across his shoulder. Ten feet away, another slept at the base of the building. At least, I assumed he was asleep. He may have been dead.

The small crowd that had spilled into the street for the second fight gathered around and prevented us from seeing most of it, but the reaction of the crowd was not the cheering and shouting I'd witnessed at the few fights at the tavern where I had worked.

Both fights were short, vicious, and each man intended to hurt the other. Knives were pulled in the second fight and in the end, one man lay on the pavement outside, ignored by all that walked past.

The crowds thinned by midnight.

"Are we going to stay here?" I asked.

"For tonight, I thought. We're scouting. In the morning, we'll see what happens around here and take it from there."

"It'll be light, then. Are you planning on staying here all day?"

He turned from the vent opening and said, "Yes. I don't want to run into whatever Grace and Jake did, so I'll go slow. If you want to return to the barn, go. I don't mind."

The last was a challenge as he threw my words back at me.

I hesitated. I wanted to leave and not face an entire day with little food, not to mention bathroom facilities or a convenient tree to hide behind. The damp and smells were sickening me.

He said, "Really, Pen, it's going to be a long night and day. Probably nothing will come of it. Go back and let Sara and Gerry know what we're up to, so they don't worry."

My flannel and jeans held enough river water they needed a day or two of sunshine to dry. Inside them, I shivered, not only from fear but cold. I considered a scouting trip to find dry clothing and decided it was too dangerous. "We're a team. We stay or go together, and by that, I mean both of us. You can return tomorrow or the day after. Now, don't give me any more shit about this."

His expression in the dim light was defiant until he drew in a long breath and gave me a single curt nod of agreement. He turned his back from me and made his way to the pull-down attic access stairs.

The smelly house, the confinement, and in truth, what I'd seen counted towards my disposition. That didn't take into consideration the fear I felt for my two friends. This part of the city was an armed camp full of men and women ready to kill for the smallest reason. It was not a place for me, and one mistake would have us captured or worse.

Danny knew me. He should understand that if we remained in the attic, sooner or later, I'd step through the ceiling and alert anyone outside, or I'd sneeze, or cough with people right outside. Something. It wouldn't take much to have the house surrounded by armed militia anxious to kill. I feared my clumsiness would get us both killed.

However, Grace and Jake were on their own somewhere in the city, perhaps hiding in an attic right across the street. My eyes strayed to those houses before I rejected the idea. I was no superhero who would swoop in, defeat a hundred enemies, and the four of us escape unharmed. No, if there was a gambler taking odds on the outcome, they would be a hundred to one that I'd get myself captured and all four of us would face the same firing squad.

"Come with me. There isn't anything else we can do here," he said. "Let's look around."

"I'm right behind you," I said. It was dark and I felt my way along. "Help me down the stairs."

As I used my feet to find my way down in the darkness, his hand brushed aside the wet hair on my forehead, a uniquely intimate action it was completely genuine and impulsive. Before I could think about it and change my mind about going with him, I leaped the last few steps and landed on the soggy carpet with a splat far too loud for a person sneaking in enemy territory.

We left the attic access pulled down and departed the house without another word.

I carefully went to the rear door and paused, listening, smelling, and watching before opening it. When satisfied the way was clear, I melded quickly into the thick, eight-foot-tall shrubbery that had once been a neatly trimmed hedge. I slipped into the edge of the forest and looked up at the rising moon.

My route would keep the sliver of light ahead and to my right. That would direct me to the river. However, it was after midnight, by my guess, and few people moved on the street. People were going to bed. The candles in the windows of the city were put out, all but a few.

The dark forest around me protected me from discovery like a cloak of invisibility. I said, "Follow me."

Mind made up; I eased my way from the trees back to overgrown shrubs, in the direction of the center of town. I found the library, a place I'd spent hours studying and flirting with the local boys with whispers and giggles that irritated the librarians. We darted across Village Way, a main street in the city, undetected.

The fire station stood ahead, and a lot of shrubberies that had grown in front of a row of houses hid us. People moved up there by the fire station. Not the raucous catcalls and drunken challenges near the makeshift tavern, but more military. The quiet arrival of several, each carrying a rifle of one sort or another gave me the impression of a changing of the guards. The men and women entering the firehouse were more interested in a bed than a drink if my instincts were correct.

Danny whispered, "We should get out of here."

My ears twitched at the slightest sound. My nose searched for human scents. My eyes explored the darkness. Leaving was not an option.

The firehouse was a natural location for people to occupy. Solidly built with kitchen facilities, sleeping areas, and easily defensible, the choice a natural for the militia. I'd wager the flat roof had a guard posted up there.

An out-of-place structure drew me closer. In the parking lot in the rear, a pair of telephone poles stood upright. A third pole connected the upright pair, probably ten feet off the pavement. From it, darker forms appeared in the soft moonlight filtered by a layer of clouds.

Five bodies.

The structure was a gallows.

We had hunkered down too far away to identify the bodies. My gag reflex threatened to spew vomit and I fought to regain control. People were near enough they would hear me. Moving closer endangered me.

Danny placed an understanding hand on my shoulder as if to calm me or perhaps to pull me away from that awful place. However, I couldn't leave the city without knowing if my friends were hanging there.

In a test of wills, two sides of my brain fought, one to flee and the other to get closer. What I wanted was to identify the dead and find none of them were Jake or Grace. I darted from the cover of the bushes in the direction of the firehouse, Danny at my heels. I made it to a large clump of shrubbery unseen, a very risky move. The bodies were clearer, but not enough I could be certain. We scooted on our butts a little farther to remain in the deep shade of the shrubs.

Movement on top of the firehouse told me that at least one guard was up there, on our side of the flat roof, so he would probably be looking our way right now. Movement is the first thing the human eye detects. I'd have to time my next moves since he seemed to be patrolling the roof in a circle. I moved behind the row of tangled growth and advanced slowly as he made his rounds.

A half-hour passed as I crept closer and closer. The gallows had been constructed out at the edge of the parking lot, so getting closer without being seen couldn't have been more difficult. Still, we didn't want to be spotted. Waiting for dawn and better light was suicide.

A pair of drunk militiamen stumbled past my location, making no pretense of being quiet. Nobody paid them any attention. It gave me an idea.

First, I formulated an escape route from the location to the river, just in case. The layout of Monroe gave me three or four nearly direct routes. Once I reached the river with pursuit hot on my tail, it was dive in, swim for the far shore, and run for my life. I doubted any of those chasing me was stupid enough to leap into the cold water after me. With luck, if we reached the river, we'd have a head start before they gathered themselves together, formed a posse, crossed the bridge, and started tracking us.

At that point, they had better be fast because I'd be running for a long time.

"Danny, if things go south, your job, your only job, will be to head for the river, swim across, and get to the area of the barn alone. It is too obvious to stay there if the militia is searching for you, so head back to Sara's parents' campsite in that hidden valley and hide. Leave no tracks. I'll find you there."

He wanted to argue. Or stall. Or object.

One part of me wanted him to do all those things—and convince me to go with him. The rest didn't. I maintained my steady gaze and waited until his head gave a single small bob of reluctant agreement. The initial part of my plan had made my breath catch in my throat while talking. The remainder unsaid. Audacious came to mind, right after foolish, stupid, and dangerous. I stood and staggered from the shrubbery before Danny could stop me.

Our hidden position had been as close to the five bodies hanging from the telephone poles as we could get without exposing ourselves. I refused to go before confirming Grace and Jake were not there. I owed it to them to find out. Perhaps they were nearby, and I could help them. The other side of that coin was that if they were hanging from the gallows, Danny and I were unnecessarily risking our lives looking for them.

"Good luck," Danny whispered behind me. I half expected him to follow and that would have pissed me off—but he didn't.

In the open, I moved several steps closer and staggered as if drunk. My eyes were watching for others who might challenge me, but few were out this late. I moved closer to the edge of the firehouse parking lot; my eyes averted from the specter of the dead.

The clouds thinned momentarily, and my eyes flitted from searching for danger around me to examining the corpses. The first two were strangers and my hopes briefly soared. However, Jake, my old boyfriend, was the third in the row. Grace hung next to him.

They were suspended by their necks with ropes. In the dim light, their bodies revealed broken limbs. Grace's legs ended in stumps. I wondered where her feet were. Jake's body had feet but no fingers on his left hand. Long cuts across their chests looked like black stripes in the moonlight. I shuddered to imagine what they had gone through before hanging.

Three rowdy people appeared in the parking lot behind me. I'd been standing there so long they were only twenty steps away when I noticed them. Two others walked out of the firehouse in my general direction. Running would draw their attention and probably pursuit. I turned away from them, bent over, and puked out what little remained in my stomach, making no pretense of hiding or being quiet. It was certainly a genuine performance.

All five detoured to move past me at a distance. One called, "You should take it easier on the booze."

Another laughed wryly and said something about how bad I'd feel the next morning. He had no idea of the truth of that statement.

I gave them a good look at my middle finger as another spasm shook me and I fell to my knees and emptied the little in my stomach. I wiped my chin and mouth with the back of my sleeve.

At the same time, my mind went to work. My actions copied those of others, and they ignored me, believing me drunk like most of them. The wounds on Jake and Grace's bodies told me they had been captured and tortured, perhaps for a long time. The only reason for doing that to them was to obtain information. The valuable information they held was the location of the sanctuary, where they stored food, supplies, and most important of all, where the weapons were.

That didn't take into account the resentment and hate that Sara had revealed towards us. We'd been the select few who had fled to safety while bombs and rockets fell from the sky. She believed we had locked the vault door to the sanctuary while people stood outside and beat their frustrated fists on it.

Sara had told of the hate for us in exaggerated stories that often held little truth. Not that truth matters when hate is the central emotion. In that brief conversation in the barn, she had revealed a contempt for us that chilled me.

She hated me. That I understood. Many others didn't like me, but hate is a strong word. She had as much as admitted she felt the same resentment for all five of us, but it centered on me, a combination of intense dislike and jealousy, in my opinion.

I'm sure Jake and Grace had held out. Or tried to. I'm also sure they told their interrogators who knew everything the two of them had known. The only heroes that never give in to torture are in fiction.

If my friends talked, as I suspected, those who ordered their torture would probably assemble a small force to pinpoint the precise location of the sanctuary door, then a larger force would march. Despite my dislike for everyone in the sanctuary, I knew them. We'd lived together five years.

I had to warn them.

The only hope I had was that they had protected the secret of the mine shaft. The interrogators might believe those inside the sanctuary had briefly opened the vault door to let us out. Had they kept that secret? If so, those below might remain safe.

The second secret they had possessed was me. Us. Had the interrogators asked how many had escaped? I remained on one knee on the blacktop and ignored others walking in pursuit of their pleasures or duties. Yes, the inquisitors would have asked how many of us there were. That meant that somewhere nearby, perhaps at this moment, plans were made to locate those who escaped.

Danny! I had to get back to him before dawn or we could both be pinned down where we were, unable to travel, which meant we couldn't warn Gerry and Sara. While Danny believed our existence was unknown, he would move slowly and cautiously.

It was time to panic.

Another thought came to mine. Gerry and Sara needed to move from the barn right away. They were sure to be discovered by those searching for the sanctuary and then the mine entrance.

I used the same ruse to convince anyone looking my way I was drunk. Walking and staggering down the center of the road made me look innocent, and if anyone doubted my condition, they had only to smell my breath or the vomit that clung to my shirt.

A few houses before the one where Danny and I had

hidden became my jumping-off point. I entered the bushes there and made my way to the back door of the stinky house with the wet carpet. I assumed Danny would retrace our original route. I entered the forest and followed the same paths as before, only a lot faster. I prepared myself to sprint at the moment of discovery.

Vines tripped me, branches reached from the dark and scratched. Uneven ground caused me to stumble, and one puddle of water was inches deeper than I believed and I fell to my knees. But I never slowed.

I heard the rustle of the river before it came into sight. As I stepped out, voices sounded to my right, maybe fifty feet away. My feet stopped without me telling them to. I strained to hear. Or see. The cloud cover was heavier now, and even the dim moonlight barely helped.

A lantern came on. Two militia faced Danny, one of them holding an old-fashioned lantern shoulder high to examine Danny's face. The other backhanded Danny after asking a muffled question and not getting the answer he demanded.

Danny's wrists were tied behind him. Blood streamed from his nose and mouth in the lanternlight. The same man repeated the question as he raised a balled fist.

My mind took another leap. I could see them. They could not see me. And worse, from their standpoint, they didn't know I was there. My gun was already in my hand.

Fifty feet does not sound like far. My pistol was probably capable of hitting a target from there. The question became, was I?

If I missed, they would toss the lantern aside and two of their guns begin firing at me, and probably at Danny. One militia stood on either side of Danny, giving me a clear line of sight without putting my friend in danger of my bullets. The fist started to swing.

I fired twice. Once at each of them. The shots sounded like cannon fire in the still of the night. Before I knew if they were even hit, I charged. I screamed like a wild thing as I rushed them, covering half the distance before diving to the ground, my gun held in front.

I fired two more times at each of them, aiming at their

chests, the shots so fast only the slightest pause came between the first two and the second. The lantern fell, but not before I realized at least the last four shots had all struck true. While I'd aimed at their chests, the largest target on each, it appeared that from my low angle on the ground all had hit their stomachs.

I came to my knees and charged ahead, prepared to empty the magazine if necessary. It was not. I cut the ropes binding Danny's wrists instead of untying him. In an almost reflex action, I relieved both guards of their handguns.

Danny said, "We have to hurry. They were waiting for me."

"Why?"

"They knew we were coming. There are more scattered all along the river."

That made sense. Jake and Grace must have told them we would follow. They posted extra guards. We'd somehow missed them earlier, or they had been posted after we crossed the river. No matter. I said, "We have to get across the river. Now."

As if to emphasize my statement, a shout came from upriver. The answer came from down river. We were as good as surrounded. They had been waiting for us to cross the river, not come at them from behind, so we had a temporary advantage. We splashed into the icy water and dived when it reached our knees. Three pistols weighed me down, and wet clothing made it worse, but I kicked and took long, powerful strokes.

We reached the other shore after about ten of those strokes. The cold had already sapped my strength, my hands and arms numb. My legs wouldn't cooperate. I pushed ahead on my knees and the current drug at me, making my progress minimal.

Danny's hand found my shirt and pulled. We fell into the shallows, too exhausted to continue. Voices behind drew my attention. At least six people were searching for us along the other bank and had found the dead we'd left behind. While they were upriver of us because the current was carrying us, we saw and heard parts of their exchanges.

They spread out and looked for where we'd gone,

convinced only idiots would attempt swimming the river in the dark. Perhaps they were right. The cold from the river penetrated our clothes and pulled any heat from us.

Danny said as his hand snaked in my direction, "Got to get to dry land."

I couldn't grasp it but managed to crawl over the sand and rocks. We reached the marshy area and got to our feet and continued. I started shivering. Waves of violent shaking swept over me, but I managed, with Danny's help to stand on my feet. Not that he was in much better shape.

We climbed a small hill covered in thick brush and the river was behind us.

Danny pulled me to a stop. He tried to unbutton his shirt and his fingers betrayed him. He ripped it open like Superman used to do. He peeled it off and reached for his pants. His hands couldn't work the button and zipper, so he pulled his knife and sliced the front. While he sat and attempted to get the pants over his thighs, I tried the Superman thing on my shirt and failed.

So, I pulled my knife and cut the buttons one at a time. Then my pants. Danny scooted closer and helped by pulling them over my feet.

We stood naked in the dim light, unashamed and scared. Bare skin wouldn't be comfortable in the spring coolness of the night, but the wet clothing would have sapped all our heat and death would have been long before dawn. The nighttime temperature might go down into the forties.

"Grace and Jake are dead. Tortured and hung," I managed to say between chattering teeth.

To his credit, Danny gathered his few things, "You lead. Tell me later what happened."

It would have been easier to walk down the center of the road, and a lot faster but I was too scared. I crept along the edges. An hour later, a whispered voice ahead stilled me.

Danny touched my shoulder, telling me he'd heard it also. I moved slower, much slower. The scent of woodsmoke drifted in the night air. In a small ravine, the remains of a campfire smoldered, the coals red and orange when a puff of breeze stirred it. Two men lay beside it. A third sleeping bag was empty.

Before moving again, I needed to know the location of the third man. If he'd stepped into the trees to relieve himself, he should quickly return and that would make it easier for us.

He didn't.

That suggested he was on watch. If he was, then the road was where he'd be and we couldn't attempt sneaking past him, so we went down the slope, fifty yards away, and circled the campsite. He was not there.

Danny said, "I'll find the one on the road. You find a position where you can shoot both down there."

He didn't have to point out who he meant. Danny slipped into the darkness.

I moved closer, still not trusting my shooting abilities. In the light cast from the glow of the fire, familiar flannel shirts and military-style gun belts like the one I wore satisfied me that we were not attacking innocents.

A single shot sounded from the direction of the road. My gun fired twice, one shot at each sleeping person, then repeated the process in case either was still alive. Sara would be horrified when she heard the increase in the body count, all of which she would blame on me.

I didn't have time to care. I rushed to the nearest sleeping bag and ran the zipper down the side. She was dead. The other was an old man, also dead. A small pile of firewood lay beside the orange coals, probably put there for use in the morning. I tossed a good amount on the firepit and backed into the edge of the forest, to await either Danny or the man who had killed him.

Danny emerged as the fire flared to life, his gun dangling from his fingers. His eyes searched for mine. I motioned to the dead in the sleeping bags.

Neither of us spoke. We stripped the two bodies of clothing, dressed quickly, and the fire warmed us as we did. We still hadn't talked. I realized that there were now six pistols for me to carry. Sitting beside the fire, I pulled the cartridges from a gun of a different manufacturer but the same caliber and refilled my original. It felt best in my hand, if for no other reason than because I knew it functioned properly and had saved my life a couple of times.

Trust is an issue in my world. I trusted that gun. It hadn't let me down yet.

One of the others was a duplicate. I made sure the magazine was full, then began stuffing my pockets with more bullets. Danny did the same. I don't know if he held on to his original weapon, but soon each of us had a gun in our holster, our pockets bulged with bullets, and we were warm and dry.

People who had heard the shots might arrive at any time. A scouting party from the city may have been formed, and they could be nearby searching for us. Danny pointed to the road, turned, and walked away.

I followed.

Danny walked fast. I kept up with him, to remain warm as much as to put distance between those I felt certain were behind us. The dry clothes were wonderful and the jackets were waterproof. We traveled for a couple of hours. Dawn drew near. The turnoff for the barn couldn't be far ahead and I didn't want to pass by it in the darkness, so found a place under a large cedar with drooping branches that hung almost to the ground. It was far enough off the road that nobody walking on it would hear our deep breathing as we slept. The soft needles under it felt as soft as any mattress.

We still hadn't spoken. I'd given only the barest of explanations.

"They're dead? Jake and Grace? I can't believe it," he repeated for the third time, trying to prompt me to talk.

I held my temper. My instinct was to growl that both were alive, and I had played a nasty prank on him. It occurred to me again that Danny knew only a fragment of what I'd seen since it had been me to sneak so close, an action that in retrospect had been more stupid than I believed possible.

Sitting shoulder to shoulder, in a voice that seemed to be someone else speaking, I described what I'd seen, the missing fingers on Jake's hand and Grace's feet, and the long slices across their upper bodies. Not in enough detail to place the horror that filled my mind, but enough for him to understand. If captured, we'd be lucky to only lose fingers, feet, and suffer a few cuts with a knife or sword for an afternoon. No, they'd probably make us remain alive a few days, at minimum. Not because they wanted us to live, but they wanted us to suffer for their soldiers we'd killed.

My eyes wouldn't stay open, my mind was fuzzy, and a headache throbbed across my temple. I sat with my knees pulled up to my chin, my arms wrapped around them to try and keep warm. Despite those efforts and the new clothing, I shivered. Inside and outside. Sleep wouldn't come but snatches of rest did.

Counting to a hundred didn't help pass the time, so I tried a thousand. When dawn finally came, we'd head for the barn. That was my plan. We'd get to Sara and Gerry and disappear. Somewhere safe, although I didn't know where that was.

The first rack of shivers took me by surprise. The trembling got worse, probably because of my imagination. It had little to do with being cold. Mental images of my friends hanging from the gallows refused to go away.

I stood and tried pacing. I promised them I'd done all I could and tried thinking of what I could have. I'd try anything.

Finally, I started walking and crossed the road to the left side, thinking that if I walked on the dirt when I came to the road that turned off to the barn, I'd have to cross blacktop and recognize it with my feet. Danny stayed at my side. We moved faster, to keep warmer. The road appeared sooner than expected. I prayed it was the right road, although I couldn't remember any others. It was darker than earlier. The moon had set, the clouds blocked out the starlight, and my eyes were as tuned to the darkness as possible.

Still, I tripped over roots or vines several times. Worse, were the unexpected holes or shallow spots. One made me lose my balance and I stumbled a few steps ahead, only to run into a tree face-first. The rough bark cut my cheek and the side of my forehead. My headache grew worse.

I ignored the blood trickling down my cheek and kept moving.

When we'd traveled about the right distance, I sat on the edge of the road and cried, too scared to move on and pass by the barn without seeing it. My friends there needed a warning. I pulled my knees to my chin and hugged myself again. I placed my forehead on my knees and tried to relax, to wipe my mind clear of all it had seen and thought about.

It didn't matter. I just needed to hold myself together until dawn.

Danny said, "We should move on."

"You go."

"Both or none." He sat beside me and placed an arm over my shoulders.

When dawn arrived, I almost missed it. I looked up and in the gray light, I could make out the tree line separating the ground from the sky. I remained seated and closed my eyes again while waiting for more light. I'd lasted all night. No sense in leaping to my feet and rushing down the dark road and hitting another tree or skinning my other knee.

During the night I'd skinned my left knee and it hurt like crazy, along with my cheek and forehead. Thinking about those injuries made me realize my palm hurt, too. I must have used it to brace one of my falls on the pavement. Touching it with the fingers of my other hand found grit.

I smeared my hair to one side. It helped some. When I looked up again, there was no additional light and I realized that what I'd been thinking for only a minute instead of an hour. Time refused to move.

I closed my eyes and squeezed out a few tears. Then I shut my mind to everything and forced it to shut down—easier said than done. Fighting with myself passed the time.

When I opened my eyes again, it was predawn, but there was more than enough light to move on the road. Danny climbed to his feet and waited.

Ten minutes later, I saw the hulking shape of the barn.

We entered the trees well before reaching the barn and circled to the back side. It was a new path, so we didn't advertise that people had used the barn today. We moved along the wall until reaching the door. I called softly into the darkness, "It's me, Pen."

Gerry answered instantly, "Come on up."

The smells and relative warmth of the barn made my tired body limp and ready for a nap, however, that was not going to happen. At the base of the ladder, I paused.

At the top, Gerry was waiting, a blanket around his shoulders. In the dim light, he took one look at me and leaped to his feet, his face full of compassion.

"What the hell happened?"

"They're dead."

"You're covered in blood. Tell me what happened."

Danny remained near the door, keeping watch. If nothing else, we'd learned how to watch our backtrail.

"Nothing serious. We spent the night in the woods, and I fell a few times on the way back here. Wet legs and feet. Cold."

His blanket swirled in the air and surrounded me. He pulled it down on my shoulders gently. He said, "You should get out of those wet clothes, but not yet. We have to talk."

That last comment caught my attention. Bare skin and the warm blanket, or maybe two blankets, and I'd warm in no time. But in his voice was a tone I didn't recognize. "What is it we have to talk about so urgently?"

"Sara's gone."

"Gone?" I couldn't comprehend what he meant in my tired state of mind.

"She wanted me to go with her."

"Where?"

"Town. Monroe. To talk to the militia. She's going to tell them about us and the sanctuary. She tried to convince me that all of you hated her and me."

"You refused and she left on her own?" I asked.

"Yes. She wants them to come here and kill all of us. We have to leave right away."

Chapter 11

The girl we'd saved from imprisonment and those evil men was going to betray us? It didn't make sense. I snapped as if angry, which I was, "Tell me more. Danny, are you hearing this?"

"I am."

Gerry went on, his voice raised a little so Danny would hear it all, "Right after you two left, she did, too. First, she asked a few questions that seemed innocent enough, like asking which direction we'd come from when we found her. Then she asked more, and I grew suspicious. She wanted to know how long we walked after leaving the sanctuary, what the entrance to the mine looked like, and stuff like that."

"And?"

"At first, I thought it was just us getting to know each other and having a conversation. Well, after a while, I realized she was picking my brain about the sanctuary and mineshaft locations. She also called you a few choice names, and Danny, too. But then she snuggled up next to me and started asking about the weapons in the sanctuary, and how it was defended."

"You didn't buy that?"

"Not for a second. I told a few lies about the location, but when you think about it, she already knows it is located up this road, which is only a couple of miles long. It takes less than half-a-day to walk it, and she knows the sanctuary entrance must be near the road because the trucks drove us right up to it, so it shouldn't be that hard to locate once you begin searching."

"Why does she want to go to Monroe?" I asked, dumbfounded. They wouldn't accept her in the sanctuary. They didn't allow any new people to arrive, and of course, none there could leave. They sealed the entrance on the bridge. Did she want medical help with her pregnancy? That almost made sense.

"She doesn't want to go there. Not herself. Since you and Danny *betrayed* her, and since we also killed the men who took care of her for so long, she said she would go into town and tell the militia where they can find guns and MREs and medication. She's going to trade that information for a house and food in Monroe, and she wants them to kill all of us as part of the deal."

"What else?" I sensed him holding back.

"She was going to tell them about Jake and Grace. That's probably why they were captured and killed."

My head had been throbbing. Now it pounded. The shivering was not all from the cold anymore. I was angry. She probably had not gotten there in time to notify the militia of Grace and Jake, but once captured, she could have told them about the guns and supplies—and that both Jake and Grace knew where they were.

She may not have gotten them captured, but I'd bet anything she caused them to be tortured. I ground my teeth and tried to sort it all out. No matter what, Sara and I would meet again. I let the information he revealed float around in my brain for a while, then said, "We can't stay here any longer."

"Monroe?" Gerry asked.

"Too dangerous and I'm beat. I need to sleep."

He gathered his few belongings and asked, "Where?"

I took a deep breath and with it came the answer as I rolled two blankets and looked for more to carry. "The camp where Sara and her family stayed."

Gerry gave it a moment. At first, he didn't like it, then changed his mind and gathered what else he could. "Okay, I guess. They were living there a few years without being discovered, and then it was by those men who stumbled on it by accident—and they were only a mile away the whole time."

"Come on, we need to go now," Danny snarled from the door.

I took the lead from the barn, intentionally heading the wrong way into the forest and leaving a trail anyone could follow, then turning in a wide circle, and still not bothering to conceal our path until we reached the blacktop road as if we were heading away from our objective. We left more than a few clear footprints in the soft mud beside puddles of water.

Still on the blacktop, and after looking at the cracks and new growth shooting up through it, I said, "Careful not to step on plants or leave any sort of evidence. Maybe it will rain enough to wash out our tracks if we don't leave too much. Step on blacktop only. No scuffs in the dirt, either."

The three of us moved slower than I would have liked, taking each step as if it were our last. The rain increased, which was a good thing as I'd predicted. It would help, but I lacked training and didn't know if following us would be easy or difficult.

The turnoff to where Sara's family had lived appeared on our left and we took to the woods long before reaching the remains of the dirt road. A wide circle brought us to it and from there we walked in wet, knee-high grass until reaching the top of the ridge where the campsite spread out below us.

The wide stream and small lake appeared serene and beautiful. They couldn't have chosen a more beautiful location. Trout probably thrived in the lake. Where their old camp stood, it now looked like a garbage dump. The destroyed RV and belongings scattered and rotting or turning green from moss and algae. I had an idea and pointed to a rocky ridge off to one side, and the thick stand of small evergreens growing on top.

"What if we make a temporary camp up there?"

"Why?" Gerry asked, neither agreeing nor disagreeing. He simply wanted an explanation.

It was a reasonable question. I said, "If we're over there in the old camp and Sara brings the militia here to look for us, we might see them as they go down and search. That's where she would think we'd be, so it would be natural to look there first. We could slip away in those evergreens and run away without them ever knowing we were close."

Danny sighed. His emotions were in ruin almost as bad as mine, his outward actions remorseful and dejected. "Okay. First, we can go down there and get a few things to help us. I want to be dry, so a few of the metal sheets that were the siding on the RV would make a good roof and we can get dry beside a small fire. I think we could take just enough supplies from down there so nobody would notice."

That reminded me of how wet and cold I was—and that night was coming and again the temperature would fall into the forties. The dry clothes and a light jacket were a blessing but not enough. I should have had the guts to unzip the sleeping bags for the pair I shot and push the bodies out. But the idea of sleeping inside with their blood seemed worse than being cold. "Can either of you make a fire?"

"Damn straight," Gerry said. "Give me a little time. Go find the place you want. Carry my stuff and I'll go down there and help find a roof for us and meet you in a while."

We split up, the two of them went to gather what they could. I headed for the pines. I cursed and worried over Sara. How could she do this to us? To Jake and Grace? We'd saved her, even freed her from a miserable life. We fed her, gave her part of our clothes. The more we did for her, the more she resented us.

We should have seen it coming.

But as I walked to the side of trees and thought about it, the signs had been there all along. She was mentally warped. Her pretty looks confused her ugly actions, as I'd heard someone else described.

The place I selected for a camp gave us a good view of the approach to the small valley and the old camping area from a small height of maybe two hundred feet. Behind the site were miles of forests and rugged mountains. We needed a bug-out bag for each of us: weapons, clothing, and food. If we had to run, we might not have much warning.

Gerry returned with three sheets of corrugated aluminum that came from the sides of the RV. He carried them balanced on his head, holding the sides. They flexed as he walked, and that goofy image brought a smile to my face.

Danny had a coil of rope over his shoulder. A dozen steps into the small evergreens, and without speaking, he quickly strung the rope between two trees, cut it off, then strung another line between two more, a little higher up. We placed the three sheets overlapping and suspended. We had ourselves a slanted roof, lower in the front.

I used a stick to loosen dirt and scooped it out with my hand until it was a foot deep. Then I gathered rocks to line a fireplace pit and used my hand to brush the dry pine needles clear for a foot around them. Campfires have a habit of burning under the needles and traveling several feet, or yards, unnoticed. I said to Gerry as I delivered another load of dry wood snapped from the trunk of a nearby fallen tree, "You're very quiet."

"The girl. Sara. She's on my mind."

I fully understood. It was a shock for all of us. "Why? Did you like her?"

"She is pretty and all that, but I was wondering what makes her mind crazy. It's like she is *bent* in some way."

"How are you thinking?" I asked, interested, and ignoring the pained expression Danny wore as Gerry talked.

"We risked our lives to set her free, we fed and protected her, and now she is betraying us. All of us."

Bent was a good description of her mind. Worse, she was out for revenge. I couldn't help but think it could be because of me. We hadn't gotten along from the first. She was jealous, that was obvious. Why, was a different matter. She was prettier, had a winning way with men, and seemed smart enough without being obnoxious or bigmouthed, like me.

It should have been me that was jealous of her—and maybe I was.

The rain fell but lightly. Just enough to keep us damp and cold. We should have emerged in the summer when there are days and days of sunshine. While I found and returned with more rocks, Gerry searched for wood. He wanted stuff wet on the outside, but dry inside. He tore off the small dry branches still attached to the trunks of trees and piled that in the center of my ring of rocks. A lighter appeared in his hand, something remembered from before the war.

"Where'd you get that?"

He pointed at the camp. "Noticed a few of them in the camper when we were here before," he grinned. "It still works. I already tried it."

No wonder he'd been so confident he could build a fire. A few clicks later and he had the beginnings of a small teepee of flame. The slope of the metal roof was lower at the front, the side that looked at the valley. Water sluiced off the low side. Smoke rose inside of the metal roof where it spread out and filtered up and out the backside. It entered the trees and dissipated even more.

"Did you do that to hide our smoke?" I asked as I peeled off clothing and hung it over a clothesline we tied between a tree and a hole in the edge of our metal roof. Steam rose from my jeans and a wool shirt. We needed waterproof oil for our boots—not to mention boots that fit our feet.

Gerry glanced at the smoke and appeared surprised. Too late to take credit for it. He seemed reluctant to strip. Danny turned his back and removed his pants without comment. His eyes never strayed to me. It was unnatural.

I situated myself half turned away from Gerry and sat, providing him a measure of privacy. I watched our small stockpile of broken limbs shrink. We might get dry but then we'd have to gather more wood. The semi-dry blanket wrapped around me felt damp, but the heat of the fire soon warmed it—and me. I turned and looked at the entrance to the valley, the first of a hundred times I'd do the same before sunset.

I worried. Oddly, I didn't worry about Gerry at all. Like any mom, I thought about teaching and protecting him. That was my attitude. I'd take care of him. I worried about Danny. He still hadn't said much.

"I've been thinking," Gerry said out of the blue while he sat with a shirt over his private area.

"Yes?"

"If we cross the road to the sanctuary, and the stream over there, then go due west, we should be able to see the bridge and road probably from inside the cover of the trees on the hill, if we're lucky. My guesstimate is it would cut off half the distance compared to taking the roads from here to there. From up there, we could keep track of who and how many people are coming and going. We might have a warning if a large group of soldiers leaves town and heads this way."

"If they are coming, it would be early in the day, tomorrow," I heard myself say as I considered his idea, which seemed like a good one.

"Why early?" he asked, which seemed a normal thing for him to do. Not objecting, just requesting additional information which was becoming normal between us.

"Because armies don't march off to battle after lunch. They start early so they don't arrive too late in the day and must spend the night before attacking. If they come this way, they'll leave in the morning and hope to return to their dry beds and hot meals before dark. Either that or they'll send a few scouts first. To look things over. Search for signs of us and maybe find the mine or entrance to the sanctuary. Probably the latter. It's what I'd do. Send scouts, I mean."

"They will also want to see if Sara is telling the truth before committing too many militias to the search," he agreed. "So, while they are spying on us, we'll be doing the same to them."

"Only we'll know that it works both ways. It gives us a little advantage."

Danny tossed a few sticks on the fire and watched the flames leap higher. "That helps us?"

"It's better than the other way around," I mumbled, lost in thought again and I didn't like where those thoughts were taking me.

Danny said suddenly, "Jake and Grace were our friends. I can't believe they betrayed us by talking. Sara, I can understand perversely, but the others? I can't get that out of my mind."

I'd heard that nobody can withstand torture. Not real torture like pulling out fingernails and lopping off fingers one at a time. No matter the resolve a person believes he or she has, they will always talk.

I said softly, drawing the full attention of both. "There's a story about old Germany or somewhere over there. Six men, bandits, were captured by the authorities and all refused to tell where the rest of the bandit hoard were camped. The king

176

ordered them all to their knees and he asked for the location. He promised freedom to the first one that talked."

Emotion choked me up as I mentally pictured my friends hanging from those poles. I fought the tears.

Gerry urged me, "Go on."

"The first bandit refused to tell, and an ax cut off his head. It fell to the ground and lay in front of the other five. The king's executioner moved to the second in line. Then the third. All three heads were in plain sight."

Gerry said, "Damn. I'd have talked."

Danny glowed his way.

I continued, "The story, as told to me, was that I was supposed to be number four. Think about it. What if I didn't tell the king where the other thieves were? I'd lose my head, of course. But the moral problem centered on the next two in line after me. That was what I had to think about. If I lost my head and the next in line talked, I'd wasted my life. Looking at the severed heads lying in the grass at my feet, I knew my next words would mean my life or death. What would they be?"

I paused there. Gerry was thoughtful, Danny puzzled and seemingly waiting for more.

I drew a breath and raised my voice a little, "The point of recalling that story is that if Grace, Jake, or Sara, for whatever reason because that is not what's important right now, revealed the location of the sanctuary, three hundred people are going to die. People we know."

I let my words stand. Yes, those people below had treated me poorly for five years. But during those same five years, a sizable percentage of the outside population had perished in one way or another. We fought a war, and we hid in a hole in the ground and avoided it. I'd been warm, fed, and provided medications when required. I'd never been whipped, beaten, or abused. And because of those people I was alive today.

There was also the matter of the death penalty that was to take place, but a case could be made that I'd known that was an option if I didn't change my ways—and I hadn't. They were protecting themselves by killing me.

Morals suddenly seem as slippery as an eel in a creek, the same one I seemed to be up without a paddle. I fought to stop the useless platitudes from filling my brain. My head filled with contradictions. I suspected the other two were similarly conflicted.

Gerry said kindly, "It all comes down to choices. For me, good choices come down to information. Does that make sense? If I have the right information, I can make the right choice."

"And right now, we do not have that information, you're telling us. I understand what you're saying." I did understand. We were going to have to gather information while deciding our futures. Sitting on a hill near the river, watching people over the rooftops, and city, we'd watch and try to make the choices that made the most sense.

Chapter 12

As we expected the militia to do, we waited until early morning to leave the camp we'd set up and headed for the highway through the underbrush. The sun barely provided enough light to travel at the beginning. An animal trail took us most of the way. We crossed the road leading to the sanctuary, paused, then sprinted to the far side. We went past the barn, or to where we could see the grass in front of the barn door. It wasn't disturbed.

That meant neither Sara nor the militia had been there, yet. I still expected her to regain her wits and return to us. It was a silly idea. With the knowledge no one had been there since we departed, the three of us headed west, deeper into the forest. It seemed to take much longer than we expected. The going was slow, and we crossed two more small roads I had forgotten about, one narrow and the other a larger one that paralleled the river.

We had discussed leaving one of us at the barn to stand watch, but there were no takers. It seemed we clung together. Where there had been six, if Sara counted, there were now three. Try as I might, I couldn't hold hard feelings against Sara. Her betrayal may have cost Jake and Grace their lives—or it might not have.

In the back of my mind, I cajoled myself that I should have examined all the other hanging bodies. One of them might have been Sara. I convinced myself, that was true and that she deserved understanding for her mental condition, not hate.

Danny said, "There was a boat launch upriver a way. Once, I went there with friends and we launched our plastic kayaks and paddled down to Snohomish where we ate at a fish-house and met a friend with a pickup who drove us back home."

It sounded like a fantasy such as riding horses in the American West a century and a half ago. Not that I didn't believe him. I did. But it had been another world five years ago.

Now, everything was overgrown and looked different. Wild. The breaks and cracks in the blacktop were only part of it. The fields that had been neatly plowed and hay cut during summer were turning wild again. A few fences remained, sagging and tilting. Where cattle once grazed, chickens crowed, dogs barked, and kids rode quad-runners or motorcycles, only trees and underbrush grew. The lawns of the few houses now resembled mini forests, the trunks of the new trees already the diameter of my wrist. In a few more years, many places would return to nature.

There had been an organization to the farms, roads, and housing despite the amount of undeveloped forest and wildlife. Now it grew tangled, overgrown, and the walls of the houses we passed were rotting and would soon disappear. About half had burned for one reason or another.

I don't know why so many burned, but instinct told me people had done it intentionally. It gave a new meaning to the idea of bad neighbors. Maybe since those who lived on farms had food and others wanted it and they fought. Maybe it was simply the anger of mobs frustrated when civilization fell. And it could have been the actions of the madmen like those that had held Sara prisoner. They may have come this way and burned their way forward until reaching their final campsite.

Gerry, thinking much the same thoughts as me, said, "Can you imagine another ten years? It'll be like America in fifteen-hundred."

It was odd that he expressed much the same as what was going on in my mind. Or maybe not. A barn ahead had a broken back. The ridge beam had snapped for some reason, and the two ends sagged to the middle. Heavy winter snow or another year or two of the beams inside rotting, and the entire structure would fall into the middle.

We reached the edge of the trees and entered tall underbrush that went all the way to the river. Across the river were the houses of Monroe and columns of smoke rose here and there. Not house fires, but from chimneys for warmth and cooking. The bridge crossed the river on our left because we were slightly upstream from where we wanted to be.

Most of what we could see was forest on the other side. "Al Borlin Park," Gerry said despite both of us knowing it was Monroe's version of Central Park in New York.

A lot of trees and acres and acres of forest. However, along our side of the river grew a strip of trees that lined the river, willows, and such. The area was larger than I remembered, and with thicker growth, if that was possible.

A trio of intrepid spies could slip into that area undetected and work their way downriver until they reached the bridge. Along in there would be many places to watch the bridge up close and see who, and how many, crossed it.

Gerry, who had not been into Monroe yet, said, "At night, we can slip into town and back out again. Explore small sections, one at a time."

Both Danny and I reacted by scowling. We'd had enough of slipping into Monroe.

That issue overwhelmed me. I turned to face Gerry. "You're free to go where you want, and I appreciate the support you've given us. What comes next will be dangerous, no matter what we do. I'd give us maybe a fifty percent chance of all three of us surviving the next few days, but there are things I must do. I have to try saving the people in the sanctuary."

Gerry swallowed hard. His face paled. He didn't answer.

I continued as I looked at the bridge. The green crossbeams had rusted, and the paint had failed, and flaked, turning a faded shade of green. "I'll see you back at camp if you decide to go into the city. I will not go in there again."

My eyes found where one of the braces stood bent and twisted. It looked fire-blackened, perhaps from where a vehicle had crashed and burned. In another five years, the bridge probably wouldn't cross the river. A critical support would fail, or a spring flood would wash it out. The whole idea depressed me.

Despite wanting to get closer, we settled in behind underbrush at the edge of a small clearing where we could see over the rooftops although we couldn't see the streets. I picked out the fire station location, and more.

"Three guards on the bridge again," Danny said, doing what we came for instead of recalling the worst of our earlier trip.

Gerry said, "Might have guessed the inmates would take over the city."

Danny shrugged and said, "Maybe. That probably happened in the beginning, but I think most of them either attempted to go to their homes or fought for control locally. There were three main groups in competition inside, and several splinter groups or gangs. I think the ones here in Monroe are more recent."

"How do you know all that?" I asked.

He said, "My uncle and a cousin worked in the prison. They used to talk about it. Inside was like three separate countries. Prisoners either joined one group or another or were marked as enemies by all three."

Gerry said, "That sounds like crap you saw on TV."

"Not everything on TV was wrong," Danny said without rancor. "I miss TV."

"This is a good time to make some plans," I inturrupted before their conversation could turn sour. "Why are we here today instead of trying to find a safe place to live?"

That question brought all conversation to a halt. They exchanged a glance that revealed neither had an answer.

Gerry said, "I'm here because of you. I already told you I need to learn to be different, to be a fighter, or this new world will kill me."

Danny said, "I came to look for my family."

Both had a reason. I didn't. Well, not one that I wanted to admit. I turned to Danny. "Listen, you already saw what it's like in the city. You can imagine what our friends looked like when I found them, but I understand what you're saying. Family is important, especially if you believe any might still be alive. I have a request."

"What's that?" he sounded hesitant.

"Don't go looking for them yet. It's been five years, a few more days won't matter."

"Why?"

I glanced at Gerry for a second. He seemed to know what I was about to say and shook his head. I plunged on, "Because if you are captured and tortured, and if Jake and Grace somehow didn't tell them about the sanctuary and us, you might."

He scowled and looked like he was going to promise not to reveal those things, but I knew he would crack under torture and quickly. He said, "I want a request, as well."

"Name it," I said.

"Two things. If we find out they do not know about the sanctuary or don't send a force to attack it in the next few days, you will help me find my family."

"The other?" I asked.

He swallowed hard. "If I'm captured or killed, you will promise to look for them and try to help them if you can. Tell my family I tried to find them."

Both requests were reasonable. "Give me your home address, family name, and the names of members. Anything that will help me locate them."

He did. Both Gerry and I memorized as much as possible. Gerry said, "I'll take a pledge to do the same, or to help Pen."

We talked a little and finally quit, at least for a while. The sky remained gray, and the air felt heavy. My legs were wet from the knees down from the water clinging to the tall grass, but the rest of me was fairly dry. I sat with my knees pulled up to my chin and dozed. It was still early, maybe an hour after sunrise.

"What's that?" Gerry asked in a hushed voice.

"Trouble," Danny said.

I looked up. Two men in flannel shirts and heavy jackets walked across the bridge. Each carried a rifle in their left hand. In their right hands, each held a leash attached to a dog. The dogs had their noses to the ground.

One was a German Sheppard, the other some kind of mixed breed, maybe a hound and bird-dog. The Sheppard strained at the leash and gave the impression of being young and eager. The other allowed slack in the lead and looked better trained.

We watched until they reached the far side of the bridge where they paused. One handler pulled something from his pocket and gave each dog time to catch the scent. I had no doubt whatever the material was, it had been clothing worn by Jake or Grace.

Despite the rain that had fallen, I'd heard that a good dog could follow a scent for days. Some said weeks. I didn't know, so asked, "How long can a dog track a scent?"

Gerry said, "A week, at least. I think it is longer, but let's say a week."

"Even after a rain?" I asked. "Will water wash the scent away?"

Gerry paused, then gave me the bad news, "I saw on the Internet that a light rain actually 'holds' scents in place and makes it easier for dogs to follow. I don't know why I remember that. Maybe because it seemed so counterintuitive when I ran across it."

Danny rolled his eyes in disbelief.

I ignored Danny and asked Gerry, "How sure are you of that?"

"Sure? I can't verify if it's true or not, but I promise that is exactly what I read."

I watched the men and dogs move along the road. From our perch, we had a clear view of the road for a long distance. I studied the area and found where we had left Jake and Grace to cross the road and begin their venture into the city. I thought I saw it and asked if either of them could verify my guess.

Both agreed to the general area. It was well within sight. The men and dogs were heading down the road a quarter of a mile away.

Danny said, "The dogs are searching for the scent. They don't have it, yet."

"When they get it?" I asked.

"If they do, we'll know right away. The dogs will alert and probably get excited and bark or howl," Danny said. "At least that's what happens in the movies."

I believed him. We said nothing. I mentally crossed my

fingers that the dogs wouldn't catch the scent of our friends because it washed away or because they were searching for someone or something other than us. I didn't believe that. I hoped it was true.

As they moved away from us, my heart pounded faster. I held my breath and then forced the air out. A glance at the two with me revealed much the same. Danny watched the men and dogs intently. Gerry did also, but his hands were shaking. He was as scared as me.

It seemed they were going to pass the spot we'd agreed on. Maybe it was a depth perception problem or parallax view, but no matter. The hound paused, crept ahead a few steps, and leaped forward so hard he yanked the handler ahead by the leash.

The German Sheppard moved another few yards ahead, then suddenly stiffened and raised its nose into the air, no doubt sniffing. My mind imagined the growl it emitted through bared teeth. It didn't strain at the lead, but its body posture became a crouch and it looked ready to fight.

Both dogs had caught our scent. The hound tried to follow it down to the river, but the handler didn't want to go in that direction. He finally managed to turn the animal and retrace where their prey came from, not where they went.

Gerry said slowly and distastefully, "That is that."

Danny was slowly nodding his head in agreement when I turned to look at them. "That's what?" I snapped.

Danny said, "Those dogs will take the handlers to the barn and then to the mineshaft. No stopping them now that the dogs have the scent."

For no reason other than because I wanted to, I balled my fist and punched him on his shoulder so hard he stumbled back and sat heavily on his butt. I turned to Gerry, who was backing away from me before I punched him also.

Gerry said defensively, "What's gotten into you?"

I growled, "That is not that. We are not finished."

Danny slowly climbed to his feet while rubbing where I'd slugged him.

Gerry said, "I don't understand."

I pointed to him, Danny, and then jabbed a thumb at me.

"Three of us. Two of them. We each have two guns and surprise on our side."

Gerry stood his ground, which sent a sliver of pride up my spine. "Those men are trained. They are part of the military. You're a bartender turned housecleaner, I wash dishes, and Danny helps with maintenance."

"And we have six pistols between us. We know they are going to follow the paved road until the turnoff, so we know where they will be."

Gerry gave it some thought. "We could cut across-country, as we did to get here, get near the barn and take up positions on both sides of the road."

Danny said, "The dogs might smell us. Will smell us."

I said, "What if we get on both sides of the road ahead of them and stay back in the woods. After they pass by, we move in from behind, all three of us?"

Gerry looked at Danny. "That might work."

Danny said, "Come out guns blazing? I can see that working."

"If we shoot them, the dogs might attack us," Gerry said.

"Then we shoot them," I said with far more confidence than I felt.

A quiet filled the air as each of us thought about the plan. Gerry finally shrugged said with a little false grin, "We all have to die someday."

To my utter surprise, Danny agreed. "I saw a movie where the hero said a line about this being a good day to die. If this is that day, we might as well do it trying to save all those lives down in the sanctuary."

None of us were in a hurry to depart that safe location. When I looked down the road again, there were no men or dogs in sight. I said, "Listen, talk is cheap. Here is my say: I'm going to do this. With luck, I might pull it off. You two can head in any direction and I won't think worse of you."

Before the words had come from my mouth, my feet were carrying me away from the town and into the forest to the trail that we had followed. I was not running, but neither did I move slowly. My mind was planning the upcoming ambush.

I didn't look behind because I heard clothing brushing

against branches and feet stepping on last fall's leaves. When I did glance back, both were behind me.

That was a bit of a surprise. Gerry and I had bonded, and I expected him to do his part. Danny had more experience in hunting and using weapons. His attitude had made me think he would leave us if given a chance. Maybe his mind was on the hundreds of lives in the sanctuary.

We knew the way through the forest this time, and we moved fast. There was a place where the secondary road had been cut through a small hill by a bulldozer. It was a perfect place to set up an ambush, therefore, we wouldn't do it there. I was learning, thanks to Gerry and his games.

Immediately past that place where the two men would probably advance cautiously, the land leveled, and the forest thinned. That was the place.

I described it to them as we walked. Both knew where I meant. Both understood.

Danny said, "When we get there, I'll make a wide circle in front, so the dogs won't smell me beforehand. You find a ditch, or dip in the ground and toss leaves back over yourselves. Nobody moves until they are ten steps past us. Don't forget about peripheral vision."

Gerry added, "We rise slowly and move out to the road, then rush ahead. Fast."

"Why?" I asked.

"Because none of us knows how to move quietly so they won't hear us. Also, because we don't know when the dogs will sense us or what they will do. They have better hearing than the men."

It was my turn to question. I asked, "So, we hit the road and run ahead, shooting? No warning?"

Danny said, "How much warning did they give Jake and Grace before they cut off his fingers and her feet?"

I said, "What if we don't hit them because we're running?"

"We die," Danny said simply. "But with three guns firing at the same time, we should be able to hit them, at least with a stray shot. If not, we pull our backups and shoot some more."

Gerry said, "The town will send more when these two do not return."

I called over my shoulder, "Maybe they only have two dogs trained."

"More men, then," Gerry said. "They won't let this be the end."

I muttered because I had no answer to his questions, "One problem at a time."

Chapter 13

We found the spot intended for the ambush. From a distance, it looked perfect, which is to say, innocent. After passing through the narrow cut in the hillside where it seemed logical for an ambush, if there was one, the tracker's minds would be at ease. The area opened up and they could relax.

Danny left us and disappeared into the forest ahead. He would cross the road in another hundred yards and work his way back to a position right across from us. We kept him in sight as we examined our side of the road for good locations.

He settled down behind a small log fifty yards from the road and gave us a weak wave before disappearing into the background. A stand of small evergreen shrubs grew in front of Gerry and me. We got on our bellies and tossed brown, soggy, leaves over our shoulders and back to disguise our shapes.

I left the 9 mm in my holster and pulled the one from my waistband. While waiting, I ejected the magazine and replaced it after making certain it was fully loaded. Gerry did the same.

The wait was a long one. The damp ground chilled my body. The moisture penetrated my jeans and shirt and wicked its way upward. As my impatience grew, a single bark from a dog snapped me awake and alert.

"They're coming," Gerry whispered unnecessarily.

I forgave him. He was as nervous and me. "We'll be okay, don't worry."

Sure, it was easy to lie. The trackers each carried a rifle and probably handguns under their coats. Chances were, they knew how to use them. We three had perhaps a few hours of training, most of it years ago.

The problem with laying an ambush is that time slows. It provides the time to think, to recriminate, to self-doubt, and consider what better plans may have been made. It raises questions. Time is an enemy.

Finally, the first man, the one with the German Sheppard, came into view. The other followed ten steps behind. Both dogs had their noses to the ground. Neither tugged nor misbehaved. They were working. The excitement of earlier had calmed, and they followed the scent of Jake and Grace, along with the scents of us three now.

All of us had walked this road together. In the future, the dogs would associate our smells with their prey. That was bad.

The man in front had slung his rifle over his head and shoulder, carried sideways at an angle and difficult to reach in a hurry. A stupid move. He would never have time to return fire if we missed our initial volley. The other still carried his rifle in his hand and could raise his weapon and shoot in an instant.

He would die first.

As they got closer, the dog in the rear acted up. It had caught our scent. It looked in our direction and growled. We didn't move.

The handler yanked the lead and got the dog centered on following the scent on the road again. A better handler would have "listened" to his animal. The first dog never veered from its task as it continued, nose to the ground.

As Danny had warned, we waited—and waited. The second man and dog were well past us, maybe fifty steps, when Danny rose and started moving to the road in a bent-over position. We did the same, like the jaws of a vice closing.

The three of us moved faster than the trackers, and I perceived the point of interception ahead. We'd be twenty yards away from the man in the rear. Sixty feet. Three of us shooting. Semi-automatic fire. The guns shooting as fast as we twitched our index fingers.

We had the element of surprise on our side. The plan was

working.

Until it wasn't.

The tracker in front must have either heard or sensed something. Maybe he simply turned to speak to the other. No matter, he turned and spotted us.

Gerry and I were more like twice our optimal distance of twenty yards away. We dived to the ground as the man shouted a warning. He was already reaching for the sling, yanking it over his head in his hurry to bring it into action.

The second man spun and brought his rifle to his shoulder.

Neither looked to the other side of the road where Danny sprinted in their direction. I fired, not expecting to hit either of them, but to cover any noise Danny made.

The crack of the rifle sounded between my shots, and then shots from Gerry's gun joined mine. I aimed at the second man, the one closest to us, the one already shooting back.

He spun a half turn. At first, I thought he'd spotted Danny, but it was too sudden a move. The rifle fell from his fingers as his other hand went to his shoulder. Either Gerry or I had managed to hit him.

Danny ignored that one. With his rifle on the blacktop and the man falling to his knees, he was no longer a danger.

The tracker fired a burst of automatic fire at us. It was a panic reaction, and the bullets flew well above. He never saw Danny coming from his other side. Danny paused and shot from ten yards away. Three times. His aim was accurate.

Danny shifted positions and fired twice more at the other man, who had reached inside his jacket and pulled a pistol that he raised.

The German Sheppard, released from the dead hands of the first man, charged Danny and leaped from three yards away.

We couldn't hit the dog. The animal was too far away, too fast, and between us and Danny.

Danny fired twice more and missed the dog.

The dog's jaws were open. It hit Danny, chest high. He went over backward.

We jumped up and raced ahead, shooting into the air as we did to scare the dog since we couldn't take a chance on shooting at it and hitting our friend. The other dog suddenly rushed directly at us from ten yards away. Gerry spun to his right and shot it with one bullet before it could leap at us. The second dog fell almost at our feet as we ran forward.

Danny was not fighting or defending himself anymore.

The German Sheppard had ripped out his throat and it now turned to face us, its jaws red with blood. We both shot the dog and continued firing until our guns were empty.

Danny was dead. His neck and part of his face were torn from his body. Leaving a bloody mess. To me, it looked like Danny's neck had snapped from the attack of the dog, and in my muddled mind, I hoped it had. That would have been a more merciful death.

I fell to my knees crying and raging at the same time. I wanted to kill something else.

Gerry stood aside, arms limp at his sides. Tears ran down his cheeks. He finally managed to say, "What now?"

That was a good question.

It pulled me away from my grief long enough to gather a few thoughts.

The militia would send more after us, perhaps a platoon, if they had them. No matter the name, they would send more men next time. Maybe more dogs. Maybe not. That gave me the idea for our next task. I said, "We can hide the bodies in the woods. The next group might not come for a couple of days and if they don't have dogs, they won't know anything happened here."

Gerry turned to me; a pained expression clear to see on his scared face. "You want to move them? Even Danny?"

"Especially Danny."

His head turned to the remains of the young man we'd known for so long. The blood-covered much of his face, but the exposed neck appeared raw and painful, despite his death. Gerry retched and shook his head.

I couldn't do it alone.

"Listen to me. That was our friend, and he would do the same for us and you know that. I'll cover his face and you lift his chest and arms. I'll get his legs. But first, let's find a good place to put him."

"I thought we were going to bury him," Gerry whined in the same voice that used to anger me so much.

Instead of answering, I walked a few steps into the forest where I had seen a dry streambed. It was close, a channel a few feet wide, and two deep. "Here."

We needed no more words. I went to the closest of the dead trackers and started removing his heavy, waterproof coat. When Gerry did nothing, I snapped. "Hey, get that coat off the other. You're going to need it."

"He's dead," Gerry said.

I paused in the struggle to remove the coat. I stood upright. He avoided my eyes. I reached down and grabbed a stick about the size of a walking cane. In one motion, I threw it at him. It struck his shoulder. I shouted, "Yes, he's dead—and that is what you are going to be if you don't get busy because I'll do what I can for Danny and then leave your ass standing right here. Alone."

"You can't make me stay here. I'll follow."

That pissed me off. Now he sounded like a petulant child. Before, I'd been so proud of him. Without thinking, I pulled the semiautomatic that I hadn't yet fired and snapped the slide to place a shell in the chamber. I didn't point it. "Refuse to help me and then try following. I'll kill you as dead as these men."

His face paled. He believed me. He should have.

I replaced my gun and put the coat on without another word. I pulled the green flannel shirt off the body and carried it to Danny. It went over his face and neck. The arms became ties to hold it in place.

Only then did I look up at Gerry, expecting an argument or at least, hesitation.

To my surprise, he stood there in the other jacket. He approached slowly, took a position near Danny's head and I moved to his feet. We lifted.

It is more accurate to say that we tried. We got his head and feet into the air, but his butt remained on the ground. Gerry attempted to pull and drag him, but from my end, it was like pushing a wet noodle. A heavy, wet noodle.

"Stop," I ordered.

We stood panting and trying to catch our breath. Gerry

said, "I can't lift a hundred pounds of weight that shifts with every movement."

"Danny weighs more than a hundred," I said between gasps for air.

"Yes," he said. "A hundred for me and the rest for you. We can't do it. Sorry."

I cried.

Gerry sat on a bank and looked unhappy. Finally, he said, "Danny would have found a way. I don't know how, but he wouldn't have quit on us."

My crying ended. My mind went to work as it should have a half-hour ago. "It's unacceptable to leave him here. We won't do that. Come on, we only need to move him twenty yards."

"A cart?"

"No." I hesitated to tell him what I was thinking. "Besides, I don't know where we would get a cart. We can drag him."

"No rope."

"By his feet. We each take a foot and pull." I didn't like the idea but didn't want to say that if we left Danny where he was, animals and insects would find him. The dead attracted them, and they would tear the body in to pieces. That wouldn't happen to our friend. Dragging him showed more respect than leaving him. I determinedly stood. Gerry did the same.

We each took a foot and ignored the blood that seeped through the shirt covering his neck and face. We pulled and he slid along the ground. Not a lot, but a couple of steps. We had to rest.

Gerry said to me as if speaking to a child, "We have to work together. Pull on three and stop. Repeat."

Taking hold of his feet again, Gerry counted slowly, out loud. On three, we pulled. Danny's upper body slid ahead only two more steps—but far easier as we pulled at the same time. Gerry counted again. And again. We got Danny to the edge of the dry streambed and had no way to lower him.

Gerry looked at me and then at the body. "Danny, sorry to say this, but you're going for a ride."

We rolled him over the edge. He landed with a thud and caved in part of the bank on his way.

Gerry said, "We should do the same with the other two

bodies and the dogs. Then try to clean up the drag marks. We won't fool any trackers, but maybe slow down others."

I didn't like the idea. Not because it didn't need doing, but I didn't want them lying there with Danny. Them being near him felt wrong. I said, "We can drag them over to the other side of the road, out of sight in the underbrush, and leave them. I mean, none of that is going to slow down people trained to follow others, but maybe they won't come over here if they locate the two over there."

He nodded his agreement but added, "When we hide the drag marks for Danny, we also cover him with dirt and maybe say a few words."

That had been my idea all along but now it didn't need me saying it.

We managed to drag the others far easier, perhaps because we didn't care if we smashed their heads on rocks or further injured them as we pulled. The bodies went into a tangle of briars and each of us pulled a dog by its tail and one hind leg to join their masters. I removed the magazines from both of their guns and handed the deer rifle to Gerry. I took the one that looked military.

Their jackets were far better than what we wore if we ignored the bullet holes and blood drying. A little dirt smeared on the blood absorbed most on the surface. We briefly looked in their backpacks and found food and blankets. The food looked like dried shavings of meat mixed with dried fruit, apples, and blackberries, maybe. I tasted it. The meat was salty, the fruit sweet, and together it was not bad. Each backpack contained several rolls of cloth around the meat.

Gerry tasted it. His lip curled. "Dogfood?"

"Probably food for the dogs and handlers." My guess was biased and hopefully true, but munching on the dried meat and fruit was far better than going hungry. The mixture would last for months and weighed little to carry.

We swept the ground where we'd drug Danny with branches as they did in the old movies. It did little good. A child could tell where the plants and ground had been disturbed. We didn't take much care at all on the other side of the road with the other two. We wanted them found as a distraction. They had no reason to believe one of us died, so they might not look for another.

Gerry stood aside and looked imploringly at me before returning his gaze to the crude grave.

I said softly after considering the words to use, "Danny, we will miss you and wish there was more we could do."

"That's it?" Gerry demanded.

"No," I lied. "I thought I'd give you the honor of saying your thoughts, too."

Gerry sputtered in confusion and frustration. He looked ready to say something nasty to me but paused and said in a softer tone as if also speaking directly to Danny, "Five of us escaped that hell below and only two remain alive after a few days. That's sixty percent dead already but you know what Danny? The last few days up here have been better than the almost two thousand we spent down there."

I cried. It was touching and he was correct on all counts.

Emotions are funny things. I'd kept my feelings to myself since my rescue. I'd known that the same deviant corruption that had earned me a death sentence would destroy any relationships with the people that had helped me to freedom. My mouth had been zipped, for lack of a better word.

What good had that done to any of us? Three of the five of our original group were dead. The remaining two were in immediate danger. One way or another, the five of us had also given information to the army of killers in Monroe about where to find and destroy the sanctuary. That probably meant killing everyone down there or taking them prisoner or making them slaves.

Thinking back, as I looked over Danny's final resting place, the thought of what had occurred because one woman, me, couldn't keep her mouth closed filled my mind. Because of me, hundreds of other people might die.

I started to count the deaths since arriving on the surface and remembering the look on Sara's face had me shutting the count down. I didn't know how many—and that should have bothered me more than it did.

Chapter 14

To my surprise, Gerry pointed to a hill taller than
those in front. He said, "Putting my gaming skills to use, the
smaller hill is too close to here if they come after us. The one
behind will give us a view and a head start to run away if we
need it."

My eyes located where he pointed. My mind recognized
the second hill. I believed it was the first one we'd climbed
during our escape from the sanctuary. His plan was a good one,
providing the maximum chance of escape if they saw our
ambush site—and we assumed it would be located quickly.

I said, "The smaller, closer one will give us a better view. If
we choose our spot well, they will come right at us. We have
rifles, now."

His surprised expression would have been amusing at
other times. I said nothing else, allowing him time to decide
what was best for himself. His face changed. It became hard.
His eyes found mine. He gave me a single nod.

"You agree? It is riskier, but provides a better field of fire,"
I said, prepared to offer him the opportunity to leave on his
own. Just because I was about to risk my life to make a point
didn't mean he had to.

When I pulled my thoughts together, he had already
turned and studied the hill a few hundred yards away. Much of
the area in front of us was a meadow with a few small trees at
random places for perhaps three hundred yards. The first hill

stood a couple of hundred feet high.

Gerry pointed off to our right. "There."

I looked. Nothing drew my attention. "Why there?"

His pointing finger moved to the left. "We walk directly to that notch over there. It's the natural place to get over the hill. They'll see that right away and suspect we went there."

"That's not where you pointed," I said.

He grinned evilly. "Anybody following us will see right away we're a couple of city-folk that know nothing about how to cover our trail. So, we head for that easy notch to reach and leave a clear path through the tall grass. When we reach the base of the hill, we turn to our right and work our away along that ridge to that spot."

My eyes followed his words. Once on that ridge, which looked more like a twenty-foot-tall granite cliff as it went down the side of the hill, nobody was going to come directly at us once we reached there. Even our handguns would hold them off from up there. They had to either follow us up there, which would again leave them in the open at very close range, or attempt climbing over the top of the hill and circling behind.

The last would be their best bet if they knew we planned an ambush. It would take the longest, however, because of that, once we opened fire, I suspected they would either retreat or charge directly ahead. Retreating would be their second-best option. Pulling back and attacking the ridge the following day when we either moved or they have reinforcements would be the next option.

But they would attack directly. I felt it deep inside.

They would know we were clumsy and lacked skills in the forest. If they spoke with Sara, she would have told them how inept we were, and then some.

I said, "When they get here, it'll take them a half hour or more to cross the open field and reach the base of the hill. With our rifles, they will be in range for much of that time."

"I can shoot a rifle," he said. "No, I mean I really can."

"But are you accurate?"

"I've shot a few times at a range with my uncle. It's just a matter of lining up the sights properly and pulling the trigger easy."

I grunted as I started walking.

"What? You don't think so?" he asked.

"I've shot a rifle a few times, too. But maybe my imagination is better than yours."

"Tell me," he said as he fell in behind me, not sounding angry but interested.

"Well, the first shot of yours might hit one of them. I'll give you that. The others in the group, however many of them there are, will scatter. How are you at hitting small targets that dart from place to place and shoot back?"

"I think I can do it."

The answer sounded about as defensive as a child who denied taking a cookie from a tray while hiding it behind his back. I said, "Listen, we have to face the problem of them shooting back at us, especially if there is a group. That changes everything. How are you going to react the first time a bullet strikes a rock near your face and sends slivers of stone into your cheek?"

I heard him behind me, walking and panting for breath, but I intentionally didn't turn around to look. He didn't answer until we neared the base of the hill and were about to turn up the ridge. He said, "I don't know."

"Nobody has ever shot at me before, either. So, I don't know what I'll do. I don't think I'm going to like it."

We reached the ridge where it was low enough to step up on top as easy as a step on stairs. There were few small plants along the edge, probably because there was only an inch or so of soil to support them. We walked to our right, where the ridge climbed higher and higher. The single step we'd used became a wall five feet high, then ten, then a growing granite cliff. At the bottom spread whatever leaves and branches had fallen over the eons, creating loose footing just waiting to break ankles.

The place we wanted suddenly appeared. The trees on either side and between us and the road were few enough to provide a sweeping view of the flat area approaching our vantage. The road was a broken line in the vegetation. Mostly knee-high grass lay between there and our position.

Gerry said, "I think I understand part of what you were

saying. If they lay down in the grass, we won't be able to see them, will we?"

"We will see the tops of the grass moving when they change positions. A shot or two in the area might spook them." The idea was to calm him. Gerry vacillated between the supreme confidence of an experienced fighter and a scared child. He posed as if brave. I suspected much of that was to impress me.

"Nearby shots might spook them. What if it doesn't? We need to see how many bullets we have for the rifles."

I had six. Four for him. The total was disappointing because the weapons had looked so powerful when we had decided to bring them along. They didn't use the same shells, and those from our pistols wouldn't fit. When shooting at targets with my boyfriend years ago, we had used the first few shots to "sight in" the rifles and make physical adjustments to them and the places where we aimed. My rifle—or me, which I hated to admit, even to myself—had tended to shoot high. After three or four test shots, my aim became a little lower and the bullets struck more or less where I wanted.

The problem we faced today was that we didn't have the luxury of sighting in our rifles. Panic rose in my overactive mind until I remembered I also had two semiautomatic pistols, each with a full magazine and more bullets weighing down my jacket pockets. The rifles were better for shooting long distances, but for shooting up closer, I had probably forty bullets.

Gerry had about the same.

It all depended on how many people they sent after us. No, I realized, it didn't. Not directly. I said, "Stay here. I'll keep an eye on what's happening but do what you think is right. I'm going to see what's behind us so we either have an escape route or we can protect our backs."

Without waiting for an answer, I turned and climbed to the top of the hill. Beyond lay another small valley with a stream winding its way down the center. In other times, a peaceful view that would have drawn an ooh or an aah from me.

This time, it didn't. I had been right. The taller hill on the other side of the valley was the backside of the one we'd been on when we watched the bears emerge from the mine entrance.

My eyes naturally scanned the nearby area for any sign of bears, then moved on to pick out several familiar landmarks. Yes, it was the same hill. A crooked tree, an exposed granite protrusion the size of a pickup, and even what I believed to be the trail we had followed came into view.

While my eyes did their thing, my mind centered on a viable path to cross the valley and the climb for a taller hill as a route to escape from pursuers. Only then, did it occur to me that I was planning a route back to the sanctuary.

That realization brought the taste of bile to my mouth. What made it worse was that I knew it was the right thing to do. To attempt to warn them. My mother had often told me that whenever a hard decision had to be made, the one that was hardest was almost always the right one. I had fought that idea for years while growing up—until realizing it was true. It's always the hardest choice that's the right one.

The hardest, in this case, was returning to the people who had wanted to kill me and warn them of impending danger. In one manner of thinking, they deserved what happened. In another, I had to live with the choices I made. I was going back to the sanctuary.

That choice either included Gerry or not. He would have to make up his mind.

On the way back to our ledge, I considered how to tell him. If he decided to move on, I wouldn't hold it against him. I understood. At least, that is what I tried to convince myself.

When I reached the ledge, he was lying down on his belly, behind three boulders as big as pumpkins that hadn't been there earlier. Between them were smaller ones, the size of my head. He had pulled a few small bushes out of the ground and placed them in front of the openings between the bounders to conceal us from sight on the level plain below.

Gerry must have rolled the boulders into position because they were too large to carry. Behind them, and the shrubs, we would be out of sight, and more importantly, almost safe from gunfire. We could shoot from between the larger boulders while protected on either side. It would take a very lucky shot to hit either of us.

He said, "This whole thing is only temporary, you know."

"Temporary, how?" I asked him, fairly certain of the answer he was going to give.

"If they only send two or three people, we can probably kill them, but more will follow later. Even if there are only three or four and even one escapes and goes back to Monroe, they're going to send a dozen or two to retaliate. So, we slow them temporarily, then what? Head south to Seattle as fast as we can travel and hope for the best?"

"We're thinking along the same lines," I admitted, even though I'd come to a different conclusion.

Gerry added, "More people are down in Seattle, and between here and there will be more armies like the militia in Monroe. We already talked about that and will have to be careful. There must be other armies or Monroe wouldn't have one to guard against."

He was planning. That was good. He might come up with a better plan than me, so I settled down behind his boulders and said, "Okay, what other choices do we have?"

He sighed. "Neither you nor I are trained to survive like this. So far, we'd made it past an angry bear, three crazies with the drop on us, and only a squeaky ladder rung in the barn saved us. Today we managed another ambush, the second one. How many more times are we going to be so lucky? Even so, with all that luck on our side, three of our group are already dead. We don't know how to find food. I think we won't last a week on our own."

"Unless?" I sensed he had more ideas and I wanted to hear them. I prayed one of them was better than mine.

He waited for perhaps ten minutes before saying, "Food is the biggie. By now, survivors have taken all the canned stuff from stores and houses. Oh, there might be a little here and there, but depending on finding it will have us starving or walking into a trap set by other survivors."

"We can hunt."

He snorted without humor. "How many animals have you seen since we've been out here? Besides, we could shoot a deer maybe, but shooting a gun tells everyone within a mile or two that someone is out there. They will investigate. And as big as a deer is, the meat will go bad after a few days with no refrigeration. That means we'd have to kill one a week."

"We could smoke or jerk it."

He gave that snort again, and the sound was becoming irritating. "Do you know how to do either of those?"

"Got any better ideas? I mean, you're right. We have to find a source of food."

"Yes. Fish. If we can get to Puget Sound, which is maybe twenty or thirty miles west from here, there are clams, oysters, crabs, and fish. Catching fish is silent. And we should be able to catch one or two a day. Not a great variety of diet, but fish will keep us alive until we figure out how to live up here."

I liked the idea. Fishing didn't have to be just sitting on a rock with a pole in my hands. Lines tied to small trees would work, and nets, if we could locate them. Maybe nets existed on fishing boats. For years, nets were plastic, not a cotton string that rotted. They lasted several years, so a few might have survived if we could find some.

I didn't mean to say it, but the words fell from my mouth. "Gerry, you're right, the militia is going to come after us again. Maybe with more people. Probably with more. They want the supplies in the sanctuary, the weapons down there, and most of all, they want revenge. They must hate us."

"Jake told me that, too. I believe him."

I paused, then plunged on in a flood of rapid words, "Listen, I can't run for the safety of the shore while knowing those people from Monroe are going to search for the sanctuary. If Sara told them about the mine entrance, they will search for that. Can you imagine ten or twenty of them entering that machinery room in the sanctuary we escaped from?"

"They would slaughter everyone and take anything useful."

"Could you live on the coast, eating your fish every day while knowing you did nothing to prevent their slaughter?"

"They treated us like slaves and worse. Hell, they were going to kill you." Spittle formed at the corners of his mouth.

The anger and defensiveness took me by surprise. I decided to let the subject lie for a while. If he didn't change his mind, I'd go down alone and meet up with him later.

The day lingered quietly on. Nobody else appeared, but I hadn't expected them to. When the pair we'd killed didn't return to Monroe by nightfall, plans would be adjusted. Reinforcements sent.

Our job was to wait here to avoid capture while down in the sanctuary. That is, if we went down to warn them. A dozen militia might arrive at any time and if we were down there, we had no escape. My basic plan, as simple as possible, would have us fend off whoever came next, then rush down to warn those below, and just as quickly, rush back up and leave the sanctuary. Then, we would head for the hills.

Waiting was not an option for us. We had to know how many they were going to send and when. If two or three more arrived in a day or two, and we killed or drove them off, we had ample time to go down into the mine and warn those people. If Monroe sent a dozen or more this time, things were different. I didn't want to get trapped with the others in the sanctuary. We'd have to make a run for it. Those below were on their own.

Gerry finally decided to speak again. "You want to warn them, don't you?"

"Want to? No. I have to."

"Taking the time to go down that mine shaft might mean when you come up again, a small army from Monroe may be waiting."

"Not trying to save their lives is something I can't live with. But yes, you're right. I can leave you up top, standing guard."

"Alone? How many of the militia do you think I can fight if they show up? One? Or do I run down the mineshaft and tell you we're all trapped and together we face the militia that is trained to fight?"

"You can warn me with a call or a shot from your gun. Sound carries in the shaft."

"Well, that's one way to let the militia know exactly where we are, I guess. Besides, those self-important people living below are going to try to kill you on sight. That's what I think. If the militia from Monroe doesn't do it, our *friends* in the sanctuary will."

He was right on all counts.

I said, "Listen to me. If the militia sends only a few soldiers, we can reasonably expect no more to arrive for, at least, another day because they are waiting to hear the report of what they found. That gives us time to locate the mine entrance and warn those people and allow them to get the hell away before a whole army arrives. I think I found the path we took when we left, so it's something we can easily do."

"What if they don't want to leave?" he asked. "Or, they don't have enough time to prepare? Besides, even if they all rush to the surface, the militia will just track them and kill everyone."

I shrugged. "That will be on the people in the sanctuary to do whatever they wish. After our warning, we can do no more for them."

"While you are down there, you can shoot Witch Hazel and do us all a big favor."

That idea had some appeal. I certainly had the weapons to do it. I wouldn't, of course, but it was a nice idea. I pictured myself striding into the dining room and pulling a gun for each hand.

Gerry scowled at my smile. He obviously had more to say. To his credit, he kept it to himself.

The afternoon drug on. We watched in silence as three deer grazed at the edge of the meadow below, two does and a spotted fawn on wobbly legs. If any militia came near, they would bolt like an alarm clock going off. After they leisurely reentered the forest, I closed my eyes and tried making my mind find solutions to our problems.

It didn't work.

I liked Gerry's idea of getting to the coast. He was right about food. For now, we had what little we'd taken from the militia but that would run out in a few days. Deer, like those we'd watched below, would live there. Fish were plentiful. In early summer blackberries grew wild. Apple and pear trees were at half the houses.

A dog. I would need a dog. Not a barker, but one to warn and protect me. The sun was setting and the air chilled. It would be another cold night without a fire.

I pulled the blanket free from the backpack I'd run off with, found it damp, but placed it over my shoulders as I chewed more of the dried meat and fruit. As my eyelids grew heavy, Gerry turned to me.

"Okay, we have not finished yet. If a lot of them come after us tomorrow, we run like hell. Run for the coast. Agreed?"

"Yes."

If four or less arrive, we let them enter our trap and hope we're able to kill them all and prevent any from returning to Monroe with a warning. Then we go down the mineshaft in a hurry and warn those below."

"Okay," I said hesitantly, instinctively knowing there was more to come.

"You and I don't waste any time. We return to the surface and head for the coast. We have nothing more to do with anyone down there, including helping them escape. They are on their own."

The vehemence in his tone jarred me fully awake. What if one or more of them wanted to go with us? Not all of them were enemies. Some, especially those we had worked with, those who were friends.

Then I saw and understood his rationale. We were in a race. A timed one. In and out. The Monroe militia was coming, we knew that. When they did, we needed to be as far away as possible, or we'd die. His reaction was not about helping or not helping others, it was about the two of us surviving.

Worse, he was right.

Chapter 15

The next day nothing happened. Nobody arrived, no enemies scouted the area, no militia arrived and searched for their friends. We could have gone to the sanctuary, given our warning, and escaped into the endless forests of central Washington. Now we committed ourselves to remain on the ledge another day.

In many ways, I hoped those arriving would be a force too great to fight. We'd decided five was the tipping point for the maximum number we could hope to defeat, but what if they sent ten, or twenty? I know what we'd agreed to.

However, my mind wouldn't quit. Four had been the maximum, then because of our location and the element of surprise, we'd changed to five. What if they sent one or two who appeared inept? Could we change to fight six?

Our basic problem was that Gerry and I were not soldiers and we knew it. Our fighting experiences were few, and our knowledge of guns limited to a few times shooting at paper targets years ago. Upon reflection, I should have insisted the tipping point of running or staying was three militia, not five.

It was going to be the inept pair of us against five experienced soldiers. Sure, we had surprise on our side, but that only lasted for about five seconds. After that, even if we killed two of them in our initial surprise attack, it was still three trained survivalists against two hapless dishwashers. The result was predictable.

By evening, we'd talked it all out a dozen times. Twice,

we'd almost left the sanctuary to itself. It was easy to suggest they deserved whatever happened, especially if it included Witch Hazel. However, each time, I eventually fell back on the original plan. If we failed, at least, we'd tried—if either of us still lived.

The soft rain started around dark and continued all night. I knew that because it was impossible to get warm or sleep. We shivered, hugged for warmth, and talked little. I used the time, which logic said would be my last hours alive, to sense the world around me. I smelled the damp earth, the wet leaves, and the moist air. I felt the soft dirt under my butt and the hard granite underneath that. My ears listened to the small drops of rain that had gathered on leaves overhead until they were large enough to pool and fall as one. My skin felt sensitive to the cold, wet, and stiffness in my legs told of tight muscles.

We talked only a little. I sensed that Gerry worried more than me. He was a detailed planner; I'd come to realize. That also mean he is a worrier, not a fighter.

As the night sky turned to early morning, he said, "If they don't come by noon, I think we should make a dash for the mine entrance, tell those below what's coming, and get the hell back up here."

"Then run away?"

"Damn right," he said firmly. "As fast as you can. Just try to keep up with me."

That told me what he'd been thinking about all night. Worrying. But he was right. We couldn't wait for another day, or two, or three. "We move at noon. Run to the mine, go down as fast as we can, tell them, and get out. Agreed."

His head bobbed in agreement. "How are you going to tell them?"

I hadn't thought of that. "Play it by ear."

"Okay, but I think a half-hour to go down there, no more than that to spread the word, and then we exit at full speed. I've been making a mental map, but it would be nice to find a real one. Too many people in Seattle and Everett, almost a solid city from one end to the other."

"I agree with that."

"North of Marysville, up near Camano Island. Not many

people lived there."

I'd once gone camping at a state park with my folks up there. He was right. "More distance to travel."

"We can do it."

"Yes," I agreed. "We can."

We sat quietly as the day grew lighter. We ate more of the jerky/fruit and I estimated we had enough for three, maybe four more days if we took it easy. I'd heard that a person can go hungry for ten days without problems other than hunger pains, but water is required almost every day. I sucked on the wet corner of the blanket over my shoulders and swallowed the moisture. If I wanted a drink, there were pools everywhere.

We were downstream of where we'd buried Danny. If the streambed had water in it, I wouldn't be drinking any.

Gerry nudged me. It was still very early.

My eyes followed his. In the distance, there was furtive movement. A dark form moved from a stand of bushes to a large tree. It paused there.

Nearby that place, another flash of movement revealed a person, man, or woman, dressed in army camouflage. I didn't move and neither did Gerry.

The movement was what had caught our attention and identified two of them. We wouldn't make the same mistake.

It was early, perhaps a half-hour after dawn, so they had either departed Monroe very early or the night before. I allowed my eyes to roam the area without looking at anything specific. They found another person inside the far tree line where others might be gathered. The deeper shadows could conceal a dozen people.

"I see three."

Gerry said, "Me too. I hope it's the same three."

I described where each was, and he agreed. We saw no more.

However, the three we watched were careful and efficient. They moved slowly, examining the ground, and chose the next cover they would dart to before moving. I saw hand signals. The rain had probably washed away our tracks or made them indistinct.

The one on the far side of the road called a halt with a

raised fist. He'd found where we drug the bodies off the road, the bent grasses, and shrubs. All three of them spread out, one following where we'd drug their friends, and one on either side looking for clues.

It didn't take them long to locate the two dead, and their dogs. They gathered in a huddle and talked.

"Now it gets interesting," Gerry said.

"They'll see our path easily," I answered.

"Yes, but will they follow us? I wouldn't be surprised if they turn around and rush back to make their report. Them or a group of others can come later today and follow our trail. That would also give us time to move to the sanctuary and beyond."

I prayed for them to turn around and go report their findings to their superiors, like good soldiers. My prayers went unanswered. They went back to the road and found where we had walked across the meadow—as we intended. From our vantage point, I could still see where we walked.

They didn't find where we took Danny. That was a plus. If they had gone to the streambed and started digging him up, I don't know what I'd have done.

They did spread out about ten yards apart and move slowly in our direction. My heart raced. My breath came in short gasps.

Gerry lowered himself to a prone position as he said, "Stay calm."

I mimicked his movements, even down to placing my rifle beside me and pulling the pistol from the small of my back. The one in the holster remained there in case I needed to use it or if we took off running, it would remain with me.

That was not my idea. Gerry had come up with it the day before. As I said, he was a planner. I watched those below move closer and wished I'd taken the time to pile more boulders in front of us, then realized that any more would look odd from below, and thus give away our location and intentions.

The three were advancing through the meadow at a painfully slow pace. They used the limited cover and paused often to watch the hillside ahead. Their attention focused on the notch in the distance that was our obvious destination. When one glanced briefly in our direction, he quickly turned back to where they expected us to have traveled.

Gerry deserved a pat on the back for that one.

Congratulating ourselves seemed premature. As I watched their progress, a disturbing thought entered my head. At the pace they moved, they would never catch up with us, if we were fleeing ahead of them. We'd gain distance—and that went against everything.

"Gerry," I hissed. "Something's wrong."

"They're going right where we want them to," he whispered back in an excited but unconcerned manner.

He was right in that our trap was set perfectly. Only three of them and they were going to be so close we couldn't miss with the rifles. Thirty or forty yards, I'd guess. Even our pistols might hit them at that range.

If we each managed a hit with our first shots, then both shot at the last one alive, the fight could be over in a few seconds. That was the optimum plan. It appeared perfect.

But that little thought in my mind wouldn't go away. They moved too slowly, too carefully. They were unconcerned at how far ahead of them we might run.

The answer struck like a blow. They were unconcerned—for a good reason. If we outran them, we would find another group ahead of us. Maybe two. A trap.

"They're herding us like sheep," I said.

Gerry spun to face me; fear etched in his features. He instantly understood. "More of them in the next valley?"

"I think so."

"Come on," he said as he started moving into the deeper underbrush as he climbed higher.

I followed, slow and easy. We reached the crest and moved down the other side a third of the way until we concealed ourselves behind a rotting log. There seemed to be nothing in the valley. Perhaps my imagination had forced us to surrender a perfect ambush location. I berated myself for allowing my fears to take charge.

A glint of sunlight off metal drew our attention. Across the valley where the floor grew wider, a person shifted position. I guessed it to be more than two football fields away. We remained still. Another figure huddled right below us, on our side of the valley.

His or her back was to us.

There were probably more. Gerry pointed to our right, in the opposite direction of where we had found the first one. There was another on the far hillside, watching the valley and almost facing us. They had set a trap and intended to flush us from cover and have us rush right into the ambush of the waiting militia. It had been a good plan.

Those behind us would follow our path to the ridge and then move along it to where we had waited in our ambush. After that, they would trail us to our present position. It was just a matter of time until the jaws of the vice closed in on us.

I mouthed, "What now?"

He motioned for me to scoot on my belly to the end of the log. He followed slowly. As if in slow motion, he used his arm to gather brown, wet leaves and scoop them over my head and neck, leaving my face clear to see around the end of the log. I felt him placing more leaves over my back and legs.

When I looked back at him, he had moved to the other end of the log and covered himself in the same way. We didn't have to talk. We waited.

If they found us, we would fight and probably die. But we would fight and the first to find us died first.

As if we had a choice. I'd seen my friends hanging from the gallows, so knew what to expect if we didn't defend ourselves. Being shot was preferable to beatings, dismemberments, and hangings. Barely.

I kept an eye on our back trail.

In the valley, my eyes picked out two more. Five of them, altogether. Without a doubt, all were better with their weapons than us. They probably had more ammunition too. A prolonged firefight was out of the question.

We waited more than an hour. I'd adjusted my position slightly, so my rifle was ready and beside my left hand lay my pistol. My plan was simple. I'd empty both and reach for my holster if I still lived that long.

A shrill whistle sounded.

Seven, not five, soldiers emerged from their concealed positions and moved to the far end of the valley where an eighth waited, whistle in hand. When all gathered in a rough circle, a conversation took place, arms waved, fingers pointed, and more than a few unintelligible shouts drifted on the still air. A few disagreed with what the leader told them. The one with the whistle took control and pointed away from us.

Almost as one, they turned their backs to us and began walking in the direction of the road.

"Another trap?" I hissed.

"Maybe. Hold still and let's give them a while." We watched all eight disappear and we located no more.

The three trackers who were on the other side of the smaller hill hadn't appeared on this side, and that worried me. Besides flushing us by moving directly at us across the meadow, this suggested it might be a feint of them leaving the area, which might draw us out into the open. I thought about the other three possibly sitting on top of the hill waiting for us to emerge.

With their rifles, they could shoot us before we knew they were up there. They would have a clear view of the small valley. Another hour passed. Then another. I was tired, my bones hurt, and the damp air and clothing had chilled me almost to shivers again. There was little patience left. I tensed and must have shifted positions.

Gerry whispered, "No. Don't move. I think I saw one of them above us."

I froze and waited, finding I had more patience than I'd believed. Another hour passed slowly. My eyes darted to one side. A man walked down the center of the valley floor carrying a long rifle with a scope as big around as my wrist. No idea where he had come from. He pulled to a stop, looked right past us to the crest of the hill, and waved. His arm outstretched and he pointed back the way we'd come.

He casually turned and followed the route the other eight had taken. He'd been there all along, hiding and waiting for us to appear after we were certain they had departed. He was their sniper and would have killed both of us easily if those three on top didn't shoot us first.

Even if they missed, there were four of them to chase us. We didn't stand a chance.

After the one with the rifle carried over his shoulder as soldiers had for a couple of hundred years, we remained still. His appearance had shaken me more than words can explain. All that crossed my mind was how close I'd come to dying if Gerry had allowed me to stand.

"Are there any more?" I asked softly.

Gerry said, "I don't think so. Want to stand up and bet your life on it?"

"No."

"Okay, it will be dark in an hour. They probably went back to a hot meal and warm beds before dark, but who knows?"

We waited some more. The waiting seemed easier to me this time. Funny how being terrified can change my outlook.

As twilight appeared, we emerged and sprinted in zigs and zags across the valley floor and darted up the side of the larger hill. When winded, we dived to the ground, waited with ears perked, and watched the darkness. Nothing appeared, made sounds, or chased us.

Gerry took the lead. We traveled the side of the hill to our left until coming to a path. He knelt and pointed in the dim light. While rounded from the drizzle, footprints were clear in the mud beside a pool.

They were true footprints, not from boots or shoes. The imprints of the bare toes were easy to see. Barefoot. They were left in the dirt and mud by five escapees from the sanctuary. Us.

It was easy, even in the dark, to follow them back. If the soldiers had searched the hillside, they would have located them. However, they were too intent on finding and killing us. They had settled into places where they had good fields of fire to shoot when we rushed over the opposing hill.

They would be back. The next time, they wouldn't be intent on setting a trap. If I were making the decision, I'd send trackers early, a few snipers to protect them, and after that, searchers. Lots of them.

They knew the general location of the sanctuary either from Sara or from Grace and Jake. The next step would be to locate it. Sending thirty or forty people would cover a lot of ground.

Five Years After

We walked mostly uphill, then finally, as my legs ached, downhill. We reached the ledge where we had watched the bears. While we couldn't see the meadow in the dark, we easily found the items we'd abandoned.

Gerry covered his hand over the lens of a flashlight and briefly switched it on. His hand glowed. He handed another to me.

"Ready?" he asked.

"Not even close, but let's do it before I change my mind."

"We can still cut and run."

"No, we can't."

Chapter 16

We climbed down the hillside following the same path we'd taken a few days earlier. I had the rifle slung over my shoulder and the spare pistol in my hand because it was easier to walk in the darkness that way, and I planned to shoot any bears with every bullet remaining in the handgun, thinking that many smaller hits are better than a few large ones.

Gerry moved slowly and confidently. Again, it struck me, how much different he was than the nerd I'd known for five years. We reached the entrance of the mine and I dreaded what came next. My foot sank ankle-deep in the muck.

We moved by feel for a dozen steps, then Gerry turned on his flashlight. I moved by his light, thinking I'd hold mine in reserve in case his ran out of power. Being inside the shaft without light was more terrifying than what lay ahead.

The sounds of our movements echoed off the stone walls. Splashes, sucking noises as we lifted our feet, our heavy breathing, and my sniffles combined to make a most unpleasant trip into the bowels of the earth.

Gerry realized I walked in almost complete darkness when I tripped again and fell face-first into the muck. He apologized for not realizing that with the light in his hand, pointed ahead, I could see little.

I followed him, down the shaft, listening and smelling for bear, and prepared to empty two full clips if one appeared. None did. We reached the poor excuse for a ladder and moved carefully down, testing each rung before moving to the next.

Eventually, we reached the wall where the hole should be, the one we have climbed through. It had been crudely patched. That didn't slow Gerry. He raised his foot and kicked. The sheetrock gave. A square piece let light stream inside.

A voice on the other side of the wall shouted a warning. They had left a guard there.

Gerry kicked again and then hit the wall with his shoulder. A piece large enough to step through ripped away. Light streamed inside, almost blinding us.

There was shouting from the hallway outside the mechanical room. Heavy footsteps mixed with orders shouted by several voices.

"They're back . . ."

"Get into position!"

"Don't let them bring their sickness inside."

"Kill them!"

There were more orders and shouts, but I quit listening.

Gerry looked at me helplessly.

I pulled the nine-millimeter from the small of my back and judged the height of the heads on the other side of the sheetrock wall along the hallway. I aimed a foot above and fired four times, with two seconds between each shot.

The sanctuary turned deathly quiet.

I shouted, "It is Gerry and Penelope. We came back to give you a message, then we're out of here."

A voice of authority, not military shouted, "We have nothing to say to you."

"Then listen. Everything up there is just like we left it. No radiation or any of that."

"You're lying," another voice shouted.

I fired my pistol again. "If there is nothing up there, where did I get this gun? Ask yourself that."

"You found it," a subdued voice answered.

Gerry stepped past me. In a motion, he slid his rifle across the floor thirty feet to the doorway. Surprisingly, to me, at least, it was on target and slid across the hallway to slap the far wall. He shouted, "You soldiers need to look at that rifle. No rust. It's been cared for."

Heated whispers were exchanged. They were arguing, but

that was normal. Those in charge would make the decisions unless the others revolted. Only one thing would make that happen. Fear. I knew the trigger to pull that would cause that fear to override their superiors.

I called loud and strong, "Monroe had been taken over by escaped prisoners from the reformatory. They have killed almost everyone and now they know you are down here. They want your supplies, ammo, and weapons. But they are also searching for anyone who was in power or who was rich before the war. They hang them in the parking lot of the fire station."

That should make the judge's knees go weak. Many of the others, too. They had all been the elite.

Gerry picked up on what I was saying. He shouted, "They will be here tomorrow. They know about the mineshaft. Anyone down here in twelve hours will never leave. If you do decide to escape, go south, not anywhere near Monroe."

To cap it all off, I shouted, "The two of us came here to warn you. That is all we have to say. We are heading outside and away before we get trapped down here with you. Good luck."

Gerry motioned with a finger held to his lips. We'd said enough.

Someone, a voice I didn't recognize, called, "Tell us more." It seemed a delaying tactic. They were up to something.

Gerry shook his head as a sign I shouldn't answer.

I agreed with him. Silence would speak far louder than words.

We backed into the mine, weapons ready in case we needed them, and once inside, Gerry took the lead while I used the flashlight to show him the way. As we neared the ladder to the upper level, a woman far behind called, "Penelope. Come back and talk to us."

We ignored her and kept on. There were more shouts and pleas to return and a few commands, but we didn't slow. While we'd told them a few mild lies, most of it had been true and intended to help them, or those who decided to leave. However, instead of calling for more information and talking it over for days, they needed to get their butts in gear and run away.

I smelled the fresh air outside before seeing the dim moonlight filtered by the clouds. The night was cool and quiet, and that last might have warned us if we were more perceptive.

As Gerry moved into the open, three shots sounded.

Three individual guns had fired almost as one. Gerry twisted and turned in my direction as if trying to warn me, but my flashlight revealed he was already dead. Part of his chest had been torn away as one bullet struck from the side. Part of his head was also missing.

Without conscious thought, and while Gerry was still sagging to the ground, I darted to one side, hearing two more shots. Both struck the walls inside the mine and ricocheted down the shaft. I dived and rolled back into the mine. My thumb fumbled for the switch of the flashlight and finally found it to shut it off but not before three more shots came my way.

My rifle was still slung over my shoulder. I moved deeper into the mine and found a vertical shelf of solid rock, probably left there as a support for the roof. I crouched and waited, a nine-millimeter in my shaking hand.

Tears came. Gerry had progressed from an inept computer geek to an emerging warrior. He'd taught me far more than I'd taught him. Now he was dead.

Worse, I was now alone. No friends, not even any below. Certainly not outside.

In the soft light at the tunnel mouth, movement flashed. A foot entered the muck and paused. Then another step and the same sound repeated.

"The floor of this damned place is covered in crap," a man said.

An answering voice said, "Go slow."

"Just two of them?" A third voice asked.

"The one outside and one carrying the flashlight. Could be more."

Three distinct voices, the last had been a woman.

I hadn't expected that but should have. Many of the women in Monroe had carried weapons and moved with the men as equals. Their sloshing gave away their positions as the three moved into the mine deeper.

Talking and making noise didn't concern them. They knew about me because of the flashlight and because they had shot at me, yet now moved confidently ahead. They must have believed I bolted or took a hit.

Shouts came from below demanding what the shooting was about. I was caught in the middle.

That was not entirely true. I could move down the mine faster than those from the surface, if for no other reason than because I'd done it three times. I was not *caught* in the middle. I *chose* to be there. At least for a while.

The reasons were anger and revenge. While I didn't wish to die, I wanted very badly for them to do so. They had killed Gerry and shot at me. Now they were chasing me, intending to kill me.

I used my ears as never before. There were three of them. Maybe more outside, but three inside the mine, no more than a hundred steps from me. A peek around the rock wall revealed their shapes against the lighter mouth of the mine.

I was in total darkness.

As if he read my mind, one man said, "I can't see shit."

"So, we come back with torches or lanterns," the woman agreed.

The sloshing ceased. They had stopped.

The first male voice said, "The two of you can stay here to guard the exit while I go for help and lanterns."

The other man grumbled, and the shapes began to move. With two posted at the mouth of the mine, I'd never get out. However, that didn't matter to me at the moment. I'd laid a trap and had wanted them to come another twenty or thirty feet closer. They were about a hundred feet from me, confined side-to-side by the stone walls six feet apart.

My mind rapidly calculated as they started to retreat. Two of them might stand side-by-side, but from the dim shapes, they were single-file, as we had been.

I shifted the pistol to my left hand and ignored the imploring shouts from the sanctuary a level below and a few hundred yards away. My right hand pulled the other pistol. I stepped into the open. The three were slowly moving away, vague shapes against the night outside.

My feet rushed ahead, not a run, but far faster than they were going. The splashes I made were either covered by their noises from walking or they didn't realize what was happening.

Suddenly, they were closer than a hundred feet: more like sixty or seventy. Inside the mine, it was hard to tell. I took a dozen more rushed steps before the woman reacted. She said, "What's that?"

They looked like one mass against the night outside. I pulled to a stop and crouched. The gun in my right hand shot as fast as my finger could pull the trigger, which was two or three times a second.

When they fired all twelve bullets, sounding almost continuous with the roar of each shot echoing off the walls and combing with others, I let the gun fall into the guck and put the other in my right hand, but didn't fire.

There had been no return fire and no people were standing ahead of me. I waited, knowing they couldn't see me and if I didn't move, they couldn't locate me by sound. They might be crouched down, waiting for me.

After a full minute, I shifted to the left wall, so my right arm remained clear and moved ahead, each splash of a step sounding like thunder to me.

I tripped over one, almost falling. It looked like two more bodies were ahead. I flicked the flashlight on and off, almost like a flash from a cellphone. One man lay face up. The other man and the woman were face down.

I pulled their weapons from holsters and collected two rifles that I slung over my shoulder. Loaded down with weapons, I moved to the mine entrance and pulled to a stop. The dark form that was my friend Gerry sprawled out there. I wished there was something I could do for him. Even the little we'd done for Danny had been something. I pulled his lifeless body to one side and left him on his back with his arms crossed over his chest and his eyelids closed.

"Sorry, Gerry. I know you'll understand." Those words were on my lips as I sprinted from the entrance in the direction the bears had taken.

No shots came. I hit the edge of the trees and slowed before I ran into one face first. I bent and threw up in one motion, not because of the pain from the tree but the horror of the experience hit me as hard as running into a cedar would have been.

I was not safe. But I was safer.

The additional guns I carried weighed my body down. Despite the different manufacturers, I managed to eject the magazines on the three handguns, all semiautomatics and probably with the same ammo as mine used. I kept one gun that was the same model and make as mine. It went into the back of the gun belt and felt as if it belonged there.

My fingertip felt the bores of the rifles. Different sizes. One had a scope. I tossed the other to the side.

"Penelope! Can you hear me?"

It was a male voice; one I'd heard often because Grainger had often hung out with Jake. They had served in the same unit before the war started. I looked back at the entrance and found a flashlight bobbing along as if he was jogging through a park in a city six or eight years ago.

"Penelope, wait up!" he shouted.

A trick? No, that didn't sound like something Grainger would try. He had been a soldier caught in the effort to escape the war like the rest of us. He never complained or made an issue of how we were treated like I had, but he was one of us. And clearly, he was stupid about how things on the surface were. His actions were likely to get him killed, if not both of us.

"Over here," I called softly, knowing that if there were probably more Monroe Militia in the nearby forests, I was leading them directly to me. There seemed no alternative.

He shifted directions at the sound of my voice.

Another figure ran behind him, one dark and small. He had to know someone was behind him, which implied they were together. That didn't make me feel better.

In the three days since my escape that I'd been on the surface, my knowledge of what it takes to survive in the new world had increased a thousandfold. Having another person, even one inexperienced in military tactics like Grainger, still put my life in danger. He had weapons training, so perhaps not as much danger as others from the sanctuary presented.

However, as they drew nearer, the one behind him

appeared to be a woman, a young, thin, woman. That description didn't match any of us who had been workers if I excluded myself. Most of the others who had been selected to survive in the sanctuary were over forty because they had *earned* the right to survive by their adult actions. At least, that was their story.

That only left four. All were the adult children of the wealthy, powerful, and select few. None of them had ever lifted a hand to support themselves, before or after entering the sanctuary. While I'd delivered beer to drunks in the honky-tonk, they had sipped white wine in their sororities.

In short, I wouldn't risk my life for any of them. I'd barely spoken to any, unless they demanded something of me, more wine, clean their rooms, or wash their clothing. I was still lost in sour thought when Grainger pulled to a stop in front of me. Panting, he said, "Good to see you made it, Pen."

The woman with him stepped between us as if that were her right. It was Carla, the blonde who had been the rudest to me. Of the four younger women, she was the last I wanted to see, except for Witch Hazel. She flipped her hair and said, "How much of what you've been telling us is true?"

"What are you doing here?" I managed.

She smirked. "Well, I thought I'd come up here and look for myself. Where are the others?"

I hesitated, then decided to tell her in the most abrupt way possible. "Jake and Grace got themselves tortured and hung after the militia cut off their fingers and feet. Danny got his throat ripped out by a dog and we buried him in a dry streambed yesterday. Gerry was ambushed when he walked out of the mine entrance just now. I killed the three people who shot him. You probably saw them all at the entrance."

Grainger pulled back as if not believing me. "*You* killed those three in the mine?"

"They killed my friend. Yes, I killed them."

"By yourself?" Carla asked in a tone that said she didn't believe me. "Anyhow, it's like it used to be up here. We could live here instead of down there."

Grainger's breathing had slowed, and he took in my appearance. His eyes went from the heavy clothing that was far too big, to the rifles slung over my back, and the holster with the nine-millimeter. He couldn't see the other in my rear waistband.

Grainger's face solidified as he put it all together. "It's true?"

"Yes."

"What do I need to do?" he asked.

I pointed to where I'd left the other weapons. "Get over there and grab a couple of handguns and that rifle, strip a couple of those bodies in the mine for clothing, and get your asses back here in less than five minutes or I'll leave you."

"Wear dead people's clothes?" Carla said, in the same manner, I would have four days ago.

She still stood directly in front of me, in a challenging manner. I took one step closer, which put our noses almost touching. "Carla, I've told you what to do. You don't have to. Me? I'm leaving in five minutes and you're only going if you've done what I said."

"I'll just follow," she snarled, using almost the same tone and words as Gerry.

I hit her. Not a slap or punch. My fist balled and the roundhouse landed on her cheek so hard it jarred my shoulder. She landed on her butt, too astonished to wail or cry. Her bare hand cradled her cheek as she looked at me in wonder or horror, it was impossible to tell which.

I said, "Four minutes."

Grainger had been about the help her. His eyes met mine.

He spun and raced for the mineshaft, leaving her sitting there.

Carla turned to watch him. Then said, "You hit me."

"If you attempt to follow, I'll kill you."

"Carla," Grainger stage whispered. "Get over here."

She cast me an evil look and said, "No wonder the judge said you should die. She was right."

The woman stood, turned, and walked away, passing right by Grainger, and using a flashlight to light the way as if nobody else could see it. She kept walking past the bodies. Grainger chased after her a few steps, then paused and knelt beside a dead man. In moments he had pulled the clothing and boots off the man.

He returned carrying an armload of clothing, two guns, and a rifle. He said, "Let's go."

"What about your girlfriend?"

"Not anymore. She's too stupid."

"She'd going to die, you know. The militia will come, and she will die with the rest of them down there."

"I know." He pulled on a heavy, wet, filthy pair of pants as he talked, then sat and pulled on the boots. More to himself than me, he said, "A little big but I'll pull the laces tight."

He stood and pulled on the shirt and coat, then slung the rifle over his shoulder. "What now?"

I started walking along a small path. "We get the hell away. They sent dogs after us before, and trackers after that. I'm afraid they'll pull out whatever they have left and hit us with it all."

"Meaning?" he asked while trying to keep up with me.

"More men, and women, maybe dogs. Probably rewards posted. Trackers on our tails for sure. Even after they reach the sanctuary, they will still want me. If you go along, you get included with my bad reputation. Your best option is to split up from me before they know who you are and make it on your own."

We walked another half hour. He finally asked, "Do you, at least, have a plan?"

Chapter 17

A plan for the immediate future. Did I have one? That was a good question. I considered before answering. Yes, I did. Sort of. Escape and survive.

"Well?" he prompted.

"I had one yesterday. With Gerry."

"Had?"

I kept walking, increasing my pace because of my agitation. The underbrush had thinned, and we progressed quickly. I talked without slowing or turning my head, "I planned to warn and rescue as many people down in the sanctuary as possible."

He said, "They are forewarned and have enough weapons to defend themselves. They should be grateful for your warning."

"Instead, they blame me."

"Understandable," he responded shortly. He struggled to keep pace.

I said, "They have weapons but only the military knows how to use them. There's only one soldier left, isn't there? And as we both know, only Jake and you had combat experience. The one left down there held a desk job five years ago. And he was a reserve, a weekend warrior earning a little extra cash."

"We were all soldiers," he growled.

I went on for a few more steps but couldn't resist. "Would you trust your life in a combat situation with that man?"

"He knows how to shoot and there are automatics."

His answer irritated me, and my big mouth simply couldn't remain shut. I pulled to a stop and said, as my fists balled in anger, "What's going to happen when twenty or thirty seasoned militia, all of whom have fought in combat for the last five years, charge down that mineshaft?"

He didn't answer.

I continued, "I'll tell you. They will bust into the sanctuary with their guns blazing, shooting everyone they see. Those below won't even have a chance to reach the armory where the weapons are locked up. The militia will shoot every person they encounter. Everyone down there is going to die."

"You can't be serious."

His face looked as if I'd kneed him in his crouch. His mouth hung open, his eyes were wide, even in the dim light the tears ran down his cheek like little sparklers. My fingers uncurled. I lowered my voice and the intensity.

"Sorry. I'm not trying to be mean."

"What can we do?"

I took pity on him. "Grainger, I already did what can be done. Gerry gave his life to warn those people. To be honest with you, even if they had listened, by the time they would have discussed it, gathered their belongings, and made their way out, it would have been too late."

"Your warning was for nothing?"

"No. It accomplished three things. It allows my mind to be at ease because I did what I could. It's not my fault they refused to listen. I also managed to rescue you. That is number two."

"You said, three things."

"I got Gerry killed because I needed to soothe my conscience. That is number three and the one that will haunt me far more than the slaughter of all those others." I fought the urge to vomit. It was true, Gerry had died because of me. If I'd have listened to him, we'd be far away by now.

I'd chosen our path to head south. Soon, we'd come to the road beyond the turnoff to the sanctuary. I had one more idea.

We reached the road and turned to our right, heading for Monroe. As the sky grew lighter, I located a hillside across the road. Not much of a hill, but a couple of hundred feet, then the ground on the other side fell off until it reached the river.

Gerry and I had spotted the place two days ago and marked its location in our minds. "Leave no footprints on the road. You go first. Leap from a log or rock to the surface of the road."

"Why?"

"Think! They are going to search for us and the first thing they will do is send scouts out along the road, probably one on each side to watch for our prints in the dirt. When you get to the far edge of the blacktop, look for a rock you can leap to. Two in a row would be better. Do not step on any plant, no matter how small."

"What are you going to do?"

"Make sure you don't leave a single telltale behind." I could tell he didn't like my answer. It was a male pride thing. Too bad. There was no time to be nice. We needed to reach the top of the hill and settle in. There were two things we needed to know. How many would come this time, and would they have dogs again. It was the dogs that scared me most. Not because they might attack, but because there was no getting away once they caught my scent.

An old boyfriend had trained them for a company that provided K9 dogs to police. His experiences said that much of what the public believed was crap. Pepper spray, changing clothes, hiding drugs in cans of coffee to hide the scent, and a hundred other ideas were flat wrong.

He'd told me people are visual, dogs are smellers. For them, a specific scent was like a man looking out over a crowd at a rock concert. Imagine that one of the crowd wore a hat made with one of those glow-in-the-dark materials, he'd said. As easily as a man could pick out the glowing hat in a vast crowd, a dog could pick out a smell. It didn't matter if there were thousands of other smells, much like it didn't matter to the man if others wore hats of different colors.

I had a rifle with limited ammunition. The rifle had a scope. I liked all other dogs but the one, or ones, that would be tracking me. I'd kill it. Or them.

It would be easier to escape from five or ten men following me than one dog. Of that, I was certain.

Grainger had asked if I had a plan. I did. If there were dogs following my scent, I planned to take advantage of a human trait and while they were trying to sneak up on me; I would do the same to them. Not too close, but close enough where my shots wouldn't miss. Far enough away that I stood a chance of escaping while the militia was confused and hiding so they didn't get a shot at me.

That's a funny thing about people searching for others. They seldom look behind themselves because they concentrate on what is ahead. I felt confident I could get very close if needed.

I learned that trick as a child playing hide and seek. You get to a temporary spot where you can see the seeker and where they look—then you go to one of those places. The second-best option for me was when someone I didn't like was "it" I'd sneak off to the park. Once to a movie.

Grainger had disturbed moss on a rock when he leaped to the road. I moved it back into place and managed to get onto the blacktop and study each of his steps, as well as my own. There were a few faint scuffs and some disturbed sand, but those may have been left by animals. Anyway, a little breeze or light rain and they would be gone.

I suspected I was not the main target. Not yet. The food in the sanctuary would last the militia for years. The weapons and ammo were almost as valuable. That was the main thrust of the search. Hopefully, I was an afterthought and Grainger an unknown.

I complimented him after we followed a game trail up the incline of the hill. It was not steep, nor high. It had one advantage. The road to Monroe curved slightly and from the side of the hill. We could watch it almost to the bridge.

If they sent more people, we'd see them long before they arrived at the turnoff. By then, we would have our minds made up as to what we were going to do.

The hill rose perhaps two hundred feet high, more than enough to look out over the tops of the trees and see the road. We settled into a position where they would come to within maybe fifty yards, then turn and move away from our position.

Grainger said, "Nice site you chose. Mind some advice?"

"Please."

"If we're going to fight, are you open to moving closer before they reach us?"

I grinned. "You're reading my mind, now?"

He returned the grin. "Otherwise, we can be over this hump before they get here and be on our way. That is if you have a destination."

I felt guilty, twice. Once for Gerry and once because I hadn't filled Grainger in on my plan. If something happened to me, or we got separated, Grainger would have no idea of where I was going.

I said, "Gerry and I talked. Food is the problem. We're going to want it every day or two. The food in the grocery stores is gone, either spoiled or taken by survivors. Hunting with a gun tells everyone, including your enemies, where you are, and that's if you can find an animal to shoot every few days. Neither of us could effectively hunt with a bow."

He pursed his lips as if he hadn't thought of that.

I went on, "Ever been up near Camano Island?"

"Nope. I know it's north of Everett, right?"

"Yes. Not many people living up there in the old days. Probably fewer now. Clams, mussels, and crabs are all over. There are salmon, flounder, and dozens of other varieties of fish. Apples in the summer and fall on trees planted years ago. Cherries, blackberries, and raspberries, too. We can dry fruit and fish for eating in the winter."

He said, "I'm not sure it'll be as easy as you think, but overall, I like it."

"There might be others with the same idea," I said to temper his excitement. "Maybe we can join them."

He scowled, then growled, "Well, they can either welcome us or fight us. If they are smart, they'll not fight."

His use of the language hinted of more education that I'd given him credit for. Who says stuff like *they'll not fight* instead of *they won't fight*? The army is a funny place for isolated and diverse people to end up. I'd met soldiers who could barely read, while others were voracious in their consumption of the written word. More than a few had partial college educations, and there were graduates.

Some soldiers were using their military service to better

themselves and prepare for productive employment after discharges, electricians, mechanics, and even cooks. And there were more than a few slackers who didn't fit comfortably into the world outside the military—and barely fit into life in the army. The man walking behind might be any of those or a combination of them.

Grainger said, "Listen, we didn't get any sleep last night. Why don't you grab a few winks?"

"What about you?"

His eyes went to the trees overhead swaying in the morning breeze. He said, "I can't sleep yet. Remember this is the first time I've seen any of this in years. It's my first morning. It's not old hat like for you with three or four sunrises under your belt."

My eyes continued to search for newness and old things remembered, and my nose had come alive again. Thousands of smells had rushed at me over the last few days and each triggered memories.

I'd stepped in a pile of poo and remembered doing the same in a park while trying to impress a boy of eleven, while I was seven or eight. I'd done a cartwheel and my left foot made the squishy landing. Yes, he'd laughed himself silly and rushed off to tell his friends.

I said, "Okay, I understand. I'll sleep but you wake me if anything happens. I mean *anything*."

My eyes closed and I went to sleep, damp, chilly, and lying on a rocky surface. It was wonderful. As my father had told me, you have to suffer a little pain to appreciate the good things. Using that as a compass, I should feel ecstatic, and I did.

Grainger's hand shook my shoulder. His voice sounded a bit frustrated as if he'd tried waking me before. "Come on, wake up, Pen."

I groaned and opened my eyes to find him peering down at me, his face contorted in a combination of worry and excitement. "What is it?"

"Trackers. And a dog."

I bolted upright. My eyes went to the road and a flash of movement. The familiar blue material of the jackets and colorful flannel shirts at the neck and front told me the man was the militia, even at the distance. He moved down the left side of the road, his rifle held loosely in his left hand. His eyes darted from side to side, examining everything at once. There was no doubt he was nervous and watchful.

Since none of the earlier scouting parties had returned to Monroe, he had every reason to be wary. The second in line was the dog handler. It looked like a hound of some kind, maybe a bird dog from a long line of breeding. It moved as if directed only by its nose hugging the ground, which was probably true.

I was not as worried about the dog as before. Chances were, I'd left nothing with my scent for it to follow. It wouldn't present a danger unless it caught the scent of us, and we were far too distant for that to happen.

As my eyes took in the third person of the scouting group, my heart beat faster.

I must have made a sharp intake or a groan or some unconscious sound because Grainger spun on me. "What is it?"

"Uh," came from my mouth. My eyes never left the third in the group. "Have we talked about Sara? I don't think so."

"Sara? No, who's she?"

I lifted my rifle and the scope found her as if knowing it was where I wanted to look. Her walk was almost a waddle, her left hand cradled her belly. The smile on her face nearly sent a bullet her way.

"Sara betrayed us after we saved her."

"Why did she do that?" Grainger asked as he watched her walk closer.

"She is evil. Jealous. And she probably traded the information about the sanctuary for food and a place to live. Maybe all that is true. Maybe something else is."

"If we get away from here, you won't have to worry about her any longer."

I placed my hand on his shoulder and turned him to face me. In a voice that even scared me, I told him, "I'm not worried about her. She needs to worry about me because I'm going to kill her."

Chapter 18

"She's pregnant!" Grainger said, shocked at my statement about Sara. "You can't kill her."

I moved my twitchy finger from the trigger of my rifle. "That fact is all that is keeping her alive. For now."

"I don't understand," Grainger said heatedly, pulling his shoulder away from me as if whatever ailed me would transfer to him.

In return, I clawed him, my grip on his shoulder so tight he winced. "We rescued that girl from three men who kept her chained to a stump and used her as a sex toy. We killed them, gave her food and shelter, and treated her wounds. In return, she took off and went to Monroe and told the militia about us, the shelter, and probably Jake and Grace. They were beaten, tortured, and hung by the firehouse where their bodies will feed the insects and worms."

Grainger gulped.

I went on, "Now she is leading them right to where we met her. She knows the direction we came from, which is a mile or two away, down the same road. They will find the sealed door to the sanctuary without any problem, but she also knows about the mineshaft. She is leading them there."

"She's going to have a baby," Grainger muttered.

That didn't slow me down. "She is leading them to where they will kill and mutilate every single person you've seen in the last five years; except the ones she already had killed—and you and me. Think about it. Every person you have seen, talked to, or heard in five years will be dead in a few days."

"The baby is innocent," he said, eyes wide and horrified.

"And that is the only reason she is alive," I handed him my rifle and pointed to the scope. "Get a good look at her before she turns up that sideroad. I mean, get a look so you will recognize her in the future. In case I die, you will promise me right now that you will swear to kill her."

"If I don't?"

I pulled my nine-millimeter as casually as I might a pair of nail clippers as I shook my head. "I'm not going to shoot you now. If you don't give me your word, I'll make us stay here until they are done killing everyone in the sanctuary—and then I will make you go down there after the militia is done and see for yourself what they did."

Grainger was a soldier but not a fighter. Not really. He didn't honestly believe what Sara had done, or what was going to happen.

In his place, I wouldn't either.

She was near to the turnoff. Without the scope, I could see the glee in her smile. She had traded the lives of all of us for shelter and food. I couldn't kill the child inside her, but after it was born someone else could raise the baby. Sara was going to die.

I'd made a threat to Grainger. My hand held my pistol. He hadn't given his word that he would kill her, so that changed things. I scooted back from him until we were five or six feet apart.

"You won't kill me," he said.

"You're right."

"Then put that gun away."

"No. I won't kill you, but I'll shoot you in your left arm." The barrel of the gun lowed until it aimed just above his elbow.

"Why? Because I won't promise to kill a young woman with a baby?"

"Yes. Because of that. But I'm going to change your mind."

"With a gun pointed at me?"

"Because you know I probably cannot kill you, and you suspect I don't want to, but shooting you in your arm is different."

"Why?" He demanded.

I glanced to my left, far behind Sara and the dog and the two scouts. A group moved along the road, between fifty and a hundred militia. The three scouts were finding the way. Those behind us were going to kill everyone and steal everything of value the sanctuary had.

Grainger's eyes followed mine.

I said, "You and I are going to stay right here and listen to them shooting everyone. Maybe that will convince you."

"No . . ."

"Yes, it is happening. Today. This morning."

"We've got to stop them," he stood.

"Get down you silly ass. There is nothing we can do for them except revenge."

"We have guns."

"If it was two of them and two of us, we'd probably lose the firefight. They are trained and have survived by killing since the war began. But it's not two against two, it is two against a hundred. If you don't sit down, it's suicide."

He abruptly sat.

His head swiveled from me to the approaching army and back again. He said, "We should get out of here."

"Not yet."

"I'll promise to kill that girl—after she had her baby."

"You don't mean it."

Sara disappeared up the side road. The main body of the militia behind her approached. My mind calculated. Two miles to the sanctuary, I estimated. Maybe three, if we traveled along a blacktop road. I'd heard a person walks three or four miles an hour. They would reach the area in a half-hour, or a little later. They would probably spread out and begin a search. Another half-hour to find the mine entrance.

Shooting would begin in over an hour, probably less than two.

Grainger said, "Your warning to those below did some good. It convinced them to have the military break out their heavy weapons and M4s. They are supposed to guard the mine entrance."

"They should use explosives to close the mine shaft. Done

right, it would never get cleared."

"The militia will also have explosives, I'd think. Lots of heavy ordnance laying around in old military depots. Hell, they could drill holes in the door with hand tools and pipe gas down there to kill the people."

"Your point?" I snapped.

He kept his focus on the people walking on the road. "My point is that not only was the location a secret, but the *existence* of the sanctuary was also. Once the militia learned of it, an intense search was sure to follow. Now that they know where it is, there is no stopping them."

"I see," I said, and I did.

The main body turned at the sideroad and followed their scouts. I noticed several carried lanterns like those we had used for camping when my dad used to take us. They burned about any kind of oil.

Grainger said, "I'll promise to come back and try to kill that girl. We should go."

I still held the pistol. "No. You mean what you're saying. For now. What you don't have is a rage building inside you that will intensify as time goes on, instead of waning. You need to hate."

"Pen, that is not healthy."

"Not for Sara, it's not."

We sat in the quiet of a damp spring morning with the scent of evergreens in the air. A few geese flew north, their honks sounding both familiar and strange. The V formations fascinated me. A chipmunk darted to the top of a boulder and scolded us. When we didn't leave, he must have called his friend the crow to tell us a thing or two.

The crow sat on a low branch, watched us, then cawed.

We ignored it and the bird danced and raised its voice.

With the echo of the first shot, the crow wisely flew off in the opposite direction. Grainger looked at me as three more shots sounded.

A burst of steady gunfire sounded, almost as one steady sound.

"M4," Grainger said. Individual shots sounded, spaced at odd times. "Militia."

Two short bursts followed, and then more single shots. I could almost see the firefight in my mind. A few soldiers with automatic weapons either inside the mouth of the mine or near it. A hundred militia with mixed rifles getting into position behind tree trunks or boulders. The sanctuary soldiers hadn't fired a shot in years.

The single shots increased as more militia settled in. Another short burst of maybe ten bullets from an M4. Single shots answered.

We heard no more shots.

"It's over," Grainger said. "They will enter the mine shaft now."

"All your army buddies are now dead as well as anyone who helped protect the sanctuary."

His jaw was clenching and unclenching. His head tilted to hear more automatic weapons fire. There were none. We waited.

Grainger looked at me. He appeared angry. I put my gun back in its holster. It wouldn't be required. Neither of us moved.

A half-hour later, muffled gunshots sounded. A lot of them.

We stood as one and turned our backs to the sanctuary.

We had a long walk to Puget Sound ahead of us. There was no telling what lay between us and there. My mind went to work again. There may be worse places and people ahead. Hard to imagine, but possible.

I finally asked, "What are you thinking? That I'm a crazy woman?"

"No. You did what you had to. I understand that now."

"You didn't answer my question."

"In training, boot camp, we had an instructor that claimed he could hit a head-sized watermelon at four-hundred yards with an M4. That's four football fields."

"Why are you thinking about that?"

"He claimed they are accurate for the best shooters up to six hundred yards."

"Again, why is that important, now?" We were walking single file, me in the rear. I had to hurry to keep up, skipping a step now and then.

He hesitated. "The armory is not the only place where weapons and ammo are stored."

"I thought it was."

"There is a secondary armory, smaller and for use in emergencies when people can't get to the main one."

"If you're thinking of going back and getting a gun, forget it. They will tear the place apart and find everything."

"I don't think so. On the floor of the quarters where they put us, there is a steel grate. It looks like a ventilation duct underneath."

"They'll pull it up."

"Nope. Locked and no, there is no key. It's keyed to military biometrics, which means only me."

"Good try," I said, "but you need electricity to use that."

"It has capacitors and batteries to recharge them. Supposed to be foolproof."

I quit walking. "Are you crazy? You'd go back down there to get a rifle?"

He sat on a boulder, his chin on the upturned palms of his hands, elbows on his knees. He screwed up his face and finally looked at me. "Yes."

"Why?" The word slipped out before I could think of something better to say.

He pointed to my rifle. "That thing is pre-World-War 2 and was maybe used in the first. It looks impressive, but you only have four bullets. That's it. No way to get more. The scope is *maybe* accurate to a hundred yards if you take the time to sight it in."

"Okay, the M4 shoots straighter. Is that worth going back down there?"

"Shoots accurately three times as far, at least. It also weighs half as much." He paused and shrugged. "There is more. I've inventoried those M4s and know there are also suppressors and plenty of ammo."

"Enlighten me."

"If you fire that blunderbuss that you're lugging around, the shot will be heard in Monroe. Three to five miles, depending on terrain and a lot of other things. An M4 with a suppressor is silent at a hundred yards, often at a hundred feet in forests or heavy cover."

Even I could understand that. My active mind pictured the devastation and slaughter of the people in the sanctuary. I realized that in other circumstances, I would be one of them. "I'm not going back down there. Not for anything."

"I'll need someone to stand watch outside the mine. That's all."

The foul taste in my mouth couldn't be ignored. I spat. "Is a new gun worth that much to you?"

He hung his head instead of arguing.

"Tell me," I demanded. "What are you thinking right now?"

"I'm thinking that you and I are different kinds of people. You're willing to run away and find a place where you can live comfortably and eat fish every day. You're willing to let what happened here go away like fog evaporating on a sunny day. As long as you can be alive and comfortable, nothing else matters."

"There are two of us, Grainger. Just two still alive. There's a good chance I don't know a single person who is alive in the whole world. My single goal in life right now is to remain alive. Well, that and kill Sara, but to do that, I have to be alive."

Grainger sighed and closed his eyes. A hint of tears glistened at the corners of his eyes. His voice was softer than I'd ever heard. "I owe Jake. And Grace, and the men in my unit that died in the last few days. In more ways, than I can explain, I owe those others who accepted us into the sanctuary, because if not for them, chances are that I'd already been dead or degenerated into one of those militias in Monroe, or worse."

"Maybe in a few days, you'll feel differently." I knew it was the wrong thing to say as soon as the words left my mouth. Not that I didn't mean what I said, but just another instance of my outspoken manners upsetting people and how the message was delivered.

"I won't," he muttered defiantly.

"Listen, I should apologize for that crack. That was not what I meant to say."

He opened his eyes and scowled.

I went on, "You and I risked more to save those below far more than they ever did for us. It's time to head for the coast and figure out how to get something to eat and how to live the rest of our lives."

"With those guns and silencers, we could shoot something and not notify everyone within miles. The scopes will accurately pinpoint the targets. They could easily mean the difference between life and death."

"You're going to do it, aren't you? You're going to go down there in all that death and carnage."

He nodded.

"I'm not."

"I just want you to watch my back, but if you can't do that, I'll understand."

Chapter 19

There was no talking Grainger out of reentering the sanctuary. He was going with or without my help. I finally said, "Okay."

That didn't mean I agreed. I clamped my jaw shut and determined to do my best for him, then I would leave. He could go or stay.

He said, "We should go back and locate a defensive position for you. We're going to have to do this quickly, then put some distance between there and us, and somehow get some sleep for ourselves."

"I could sleep a week."

We stood and began the trek back. On the same hillside, we watched the last of the militia carry out sacks of food carried in sheets bundled over their shoulders as if they were a string of Levi-wearing Santas.

As if to help us know when it was safe to return to the sanctuary, a lone guard called out to one of them, "Are you the last?"

"That's me," he chuckled, "Always last."

"It's getting late. I got the word for everyone to return tonight. We'll be back tomorrow," the one who seemed in charge bellowed.

They walked away together. When the pair were out of sight, Grainger said, "That was nice of them. I would have hated to get down there and found a dozen or so still gathering plunder."

We were on the same ledge where our outdoor adventure

had started a few days ago. We'd watched the bear kill the first person I'd ever seen die. I situated myself behind the same boulders I'd used before and placed my spare pistol in easy reach, as was now a habit. Grainger had one of the three flashlights we'd left lying there, along with other miscellaneous stuff we hadn't thought we'd need again. I said, "Better take them all. Nothing worse than being in the dark."

He picked up the other two flashlights and stuck them in his waistband. "I'm not looking forward to this."

"Better now than it will be down there in two or three days."

"I suppose so," He said, avoiding the mention of the rotting bodies of everyone we knew. "If any of the militia come back, fire one rifle shot down the tunnel to warn me and run away as fast as you can. I'll try to catch up on the coast."

That was the extent of our plans. Simple. Direct.

In the twilight, he made his way down the hillside and I saw the flashlight turn on after he entered the mineshaft. The little slip of light made it easy to follow until he rounded the first corner. Sleep and exhaustion overwhelmed me. I could close my eyes, *just for a moment.* I shook my head violently. I'd almost fallen asleep. That put both of us in extreme danger. I stood, despite knowing that movement is the first thing people see. It was not yet full dark and the move dangerous.

On my feet, if I fell asleep, I'd stumble and fall, and wake. I berated myself for being weak. Worse, less than ten minutes had passed.

I didn't know how long it would take Grainger. At least, two hours to go down, locate the place he believed more weapons were kept, and return. I had no watch. Counting didn't help because I kept losing track of my count. My feet walked me along the ridge, pacing if you will. It's hard to pace in the dark because of stumbling. It should be called p-stumbling. Or stumble-pacing.

Those sorts of thoughts indicated how tired and confused I was. I fought to remain upright and awake. An hour passed. Then another. Or maybe instead of two hours, it had only been a half-hour. There was no way to tell.

As I finished my pacing in one direction and turned, I

jerked myself awake. There was movement out on the road.

It might be a deer.

It was not. It was a man or woman edging closer and as the person moved, enough light struck to tell me it was human. One.

I searched the darkness for another. There didn't seem to be more. Had they left a lone watchman? Or sent one person back to keep an eye on the mine entrance? No matter, we were not alone. Not anymore.

Grainger had left me orders to fire one shot into the mine. If two hours had passed and I did that, he might be returning any moment. The ricochet of the bullet might hit him. The newcomer moved slowly, carefully. I tracked his movements and remained perfectly still except to move the barrel of my rifle to aim at the intruder instead of the mine. It moved like a man, but that might be my imagination. Any thought of sleep fled, replaced by fear.

He or she came to an abrupt halt. Maybe there had been a sound from inside the mine. Perhaps a flash of light. Something. I held my breath.

My finger moved to the trigger. Eighty yards away, a vague target the size of a man stood out. The starlight and moonlight provided just enough illumination to use the scope. My shot would be in the center of the dark shape, my second shot, too. If I missed with both, I'd shoot the other two remaining bullets and abandon the rifle because of not ammunition.

Moving myself closer would give me a shot I couldn't miss. It would also tip off the person because I couldn't even move quietly during daylight. Hell, I couldn't walk without tripping on blacktop every dozen steps. I remained where I was and waited, all thoughts of sleep gone.

The figure below had blended in with the shadows and disappeared.

Which presented me with choices. Ones I didn't like. The obvious was the militia had sent someone back to watch the sanctuary and probably be on the lookout for me. They didn't know about Grainger. It was me they were after.

The second, an idea almost equally obvious was that someone living in the nearby area and who was not associated with the militia came to investigate all the gunfire. That person was innocent of the slaughter below—but still may present a danger to us. He or she might shoot Grainger as he emerged. Or not.

Thus, my choices. If it was someone sent by the militia, I should shoot. If not, killing an innocent would haunt me.

I decided to wait. Hopefully, the intruder would do something to indicate his intentions. My eyes and ears strained.

A flicker of light came from the depths of the mine. It had to be Grainger.

In the soft night sounds of the forest, a series of four soft metal-on-metal clicks sounded. The bolt of a rifle inserting a shell into the firing chamber. That readied the rifle below to kill.

I searched without the scope again and failed to find the shooter. I peered into the scope and carefully moved it about, failing to locate the person again and again. From the side of my vision, the flickering light in the mine appeared brighter.

The action of the bolt had made my choice and if I located the person below, I'd shoot. My rifle could be heard as much as five miles away, Grainger had told me. The bullets were as large as my little finger. However, the nine-millimeter bullets in my pistol were stubby little things, a third the size. While we had not discussed how far the sound of them carried, I'd guess it was far less.

I took my spare pistol and aimed at a spot a few feet above the mine shaft but didn't fire. Not yet. I kept my attention on the spot where I'd last seen movement in the shadows.

The flickering light grew more regular, and brighter. Reflected light off stone walls. When the first flash of direct light from the flashlight came, I fired my pistol with my left hand, while watching below.

Almost instantly, a shot came, not aimed at Grainger as expected, but at me!

It struck well below my location as if it was a snapped shot, one fired in reaction to mine. The flash told me where the shooter was. I used the scope and found a dark figure prone, scooting quickly under cover in the shadows. I fired.

The recoil slammed into my shoulder. The sound was that of a cannon. The militia in Monroe would have heard it. If there was militia in Everett, twenty miles away, they may have heard it. My ears rang. My eyes squinted into the scope.

The figure lay still, half in shadow, half dim light, unmoving.

"Grainger, come on out," I called softly. My eyes searched for others. Found none. "I think there was only one."

He didn't use the flashlight. Grainger darted from the mouth of the mine to the nearest trees and paused. He sprinted up the hill and dived behind a stump. Nobody fired at him. He moved to his right, then dashed to a small hill and settled in behind.

I saw nothing.

He finally rushed up the side of the hill in my direction and disappeared in the heavy underbrush. I climbed to my feet and moved to meet him, my feet placed carefully for each tentative step.

"Who was it?" he asked.

"I don't know. I think it was a man. One. He had a bolt-action rifle, and he inserted a shell when you were coming out. I shot him."

"How long had he been there?"

"Half-hour."

He reached out, took my rifle, and placed it against a nearby tree, standing, the barrel leaning on the bark. He handed me a replacement, half the weight and far smaller. "I'd like to go see who it was, but that's unimportant right now. We've got to get out of here."

"Okay," I said with a voice that quavered. I'd just shot a person. Killed a person. It may have been a friend, a lawman, or anyone else. I didn't want to know, just in case, it was an innocent. I'd done what I needed to do. Grainger had been safe.

The dead person had sealed his fate when he loaded the shell into his rifle. Until then, I'd have waited until the situation developed. When he fired at me, reflexes had taken over. It was not an innocent, in that regard.

My hands were shaking. They were not listening to my head.

Grainger handed me a backpack and helped me put it on. It was too loose, but little things like adjusting it to fit would wait. It had probably ten pounds inside, maybe more. I used the sling of the rifle to fit it over my shoulder as I followed Grainger back up the same hill we'd traveled earlier.

"Was it bad?" I whispered.

He pushed through the brush and low-hanging branches, not even trying to avoid them or hide our trail. "Worse than you can imagine."

That was enough talk. We located the highway but instead of crossing it, we moved parallel, keeping to the higher ridges and hills. Two streams and probably two miles were behind us when he pointed ahead. "Up there."

The moon, or half of it, was out. *Up there*, where he pointed, stood a hill taller than most. The trees that had once been there having either been logged or a fire had burned them. The peak was bald.

Tiredness kept me from asking why we wanted to climb what looked like a thousand feet of the steep mountain. I put my head down, recovered from several trips without falling, and hardly slowed Grainger up. He was tired, too. But he was the kind of soldier that once had a goal, refused to quit. He reminded me of brave soldiers in world war two movies set in the Pacific islands. Marines. No matter the odds, they kept moving ahead.

We walked and stumbled for another couple of hours. Always upward. The trees ended abruptly. It had been a recent fire that left the top of the mountain clear of trees. Blackened stumps and fallen trees made progress almost impossible. We kept moving.

Grainger pulled to a stop. "Here."

That was the word I wanted. I sat heavily. He fell to his knees and leaned closer as he said. "We left a trail a blind tracker could follow."

"Couldn't be helped," I panted. "Right now, I think moving fast is more important. Besides, neither of us knows how to hide our trail, not from a good tracker."

He smiled without humor. "I want them to see how bad we are at this. Instead of going slow and being careful, they're going to think we panicked and ran."

"Which is pretty much what we did," I managed to slip into the conversation.

"So, they will chase us at full speed, to make sure we don't get away."

"This is a good plan?"

"It is. Daylight will be here soon. They will come across that valley down there and up the side of this hill, hopefully, without looking ahead or anticipating an ambush."

I saw his idea and approved it. My breathing had slowed, and my brain went back to work. It was much like the ambush Gerry and I had done, but with one huge difference. We now had the M4s. When the enemies were within a hundred yards, we could pick them off as easily as shooting spinning targets at a carnival.

Besides easily killing people, the difference was the *possession* of the M4s. Light, plenty of ammo, accurate, almost indestructible. What person alive in a post-holocaust world wouldn't want one? *That was the problem.*

Once the idea entered my head, it remained. Anyone, Monroe militia, civilian, hunter, raider, or outlaw, that saw our weapons instantly became an enemy because each would think or act on how they could possess our weapons. Our weapons, in any gunfight, could mean the difference in survival or not. The problem was that all those other people understood that— probably better than me.

We didn't have to fight them. If a hunter hid in the forest and we slunk past, they would recognize our weapons. Some, maybe not all, would follow us. Sneak up on us at night, kill us and steal the guns. Or they would set up their ambushes and kill both of us before we knew we were in danger.

Having finally sorted that out in my mind, there remained the problem of how to tell Grainger he had risked his life and gone into the sanctuary to see terrible things he couldn't ever forget, but the reward in the form of better guns placed our lives in far more danger than old rifles that were falling apart. Perhaps it was time for me to use tact. Step lightly instead of stomping on the subject.

He said, "Something is wrong."

"Out there?" I asked, searching the horizon for danger.

"Not there. With you."

I tried to look innocent and failed.

"What's on your mind, Pen? Don't try to deny it, I've been watching your face and eyes."

No use in not talking about it. "It's the M4s."

"You think I should have taken more? No worries. I locked the compartment again, and nobody is likely to find it. We have ten more and thousands of rounds of ammo down there, waiting."

He was so happy and proud. I shifted my gaze to the far end of the meadow. A hint of movement had drawn my attention but now nothing out there was to be seen. I glanced back. "Every soldier, hunter, and survivor of the war wants our rifles. They will kill for them."

I cringed at the expected reaction. His face solidified and his eyes narrowed dangerously. He nodded slowly. "You're right."

"I am? We're getting rid of them?"

"Not so fast. Let's think about it for a while. He held his M4 in front of himself and examined it as if for the first time.

"What are you thinking?"

He pointed to the round handle projecting downward from the barrel in front of the magazine, a distinctive design. "This can be removed. A wood stock from an old rifle, even one carved from soft wood like pine, could be fitted instead of the extendable one."

I liked where the conversation was going. "Even an old rag or canvas tube sewed around the front stock would change the appearance. Maybe a few flat pieces of wood held on with some black electrical tape if we can find some. Enough to change the general appearance."

In my mind, I pictured the nasty-yet-familiar outline and melded it slightly with the exterior modifications. The odd little scope couldn't be changed without defeating its purpose. But Grainger was right. A two-by-four and a few hand tools and we could change the outline of the M4 into a seemingly homemade beast nobody would think twice about wanting. A piece of canvas or bedspread, a needle and thread, and an evening beside a fire with the tools would be enough to begin the transformation.

It might work.

He pursed his lips and instead of snarling at me as I'd expected, said, "Nice catch, Pen. You may have just saved our lives."

I was still congratulating myself when my eye caught movement near the same place again. "I saw something."

As if the gods of the afterworld intended to slap me down for being so pleased with myself, a deer broke from cover and bounded in our direction. I relaxed. It was just a deer.

Grainger hissed, "Don't move."

Five or six birds took flight from a still-standing dead tree in the same area.

Grainger pulled me slowly downward until we were shielded by the log we'd been sitting on. It had fallen in a windstorm and the top of it hung in the crotch of another tree. Leaving one end suspended from the ground. We eased back under it, and knelt, our rifles braced on the top edge of the log, our eyes focused on the powerful scopes and the far end of the meadow that filled the valley.

"I see two," Grainger said.

"One," I added. "No, there are two more over near that big fir."

"I see your one."

They waited as if expecting us to be watching. Finally, after almost a half-hour, one of the pair advanced. He was the rabbit. His job was to draw fire so the others would locate us, and he knew it. At first, he stood upright and walked naturally, if a little stiff. He must have estimated the time it would take for a rifleman to spot, aim, and ready himself.

The rabbit dived to one side into the tall grass. He didn't move.

After a couple of minutes, he stood and ran directly at us before diving again. His next appearance took him off to the right where a small stand of trees hid him. I'd forgotten about the other two. When I looked, they were gone.

Damn.

I must have grunted it out loud. Grainger seemed to

understand and said, "They moved left."

The rabbit went right and had drawn my attention while the others moved to their left. As intended, I'd fallen for it. They were far better at the game we played than me. "Tell me what to do."

"You follow the one on our right, and I'll follow the other two. Do not lose him."

"I already have." It was better to tell the truth. Far better.

Grainger said, "Find him."

Ten minutes went past. Twenty. Then, at the very edge of my vision and much closer to us than expected, I saw him. "Got my eyes on him."

He was crouched over, his rifle held in both hands in front of him, moving from one patch of cover to another in darts and dashes. He moved while on the ground, never appearing where he'd disappeared. I wanted to look at the other two, but resisted the temptation.

Grainger said softly, "Careful. We're at the extreme distance their weapons."

What that said to me sounded more like, *they're getting close enough to kill us*. My heart pounded. I wanted to turn and run. Doing so would only mean they would catch up with us later, and probably to their advantage.

Grainger didn't turn to look at me as he spoke, "I need to ask you something."

"Ask away."

"Can you think of that man as a target? Or that he is trying to kill you and within a few minutes one of you dies?"

"I'm thinking that, now. So what?"

He harrumphed a crude laugh. "Can you shoot him? I don't mean, *can,* but *will* you? No warning. No call to surrender or any of that nonsense? Just aim and pull the trigger. Can you do it?"

I gritted my teeth. "I can and will. I already did it back at the mine, remember?"

"Okay, okay. Calm down. When you think you have a clear shot, take it. Don't hesitate. Tell me right away if you think you got a hit."

"What are you going to do?"

"When you fire, I will too. Give me a three-two-one, if you can."

Instead of thinking of killing a man in cold blood, I thought of what that man out there would do to me if he caught up with us. I thought that it takes two to fight, and if he would go back to wherever he came from, we wouldn't be doing this. He was hunting me, not the other way around. In other words, it was his fault.

He shifted positions again. It had become a pattern. Leap up, run twenty steps, and dive. Roll over a few times, and maybe crawl ahead a few yards, then repeat. I watched and counted to myself. On thirty, he leaped up right where I expected and charged, angling to his right. He dived.

On thirty again, he appeared where I expected, running to his left and diving. I moved the barrel slightly, to where I believed he would appear. He would run right this time. His head came into view.

"Three, two, one." He stood. I fired. He spun as he fell. "I think . . ."

Three shots sounded from Grager, equally spaced, about a second between them. "Stay where you are."

We hadn't put the silencers on the rifles. We should have. The shots were loud, like cracks of thunder in a spring storm. Instead of thinking about the man I'd probably shot, I concentrated on yelling at Grainger for not putting the silencers on the M4s. It's things like that he is supposed to know.

My ears were ringing. I turned to him.

He was still in position, his eye to his scope, examining the far edge of the meadow—which is what I should have been doing. I put my eye to the scope and slowly moved my field of sight from left to right, then back again. "I don't see anyone else."

"Doesn't mean they aren't there," he said evenly.

I kept looking. A slow twenty minutes passed. He said, "We should pull back."

"Are we going to see if we killed them?"

He gave me one of those looks you give to people when they say something really stupid. Trying to sound mature in the fact that dead or alive, I'd just shot a man, I said, "I'll follow you."

"Good enough." Grainger turned and started up what little remained of the hill, me right at his heels. We moved steadily, if not fast. As we reached the peak, the view revealed the small city of Monroe in the background, the river as the dividing line, and the industrial-looking walls of the prison closer to us.

He said, "Feel any need to go into the city?"

Chapter 20

Go into Monroe? That was what he asked. Did I feel a *need* to go there? The short answer was no. No *need*, no *desire*. My immediate *want* was to put as much distance between the city and myself as possible. "Let's head for the coast."

"Due west?"

"West and a little north."

We moved down the hill and into the flatter lands that had once been pastures and farms. Grainger didn't seem able to let it go. "You have family in Monroe, right?"

"I did, before. If any are alive, I doubt they live there. What about you? Family near here?"

"Brought up back east. Not married, so nobody."

I felt I owed him an explanation if only a brief one. "What little family I had wouldn't have survived what I see there now. They may have escaped to somewhere safe, but there is no way for me to know where that might be, and realistically, there is not much chance of that."

"Okay, I understand that. Why go west?"

"Puget Sound. In a few days when our supplies run out, and we will have to gather enough food every day. Gerry came up with the idea of the coast. Eating fish might get boring after a while, but that's better than not eating for a week or two at a time. Gerry felt we could find crabs, clams, and fish to supplement our diet. Berries and fruit in the summer."

"Others might have the same idea. Probably will. It might

be crowded."

"I'm open to a better plan," I snapped. Grainger had a habit of contradicting everything I said. It was getting old already.

He moved on without answering. We spotted the remains of a house ahead, the roof nonexistent. Only the walls remained. The missing or broken windows seemed like eyes that watched us. A barn or large garage had once stood beside it. A few of the blackened timbers stood upright like fingers pointing into the sky.

We'd crossed open fields that had been pasture or used for crops. Now there were small trees here and there, none over eight feet tall with trunks not as large as my wrist, however, in a few more years, the vegetation would take over the whole area and the forest would return as if people had never existed.

Grainger took us on a wide circle around the house before moving in closer. It appeared that nobody had been there for months, or longer. No traps or ambushes waited. The missing roof had allowed water to enter. The foundation of the basement contained it like a shallow pool and a few items floated in the turbid water.

Aluminum cans and various plastic items gathered at one edge or rested on debris coated with brown slime below the surface. Grainger read my mind. "Nothing here for us."

That was not entirely true. The aluminum cans could act as cups for drinking or boiling water. A little imagination revealed dozens of useful items. Assuming they would be available later, I said nothing, which seemed to be my model of operation lately. We moved on. I made it a practice to look quickly behind us, thinking that if Grainger watched where we were going, I should make certain nobody followed. He caught me doing it and gave me a silent thumbs up.

We were still well away from what had been population centers. Seattle lay to the south probably twenty miles and Everett due west maybe ten. I would avoid both. Hopefully, Grainger agreed.

A single shot sounded. We paused as it echoed.

I said, "Probably a hunter. One shot means he hit his target."

Grainger nodded. "I've heard that said. It might also mean a tracker had found our trail and is calling others to join in the hunt."

"Well, aren't you a bowl of cheer?" Despite my words, I knew he was correct. "What do we do now?"

"Bypass as much civilization, or what passes for it. We should be coming up to highway nine before long, later today or early tomorrow. We'll follow the old Snohomish Monroe road until just before we get to the town of Snohomish. I think we should follow Highway nine north fifteen or twenty miles before turning west to the coast."

"Avoiding all people along the way? I like that."

He kept looking behind as if I wasn't doing it often enough. Either that, or he was far more scared than I'd believed. We found the old highway shortly after that. There were signs of travel on it. While the pavement had cracked and pieces were uptilted, in the level areas two or three paths wound their way along it. There were farms, or what had been farms, but nothing looked like anyone presently worked them.

We didn't venture out on the roadway itself. A path paralleled the road and it looked like another was on the other side. The chances of meeting someone coming the other way seemed too great to remain where we were. Grainger pointed at the ground. "Horses."

The clear impressions of horseshoes instantly indicated a few things, none of which seemed welcome. People rode horses. That implied they did it with impunity as if they had no fear of exposing themselves from high up on the animal's back. That said there were "rulers" in the area. Rulers who had the skills to work iron into metal shoes for horses and ride them without fear.

While none of that specifically indicated the people riding horses were after us, it was unsettling to see them. I'd grown used to the idea that society had regressed to the stone age, and now that appeared untrue. It brought up the idea of what else had I been so wrong about.

Those clues in the mud also revealed who the militia in Monroe might fear. Horsemen versus militia. It was a natural leap of conclusion, likely to be completely wrong. But maybe not.

I was cold, wet, and tired. My anger centered on one item and that affected all thought processes. "Grainger, are we ever going to be able to build a fire and get warm?"

"Smoke tells the world where we are."

"I don't like this world we're in."

"Don't talk like that."

I was not a child to be shushed. "We should move off the road further. Just keep it in sight every now and then."

For once Grainger didn't have anything to say or add. It felt as if I'd won something as he angled away from the road. It was the old road that went west to Snohomish, a winding strip of blacktop that had seen better days. I looked over my shoulder again as if fearing a small army had managed to sneak up on us.

The land was either flat or small rolling hills. Lord Hill Park rose on our left, flat floodplains to our right. Somewhere far to our left, a mile or two, flowed the Snohomish River. The forest grew right up to the pavement and sometimes all the way across. Dirt coated all of it, and puddles of standing water were common.

Grainger finally said, "If we cross the road, we might find a sheltered place inside the forest over there. Lots of trails and walkways, or there used to be. That was a park for hiking trails."

Ahead, to our right, were the remains of more farms and pastureland. I wondered where the horses lived. My mind centered far more on the horses than the owners. "Hey, if we stole a couple of horses, we could make better time."

He grumbled but changed directions to take us across the road and away from the horses, as he'd suggested.

"I'm serious," I persisted, struggling to keep up.

He entered the thick underbrush and paused in a small clearing, where he sat on an outcrop of granite, leaving me no place to sit but in the wet grass. I sat. The clearing was perhaps twenty feet across, deep enough in the forest we couldn't see out, and therefore nobody could see us. We'd walked about a quarter of a mile, so even our voices couldn't be heard, unless others were living or camping nearby.

As I tried to sort things out, Grainger spoke as if he was a teacher and I was a third-grader, "Stealing horses sounds romantic but it's the last thing we want to do. They would leave tracks anyone could follow. The owners will have other horses. I don't think we could get more than a few miles before they would catch up with us or others would kill us and take the horses."

I crossed my arms over my chest and scowled. Yes, I must have looked bratty.

He did much the same, his mind made up.

I said, "You are making all the decisions."

"I guess I am if you say so."

"I don't like that," I said, expecting him to relent and give me a little respect.

"If you like," he began apologetically, "we can divide what little we have and go our separate ways."

It sounded like he was dumping our relationship. An old boyfriend had used almost the same words and tone as he split up with me: Divide our things and go our separate ways. If I didn't know better, I'd think I was being dumped again. But there was more. I became suspicious of Grainger in a way that hadn't been there earlier.

It seemed more than just exhaustion. "What's this all about?"

"You."

"Explain."

He inhaled deeply and expelled it all before saying, "You started all this, Pen. Your actions got everyone in the sanctuary killed when it was only you that was supposed to die."

"Well, I'm sorry that I stayed alive if that makes you feel better. Or maybe they should have fought harder."

"No, that all came out wrong, Penelope. There is something I didn't tell you. When I went down there in the tunnels to get the rifles, everything was missing from the armory. Stripped bare. Dozens of rifles, thousands of rounds of ammo. Everything."

"You expected that."

"True. What I didn't expect was that the door hadn't been blown open with explosives or forced open. Somebody opened it for them."

That didn't make sense. Well, maybe it did. There were only a few people that had the codes to the door and one of them must have been tortured to tell the invaders. I said so, trying to keep the snark from my tone.

He shook his head. "No. How would they even know who to torture? Besides, there was no time for them to do that. They were in right away and out within a few hours."

"Then, what happened?"

"Almost everyone down there had been gathered into the eating hall and killed. One big killing floor. Oh, there were a few others on the hallways, but not many."

"Keep talking." I could see from his face that there was more unsaid.

"They were rounded up and put in there. Six were missing."

"Missing? You didn't look everywhere. You didn't have time to count everyone. They might have hidden or been killed somewhere else. And you can account for six easily. The five of us that originally escaped, and you."

"Six others. Not us. Besides, that doesn't explain the open lock on the door to the armory and the same for the locked doors to the supplies. All had been opened, not forced. Those raiders knew the codes."

I found myself on my feet. "You don't think I had anything to do with it, do you?"

"There were five of you that escaped and had time to make contact with the militia. Only the five of you had time to make a deal with them."

My fist was balled, but I managed to hold onto my reactions enough to snarl, "You are a real dumb-ass. Grace, Gerry, Danny, and I, were the scrubs down there for five years. Do you think any of us had the security codes for any locked door to food supplies or ammunition and guns? Do you think they would have trusted any of us with them? We were slaves."

"You didn't mention your old boyfriend, Jake."

"Jake was tortured and hung by the militia. They cut his fingers off. He didn't make any deals with them and anyhow, there was no time for them to torture him enough to make him talk. Besides, he wouldn't have had the security codes for the doors to the supply rooms, even if he did have the one for the armory. None of the rest of us had any codes."

Grainger seemed to deflate.

I said, "That was a stupid idea, and it was even stupider for you to say it out loud without thinking."

"I guess so."

I sat again but refused to look directly at him. I might never do so. Maybe I should take him up on his idea and split up. He was the only other person to survive, except for myself. My fake trial had caused the death of everyone in the sanctuary except the one that was supposed to die. And Grainger. And if he kept making stupid comments, he might not last long. I felt like shooting him where he sat.

I said, "Listen, you're free to go. Alone."

"Nowhere to go and it sounds like your plan to eat fish for the next thirty years is better than any I have."

I knew it was time to shut up. While we didn't seem to agree on many things, surviving on my own became far more precarious without him than with him. Being stubborn and headstrong has advantages—and detractions. If we split up, my chances of living another week severely decreased.

That didn't mean I had to like it. Grainger had some good points, not the least his military experience. He knew how to use his weapons and how to hunt. My immediate future depended on him. I'd work to change my limitations. We probably wouldn't be together for the full thirty years he'd suggested.

"I'm sorry," I told him. Right now, I needed him. Hopefully, he felt he needed me.

As my voice sounded, he leaped to his feet, startling me. My apology couldn't be that upsetting. He spun away and looked at the trees behind us. He grabbed for his rifle.

"What is it?" I asked, suddenly as scared as he looked.

The three shots that killed him seemed to come from three directions. As he fell, militia emerged from the underbrush and moved forward, at least five of them. All held rifles. All were pointed at me.

My last friend in the world was as dead as my insides felt.

We were never going to catch fish and live peacefully. My eyes refused to look at Grainger.

One man advancing with a rifle pointed at me shouted, "Don't reach for your weapon!"

Chapter 21

I remained sitting on the wet ground, in shock. Grainger was dead at my feet. That made everyone I had known in the last five years dead.

"That's her," one man growled.

"Tie her up," another ordered.

The initial five militia moved forward as more emerged from the forest, until nine faced me, standing in a round semi-circle. All held weapons, most rifles, but a few pointed handguns loosely in my direction. All eyes were on me as if poor Grainger had never existed.

One pulled me to my feet, ignoring my weak knees. While he held me upright, another reached around from behind and pulled my hands and arms behind. Before I thought to protest, I had been tied, my weapons removed, and a man slapped my face with his open hand.

It stung but didn't hurt.

My eyes went to Grainger again. He might be the lucky one of the two of us. Any fight that had been in me dissolved. I was too tired to fight anymore. Too dejected.

A middle-aged woman who had the shoulders and bulk of a linebacker moved to stand in front of me. She wore a heavy outer coat, stained and muddy. It looked waterproof, a gray-green color that blended in well with the trees. She might be thirty, or forty, it was impossible to tell. She asked softly, which surprised me, "Your name?"

Who cared about that? I could give her any name I wanted

and there was nobody alive to refute it.

"Pen. Short for Penelope." Yes, force of habit and I didn't see any advantage in lying.

She turned to face the ring of others as if to refute my thinking. "It's her. Todd, you and Mark take off and carry the news to Chance. We'll spend the night here and leave at dawn."

Two of the men stepped away from the group and melted silently into the forest. The woman then said to the rest as if she was used to giving them orders and they were used to obeying, "Make camp here. Get a fire going and set out guards."

There could be no doubt she was in charge, or that the others respected her. While one remained standing a dozen feet away with a revolver pointed at my middle, the others broke away and started gathering wood. In minutes, a pile of broken limbs grew to waist high. Bedrolls were spread. All done silently. The fire burned, small and almost smokeless. Watches for the night were agreed upon.

These people knew what they were doing.

I slipped to the ground and waited. When I turned at the approach of someone behind, I realized Grainger's body was no longer lying there beside me. It had been moved while my mind had quit on me. I looked up at the woman who seemed in charge. "Why didn't you shoot me too?"

"Orders."

Orders? What the hell did that mean? I would have preferred to be dead. My mind leaped to the bruises and cuts Jake and Grace had on their bodies, injuries before they were hung. My future didn't look great. If we went near a cliff, I might throw myself over, if I found the nerve.

"What do you mean by orders?" I asked.

"We were told to bring you in alive. That's all I know." Her scowl told me she didn't have more to say, and my last question had irritated her. I watched the others gather near the small fire and reach into pockets or bags and draw out handfuls of food, dried meat, fruit, and nuts, from the looks of the granular concoctions. None offered me any.

My stomach growled a time or two. I changed positions and found a place to put my head. The cold seeped through my clothing but my depression and exhaustion prevented me from suffering. The last few days, and lack of sleep, had worn me out, mentally and physically. I passed out.

A foot shoving my shoulder woke me. The cold gray of morning greeted me like the village executioner five hundred years ago, in the same way, funerals are always held on rainy days in the movies. It foretold what to expect.

"On your feet," the man growled.

The others were awake and eating as they folded their bedrolls or stuffed them in backpacks. Talking was kept to a minimum and so soft I heard little of the actual words. They were not happy, nor unhappy. Just people doing their jobs. All were dressed in new-appearing jeans and long sleeve flannel shirts, all different colors, all plaid patterns.

Beyond that, they were individuals. Different boots, although all wore boots of one sort or another, different rifles, most wore nine-millimeter semi-automatics of the same manufacturer on their hips. All that indicated they drew much of their supplies from the same place. They were the Monroe Militia, but they were the worker-bees. I suspected many were ex-cons from the penitentiary, and the exposed tattoos suggested I was right, but you can't go by that anymore. Still, someone else was running things.

Unless I misunderstood, which was entirely possible, I would meet the leader, or leaders later today. Again, nobody offered me a handful of their food. One was tall and glanced my way. That reminded me of Jake. Could that have been only four or five days ago that we'd escaped?

I rolled and attempted to get to my feet without assistance. With my hands tied behind my back and cramped muscles, I failed. I stumbled back to my knees. The linebacker of a woman strode to me and pulled me to my feet. If I hadn't wanted to stand, it was too bad because her hands on my arms demanded it.

Also surprising, she pulled me to one side, behind a few low shrubs, and unfastened my pants, and pulled them down from behind. I didn't hesitate. I squatted and took care of business.

On my feet again, I asked, "Breakfast?"

She was full of surprises. "Later. No way for you to eat without hands and we're not untying you for any reason. Our intel says you've killed a dozen of us." She barked at a nearby man, "Tyler, you still got that piece of rope on you?"

"In my backpack."

"Get it and tie it to her wrists. You get the honor of holding her leash all the way back."

He was digging in his pack and came up with a long, coiled rope about a quarter of an inch thick. He said sourly, "Gee, thanks."

Still, I noticed that he smiled as he said it. That respect thing for the woman again. If he complained, I had the feeling she might shoot him between his eyes without missing a beat.

We started walking. I, of course, walked ten steps ahead of Tyler. He tied the other end to his wrist and kept the slack from dragging the ground as he followed me.

When we reached the pavement again, I noticed one of the reasons it looked so strange. Not only were chunks upended for whatever reason, and grass and shrubs grew haphazardly, but for the first time, I realized how narrow it was. The dirt at the sides accumulated and plants took hold there. The road remaining was barely wide enough for one car.

However, there were twin ruts. Wagons, not cars, still used it. Wagon transporting food from farms, I'd bet.

I saw an old hoofprint that seemed to confirm my idea, but instead of feeling cheered, I almost vomited. It was the first time I had thought of Grainger today. He and I had discovered hoofprints only yesterday and today I didn't even think of him.

My clothing was damp. More than damp, it was wet and cold. My mind acted sluggishly. Facts didn't seem to connect.

"Faster," Tyler growled.

"Or what?" I heard my voice. "You've got orders to keep me alive, remember?"

The linebacker-woman chuckled and called to me, "Yup, orders to bring you in alive, but they didn't say how much damage we can do to you on the way, Missy Penelope."

A couple of militia soldiers chuckled dryly but I got the idea they wanted to return home, get on dry clothing, and eat a warm meal. A couple eyed me as if I was a raw steak and they were starving. I'd seen men look at women like that. It scared me.

But it didn't slow down my angry mouth. I called out, "Anybody here knows any good stories they can tell while we're out for this walk?"

The linebacker turned and flashed a grin in my direction. She said, "When I was locked up, I had a cellmate a lot like you. She died in less than a month. Too bad. I enjoyed her tales—most of the time."

I didn't believe for a moment the cellmate was executed. I did believe my captor had killed her. My tongue decided to take a rest.

The Monroe skyline, what there was of it, and the familiar metal bridge I'd crossed a hundred times in earlier years, came into view. I trudged along, now wanting to arrive and afraid to move slower for fear of being beaten.

I glanced up at the blue sky in awe, now that the fog had lifted. Blue skies in Washington are like nowhere else and worth the wait. The beautiful day seemed to affect the rest of the militia escorting me. A few joked. Others smiled.

I had nothing to joke or smile about.

Three guards were standing at the end of the bridge. One stood a head taller than the others. Prison tats rose up his neck like they were beasts trying to escape from inside his shirt. He grinned with wide yellow teeth. One in the front was missing and ruined what might have been an engaging smile.

Even under his coat and shirt, his massive chest strained the zipper to bursting dimensions. A weightlifter, I told myself. Prisoners in penitentiaries often have the time to work on their upper bodies because they have little else to do. He came forward and motioned for my escort to untie his wrist. The giant took the end of the rope and pointed across the bridge with his left hand.

We walked ahead of the others, who were now oddly quiet. The few on the street glanced our way. Most ignored us after that initial brief acknowledgment. We moved down the main street in the old section of town, then turned in the direction of the firehouse, not a good sign.

One woman whispered to another, "That's her."

We arrived at the front and walked inside the bay where the firetrucks used to be. There were blankets hung from ropes strung across the floor, a fire pit in the center with a pile of split wood that must have been half a cord. People sat in folding or lawn chairs. Some were eating, others already drinking, and most smoked. The room reeked of weed.

The once polished floor was littered with refuse. It smelled awful, worse than most sewers. However, we didn't pause. My escort must have expected the stench because none made a mention of it. We moved up a set of concrete stairs to what had been the administrative offices, kitchen, common room, and sleeping areas. It smelled far better, if only because a filthy man had a small fire burning in the sink and was roasting what looked like a couple of rabbits. A haze of greasy smoke filled the area.

My tall escort pushed me through a door and into an office, probably one that had belonged to the fire chief at one time. Inside were five people, three sitting on a sofa, one in a recliner, and one in an office chair with his feet propped up on his desk. Only a small amount of light filtered through a small window.

I was yanked to a stop in the center. Nobody spoke. My eyes adjusted to the dim light and the features of the people became defined.

"Hello, Penelope," a familiar voice said from the sofa.

Chapter 22

I started at the mention of my name. It came from the sofa and I spun to face my old nemesis, Witch Hazel, who I'd last seen acting as the head judge for my trial.

"You," I spat with all the venom possible. "You're alive?"

She smiled sweetly, "We find ourselves in familiar circumstances as the last time we met, you a prisoner and I again have the power of your life and death in my hands."

Words wanted to tumble from my mouth, so many that only gibberish would emerge. Instead, I clenched my teeth and waited. She couldn't help gloating and wouldn't be silent for long.

She said, "And then, there were two. I think that comes from an old book, although there are more than two of us, you get my meaning."

That information came as a shock. Suddenly, I understood part of what had happened. I scowled. "You gave them the combinations."

"In return for the lives of the most important people in the sanctuary. Surely, you can see that."

I felt my stomach turn and fought to keep from vomiting. If I felt it coming up, I would face her. "Those who died, would they agree who was most important?"

The man with his feet on the desk laughed. Two others belatedly joined, as if to please him. When he finished with the guffaws, he said, "Got some balls on you."

My eyesight improved as I became used to the dim light after the brightness outside. The recliner against the wall held another woman, one familiar. She had once been the wealthiest woman in Monroe, and her husband a high-ranking official in Washington DC. In our five years together, she had never uttered a single word to me, although there had been times when she had pointed to a half-empty wine glass for me to fill it. I'd cleaned her room a few times, but she preferred others to do it. She hadn't liked me.

That accounted for two of the people from the sanctuary. The man with his feet on the desk and the pair flanking Witch Hazel on the sofa accounted for the other three in the room. All of them were unfamiliar.

"Why am I here?" I asked.

The man at the desk lifted a glass that contained an amber fluid, probably some sort of whisky. He said with all traces of humor gone, "I believe you are responsible for the deaths of several of my people."

"I believe your people were killed by a young girl with no experience with weapons, so my question to you is, were they stupid or just poorly trained by you?" I knew my mouth would get me into trouble, but after rethinking that for an instant, how much more trouble could I be in? I continued, "Not to mention three hundred of my friends that you had killed."

"You got a point, I admit." He sipped his whiskey, bourbon, or whatever.

We stared at each other.

Witch Hazel said with almost a chuckle, "I told you she had a mouth. Kill her."

He slammed the glass down on the wooden desk so hard I didn't understand why it didn't shatter. Superglass or something. He looked away from me and at her. "Shut up."

"I said, kill her," the judge who had dated my boyfriend and gave me a death sentence repeated.

Faster than I could react, he reared back. One hand grasped the glass, and he threw it. Not at me. At her. She may have ducked, but I didn't think she had time. The glass buzzed over the top of her head spilling the contents at the same time.

Witch Hazel still looked at me with hatred as she wiped the liquid from her hair and face. She said as her eyes danced, "I enjoyed dating Jake right in front of you, you know. Had him almost daily while you scrubbed my toilets and floors. It made me laugh to have you clean up after me, which was what you were unknowingly doing when I let Jake spend time with you. You were cleaning up after me."

I shifted my weight to attack.

The man at the desk caught my attention and wagged a finger. He knew what I was going to do. Then, he surprised me. He said, "Whatever Pen *was*, the fact of the matter is that right now, Penelope did not turn traitor to her people. You did. So, which person do you think I respect more?"

"We have a deal," she growled, not intimidated at all.

"Yup, we made a deal." But he was again looking at me. "What do you think of deals made with people who trade the lives of their friends for their advancement?"

"You can't trust them."

He smiled at my answer. "Tell me about her."

I stood up straighter. "She would have you killed right here, today if she could take your place. Trust her, and you are a fool."

He reached down behind the desk and I feared he would come up with a pistol. Instead, he lifted a nearly full bottle of a familiar bourbon on the desktop. He unscrewed the cap and tossed it aside, then nudged it in my direction. "Drink?"

"My hands are tied."

He nodded to my escort. My hands were released. I went to the desk as I looked for glasses, which were in short supply, as in none. I knew where one had shattered. Despite disliking all hard liquor, I lifted the bottle by the neck and allowed a trickle to enter my throat. It burned. I smiled and placed it back on the desk.

He gulped a huge swallow as if to show me how it was properly done. He said, "You don't seem to like her much."

I thought about the right answer. "She allowed all my friends to die, and that is after she rigged a phony trial that ended with her pronouncement that, I'd get a lethal injection."

"Would you kill her if I allowed it?"

I turned and looked. The man on either side now pinned her arms to her side. Her eyes were wild. I turned back to him, determined to tell the truth. "I'd like to think I could and would. I'm not sure if that would happen, but yes, I hate her."

His eyes shifted to Witch Hazel. "You were a judge before living down there? You never said anything about that."

"Traffic court."

"Down there in that hole in the ground, you gave Penelope a death sentence?" His voice was as smooth as the bourbon on his desk was supposed to be, and I suspected the underlying harshness to be the same.

"She broke our rules, repeatedly. She deserved to die."

He leaned back and looked up at the ceiling instead of at us. His mellow voice said, "I'm going to tell you a short story, Judge Hazel. A judge once sentenced me to death, just like you did to her, so I know how that feels on the receiving end. Helpless. Sad. Angry at the world. Me? I'd kill that judge by a slow death if I came across him today. Know what I mean?"

I didn't know if the question was for her or me. I decided not to talk unless asked to.

Witch Hazel didn't seem to understand how the tables had turned. She lifted her nose slightly and said, "I suppose I do know but I would remind you we have a deal and I expect you to keep it. Without me, you'd have blown half the sanctuary to hell and probably ruined the weapons and supplies in the process."

He slipped his feet to the side and they fell to the floor with a crash of the heavy boots he wore. He sat upright and looked at her in disbelief. "Lady, before the war, I killed four people, one at a time, until the cops caught me, or I'd have done a few more. Keeping that in mind, how much do you think that deal of ours is worth now that I know it could have been you that sentenced me?"

She drew back as if confused, her arms crossed over her chest. Her tone was sharp and defiant. "I was a traffic judge. Aside from that, we made a deal. I gave you the combinations and I expect to be repaid as we discussed. Catching Penelope and killing her was one of the conditions. Setting me up for life, another."

He turned to me. "What do you think of her deal?"

I ignored the snicker from the wealthy woman sitting in the recliner. I said to Hazel, "I think six of you made it out together."

"Six, yes. Two died rather violently when they refused to work with the militia. Mister Marsdon and Mister Wayne seem a little more cooperative and are now working with our rescuers, as am I."

Rescuers. I felt ill again.

The man at the desk fell into his chair and lifted his feet back on the desktop one at a time. He said to me, "I asked you a question about the deal we have."

"You already know the answer."

"I want to hear you say it."

I faced Witch Hazel and then turned to look at a place between her and the older woman in the recliner. I steadied my voice. "These two sold out the lives of three hundred so that they could live well and resume their elite positions. Do you really want to know what I think? I think the same thing you do. If either of these two ever gets the opportunity, they will sell you out just as fast."

"I agree," he thundered.

"You should shoot them. Now. Two bullets. One in each forehead should do it." I couldn't believe the words had flowed from my mouth as easily as asking for a glass of water.

The three men in the room howled in laughter.

The two women stared blankly at each other. Better said, they returned my glower with stoic expressions.

Witch Hazel said as the laughter died down, "You've had your jest, Chance. Kill her."

Her voice had wavered just the smallest amount. I sensed that she was suddenly scared. The men on either side kept her pinned between them, almost as if she was the prisoner and not me.

The man behind the desk removed a huge revolver from a drawer and dramatically pointed it at the ceiling. His thumb operated an ejector rod. A shell appeared and fell to the surface of the desk. He did that five times, then on the sixth, he caught the shell and reinserted it.

He wore a small smile that made him almost look human, in a grandfatherly way. His eyes twinkled. Like at my trial a week ago, I decided to show no emotion. I gritted my teeth and

274

refused to beg. It wouldn't do any good and Witch Hazel would enjoy me doing it, so I wouldn't.

The man made a "gun" of his forefinger and thumb, to the men on the sofa and both removed their pistols, ready to use them if needed. They released her arms and pulled away. Instead of shooting me, he slid the revolver across the desktop. It came to rest directly in front of Witch Hazel.

His expression never changed. "You do it."

"Huh? You're supposed to kill her, not me."

"Your exact words when we made our deal were, she has to die."

"That meant you would kill her. Not me."

"Around here, we do our own dirty work. Kill her or don't."

I turned slightly and faced my nemesis. Her eyes were on the pistol as if it was about to attack her. She pulled away and shook her head. "I can't."

"Do it," he growled softly, the warning in his voice clear.

"No. You kill her. That was our deal."

He sighed and turned his attention back to me. "Beg for your life."

"Go to hell."

He slowly and deliberately reached his right hand down and lifted a semiautomatic into sight. "Beg."

"No." The word came out firm and strong, but not a shout. Inside, I quaked. If Witch Hazel hadn't been there, I'd have asked for my life, maybe, but her presence made all the difference. I resigned myself to death since there was nothing that I could do to prevent it.

Begging wouldn't change things. I couldn't leap across the desk and heroically grab his gun and turn it on him. There was one in reach and the pair on the sofa had shifted slightly so there was no chance to reach either of them. With three semiautomatics aimed at me, the men six feet apart, the outcome was clear.

The leader said softly, his eyes penetrating mine, "I respect strength. In this world, the weak die."

The barrel of the semi-automatic lowered and shifted from me to her. He shot Witch Hazel in the forehead, then a second later, the older rich woman. He carefully replaced his weapon in his holster while my ears rang, my eyes burned, and I smelled gun powder. For the third time, my stomach revolted. I held it in check, barely.

"Why?" I asked.

"You were right," he said. "Traitors never change. At the first opportunity, she would have turned on me to improve her situation. Some people hate thieves. Others, liars. I hate those who betray their friends."

"Uh, that's quite a speech," I muttered as my mouth continued to betray me and say what should have been a thought that never passed my lips. My eyes hadn't left the lifeless body of Hazel. The blood no longer oozed from the small hole just over her left eye.

I didn't feel elated to be alive. Nor did I feel happy she was dead. I had few feelings at all, just a stunning sort of existence as if in a terrible dream.

"Agreed," he said. "Get those two bodies out of here."

The man on the sofa closest to the door put his weapon away as he stood and walked into the hallway. I heard him speaking to someone unseen, and he returned.

"You have questions?" the man at the desk asked.

"No. Yes. I don't know. Can you ask me that later?"

He laughed again, with genuine humor. He pushed the bottle of whiskey closer and this time I swallowed a slug. It made the room swirl. Not from alcohol, but the overall sensation combined with what had just happened and my empty stomach.

Three burly men entered the room. With hardly a glance, they walked to the women. The one in front, well over six feet tall and probably near three hundred pounds, lifted the formerly wealthy woman by placing her arm over his shoulder and shoving his shoulder into her middle as he lifted. He stood, her slim body seemingly not bothering him at all as he strode out.

The other two lifted Witch Hazel, one taking her wrists, the other her ankles. They dropped her just before reaching the door, her head thumped on the floor, and they roughly picked her up again. I found I still had no feelings for her.

"Want to sit down?" the man at the desk asked.

I looked where they had sat and shuddered.

"Maybe another chair? Will one of you guys get her one? By the way, call me Chance."

"Because that's your given name?" My tone was bitter, the words sour in my mouth.

"Nope. That is, I used to have one of those bland names, like Bill, Bob, or Jim. People started calling me Chance about the time I killed that first one man who disrespected me."

"The name came from nowhere but suited you?" Why was I challenging this man?

"Because I told them to call me that."

"Or you'd kill them?"

"That may have been implied," he smiled.

A straight-back chair arrived. I sat.

Chance asked conversationally as if he shot two people a day, and indeed, maybe he did, "What are your plans for the future?"

"I haven't given it much thought." I reached for the bottle again and paused, asking his permission.

He nodded.

I said, "Everyone I know is dead. Well, not everyone. There was a girl we helped."

He nodded. "You killed her captors, cut her free of the chain that held her by her neck, and cared for her wounds. She repaid you by coming here and telling us all about you. She wants you dead, too."

"That's the short story."

"Pretty girl. Pregnant."

"Yes."

He rocked back and looked at the ceiling again. "Are you going to kill her if you see her?"

"Probably not. But that's not a guarantee, and I may slash her face with my fingernails."

He chuckled again. "It's good to hear someone speak the truth, for a change. The girl is now one of mine. I protect her."

"Maybe." There went my mouth again. I almost apologized, but he held up his palm to stall me.

"Hear me out. She is mine. The girl will work twelve or fifteen hours a day in the kitchens until she gives birth. For a month or two, she will be on light duty, if that's what you call taking care of an infant. Then she will work the kitchens in the mornings and provide sexual pleasures to my men in the evenings, probably until none want to bed her after a few years."

"Damn."

"I thought you might like that. A fitting punishment for another traitor, don't you think?"

I remembered my five years serving others. Not sex, but all the rest. Humiliating. Five years seemed like a lifetime. Her lifetime expectancy was thirty, forty, or fifty years. Ouch. Then, it occurred to me that her chances of living that long were slim.

"Now I feel sorry for her," I said, my eye on the bottle of whiskey I might need.

He chuckled and his men joined in again. Finally, he said, "You would figure out a way to kill any man who forced himself on you, I suppose. If I put you in the kitchen, I hear all the others will learn to hate you because of your sharp tongue. Same with most other jobs. Besides, you'd probably find a way to slip poison into my food."

"That's all true enough," I agreed.

"You got any ideas?"

His demeanor amazed me. It was as if we were having a pleasant conversation, yet I understood that one wrong phrase, and there would be a new bullet hole in my forehead. Based on the experience so far, I determined that telling the absolute truth was my best option. "I have been squirreled away in that underground sanctuary for years. Until a week ago, I believed it was a radiated desert up here with no people and only rabid creatures. So, no. I have no ideas because I don't know anything."

"What were your plans before we captured you?"

"A soldier named Grainger and I were going to the coast around Camano Island because it is pretty unpopulated and there are fish to eat. We thought starving was our biggest risk."

Chance turned to the man who seemed to be his second in command. "See? I told you."

"Yup," he grunted.

"What?" I asked.

"Smart. You'll do. Just don't you kill anybody for a few days unless you check with me, first. Deal?"

"What does that mean?"

He pulled another semiautomatic from his drawer and slid it my way. For all I knew, he had a drawer full of guns. I ejected the clip, found it fully loaded, and reinserted it. It fit my holster perfectly. It never occurred to me to shoot him.

As I settled back in my chair, I noticed both men held their weapons pointed loosely at me. I wouldn't have leveled the gun without dying.

He smirked. "Here's my thinking. You know nothing about what is happening up here. I am considering that as a possible advantage. New eyes, and all that. What I would like from you is to understand that we are at war and losing. I'd like you to spend a week or two here with us. Meet with me every day, or so, and give me your ideas."

"Ideas? I don't know anything."

"You do. You just don't know it. There is room for a lot of improvement around here. You might make things better. Sitting beside you is Benny. He's the old, ugly one. Benny will move around with you and keep you safe."

"Then what?"

"Give me two weeks of your honesty. Then, if you want, you can still go to Camano. I'll even provide an escort and horses."

I knew my mouth would do it again, but not so soon. "I've seen how you keep your deals."

"Fair enough," he said without humor. "What you have not seen is how I treat those who are loyal to me. Benny?"

"He would die for you," Benny said for his first words in a gravelly voice. "No shit."

I believed them.

Chapter 23

The old man known as Benny escorted me from the office in the firehouse. He turned to the rear parking lot where the gallows were located, the one still holding the bodies of my friends, I assumed. I steered him around to the front entrance without explaining why I didn't want to go the other way.

It was midmorning. The sun was still out. In other times, it would be a perfect day and I reminded myself to keep out of the sunlight to prevent getting burned. My skin looked pasty. Only the long sleeve flannel shirt kept my arms covered. I said, "Got a hat around here?"

Benny pointed. We walked down the street, drawing curious looks. I ignored them. Benny spoke to a few but never mentioned me. Just good morning, sort of greetings. Once, he questioned a young man about troop strength.

We headed for what had been a superstore at one time. Once inside, I found it still was, only more so. The shelving had been rearranged. Rows were only a couple of feet apart. No more wire baskets on wheels. The units were mismatched, probably brought in from other nearby stores. I saw where the refrigerated cases had been, now replaced with additional shelving. The side of the store that had held food now contained clothing. It was all clothing, the shelves stacked double high. Shirts of all kinds, but especially flannel, to the left. Jake and I had been right in our guess about that. Jeans of every style and color were stacked on shelves by size. Coats over there, socks, underwear, and everything else stored by function.

Benny called out, "Who's here?"

"Me," a kid of about ten called and appeared, carrying a stack of tee shirts.

"Hats?" Benny said.

The boy pointed. "Over by the wall."

Benny led the way.

I paused at the ballcaps, thinking a ponytail to stick out the back and I'd be set.

Benny shook his head and moved on down the row. He motioned for me to join him. He grabbed a tan, floppy thing with no style. A sagging brim went all around. He tried to put it on my head.

I moved away. "No, a ballcap is better."

"If you want to get your damn ears burned off and you like water running down your neck."

He had a point. Two points. I tried it on, and it slid down over my forehead to cover my eyes. He yanked it off and found a smaller one that fit. No ponytail needed. It had a chinstrap that did the dual duty of holding the two sides rolled up. In my imagination, I decided it made me look cute.

"Okay, you were right," I conceded. What next?"

"Hungry?"

I was. As we walked, I started looking at people in what remained of the city. How they were dressed, their hair, expressions, and attitudes. I quickly noticed whole areas and neighborhoods had burned, along with the odd house here and there.

I also noticed a strange smell. As we approached the areas where more people lived, the smells turned to stenches, reminding me of outhouses that hadn't been emptied in hot summer. The people and their clothing were not in much better shape, as if water were hard to locate in the river flowing right past the city.

I also watched for familiar faces. Not people from the sanctuary, but high school or customers at the tavern where I had worked. The women were few, and the men all wore beards, so even if I saw one, I might not recognize her or him. All wore weapons as comfortably as they used to carry wallets.

They probably never left home without them.

Above all that, was a different sort of thing that I'd identified on my last trip into Monroe. An air of expectancy permeated. Or fear. People were jumpy. Not at each other. Tempers flared. A fistfight held our attention for a few moments, but it ended.

No, it was a smaller thing, I was noticing. Someone dropped a glass jar. At the sound, people reached for their weapons. Their knees flexed; their eyes searched. Scared. That was the way I'd describe them. A city filled with fear.

"In here," the less than talkative Benny said.

Once, it had been a lumberyard, one of those national chains. Now it held picnic tables made of the wood that it had sold. Rows of them. Along the rear wall stood barbeques with tall pipes leading up through the ceiling in a pattern Doctor Suisse would have approved of.

However, it smelled fantastic. Meat roasted over wood fires in the barbeques. Pots of beans simmered on others. Bread baked and spread the goodness of those remembered scents. My stomach roiled.

Benny said, "Grab a bowl and serve yourself. Only get what you're gonna eat."

I gave him a look that said I was an adult—or hoped it did.

He said, "We don't waste food. You can go back for seconds."

Four stacks of mismatched bowls of every color and shape waited at one end, along with a tub of spoons. No forks or knives. I selected a medium bowl although I wanted a large and followed Benny. He lifted the lids on three barbeques before selecting the fourth. He removed two long strips of meat covered in a thick sauce. I took one. He checked the pots of beans and pointed to the red sign above that said *hot* as he shook his head at me. I understood. Both other pots had meat, however, one also had what looked like potatoes and carrots.

Potatoes and carrots! I ladled out half a bowl. Getting seconds didn't mean it had to be the same as the first time around, I guessed. At the end of the line, a table covered in a white sheet was Benny's next stop. Bread. Two kinds. Rolls, soft and hard. Butter.

Food to die for, if I used an old expression that I should forget. We sat at a picnic table by ourselves. If I had a knife, I thought I'd carve a dirty word into the surface like everyone else seemed to have done. Words I hadn't heard for years brought a smile to my lips.

The first taste of the beans did too. At least three different kinds, chunks of vegetables floated in a brown sauce more like a stew than beans. The end of the meat stick extended from the side of the bowl and the rest lay inside because of no other place to put it. I extracted it and nibbled on the end. Sweet and spicy. I took a larger bite.

The bread, I held out for last.

Benny watched me without saying a word.

"What?" I barked.

"You ate dried shit below?"

"That or go hungry."

He ate his beans with dignity. I gulped mine and flashed a smile his way, just to show him I was not an animal. He said, "You're now the sole survivor, you know."

That brought me down to earth. I'd just watched the other two die in front of me and I was more concerned with a bowl of beans. What did that say about what kind of person I'd become? I should feel guilty. I didn't. Maybe that said more about me than it should.

I tore off another bite of meat with my teeth while eyeing the bread. I said, "Things change. A week ago, I was lower than a servant, almost a slave. No, I was a slave. Either work or starve is how Witch Hazel put it."

"Chance didn't take to that woman from the start. My advice is, don't ever lie to him and don't try to cover up anything. He might slap you around if you screw up, but he'll do worse if you lie. And he will kill you for lack of loyalty."

"I see."

"Your friends, Hazel and that other woman didn't."

I used the bread to soak up the last of the soup. Then I sat back and ate the meat stick like I used to do with beef jerky, taking time to enjoy each mouthful. I wouldn't dare ask what the meat in my hand was. Instead, since Benny was talking more than he had, I asked, "What the hell is everyone so scared of?"

"Territory. There's a group of thugs that come over the pass in the summer. They want to take over Monroe, so they have people on both sides of the mountains. They need people to work the orchards and farms over there. Pick the crops. So, they hire slavers to round up workers."

I gave that some thought. At least, they were growing food. That was on the positive side and if they could get people to do the work, more would have food to eat. I saw and understood both sides of the problem.

Benny continued, "There's a powerful army in Everett to the northeast that is expanding this way and hoping to take over part of north Seattle. Army, gang, militia, whatever you want to call it. Two or three of the same from Seattle are looking to stop Everett from doing that and taking us over will help them bottleneck Everett."

"Geography," I said. Monroe lay at the crossroads. Whoever took it over gained an advantage because of location. Simple.

"You got it. The old war is over, and we're recovering but there isn't a central government, county, state, or fed. Everyone's on their own."

"Gang warfare," I added as I licked my fingers.

"More like feudal Europe a thousand years ago."

Unfortunately, I understood that too. The citizens of Monroe probably did also, on some level. I noticed others taking their bowl and spoon to a common table after eating, probably for washing. I stood and said, "Give me a tour?"

Benny silently agreed. After depositing our bowls, during which I didn't see Sara the pregnant girl, we walked into brilliant sunshine. No matter where I'd traveled, none compared to a sunny day in the Pacific Northwest. We walked west and north to where most of the new construction had been. Decay, blackened structures, cracked pavement, and listless people walking while a few rode horses described the city. The little laughter was coarse, vulgar, and lacked humor.

Boys were wrestling on the grass and pretending to shoot imaginary rifles, and teenagers lugged around the real things. There were little girls, some doing the same war games as boys, but they were noticeably absent as teenagers. The militia had many older women, meaning over thirty. It was only the young, pretty ones I didn't see.

As we moved from place to place, I maneuvered our route to pass by my old home. It was a blackened heap of ash with new green plants already ten feet tall. I held back the tears. While I'd expected to find much of what I did, the sheer shock of it struck me like something physical.

I assumed from the growth of the vegetation my home had been one of the original buildings the war claimed. My family had either died within it or soon after. They were gentle, friendly people who wouldn't adapt to this world. They wouldn't like it, either.

"What else do you want to see?" Benny asked.

"Were you a prisoner?" I asked the question without forethought or intent. It just came out.

"That's a question we don't ask around here. Why?"

I glanced at his bare forearm and the crudely made tattoo there.

He pulled his sleeve down to cover it. "Alright. Financial embezzling. Satisfied?"

"Guilty?" I asked, suspecting the truth but wondering if he would admit to it.

"Of course."

"I thought all you guys were innocent."

"None of us were. I never met an inmate who was there by mistake."

"Did you embezzle a lot?"

"Too much. That's what got the finger pointed at me, otherwise, I'd have never been convicted."

"Really?"

"Nope," he said seriously. "I had a brother-in-law who would have been fingered if anyone managed to figure out money was missing in the first place. Never did like him and he dissed me in front of my family. It was all set up for him to eventually take the fall. I even had him sign documents he never knew authorized the transfer of funds into an account I set up in his name. Only I knew of the account and the passwords, and I kept the originals he signed."

That was the most he'd said all day. He'd also said it with pride. The world was a different place. I said, "I went to high school here."

"I was non-violent and did work release around town. We might have run into each other."

"And now you're the second in command of a gang that runs the city and enslaves the residents you don't kill?"

That drew a reaction. He took my upper arm in a grip of iron and spun me against a brick wall. The few people nearby either changed directions or ignored us. His face had turned to one of pain. His teeth were showing like those of a German shepherd watchdog as if he wanted to take a bite out of me.

His voice was hoarse. "You have it all wrong, Miss Penelope. Without us, without the organizational skills of Chance, most of the people you see around here would be dead. We provide food, shelter, clothing, and relative safety. Anyone can walk away from here. The problem is that they won't last a week outside the city. It's like you said, there is not enough food to feed people unless they work together. Everyone can't go to the coast and fish."

"Okay," I said, trying to free my arm.

"No, not okay. There is more. A mile outside this city are bad people, the kind that kills and eats you. The kind that lurks in the dark and looks for a weakness to take advantage of. Remember all those stories you heard about what you thought was up here? Let me tell you, it's worse."

I felt a tremble. Not from him, from me. I couldn't swallow. The food I'd eaten wanted to come back up—again. That seemed to be a regular thing in the last few days. His grip released me.

He said, "I'll take you back."

"No. I want to see more." I slumped against the brick wall and asked myself when I'd learn to think before speaking.

"Not much more to see."

"The prison?"

"Reformatory," he corrected. "We finally got out of there. We're not interested in going back."

"Does anybody?"

"No."

I held my tongue as we walked. I looked at the people of the city in a different light. Yes, they were scared, but none were starving, all wore similar clothing, and the food was served daily. Nobody guarded the city against anyone wanting to leave, which would be impossible. If a person wished to go, there were a hundred ways. These people were here because they wanted to be. It was that simple.

Still, my friends had been beaten and hung by them. They were not my people. Not anymore.

"Something still bothering you?"

I stalled, choosing my words carefully. "Did you go down in our sanctuary and help kill all those people?"

"Yes."

"You could have lied."

"It doesn't work that way. Trust, I mean. Lie to me once, you might as well do it a thousand times. A few questions to anyone here and you'd have found out the truth, anyway."

"Did you have to kill them all? What'd they do to you?"

A pickup truck with four flat tires sat nearby, the tailgate down. He walked over to it and sat, using it as a bench. From there we could see most of the street. I suspected he had sat there before.

After I sat beside him, he said, "Yes, we did have to kill them. There were rumors of that place, but nobody knew for sure if or where it was. What we did know was that bombs and missiles fell all over this area. The major cities and military bases were hit hardest. What we believe were low yield atomic bombs sent those mushroom clouds into the sky, so many of them they ran together like colors on a kid's watercolor painting."

I said nothing. It must have been horrible.

"Planes flew over for a month, day and night. Those were the worst. At night we could see parts of the world explode. We felt the vibrations here, and the orange explosions meant later we would hear the booms and sometimes feel the blasts when the ground shook."

"What happened? I mean, why did it stop?"

"Rumors say we unleashed a boatload of missiles of our own and destroyed their main cities. That's the rumors, but it's anybody's guess who it was. At least, I don't know."

"That is terrible."

"Yup," he said, his eyes averted. Then he turned back to me. "Want to know what is worse?"

Did I? Maybe. I nodded slowly, expecting the worst to be something other than what he told me.

He said, "During all that, while all those people died and we stayed up all night waiting for the next plane to pass over the top of us and drop bombs, there were people safely below ground sipping champagne and watching old movies. They missed all we lived through. The collapse of the food chain, the fighting and killing over a can of soup, the people who needed medication and died, the infections, rampant disease, and a hundred other things."

"While we sipped champagne in the safety of our shelter."

His shoulders slumped and his tone softened, "You'd be dead too if those others hadn't told us about you. How you refused to serve them and finally escaped. You're more like us prisoners from the reformatory than them."

"You would have killed me if I was still down there?"

"Without hesitation. Or Chance would have. Or most anyone you see on this street."

Chapter 24

Benny routed us back to the stinky firehouse. We went up the stairs and into the same office as before. Chance had his feet up on the desk again, his eyes closed and soft snores and snorts that made us smile. The bottle of whiskey was half empty.

"Time to wake up," Benny said.

Chance's head came up off his chest and his eyes locked on me.

"Good nap?" I asked.

"Better than some," he grumbled.

I still wore the pistol he gave me on my hip. It struck me as odd. He couldn't trust me that much. It reeked of a test. His other bodyguard was gone, so it was just the three of us, Chance who was half asleep, Benny the old man, and me. I could easily pull my gun and shoot Chance, then Benny.

But what would that get me? Looking at it from my standpoint, nothing. Others would track me down and kill me in an hour or two, but it dawned on me that Chance wouldn't take that sort of risk, or he wouldn't be in the position he was.

I sat in the same chair, avoiding the sofa.

Benny sat at one end of the sofa after looking for blood. As usual, he said nothing.

Chance rinsed his mouth with whiskey and spat it out at the wall to his side. No wonder the room stank. I wondered where he peed. However, I sat as quietly as Benny while my mind sorted out the wrinkles in my world.

Chance said, "What do you know?" It sounded like *waddayano*.

I pulled the pistol from my holster and ejected the clip again.

"Something wrong?" he asked, no longer looking sleepy.

"Do you trust me?" I asked innocently.

"No."

I found myself smiling. "I didn't think so. You'd be a fool if you did."

Now he was also smiling. "And you don't think I'm a fool."

Just in case I was wrong, I racked a shell into the chamber while watching him. I pointed the gun at the little window on the wall above him and pulled the trigger. Nothing happened. I handed him the gun back by sliding it across his desk.

He reached into that drawer again and slid another to me. "Please don't break my window by shooting that one. It is fully functional. What did you try to shoot to find out?"

"To figure out the gun was a dummy? Nothing. It only made sense. You removed the firing pin or something." From the corner of my eye, I saw Benny give a single nod of agreement to my words. I now held a fully functioning weapon and Chance was alright with that.

"Have a good tour?" he asked.

"I did. And a meal."

"Did Benny outline our situation?"

"About being in the middle and having other armies trying to take over Monroe?"

"Yes, that. I'm tempted to take a few good people and head up into the mountains. My spies tell me Everett is already moving this way in a few weeks, and so is one of the Seattle gangs. Those damn Wenatchee devils will cross the pass when the snow melts, so we have three armies coming this way, all stronger than us."

"Benny told me that."

"I want your take on it."

"First, that is a silly idea about running off. I'm no military person, I have only second-hand information, mostly provided by you, and even asking me to examine the situation shows your desperation."

The room went quiet. I could hear Benny's deep breathing, my heart pounding, and nothing from Chance. It stayed that way for a long time.

I was angry. Who was this killer to ask me what his future should be? He admitted to killing people before the war, I'd seen him shoot two only this morning, and there were undoubtedly dozens of others. I allowed myself to review all I'd seen today and tried to pull any one item that might help.

The room remained quiet.

I adjusted my chair, which sounded like a baby crying in a church. I tried to stare him down and failed. Two things came to mind as if conjoined at the hip. If escaping with a few of his closest friends was not an option, there remained only one.

"Well?" he demanded.

"What?"

"Your eyes lit up," he said.

"Did not."

"Tell me what you just thought of."

"If you don't like it? How much trouble am I in?"

He sighed and threw his arms wide. "Everybody thinks I'm a bad guy."

"You did shoot two women in this room today."

He laughed. Not a snort or giggle, but a full belly-laugh. He said, "Let's make a deal. No, you don't think I keep my end, so I will give you this. On my honor, you can stand up and walk away right now. We part as friends and I try to solve my problems as best I can. Or you can tell me what you are thinking and maybe we can save the lives of some of these people."

"I don't have answers, just a couple of observations based on what you've told me, and what I've seen."

"Go on."

"Assuming you are right about two or three armies coming this way, you lose. They will win. Sorry, but if something drastic doesn't change, you lose. Summer will be here in a couple of months."

"That's what I'm telling you and I agree. Go on. You have an idea."

"Two of them. I'd guess that both Seattle and Everett have

a lot more soldiers than you."

"I've recruited about all I can, and yes, both are larger. We have a good defensive position and thanks to your people, a supply of quality weapons and ammo. But the fact is, attacking us with a larger force will not change the outcome. We will lose."

"Not if you join forces with one of them."

He smiled. "I already tried that and failed. They want it all so they can continue to move north or south. We're just a thorn in their side."

"Not my point. You don't want either of them. You want the Wenatchee devils to join with you. If Everett or Seattle take over Monroe, the Wenatchee people lose access to the west coast. It is in their interest to help you. Have you talked with them?"

He slowly shook his head. "No, just Everett and Seattle.

"I would guess Wenatchee is smaller than you but combined you are larger?"

"We'd still be smaller than the armies they are bringing. Good idea, but it won't work."

"That's because you are stubborn and still don't see your biggest asset."

He squinted as if imagining all around and shrugged.

"The prison, you idiot," I snapped.

"I spent eleven years in that damned place, so I know every brick in it. What are you talking about?"

"You're thinking about it inside-out. Imagine the buildings and walls. It is a fortress. Sure, it was built to keep people inside, but it will also keep them out. One good man with a rifle up on the top of the wall is worth a hundred outside."

Benny leaned forward. "She's right. We could use wagons and move all our food and stores from the city inside the walls of Supermax. Water is right there at the river and the water table is high. We could dig a well or two."

Chance scrunched up his face and his eyes looked unfocused. He finally said, "We could hold them off from there. Set fire to the forest around the prison and we'd have a clear field of fire."

Benny said, "Hell, the cells could be made as comfortable

as the barracks we use now. We don't have to defend the entire complex, just the Supermax. She's right. Put a dozen men on the walls with the M4s and it would take hundreds, maybe thousands to get inside, if at all."

A thoughtful smile formed on Chance's face.

Benny continued, speaking excitedly, "Winter is over. The snow on the pass is melting. A small group of us could go over the hill and talk to those devils over there. If either Everett or Seattle takes Monroe, they are cut off. Totally. Besides, that, Everett or Seattle would soon be using the pass to attack them. But if they help us, we can offer them free access to this side of the mountains and protection from invasion. Hell, we can even offer them rooms in the reformatory and food. Any prisoners we jointly take can be sent as slaves to their farms. It's an offer they can't refuse."

Chance pounded a fist on the desk. "Yes, that's our answer. Why didn't we see it?"

"Maybe because neither of you ever wanted to set foot inside those walls again?" I said in my most snarky manner. "Some might even say I'm smarter than you. No, you can laugh. That was a joke."

Chance ignored me. "Benny, you know the best soldier to make a hard trip to Wenatchee. One who can speak convincingly for us. Find him and let's meet downstairs in the bay where the firetrucks used to park. Also, we need two or three others who can negotiate and sell the deal to the devils across the mountains. Also, I need to stop calling our new allies that name. Working together will benefit us all."

"When do you want them here?"

"Tonight, at dusk."

Benny got up and as he walked past me, I felt his hand briefly on my shoulder. It was no accident. A warmth flowed through me that hadn't been there for a couple of years. Just that one touch meant so much.

Chance said, "Your idea will work, Pen. We owe you for this. Is there anything we can do?"

"You could start by cleaning up this dump of a room. At least, so it does not smell so bad, or move our meetings somewhere else."

"Our? You're saying you'll stay and help us?"

"I have nowhere to go and maybe I can do some good here. If nothing else, I can help with the move of everyone to the prison. I'm good at organizing, but please don't ask me to do the heavy cleaning. I've had enough of that for a while."

Chance said with a smile, "The word of this idea will spread, and people near here will love you. More than me. If we held an election in a few days, you'd win. That makes me uncomfortable. I'd better watch out or you'll be telling me what to do."

I smiled back. "If that happens, they elected the wrong person to lead them. I'm just a girl who serves beer with a smile."

We grinned at each other until he asked, "Hey, are there any more sanctuaries around here? We could use some more guns and ammo."

My smile faded despite my efforts to hold it in place. It was going to be interesting around Monroe for a while.

The End

*Any book in the *"After"* series can be read in any order. The setting and world described in them allow for people in other sanctuaries and locations, and the times spent in them vary. They eventually emerge and explore what they find on the surface—possibly even meeting some who survived living in other sanctuaries.

If you enjoyed this book, please consider leaving a review with Amazon at the following link. If you didn't enjoy it, skip over the link (actually, review it anyhow, and tell me why you didn't like it so the next in the series will be better).

ABOUT THE AUTHOR

LeRoy Clary

LeRoy currently lives in Washington State with his wife, youngest son, and a dog named Molly. He spends his time doing what he loves the most: writing about an action-packed fantasy world of dragons, and magic, and science fiction. LeRoy spends his leisure time traveling and exploring the countryside in the Pacific Northwest from high desert to forests and coast.

Writing has always been one of LeRoy's favorite past times and passions; mostly fantasy and science fiction. He's been a member of several author critique groups both in Texas and in Washington State.

*In recent years, LeRoy has published over a dozen fantasy books including a book called **DRAGON! Stealing the Egg** which began the idea of how to live and survive in a world where dragons are part of the landscape. **The Dragon Clan Series** is unique in that it introduces a new main character in each of the seven books of the series. The book entitled **Blade of Lies: Mica Silverthorne Story** was a finalist in an Amazon national novel writer's contest in 2013.*

Learn more about LeRoy at:
Facebook: www.facebook.com/leroyclary
Website: www.leroyclary.com *(join his email list)*
Email: Leroy.clary@gmail.com

Made in the USA
Las Vegas, NV
11 September 2022

55062033R00167